RANGERS OF THE LONE STAR

Also by Zane Grey
in Large Print:

Arizona Ames
Black Mesa
Horse Heaven Hill
Stairs of Sand
To the Last Man
The Thundering Herd
Shadow on the Trail
Lost Pueblo
Knights of the Range
A Grave for Lassiter
The Vanishing American

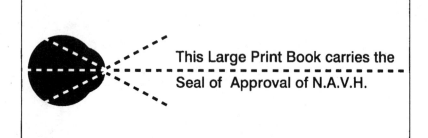
This Large Print Book carries the
Seal of Approval of N.A.V.H.

RANGERS OF THE LONE STAR

ZANE GREY

Thorndike Press • Thorndike, Maine

Published in 1998 by arrangement with
Golden West Literary Agency.

Thorndike Large Print® Western Series.

The tree indicium is a trademark of Thorndike Press.

The text of this Large Print edition is unabridged.
Other aspects of the book may vary from the original edition.

Set in 16 pt. Plantin by Al Chase.

Printed in the United States on permanent paper.

Library of Congress Cataloging in Publication Data
Grey, Zane, 1872–1939.
    Rangers of the Lone Star : a western story / by Zane Grey.
      p. cm.
    ISBN 0-7862-0771-X (lg. print : hc : alk. paper)
    I. Large type books. I. Title.
    [PS3513.R6545R36 1998]
     813'.52—dc21   98-24417

RANGERS OF THE LONE STAR

Foreword

This is one of the three "Stars" of what might be called the Lone Star Trilogy. Most of those readers who have read Zane Grey's THE LONE STAR RANGER are probably not aware that it was the result of the combination of parts of two other full-length novels that have been around for eighty years but that have never been published separately in book form. Notwithstanding, THE LONE STAR RANGER has enjoyed great success, even though it was not my father's best Texas novel. Those who have read the most powerful of the three, LAST OF THE DUANES, published by Five Star Westerns in August, 1996, will have seen in the Foreword to that book what happened to create three books instead of one. However, readers of this volume should also be acquainted with the circumstances that led to its being written and eventually, also, to its being published as a Five Star Western.

LAST OF THE DUANES was written in the summer of 1913, not long after Zane Grey had visited Captain Hughes of the Texas Rangers in San Antonio and had formulated his ideas for a book. It is likely that my father also read historical accounts about the exploits of the famed Captain McNelly — whose name was changed to MacNeal in the present book — who not only restored the Texas Rangers to legitimate status in the state, when heretofore they had been branded as being virtually outlaws, but who also was instrumental in leading them to clean out the notorious bands of outlaws in Pecos County from what was called the Neuces Strip. I do not know what sources my father used, but as far as I am aware his historical data underlying the story is reasonably accurate. When he finished the novel, he immediately sent it off to his friend and one time mentor, Bob Davis, who at the time was the editor of *Munsey's Magazine*. Dad was literally stunned when he received a letter from Davis, suggesting that Buck Duane, the central character, was far too "saturnalian" and that killing eighteen men in one book was just too much violence for readers to swallow.

When one considers the level of violence that goes on in TV programs and even in some Western stories today, this seems ludicrous. But in 1913 Davis may have been trying to avoid having his magazine labeled a kin to the dime novel or the pulp fiction

Westerns that abounded in those days where shootings occurred regularly and practically on every page.

About the same time Dad received a letter from Ripley Hitchcock, then editor of Harper and Bros., who had probably talked to Davis and who suggested that, though he had not read the book himself, there was probably too much "pistol play" in it and Dad should write something along the lines of LORNA DOONE. Despite having already had behind him such outstanding successes as THE HERITAGE OF THE DESERT, RIDERS OF THE PURPLE SAGE, and THE LIGHT OF WESTERN STARS, Dad probably was still not that sure of himself as a writer. Perhaps he was also suffering from the malaise that often afflicts many writers: they are really never quite that convinced of the value of their work. This may be just as well since to a degree it is what impels them to move on, to strive for higher levels, and to write more books. In Zane Grey's case he dutifully adhered to Hitchcock's and Davis's admonitions, sat down, and wrote this novel, RANGERS OF THE LONE STAR.

Though dealing with somewhat the same set of circumstances, as is evident after reading LAST OF THE DUANES, this present novel takes a totally different approach. Perhaps one of the most interesting distinctions between this and all of Dad's other books is that RANGERS OF THE LONE STAR is the only Western story Zane Grey wrote in the first person. I also believe that the character of his narrator, Russ Sittell, is somewhat autobiographical. Dad was only five feet eight inches tall, slightly above average for American males at that time. In this story Sittell is five feet six inches in contrast to Vaughn Steele who is a giant among men. In appearance Steele reminds me of the only Texas Ranger I have met, Carlos Jackson, who was about six feet five inches tall and probably weighed 275 pounds (appearing to me to be all muscle) when I visited Fort Davis, Texas, on the occasion of the Zane Grey's West Society Convention in 1992. I remember when we took an old-fashioned carriage ride from the lodge to the scene where we had our traditional Monday evening barbecue. Jackson sat on the right side of the carriage, opposite the driver, my wife, and daughter, and I sat on the left-hand side, and the wagon still tilted perilously in his direction.

In this book, although Russ Sittell functions primarily as an observer to recount the exploits of Vaughn Steele, I think Dad's romantic impulses got the better of him. Sittell turns out to be quite a hero in his own right. Also, in order to provide romance, there are two heroines introduced in the story, one the daughter of the wealthy rancher who ultimately turns out to be an outlaw leader, and the other, her cousin, who becomes the object of Russ's amorous attentions.

One of the aspects of Zane Grey's writing that sets him apart from any other Western novelist is his monumental description of the land with all its primitive and harsh grandeur that so frequently influences the manner in which human beings and animals behave. When I visited Fort Davis, I did not take the tour to Big Bend National Park — I was probably fortunate because the air conditioner in the tour bus broke down and some of my friends almost died from the heat. But they did say that what they saw was one of the most awesome spectacles they had ever witnessed, perhaps only rivaled by the Grand Canyon. The Big Bend country is still as wild and inhospitable today as it was in the days when the characters in this book were presumably alive. In fact, I asked Carlos Jackson, who was the head of the Rangers in that area and whose territory comprised literally thousands of square miles, whether he had difficulty curbing illegal aliens from crossing the border in that terrible and inhospitable terrain. His answer was that he paid very little attention to them because there were so few. His main concern was drug smuggling all along the part of the Rio Grande that forms the border between the United States and Mexico. Although it is certainly mentioned, there is much less description of the Big Bend's wildness in this novel than you might expect, especially since it served as a hiding place for the rustler gangs operating in that section of Texas. Still, the action in this story is well paced, and it moves along in an eminently readable fashion.

Though this novel was published in a somewhat abridged form in *Cavalier* and *All-Story Weekly* magazines in 1914, today the manuscript as my father wrote it engenders a mystery and one that I have not been able to solve, even though I have read all of the correspondence to be found on this matter. When the time arrived to publish the Harper's version — what became THE LONE STAR RANGER — evidently the Harper editors did not really like either of these individual stories by itself. They literally pasted together — I say *they* because I can find no evidence that Dad or Mother had anything to do with it — the first half of

LAST OF THE DUANES with the last installments of this book. In their version they substituted Buck Duane for Vaughn Steele, eliminated Russ Sittell entirely, and "lost" Jennie Lee in the process. The result was THE LONE STAR RANGER which first appeared in 1915. Despite its origins, this dubious book has remained one of Zane Grey's bestsellers to this day.

Although neither novel ever appeared as my father wrote it until they were published by Five Star Westerns, both LAST OF THE DUANES and RANGERS OF THE LONE STAR served as the basis and have a record for having jointly been made into more full-length films than any other literary property in motion picture history. LAST OF THE DUANES was filmed four times, the last version in 1940 starring my good friend, George Montgomery. In the years between 1919 and 1940 the hybrid, THE LONE STAR RANGER, was also produced and released four times as a motion picture.

So here at last is the fully unexpurgated version of RANGERS OF THE LONE STAR. How much actual history is contained in these pages is perhaps a subject for historians to debate. However, it is quite true that Captain McNelly, the most famous Texas Ranger of his time, was given the task of cleaning up the Neuces Strip in those wild, turbulent, lawless days in early Texas, and he proved successful in this task. And what also resulted are these three novels, eight films, radio and TV adaptations, and all the lore that has become so much a part of the Zane Grey legend.

Loren Grey,
Woodland Hills, California

Chapter One

THE FUTURE OF THE SERVICE

"United States Deputy Marshal Sittell to see Captain MacNeal of the Texas Rangers." I spoke with more force than politeness, and I flashed my shield at the block-headed attendant who had denied me admittance to the adjutant general's office.

In Texas, where nearly every man was such a giant that he had to lower his head to enter a door, it was exasperating to be only five feet six. As my business was to impress a class of men exceedingly hard to impress, and as I, despite my size, had some little reason for pride, I was naturally nettled by the manner of the attendant. Mildness of disposition was not one of my strong characteristics.

"Marshal Sittell, excuse me!" the attendant quickly replied with a vast change of demeanor that somewhat assuaged my wounded vanity.

He led me into an anteroom from which I could see into Adjutant General Weed's office. Motioning me to a chair, he passed into the office, evidently to announce my arrival. Voices sounded from within. Directly the attendant returned and now approached me with a show of respect.

"Captain MacNeal will see you presently. He is about to leave an interview with Adjutant General Weed and Governor Stone. You are to listen, hear what you can."

Then he went out, closing the door behind him.

I sat down, decidedly interested. There was something in the wind. Captain Mac-Neal's summons had been urgent, much in the nature of an appeal. I had been one of his rangers for three years before my service had earned me a higher post. Our relationship had been something more than that of ranger to captain, and my respect and admiration for him were great.

Since MacNeal had been leader of the rangers, he had not only been fighting the horde of outlaws, west of the Colorado, but a political faction at Austin that opposed the ranger system. MacNeal had so far accomplished wonders, making sections of that wild and vast Southwest habitable for pioneers and ranchmen. I did not doubt that he had some unusual task in the accomplishment of which he hoped to enlist my aid.

The door to the inner office was open and

I overheard the earnest voice of the adjutant general, whom I knew.

"Governor Stone, this is Captain Mac-Neal of the Texas Rangers."

Both men courteously acknowledged the introduction, and the governor said that, of course, he was familiar with MacNeal's splendid record, won during the Rebellion. "And Captain MacNeal," he added, "I shall be pleased to hear what you have to say."

"Governor Stone," replied MacNeal earnestly, "I sought this interview to try to show you what a great . . . a fatal error it would be now to discontinue the ranger service. I have no axe to grind. I'm independent of salary, and I'm not seeking anything for myself. I love the great Lone Star state. Although I am doing a great deal, I want to do something more for it.

"When I heard about the possibility of abolishing the ranger system, I scarcely credited the rumor. But, now that there seems reason to believe it, I am here to place my case and make a fight. Governor Stone, I want to ask bluntly . . . do you know anything about the ranger system . . . about the rangers? You are from eastern Texas. We needn't beat about the bush. It's well known that between east and west Texas there's differences of opinion . . . political and otherwise. Eastern Texas has no need of a ranger service. But as for the western . . . the wild Panhandle, the Staked Plains, the Rio Grande . . . that's a different matter. Will you be kind enough to give me your idea of the Texas Rangers?"

That certainly was blunt. It brought back to me strong recollections of MacNeal's personality. He was a man. I warmed to his side of what I sensed might be more than an argument.

"Captain MacNeal, since you ask me directly, you are welcome to my opinion," replied the governor coldly. "Personally, I know nothing of the rangers. But I've been told by good authorities that as a whole they are a lot of swashbuckling adventurers and gunfighters, looking for somebody to kill. The sentiment in certain parts of the state makes heroes out of them, a fact which they are not slow to take advantage of. They have too much power. They are too much a law unto themselves. The sheriffs ought to be able to cope with any lawless element in western Texas, as they do in the eastern part of the state. There is a bill pending in the legislature now for the abolishment of this ranger service, and unless very strong evidence is put before me . . . great enough to change my mind . . . I shall sign the bill."

18

"Thank you for plain speaking," replied MacNeal, and the tone of his voice told me how cool and tense he could be when feeling anger or resentment. "You will remember, Governor, that the original bill provided for a ranger service operating only west of the Colorado River. If you are not familiar with the conditions in the remote and wild sections of the border, it is time you were availing yourself of reports sent monthly to Adjutant General Weed.

"I have this to say, pointblank. Sheriffs cannot deal with the situation as it stands today. There's a horde of criminals along the Rio Grande. I have a record of three thousand. The Panhandle and Staked Plains are also overrun by outlaws and desperadoes. There are honest communities . . . towns . . . whole counties under the dominance of clever, unscrupulous rustlers. A band of militia could not clean up these places. If it is to be done, the rangers must do it. As to my men . . . well, some of them *are* gunfighters. I have tried to find that class of men. I have rangers who have been outlaws. A reformed outlaw who has been a famous gunfighter makes the best kind of ranger. His fame is as much help as his actual work.

"You will not understand this, because

you know nothing of the class of men who harass the border. I think a careful study of the reports sent in by my rangers will open the eyes of any unprejudiced person."

"Let us see one of these reports," suggested the governor.

"Adjutant, get that last one of Vaughn Steele's I sent in. It's a case in point, and, besides, I'll have something else to say about Steele."

I heard the opening of a drawer and rustling of papers.

"Here it is. Steele certainly does things. You can see that by what he leaves out in his report," replied the adjutant general.

"Read it to me," said Governor Stone.

"Please take note that this is the report of one ranger's work for one month," put in Captain MacNeal.

The adjutant began by naming the town of Del Rio, where evidently the report had been written, and the date; then, after a pause, he read:

El Paso to Valentine to Del Rio. Arrested three Mexicans . . . cattle thieves. In absence of sheriff guarded them till his return. To Ensign. Called by attack of schoolteacher. School house burned in

fight. No arrests. Brought teacher to Del Rio. Prevented lynching of Negro. Arrested sheriff in getting Negro to safe place. Traced down rumor of Mexican raiders operating on this side border. Unfounded. Arrested white man named Jinks with boatload of stolen goods. Chased the outlaw, Mott, across into Mexico. Killed my horse. No arrest. Assisted rancher. Found bunch of cattle hidden in brush along river. Enlisted cowboys. Drove herd to owner. Nursed maltreated Mexican. Got him home over river. Arrested four Negroes for attacking him. Shot two . . . not fatally. Called to Ensign. No arrest. To Del Rio. Arrested rioters in gambler's resort. Chased them with posse. No arrests. To Ensign, to Cargo, to Junction, to Del Rio after the outlaw and murderer . . . Chick Owens. Was shot making arrest. Jail torn down by Owens's pals. Wounded again in fight. Had to kill Owens. . . .

"There! That's quite sufficient," interrupted Governor Stone. "I don't want to hear any bloody details."

"The half is not told here," said Captain MacNeal. "But I can read between the lines. This ranger rode seven hundred miles last month. He simply states . . . To El Paso, to Valentine, to Del Rio, *et cetera.* But that means the hardest kind of riding over desert country. He merely states he was wounded twice. No particulars. He . . ."

"I gather the report must have been a chronicle of a most remarkable month's work. But is it . . . er . . . true?"

For a moment, following the governor's cold question, there was silence in the other room.

"Governor Stone, I believe you can rely on these reports," replied the adjutant.

"He must be an able fellow. Where is he now?"

Here I pricked up my ears and listened a little harder. I had never met this magnificent ranger, but I, like every other outdoor man in western Texas, had heard all about him. Some of Steele's jobs had given me jealous qualms, yet thrilled me through and through.

"I have just sent Steele upon the most difficult and, perhaps, dangerous service he ever undertook. Certainly it is the most important one. It is one I would have undertaken myself, had I had the confidence and ability needed."

"What is the service?" inquired the governor.

"Have you ever heard of Fairdale, Pecos County?"

"Let me see . . . Fairdale? Why, yes, indeed, I've read things in the papers. Somebody has spoken to me about Fairdale. A remote town or settlement, rich but exceedingly lawless."

"Lawless!" Captain MacNeal uttered a short, grim laugh. "Fairdale is far to the southwest. I've never been there. It's a good-sized town, located west of the Pecos River. Pecos County is merely a name for a great wild barren. Fairdale is favorably located in a rich, well-watered valley, and the ranchers are prosperous in spite of the raiders.

"For a year now, from time to time, I've been receiving anonymous letters. They are from persons afraid to sign names . . . persons whose friends and families have been robbed, assaulted, murdered. In every case I was importuned to send a company of rangers there. I sent an unknown ranger to make an investigation . . . to be careful and secret . . . and to return with a report.

"He did so. Used as I am to reports of lawlessness, this one amazed me. All the deviltry common to the border goes on there by day and night. More than that, and more interesting, was the ranger's report that Fairdale must be a center for the most secret, powerful, mysterious, and dangerous band of criminals operating in the Southwest. I decided to send Steele there, to ferret out this lawless gang and break it up."

"Sir, you don't mean to tell me you've given one single ranger such a job as that?" queried the governor incredulously.

"I expect to send him another ranger . . . that's all," replied MacNeal.

"But, man alive, it's absurd! What you ought to send is a company of militia!"

"That would entail great expense, and that is what this new legislative bill is aiming to cut down, isn't it?"

"That is the aim . . . yes."

"Well, anyway, soldiers would be powerless, even if you did send them. So also would a whole company of rangers. What this job needs is a couple of keen, resourceful, implacable, dangerous men!"

"But how can they . . . alone . . . break up a powerful gang of ruffians?"

"Perhaps they're not all ruffians. I've known respected and intelligent citizens to be mixed up in shady deals. I have detailed Steele to go to Fairdale, openly as a ranger, and to begin work. I'll send another ranger to help him. If they are not killed, they will clean up the town. My men have made more than one town safe for the decent people to live in. Of course, not such places as Fairdale, but bad enough to show their capacity for dangerous work."

"Captain, your confidence is beyond me," commented the governor. "Frankly, this is the most extraordinary undertaking I've ever heard of."

"If you knew the ranger, it wouldn't seem so strange," went on Captain MacNeal. "I expect, of course, to lend them every assistance possible. Steele asked for a nervy and clever man to be sent to Fairdale as a secret aid. I've had the man in mind, and he's now waiting outside."

"Another ranger?"

"No, not now. Formerly he was with my service. But at present he is a special officer, United States deputy marshal."

"Call him in," said the governor.

It was the adjutant general who came into the anteroom for me. His greeting made me believe he sided with MacNeal in this matter. I went with him.

MacNeal seemed the same slim, erect, and soldierly officer I remembered so well, and his dark face surely expressed welcome and pleasure at sight of me. We shook hands as we greeted each other.

Then Adjutant General Weed introduced me to the governor. I saw a tall, pale man with a pointed beard and an aristocratic bearing that reminded me of a rich Louisiana planter. The way the governor looked me over with his cold, blue eyes was not especially to my liking. He did not offer his hand, though from habit I had made a move to extend mine.

"Does the . . . er . . . the marshal know yet of the dangerous mission upon which you would send him?" asked Governor Stone of MacNeal.

"I heard your conversation," I replied bluntly.

"Will you care to accept Captain Mac-Neal's proposition?"

"I'll be glad to go. Adjutant General Weed can authorize me, if he sees fit."

"You, of course, appreciate the danger of this work?" queried the governor.

"The more the danger, the better I'll like it," I rejoined.

My tongue sometimes was swifter than it ought to have been, and I had a hankering for the governor to take me for one of those swashbucklers that had so disgusted him.

"Do you know this Ranger Steele?"

"Only by reputation."

"And what is that reputation?"

"Steele's known on the border from El Paso to the mouth of the Rio Grande. He is feared."

"Do you entertain any conviction of his success in this service?"

"He'll clean up Fairdale."

I put it strongly, without a shadow of doubt. I was eager to help MacNeal's argument.

"Ah! Indeed! You seem to share the captain's confidence. I see you wear a gun there, under your coat. How is that . . . carrying a weapon here in the capital?"

"I always pack a gun. Any minute I might run into men."

"Men you want to arrest, I presume?"

"No. Men who are hankering to kill me!"

"Indeed? May I ask what for?"

"Because I did arrest them once, and now that one thing or another . . . perhaps political influence . . . has helped them out of jail, they'll be looking for me."

Plain it was that Governor Stone was impressed with me, but scarcely favorably.

"No doubt you've had victims . . . er . . . you've killed men?"

"Only a few. I never counted."

That sickened the aristocratic governor from eastern Texas, and he turned to the others. "Gentlemen, manifestly the United

27

States deputy marshal will be an able lieutenant for Ranger Steele." He turned his face to MacNeal. "Have you anything further to say to me about the matter?"

"Only this, Governor Stone," replied MacNeal quickly. "Will you make a test case of this? Will you wait till Steele has succeeded or failed in his attempt to make Fairdale a law-abiding town? I shall find means to furnish you with authentic details of his work. Will you hold off signing this bill for a while?"

"Captain MacNeal, that is a most fair and reasonable request," replied the governor with some warmth. "If you are satisfied to make this a test of the ranger service, I shall be glad to wait, even a year or more. I remind you, I am open to conviction. You have made some remarkable statements in regard to your rangers. For the welfare of Texas I hope and pray they are true."

Governor Stone bowed to the captain, then to me, and in company with the adjutant general he left the office.

When Captain MacNeal turned to me he was white, and his jaw was working. "Russ!" he exclaimed passionately, calling me by the familiar name once common among my ranger comrades, "Russ, the future of the service depends on you and Vaughn Steele!"

Chapter Two

TWO FAIR LADIES

There never lived a more indomitable man than MacNeal. His agitation showed me not only the apparent hopelessness of this ranger venture, but also how his whole heart was in the service. It made me glad the captain had appealed to me. Right there, I conceived a strong desire to help him. And at the same time I had a strange feeling — something amounting to a premonition — that this undertaking with Vaughn Steele was to be a significant and fateful one in my life. So from the start I found the spirit that would encourage MacNeal.

"Well, Cap, if the future of the ranger service depends on Steele and me, it's in good hands."

He brightened at that and began to pace the room. "Yes, yes. You're right. I know him, and I know you. If it were only an ordinary job! But that report my ranger brought from Fairdale . . . here, read it at your leisure. It'll make you cold in the pit of your stomach."

"Not me, Cap. I never get sick that way." Then I grew earnest. "MacNeal, I like the job. I know I'll be proud to help Steele. I always wanted to work with him. This is a big thing, aside from what political move may hang upon it. But I have only one concern. Will Steele like me? I've heard of his patience, his forbearance, his reluctance to fight. You know, I've a temper. And I'm quick to pull a gun. My only concern is . . . will I suit Steele?"

The captain laughed and dived into his pocket to produce a paper. "Rather," he said. "Here are the names he asked me to pick from. The number of men named shows how difficult he expected it to be to get a man to tackle this job with him. And what he thinks of their fitness shows in the order he named them."

Russ Sittell was the first name on the list. That gave me a warm thrill, and more than a little surprise. Steele did not know me. To be sure, I had served the state, but as a ranger I had never been in Steele's class. However, as he was in a class by himself, and as he had chosen to elevate me to it, I gathered considerable pride from the fact and suddenly found myself bound to him by strong ties.

"Good!" exclaimed MacNeal, who evidently had been watching my face. "Russ, it's settled. The adjutant is glad to let me send you."

"Sure is good," I replied. "So, I'm to go in my capacity as United States deputy marshal, taking orders from Steele?"

"Absolutely. You're to obey him, trust him implicitly, help him all you can. Steele has a free hand. You both have free hands. You will never get a single order from this office. You have all the authority the adjutant can give and papers to prove it. You can arrest anybody without warrants. You can search any house or place without warrants. You can swear in any men as deputies and give them orders. You can . . . and you *must* . . . shoot when it's necessary.

"I'm glad you're quick with your gun. For Steele, with his damned stony nerve, risks his life too much. You'll obey him, yes. But tell him that in one sense I'm giving you a free hand with a gun. See?"

"Cap, the job grows on me," I said. "How about letters, reports, money?"

MacNeal went into his pocket again, but this time I made note that his hand dragged a little. No wonder, for it came forth with a huge bundle of greenbacks. I did not need to be told that it was his own money.

"Here's five thousand dollars. Take it to

Steele. Tell him to exercise care in spending but not to hamper developments by stinginess. There's more money, if it's needed.

"Now as to letters and reports, I think Steele will decide how and when they are to be sent to me. I gathered that he wanted you to be a secret aid. You will have no open relation with him. You'll not be known as an officer at first. Probably Steele will want you to pretend you're a cowboy or gambler or rustler . . . to make yourself known to mingle with this or that crowd. It seems to me, Russ, you're in for an adventure. I remember you always liked to be detailed on a job that promised adventure. Perhaps you'll get enough now, for once."

"Cap, I can stand a lot," I replied cheerfully. "This promises a lot, too. I'm eager to start. When?"

"At once. Wait a moment till Adjutant General Weed returns. Just a matter of form."

The adjutant general entered the office at that moment. He carried a card in his extended hand, and his face wore an expression of interest and expectancy. "Gentlemen, look here," he said, laying the card down upon a desk before us.

The captain and I bent over. Cards were

not frequent in those days, and I had never had my name on one. Upon this one I read:

COL. GRANGER LONGSTRETH
Mayor of Fairdale,
Pecos County, Texas

Both MacNeal and I were too surprised to speak. Straightening up, we looked at the adjutant.

"Quite a coincidence, isn't it? This man, Longstreth, is waiting. I haven't seen him. His card was brought to me. He wants to call on Governor Stone. The name Fairdale caught my eye, and it struck me that you gentlemen might be interested in the mayor of Fairdale, Pecos County, Texas."

"By George, this's luck!" exclaimed Mac-Neal. "Russ, I knew you'd bring luck. You always were the luckiest fellow. Here, let me have the report I gave you."

I returned it, and the captain, hurriedly turning over closely written pages, found the place he sought.

"Listen to this. 'The biggest man in Fairdale is Longstreth. He's rancher, cattle buyer, merchant. Of all the rich men about Fairdale he's the richest. He owns the inn. Rumored that he owns the biggest gambling resort. Couldn't substantiate rumor. He lives at his magnificent ranch, the finest in southwest Texas. Is often absent from home. He is the mayor. A splendid man, esteemed by his townsfolk. The only reason he has been given space in this report is because he's mayor of Fairdale, and Fairdale is wide open for all kinds of crime.' "

MacNeal closed the report and, returning it to me straightway, became thoughtful. Finally he added: "Steele hasn't reached Fairdale yet, so, of course, he knows nothing of this Mayor Longstreth. Equally sure it is that Longstreth knows nothing of Steele. I imagine that we can get some kind of interesting point of view from the mayor of the town we expect to clean up. He may be as honorable as any man and worthy of the esteem mentioned in the report. But . . . Fairdale is wide open. That sticks in my craw.

"Now, Adjutant, I'll suggest something. Let Sittell and me hide somewhere. I'll go behind that screen. Sittell will go into the closet and leave the door open an inch or so. You have Mayor Longstreth shown in here. Receive him cordially. Draw him out. That is, help him to talk.

"He has some motive for coming. Perhaps it's only to make a social call . . . to go home and be able to say he called on the governor. Whatever it is, you lead him to talk about

Fairdale. If he admits Fairdale is wide open, overrun by a bad lot, and that he can do nothing, why he'll be honest, and it won't hurt our case to favor his desire to meet the governor. But, if he laughs at any casual query of yours . . . if he makes light of your repetition of rumors regarding the viciousness of Fairdale, steer him off . . . don't let him meet Governor Stone. We know positively that Fairdale is a nest of secret and dangerous criminals. Now, Adjutant, what do you say?"

Weed entered readily into the little scheme. After MacNeal was placed behind the screen and I was in the closet, he rang for his clerk and bade him to show in the waiting gentleman.

I placed my eye to the narrow slit in the nearly closed door and had a good view of the larger part of the office. Presently the clerk entered and, to my surprise, was followed by two girls, one tall and dark, the other petite and fair. I wanted to bestow a second glance on them, but the entrance of a striking-looking man drew all my attention.

"Adjutant General Weed?" he asked, stepping forward.

"Yes. You are Colonel Granger Longstreth? Mayor Longstreth, I am pleased to meet you," replied the adjutant courteously.

"That honor is mine," said Longstreth, bowing. "Permit me to introduce my daughter, Ray, and my niece, Ruth Herbert."

My gaze leaped swiftly back and forth from this handsome, dark man to the daughter that resembled him and then to the niece, who, as she blushed at the adjutant's greeting, appeared to me to be about the prettiest girl I had ever seen.

"Will Governor Stone receive me?" asked Longstreth.

"I shall see. He is exceedingly busy. But, perhaps, I can arrange it. Please be seated." As he spoke, the adjutant brought chairs for the ladies. "Let me have the pleasure of a little chat. It is seldom, indeed, that I meet anyone, especially ladies, from so remote a corner of our great state as Fairdale. I have heard, too, that Fairdale was such a wild, uncivilized place. That must be a mistake."

The adjutant general smiled winningly. He was, indeed, very pleasant and likable in that mood, and his glance more than his words implied a compliment. For my part I would certainly not have expected these girls to belong to western Texas.

"I've never been to Fairdale," said Miss Ray Longstreth. Her voice surprised me. It was low, sweet, deep, like that of a singer who had thrilled me once. "Papa says it's a terrible place. But it's his home and is going to be my home."

Granger Longstreth laughed, and that laugh broke up a certain hardness of face I had been studying. "Adjutant Weed, my home town is the worst corner of Texas," he said. "There's no place on the Rio Grande that can hold a candle to it. No place for my daughter and niece. But they will go out.

"You see, I am a Louisianian by birth. Went West years ago, after the death of my wife. Have succeeded out there. My daughter has lived with relatives, except the last few years, which have been spent at school in Atlanta. I occasionally visited her, and, upon this last visit, she calmly announced her intention of going home with me. I stormed and pleaded. It was of no use. She's her father's daughter. She's going out to the ranch."

"Very commendable, I think," replied the adjutant. "And you, Miss Herbert, are also going out for a visit?"

"Yes. I'm crazy to ride broncos and meet cowboys," she said.

She had a lazy, Southern drawl, altogether charming to hear, but it was what she said, rather than her tone, that most interested me. I looked closer at her. She had chestnut hair, curly and unruly, gray or hazel eyes, a sweet, red mouth, and altogether a saucy arch kind of prettiness that made me feel I would not soon forget her.

"I envy the lucky cowboys," remarked Adjutant Weed with smile and bow. "If Fairdale is such a wild and dangerous place, there may be opportunities for cowboys to play the gallant." Then the adjutant turned to Longstreth. "Seriously, Mayor, what kind of a . . . a country is this you live in? We are very ignorant of life on the frontier of Texas. I have heard a rumor now and then about Fairdale and its lawlessness. But rumors only, very vague. We hear so much authentic news about places famous for rustlers and gunfighters that we have no time to trace rumors."

"Well, sir," replied Longstreth, "Fairdale is unique. I know Texas. And there's no town like it. We have about twenty-five hundred people. We have a rich country and are prosperous. There were a hundred thousand head of cattle in the valley when I left home. Then, we are close to the great ranges south of the Pecos. Naturally we attract the vicious element. But every isolated town does that. The queer thing about Fairdale is that every man looks askance at his neighbor. Each one personally is honest, it seems, but doubts the other. However, there is no open doubt. That wouldn't be healthy. When I was elected to office, there was no law. I have maintained a little. If I didn't, there would be no law at all. I have a county judge, a justice of the peace, and two sheriffs."

"Well, I suppose conditions, such as you mention, are certain to arise in the development of wild ranges," observed Weed.

"They are indeed. But I take a hopeful view of prospects. We are slowly progressing. The pioneer can't be stopped. Meanwhile, the gunmen are killing each other. And in time the outlaws and rustlers must go."

"I hope so . . . soon. While they're passing, it's hard on the honest pioneer." The adjutant paused a moment and played with a paper-knife upon his desk. Then he looked at Longstreth rather intently. "Colonel Longstreth, do you imagine a company of Texas Rangers would be of any use to you out there on the frontier?"

"Hardly. One of two things would happen. Either the lawless element would leave the country temporarily, until the rangers had left, then return to make us suffer all the more, or they would band together and annihilate the rangers."

The adjutant general raised his eyebrows in surprise. "Is there a large enough force to do that?"

"I believe there are a thousand badmen in Pecos County."

"Well, we can't spare a whole company of rangers, even if there were a chance to clean up Fairdale. I wonder how it would do to send . . . say, *one* ranger?"

Weed gazed with innocent, clear eyes straight at the mayor, and for his pains he received an incredulous stare, then a mellow laugh. While Longstreth's head lay back, as he was shaken with mirth, the adjutant turned away from his visitors, and I was sure some kind of signal passed between him and MacNeal.

"But, Colonel," rejoined Weed in expostulation, "you don't know rangers. Let me read a report from one ranger about another ranger's work. Miss Longstreth, and you, Miss Herbert, will surely find this interesting."

The adjutant picked over some papers, and, selecting one, he began to read. He had not progressed far before I realized that he was fabricating such a report as was never in the world written by any ranger. The adjutant showed a quick mind, and he was clever. As he read, the color came to Miss

Herbert's cheeks, and Miss Longstreth listened with mounting interest.

What purpose Weed had in mind, I could not divine, but he detailed accounts of hard riding, arrests, rescues, and fights, with a series of remarkable doings entirely new to me as a ranger. As far as these details were concerned, what puzzled me most was how he ever made them up. As he concluded and carefully replaced the papers on his desk, there was a significant silence.

"How splendid!" exclaimed Miss Longstreth. "What a noble fellow."

Her deep voice, sweet like a bell, made me look closer at her. I had at first noted her pale face and dark eyes and hair, but that was all. I had not really looked at her. This time I saw pride, fire, passion in her, and something that made me sure she had French blood. She had beauty, as I had never seen it in another woman. Then my gaze shifted to Miss Herbert, and the expression on her arch face gave me a feeling that was new to me. I must have been jealous of the adjutant's fictitious ranger.

"A ranger! I want to meet a man like that," she burst out. "I think I'd prefer him to the cowboys."

Somehow I gathered from Miss Herbert's tone that generally she attached persons she liked to her train, and I did not wonder at that.

"A remarkable report . . . almost inconceivable, unless you know character west of the Colorado," said Colonel Longstreth. "Is that the ranger's name, Steele . . . Vaughn Steele?"

The adjutant general showed surprise, but I was not surprised. I knew something of Steele's fame on the border. What did surprise me was to see Weed nod his head. "Yes, Steele's the ranger," he said. Probably he wanted Longstreth to carry back to Fairdale as strong an impression of the ranger as it was possible to give.

"I've heard of Steele," the colonel mused. "He's called the Lone Wolf Ranger. No, it's the Lone Star Ranger. That report about him is a remarkable document."

"Vaughn Steele. Lone Star Ranger," said Miss Longstreth dreamily. "Truly, I know little about the state and the country where my father lives. I'm to make my home where such a man as Vaughn Steele is needed. It's very strange. What is he like?" She asked the question suddenly.

"Steele? Oh, he's a magnificent fellow, Miss Longstreth," replied the adjutant, and it was evident to me that he meant to impress the daughter further, if possible. "Why, he'd

42

have to stoop and almost turn sidewise to come in that door. I think you ladies would find him too somber-faced, too stern to be handsome. He can talk, for he is well educated and has a fine mind, but he seldom talks unless it has to do with his work. He does strange, chivalric things. He is gentle, kind. Captain MacNeal tells me Steele's the best nurse among the rangers. He's brave as a lion. In fact, he's a composite of many traits. I suppose, more than anything else, his fame rests upon his marvelous quickness with a gun. That's his best asset as a ranger, and quite naturally the one least calculated to interest you ladies."

"Then he has killed men?" Miss Longstreth asked, shrinking, yet fascinated.

"Yes."

Weed let the single word stand with all its force. I would have liked to tell Miss Longstreth what MacNeal had said about Steele's reluctance to kill a man. But obviously the adjutant's purpose was to let the ranger appear, apart from his noble attributes, as a stern, ruthless, wonderful officer.

"Don't send Steele to Fairdale," interposed the colonel with a little laugh that made me start. "He's too valuable to your ranger service. Adjutant Weed, I thank you for your courtesy. Will you ask Governor

Stone to receive us now?"

"I'll have you taken in at once," replied the adjutant, rising. "I've enjoyed meeting you. May I ask when you leave?"

"By first stage tomorrow . . . to San Antonio."

The adjutant shook hands with Colonel Longstreth, then turned to the ladies. "Miss Longstreth, I wish you a pleasant journey and hope that you will like your new home. Miss Herbert, I'm sure you'll have your desire fulfilled. You'll ride broncos and work sad havoc among the cowboys. And you may meet the Lone Star Ranger. *¿Quien sabe?* Good bye."

He rang for his clerk, who led the party out. When they were gone, Weed closed the door, and MacNeal came forth from behind his screen and I out of the closet.

"What did you make of Longstreth, mayor of Fairdale?" queried Weed of the captain.

"He's not much of a mayor. Lax, I'd call him," replied MacNeal.

"He certainly wasn't backward about admitting the lawlessness at Fairdale. Say, but that must be a place! Russ, what did you think of Longstreth?"

I was non-committal on that score, but I said I was willing to tell what I thought about the colonel's daughter and his niece.

44

"You'll be on that stage tomorrow?"

"I sure will."

"Well, Marshal," said Weed, with his engaging smile, "your lot appears to begin pleasantly. Make the most of it."

Chapter Three

NEARLY A HOLD-UP

It did not take me long to show the wary captain that I could take the stage ride to San Antonio without danger of being recognized as a United States deputy marshal. I seldom visited the capital, always riding to and fro on horseback, and had few acquaintances. Having allayed his fears on this point, I talked to him a little more about our plan, asked his advice on this and that procedure, received it in good measure, and a stern parting reminder not to be backward in pulling my gun on behalf of my own and Steele's life, and then we said farewell.

Never had I faced a ranger assignment or any other kind with such a stir of blood and speculative mind. First, I sold my horse, pack, and trappings, keeping out from my old outfit only a few articles that I used in disguising myself. In my official capacity a disguise was often necessary — and healthy, to use Longstreth's expression — and I imagined the Fairdale enterprise might call for all manner of strategy.

I bought another gun, a small one, easily carried in a coat pocket, and that done I thought I had completed my preparation. But it developed, somewhat to my surprise, that I had a sudden and unaccountable dissatisfaction with my clothes and, for that matter, with my whole personal appearance. Not until I had purchased new suit, sombrero, boots, and other necessary articles, did I discover that I had been prompted by a strange desire to look well in the eyes of Miss Ruth Herbert whom I expected to meet on the stage ride to San Antonio.

The interest I felt in her was not amazing. I had observed similar symptoms, often before, but not lately. What amazed me was the realization that this time, and before I really thought about it, I was doing unprecedented things. At first it seemed funny. A man old in hardened experience, an adventurer, ranger, marshal of the wildest state in the Union — a gun-thrower without scruples — a fighter whose softer side must long ago have become blunted to finer feelings — an outlaw-hunter almost as alien as those he hunted — what business on earth had *I* to want to appear well in the eyes of a charming, arch-faced girl? After all, it was not in the least funny, and I experienced a depression unusual to my buoyant spirit. But I did not remain cast down for long.

The remainder of that day I kept to myself at the inn where I stayed and went to bed early. Next morning I was up with the sun, ready and eager for the ride, and what was to come after. My mind was strangely fertile with possibility and conjecture.

The stagecoach started from another inn, across town, and, when I got there, I found all the inside seats reserved, but I might ride on top of the coach with the driver. This did not please me, still, I had to make the best of it. Even in my disappointment I felt a little relief, the reason of which was not clear to me.

The stagecoach was a huge, lumbering affair, littered with baggage on top and tied behind, and already was nearly full of passengers. I imagined that, when the Longstreth party arrived, they would find it a tight squeeze in the coach.

I took my little pack of luggage and climbed up in front. It was the loftiest vehicle I had ever been on, and the seat was wide and comfortable, with a back rest. A rifle lay on the seat, and it reminded me that not by any means was it beyond the bounds of probability for the stage to be held up by highwaymen. The eighty-mile ride to San Antonio might be interesting for me from various points of view.

Four splendid horses were being hitched to the coach by stablemen. The stage driver, however, had not put in an appearance. Naturally I presumed, after the nature of stagecoach drivers, he was in at the bar, taking long odds against a future thirst. I was curious to see this driver I had to ride with, for I wanted to get along well with him. How pleasant it would have been if my old friend Joel Harkness, most noted of Texas stagecoach drivers, had been the one to handle the reins on this ride.

Scarcely had I had the thought when a grizzled and bronzed Texan in corduroys, high boots, and black sombrero full of holes strode from the inn. He wore a six-shooter and a belt full of cartridges, and he carried a long whip in his hand. It *was* Joel Harkness, and I remembered what MacNeal had said about my luck. Turning my head aside so Joel could not recognize me, I awaited developments.

"Say, who's thet up there on top?" I heard him ask somebody.

He was told that it was a passenger for San Antonio.

"Wal, he shore 'pears like one of these heah flash Mississippi River gamblers . . . all spick an' span," remarked Joel, not exactly in an undertone.

I was considerably crestfallen at the impression he had gathered from my new attire. The arrival of the Longstreth party, however, made me forget myself. They alighted from a hack. While the colonel went into the inn, probably for the same reason that made all stagecoach drivers and passengers late in starting, the ladies, both wearing long, gray ulsters and veils, got into the stage.

Joel clambered up on the seat, gave me a shove that was as unnecessary as it was powerful, and then he gathered up the reins, grumbling to himself. By dint of some strength of hand and no little dexterity, I regained my balance without falling off the stage. Then I turned to Joel, swore softly into his ear, and prodded him in the side with the gun I had in my coat pocket.

"Wal, dog-gone me!" he ejaculated. "If it ain't Russ . . ."

"My name's Russ . . . just Russ, on this ride," I whispered. "And I'm a tenderfoot or a cowboy, whichever you like. Savvy, Joel?"

He crushed my hand with his great paw. "Heah in Austin. Wal, I shore am surprised an' glad," he said. "Say, it was down Brownsville way I run into you last. I like this new job better, Russ. Shore there ain't so much dodgin' of bullets. Wal, what air you doin', Russ? Never seen you so togged out. Ain't been an' gone an' done took a pardner for life?"

"No. Same old job, Joel."

"Chasin' some o' the poor homeless cusses. I was on the dodge onct."

"Well, Joel, I'm after some cusses, sure, but they're not poor or homeless. They're rich and own a whole town."

"Wal, I shore seen thet kind of a bunch more'n onct in this heah Lone Star state. Say, who's the tall gent? Is he a passenger?"

Joel had caught sight of Colonel Longstreth who appeared, walking briskly toward the stage. He carried something in his hand.

"Hello, the new driver," he said, looking up. "You're Harkness, eh? Glad to make your acquaintance. My name's Longstreth. From Pecos."

He shook hands with Joel and gave him a flask, which the driver took beamingly. Then Longstreth, waving his hand, stepped up into the coach.

"Uncle, I want to ride outside . . . on top of the coach," spoke up a voice that made me start.

"Ruth, you'd better not," replied Miss

51

Longstreth. "It'll be dusty and sunny up there."

"But Ray, I can't breathe in here," protested Ruth. "It was bad enough before Uncle got in. Now, I'm squeezed to death. Uncle, won't you ask if I may ride outside?"

"Ray, it's pretty crowded. Let Ruth go up. She likes that kind of thing," said the colonel. Then he raised his voice. "Hello, driver, will you make room up there for my niece?"

"Now, Mister Longstreth, I'm shore deelighted," replied Joel. "There's room for her an' a nice easy seat."

Miss Ruth lightly leaped out.

"Wait, Ruth, I'll give you a lift," said the colonel.

But she did not need any. She gathered up the long ulster, disclosing little feet and shapely ankles, and climbed like a boy. It was my hand that caught and steadied her, and I moved over toward Joel, leaving my seat for her.

"Thank you," she said, and she looked at me.

"Wal, we're off," called Joel cheerily, and he cracked his whip.

The horses started, the coach rattled, and presently we were going at a trot down a good road toward the open country.

I had faced the open on many a ride but never with the sensations that beset me now. The close proximity of this girl had a strange effect on me. At every jolt of the coach her arm touched mine, and sometimes we bumped shoulder to shoulder. I could see out of the corner of my eye that she had tucked the veil back from her face. I wanted to look directly at her, but, as I thought that would be imprudent, I refrained.

"Miss Longstreth . . . ," began Joel.

"Herbert . . . Ruth Herbert," corrected the girl. "I'm Colonel Longstreth's niece."

"Aw. Wal, now, Miss Ruth, it's shore powerful fine to hev you up heah. This gentleman's name's . . . Russ. He's an ole acquaintance . . . a cowboy . . . an' I'm shore sorry to say, out of a job. Reckon he's as glad as me to hev company."

My vanity suffered a little shock at Joel's naïve manner of introducing me, but it was forgotten when I looked at Miss Herbert.

"Mister Russ," she said demurely, and bowed.

I bowed, too, spoke, and with sound of my voice suddenly lost all stiffness and embarrassment. If ever I had met a born flirt, it was then. Her eyes were hazel, clear, roguish, with a devil in the deeps of them. Her face was round, but not plump, with a fine

53

skin, just a little tanned by sun and wind. Her lips were red, sweet, extremely thought-provoking. She had a good, square little chin, denoting a will of her own. This close sight of her made me think she was less pretty than I at first had believed, but it gave me a feeling of spirit more attractive than any prettiness.

After an interchange of commonplaces usually incident to an introduction, Miss Ruth gave me a theme for conversation by expressing fervent admiration for Joel's splendid horses. I knew horses almost as well as if I had really been the cowboy Joel had pretended I was. So I talked about horses. However, the talk was not one-sided, because Miss Ruth loved horses, had owned and ridden many, and was gifted with what a cowboy called horse sense.

We began to get pretty well acquainted, although I did not see that there was any change in a certain subtle something that I had before encountered in Southern girls of quality. There was a considerable difference between the niece of a rich rancher, who evidently belonged to a family of blooded Louisiana planters, and a cowboy out of a job. Time and again I caught Miss Ruth looking at me, neither hiding her interest nor something that puzzled her. This occasioned me to redouble my efforts to be worthy of such attention.

Joel put in his big voice occasionally, telling things about the road and the country, sometimes sandwiching in a little anecdote. There was no doubt that, between the two of us, Miss Ruth passed a morning far from dull.

At noon Joel pulled up at a water hole and called all hands to get down for a rest in the shade and lunch while the horses were feeding. Nobody lost any time complying. Besides Colonel Longstreth and his daughter there had been five other passengers inside the coach — one woman and four men. These last were not interesting.

Miss Ruth introduced me to her cousin and her uncle. I was aware of a keen scrutiny from the genial rancher. The girls laid aside ulsters, veils, and hats, and appeared to be more comfortable. Certainly they looked better. When Miss Ruth went to the little brook and began to bathe her face, I ventured to say that alkali water was decidedly not good for the complexion.

"I don't care. It's cool," she replied, and I liked her the better for it.

It appeared, presently, that everybody except myself had brought lunch. Miss Ruth called her cousin's attention to my lack of lunch, and I was promptly asked to share theirs. The opportunity thus presented itself for me to take a good and unobtrusive look at Miss Ray Longstreth.

She was slender, but the womanly development of her figure made me think she was twenty years old, at the least. She had the most exquisite hands I had ever seen, and her wrists and arms were molded in like symmetry. Close by, she did not resemble her father so much. She looked tired, quiet, even melancholy, yet that did not detract from her beauty. A finely chiseled oval face, clear, olive-tinted skin, long eyes set wide apart and black as coal, beautiful to look into, a slender, straight nose that had something nervous and delicate about it which made me think of a Thoroughbred, a mouth by no means small but perfectly curved, and hair like jet. All these features proclaimed her loveliness to me and confirmed my first impression. She was a descendant of one of the old French families that had settled Louisiana.

She was gracious to me, and there was not any of the aloofness that I had felt or imagined I had felt in her cousin. Strange to me was this quality I sensed in Miss Ruth, who I believed was ready to flirt with me. Somehow, Ray Longstreth made me feel how a man could fight for a woman. I liked her. And thinking of that, I was surprised to find that I disliked her father. There seemed absolutely no cause for it.

My instincts were queer, and, though I had not learned to understand them, I had lived to find out they rarely directed me wrong. After lunch I went over to where Joel sat and talked with him. There was to be an hour of rest. The month was April, and in the middle of the day it was sultry, hot, without a breath of wind.

While I was with Joel, I heard Miss Ruth tell her cousin that I was a cowboy out of a job and that she had supposed cowboys were all illiterate, ignorant. I thought she said something more about me, but in too low a voice for me to hear. Most shamelessly would I have listened. When Joel finished his pipe, he appeared inclined to a little nap, so I left him and found for myself a comfortable seat located under a mesquite, where I could see, yet not readily be seen.

How interested I was in this Longstreth party! It occurred to me that I ought to tell them I was on the way to Fairdale. But whenever I met ladies the worst of my job manifested itself — I had to be the deputy marshal, the hounder of criminals, before I could be the gentleman. That keen instinct

57

of mine told me I would have more to do with the mayor of Fairdale and his daughter and niece, but I had no inkling whether that relation would be friendly or otherwise.

I had taken him at his face value — a fine, genial, Southern rancher, good-natured and apparently lax in certain principles. I imagined he cared more for mint juleps and horses than he cared for his family. But that might have been imagination only, in line with my instinctive dislike.

What did he intend to do away out there in the Pecos country with this beautiful daughter? Probably, as he had intimated, he had no choice in the matter of her going. The cousin, I supposed, would visit them for a while, then return to Louisiana. But Ray Longstreth struck me as a girl close to womanhood — one who had strong ideas of duty and who would be hard to change. She would stay in her father's home, if it lay in the middle of the Staked Plains.

Again there came over me that subtle and unintelligible promise of the future. In a way, like nearly all men used to lonely lives, I was a dreamer. Dreaming never interfered with my practical duties, and it often enabled me to forget much that I did not want to remember. If Vaughn Steele and I were ever to be mixed up with this party I had so strangely fallen in with, what kind of a relation would it be?

For myself, I admitted straight out that I could not very long resist the demure Miss Ruth. She had a petiteness, a fragility, a prettiness that appealed to me, and I believed she had a temper as well as a coquetry that would tantalize my heart out of me in a day. For Steele, I could not speak, though I could dream. He was young. I had heard that he never approached women except when his ranger duty demanded. Still, I imagined that one look at Ray Longstreth would be his undoing.

Even while this dream conjecture held me, I thought that it was silly and sentimental. Likewise, I thought it might just as well be my prophetic sense of things to come. Anyway, dreams aside, the situation at Fairdale was bound to be absorbing. Here was Steele, a wonderful instrument for the subjugation of criminals, let foot loose on the most vicious settlement in the wilds of Texas. Here was myself, confessedly an adventurer, yet one who could love his comrade. Here was Colonel Longstreth, a lax mayor, sure to oppose ranger interference in the law and order of his town. Here was Ray Longstreth, a beautiful girl, bordering on womanhood, proud, fiery, surely passionate in her devotion to her kin, surely gentle and noble, surely one who would hate any form of wickedness. Lastly, here was Ruth Herbert, a piquant little disturber of man's peace. Verily that was a combination of characters and possibilities calculated to make even me draw a deep, full breath of pure joy and face the future with all my spirit aflame, yet with a graver something, an earnestness never before felt, knocking at my heart.

Joel's call roused me out of my reverie. I helped him hitch up. The passengers betook themselves to the coach and settled themselves for a long ride. Miss Ruth patted the horses. I awaited her pleasure while Joel climbed to his seat.

When she did get ready to climb, I offered to assist her, but she shook her head. As my luck would have it, she slipped on the second step and fell into my arms. There was laughter then, and embarrassment, and no further refusal of my help up to the driver's seat. Miss Ruth had more color in her cheeks, too.

This time she took the middle seat next to Joel, and, for all the attention she paid to me, I might not have been on the coach. Her manner occasioned some reflection on my part. What I had done on the spur of the moment, when she fell into my arms, I had no idea, unless it was that I might have held her just a moment too long. I made one or two unsuccessful attempts to enlist her attention again, or a little of it, and then I gave up trying. I threw a robe back on top of the coach, and, climbing over the seat, I lay down.

My intention was to go to sleep, but it was frustrated by a rather active mind, so to carry out my idea of indifference, I pretended to sleep. Under the edge of my silk scarf, with which I had covered my face, I saw Miss Ruth turn twice to look at me and heard her tell Joel something.

"Wal, he's all in, poor boy, no wonder," said that worthy with a most amazing solicitude. "Grand boy, Russ is, Miss Ruth, but he's jest onable to hold a job."

"Why?"

"Because he's plumb wild."

"Wild? Why, he seemed so . . . nice," she said. "My cousin thought so, too."

"Nice? Wal, reckon Russ's the nicest boy thet ever punched a steer. Comes from good family, Russ does. But he's jest wild. Why, if I'd tell you some of his cowboy stunts, you'd think Joel Harkness shore an ole liar."

"Tell me some," she said.

Joel was noted for his loquacity and his stories. He began to talk, and he made me the hero of more fights, more conquests of fair ladies, of more rescues and wild rides and strange adventures than could possibly have been the experience of a dozen cowboys.

"But if only Russ'd fall in love with a nice girl, one as could boss him an' put a cinch on his wildness, wal, he'd shore be saved," said the old villain in conclusion.

"Maybe," returned Miss Ruth, with a glance back at me. "But wouldn't it be risky for the girl?"

At this juncture I quickly lifted the scarf and met her gaze full. Disconcerted and flushing, she whirled away. Then the shaking of her shoulders and a sound like smothered mirth furnished more food for reflection.

That roused me to an Homeric mood. She would probably laugh at me more, unless I did something to justify to some little degree the reputation Joel had given me. So I resumed my seat beside her and, if anything, sat a little closer.

"Didn't you say you were crazy to meet cowboys?" I asked abruptly.

"Sir!" she exclaimed with a start.

"Now, honest, didn't you ever say that?"

The pink cheeks shaded to red, and she turned to me stiffly, yet she was not far from laughing. "Yes, I said that," she replied.

"How on earth you know, I can't imagine. You guessed it! Well, I *was* crazy to meet cowboys."

The emphasis on the past tense was not lost upon me.

"You don't seem to be making the best of your opportunity," I retorted.

At that she faced straight ahead and made no reply. But she looked anything except dangerous.

Leaning a little nearer to her, I said in a low tone: "Do you believe in love at first sight?"

"No," she replied with stinging coldness. Then she turned her back upon me and engaged Joel's attention.

I had made her angry and was glad of it. The remainder of the ride apparently would be lonely for me. It certainly was monotonous, so far as scenery was concerned. The road was level and smooth. The horses kept at a steady trot. On each side spread a scant growth of brush, with occasional mesquites, and far into the distance stretched the green and yellow plain to merge into dim hills or clouds on the horizon. There was not a living creature to be seen. I looked and mused, tried to be oblivious of the girl so close to me, tried not to hear her vivacious talk and occasional merry laugh.

After a while two dark specks appeared against the green, far down the road. They were horses. I spoke to Joel and pointed.

"Jest seen them," he replied, "but wasn't shore what they was. My eyes ain't shurp fer distance any more."

"Do you meet any travelers between Austin and San Antonio?" asked Miss Ruth.

"Shore. Allus meetin' some. That's the wust of this trip. You jest never can pick out the road agents."

"Road agents. What are they?" queried Miss Ruth.

"Highwaymen! Robbers!"

"Oh, you never meet any?" she said with eyes wide.

"Lots of them. I've been held up twice this side of San Antonio."

"How dreadful! What do road agents usually do when they . . . hold you up?"

"Wal, they jump out from the brush or drop out of the clouds, so to say, an' surprise me before I can pull a gun. One feller holds the hosses an' the others make the passengers git out an' line up an' deliver. I've met some pretty decent road agents . . . fellers thet wouldn't rob a lady."

"Joel, those horses have gone out of sight," I interposed quietly.

"So they hev. Mebbe hid by a bend in the

64

road or dropped behind a hill."

"Perhaps. But the road looks straight and level, far as I can see."

"Them horses was all of five miles off, wasn't they, Russ?"

"More than that."

He said nothing further, and I made no other comment. Miss Ruth looked from Joel to me, with something of alarm in her glance. Then I gazed ahead, trying to espy the horses that had disappeared.

The incident might not have any significance, and then again it could mean a great deal. There was an even chance. So I would have been relieved to see the horses show up again. They didn't. When we had covered two miles, I began to consider the disappearance unusual, and another mile brought misgivings. From the lay of the land ahead there did not appear to be any good reason why travelers should turn off the road out of sight.

"Stop the stage, Joel," I said.

"Reckon that'll be about the deal," replied Joel gruffly, as he hauled on the reins. Presently he brought the stage to a halt.

"Miss Herbert, would you mind hiding my money somewhere about you?" I asked her, producing my roll of greenbacks. "If we're held up, there's a chance they won't

65

search such a demure and innocent little maid as you are."

She missed entirely the satire in my remark, and I felt a little ashamed. As she took the money, there was fire in her eye. "I'll hide it all right," she said.

Then with swift directness, and as absolutely unabashed as if I had been her brother, she lifted her skirt. Swiftly, as I tried to turn away my eyes, I could not help seeing the little foot and shapely leg thrust out. I jumped down off the coach.

"What's up?" asked the colonel sharply.

"Reckon we ain't shore," replied Joel. "But we want Miss Ruth to go inside. If you heah me yell, put the women down between the seats, an' them of you as has guns git busy."

That was all from Joel. Colonel Longstreth laughed, which fact struck me as odd. His daughter murmured plaintively. Some of the other men muttered. I helped Miss Ruth down and into the coach. Then I climbed back. Joel cracked his long whip, and we resumed our journey.

Joel had his rifle across his knees and his gun by his side on the seat. I held both my guns in readiness. We were just as liable to be held up as we were not. The fact was that travelers usually were wary about carrying considerable money or valuables. That five thousand dollars of MacNeal's suddenly became a white elephant on my hands.

Joel kept the horses at a steady trot, and we covered another couple of miles. Just ahead the road turned slightly at a point where the brush grew thick and straggly clumps of mesquite marked lower ground.

"Hit the pace now, Joel," I said. "If we're jumped, it'll be hereabouts."

"Keep your eye peeled, boy," replied Joel as he put the horses to a brisker trot.

Fortunately, here the road ran somewhat down hill, and the sharp gait of the horses might appear natural. It would never have done to race by that dangerous point. For, if there were robbers awaiting our approach, they would shoot the leaders of a running team.

I peered ahead from side to side of the road, looking low down between the trees and bushes, trying to spy out dark figures or the legs of horses. At the same time I had a sharp eye sweeping the side of the road. Just before we reached the bend, I discovered fresh horse tracks leading into the brush. Joel, too, saw them. But no riders or horses were in sight.

We bowled along, turned the curve down into a little swale where water ran in wet season. Here, if anywhere, would be the place. Certainly I expected to hear the harsh "Halt!" ring out, and I meant to shoot at the voice. But nothing happened, and we trotted out of the swale to level ground once more.

"Looked us over an' shore lost their nerve or rid ahaid to make a stand somewheres," said Joel.

We agreed on that. However, the situation was less critical. We entered upon another long level stretch, bordered by both dense patches and open places. After we had passed the first few thickets, we began to feel easier. Joel drew the horses to a less wearing gait. Still we did not lack vigilance, and for me, what with the excitement of keen watching, the afternoon passed swiftly.

It was just sunset when we made out a cluster of adobe houses that marked the half way point between Austin and San Antonio. Here was stationed a comfortable inn for wayfarers and the home of an acquaintance, with whom I had stayed once. This place was the last where I had any reason to fear being recognized before the Longstreth party, and, accordingly, I made my plans.

It developed, when I questioned Joel about my acquaintance, that I need fear no risk at all, for he had moved to Austin. Presently we drew up before the inn, where the landlord and his family and a number of loungers awaited the stage with that interest common to isolated people upon the arrival of the one daily event of consequence. I entered the inn without waiting for the Longstreth party.

Supper was soon ready, and at table I found myself next to Miss Herbert. She appeared to be looking for me — apparently she had forgotten her annoyance. I did not mention the money she had of mine, and I divined she wanted to speak of it, but found the matter a little difficult to approach.

Supper was usually merry when it was eaten in a wild country, half way between civilized points. Joel Harkness was at his best. I had to kick him in the shin to shut off further encomiums calculated to bring me into notice. Miss Ruth heard me kick him, and it made her thoughtful. Colonel Longstreth was inclined to joke about the incident of the afternoon.

Miss Longstreth enjoyed her supper and was evidently excited about the journey. It was something to hear her low laugh. She appeared interested in me and asked me what way my path led beyond San Antonio.

I replied that I was out of work and did not know what I was going to do or where I would head for.

She looked sympathetic, and so did her father. Manifestly I had given an impression somewhat at variance with the one Miss Ruth had. For I caught her grave questioning look and suddenly remembered again the huge roll of money I had given her for safekeeping.

After supper we all assembled in a big sitting room where an open fireplace with blazing mesquite sticks gave out warmth and cheery glow. I had gotten hold of a paper and was reading at a table in one corner of the room when Miss Ruth came up to me. She had something in her hand wrapped in a handkerchief.

"Haven't you forgotten your money?" she asked.

"Why, so I had. But it was in a safe . . . in safekeeping."

She blushed. "Isn't this an awful lot of money for a poor cowboy, out of a job, to be carrying around?" she asked severely.

"It's all I have in the world," I replied, as if it were two dollars. "I'd rather no one but you knew about it. Please don't tell."

"Certainly not," she replied. "Mister Russ, I don't know about you," she went on dubiously.

"If you hadn't been so cold, you'd have known all . . ."

"Here's your money," she interrupted.

Hastily I took off the handkerchief and put the bills in my pocket. "Thank you," I said. "But I almost wish we'd been held up and robbed."

"Why?" she asked blankly.

"Because I'll treasure this money now. I can't ever spend it. How could I? And I'll always think of . . ."

She silenced me with a look and turned away.

As I glanced after her, I saw two dark-faced men, strangers who had not appeared before, and they were watching me from a doorway. As I caught a glimpse of them, they stepped back out of sight.

Chapter Four

FLOYD LAWSON

It flashed over me that the strangers had seen the roll of greenbacks pass from Miss Ruth's hand to mine. This fact disturbed me. In Texas in the 'Seventies it was always bad policy to let strangers see any considerable sum of money. If it had been my own, however, its possession might not have given me so much uneasiness. I pondered a moment. Then, with an assurance that was my nature as much as it was the habitual sense of my authority, I went to look over these two men.

The doorway opened onto a patio and across from that was a little dingy, dim-lighted barroom. Here I found the innkeeper dispensing drinks to the two strangers. They glanced up when I entered, and fell to whispering.

I imagined I had seen one of them before. In Texas, where outdoor men were so rough, bronzed, bold, and sometimes grim of aspect, it was no easy task to pick out the crooked ones. But my years of ranger and marshal service had augmented a natural instinct or gift to read character, or at least to sense the evil in men — and I knew at once that these strangers were dishonest.

"Hev somethin'?" one of them asked, leering.

Both looked me up and down. Probably they were puzzled to understand why my clothes gave an impression that did not fit my face.

"No, thanks . . . I don't drink," I replied, and returned their scrutiny with interest. "How's tricks in the Big Bend?"

Both men stared. It had taken only a close glance for me to recognize a type of ruffian most frequently met in the Big Bend of the Rio Grande, an outlaw-infested region. These strangers had that stamp, and their surprise proved I was right.

Here the innkeeper showed signs of uneasiness and seconded the surprise of his customers. No more was said at the instant, and the two rather hurriedly went out.

"Say, boss, do you know those fellows?" I asked the innkeeper.

"Nope."

"Which way did they come?"

"Now I think of it, them fellers rid in from both corners today," he replied, and he put his hands on the bar and looked at me. "They nooned heah, comin' from Santone, they said, an' by Josh! they trailed in after the stage."

If I needed to know any more, that was enough. These fellows had met the stage, which for some reason or other they had not halted, and they had followed us back with evil intent that waited upon opportunity.

Might I have been mistaken? In my ranger days I had acquired the habit of always anticipating violent action, dark deeds. But that was not unnatural. I knew Texas. I gravitated toward criminals. I had knowledge. A resident of eastern Texas would have found in me a cheerful presager of fights, hold-ups, assaults, and killings, and he would have been aghast, possibly disgusted, as had been Governor Stone. The truth was, I seldom made mistakes, and I did not intend to give these dark-faced strangers the benefit of a doubt.

When I returned to the sitting room, Colonel Longstreth was absent — also several of the other passengers. Miss Ruth sat in the chair I had vacated, and across the table from her sat Miss Longstreth. I went directly to them.

"Miss Herbert, I was rude today," I said in a low, earnest voice. "But only teasing. I ask your pardon now, because I want you to take me seriously."

I paused, while Miss Ruth looked up in amazement, and her cousin leaned forward in sudden interest.

"The men whom we expected to hold up the stage today have followed us here. I've just seen them. They mean evil. I want to warn you to be careful. Lock your door . . . bar your window tonight."

"Oh!" cried Miss Ruth, very low.

"Thank you, we'll be careful," said her cousin gratefully. The rich color had faded in her cheek. "I saw those men watching you from that door. They had such bright black eyes. Is there really danger . . . here?"

"I think so," was my reply.

Soft, swift steps behind me preceded a harsh voice.

"Hands up!"

No man quicker than I to recognize the intent in those words! My hands shot up. Miss Ruth uttered a little frightened cry and sank into her chair. Miss Longstreth turned white, and her eyes dilated. Both girls had glances riveted behind me.

"Turn around," ordered the harsh voice.

Like a soldier I pivoted. The big, dark stranger, the bearded one who had whispered to his comrade in the barroom and asked me to drink, had me covered with a cocked gun.

He strode forward, his eyes gleaming, pressed the gun against me, and with his other hand dived into my inside coat pocket and tore out my roll of bills. Then he reached low at my hip, felt my gun, and took it. Then he slapped my other hip, evidently in search of another weapon.

That done, he backed away, wearing an expression of fiendish satisfaction that made me think he was only a common thief — a novice at this kind of game.

His comrade stood in the door with a gun leveled at the other two men, who stood frightened, speechless. "Git a move on, Bill," called this fellow, and he took a hasty glance backward.

A stamp of hoofs came from outside. Of course, the robbers had horses waiting. The one called Bill strode across the room and with brutal, careless haste began to prod the two men with his weapon and to search them.

The robber in the doorway called: "Rustle!" and disappeared.

I wondered where the innkeeper was and Colonel Longstreth and the other two passengers who had ridden with us. The bearded robber quickly got through with his searching, and from his growls I gathered he had not been well remunerated.

Then he wheeled to us once more. I had not moved a muscle, stood perfectly calm, with my arms high. He strode back with his bloodshot eyes fastened upon the girls. Miss Longstreth never flinched, but her little cousin appeared about to faint.

"Don't yap there!" he said, low and hard. He had thrust the gun close to Ruth.

Then I knew for sure that he was no knight of the road, but a plain cutthroat robber. Danger always acted strangely upon me, made me exult in a kind of cold glow. But now something hot worked within me. I had the little gun in my pocket. The robber had missed it. And I began to calculate chances.

"Any money, jewelry, diamonds?" ordered the ruffian fiercely.

Miss Ruth had collapsed, so he made at Miss Longstreth. She stood with her hands at her breast. Evidently the robber took this position to mean that she had valuables concealed there. But I fancied she had instinctively pressed her hands against a throbbing heart.

"Come out with it!" he said harshly, reaching for her.

"Don't dare touch me!" she cried, her eyes ablaze. She did not move. She had nerve. It made me thrill.

I saw I was going to get my chance, if I

could only wait. Waiting has been a science with me. But here it was hard. Miss Ruth had fainted, and that was well. Miss Longstreth had fight in her, which fact helped my chance, yet made injury possible to her.

She eluded two lunges he made at her. Then his rough hand caught her waist and with one pull ripped it asunder, exposing her beautiful shoulder white as snow.

"Mister Russ!" she wildly appealed.

The prospect of being robbed or even killed had not shaken Miss Longstreth's nerve as had this brutal tearing off of half her waist. My icy control seemed to crack as if with heat. The ruffian was only turned partially away from me. For myself, I could have waited longer. But for her!

His gun was still held dangerously upward, close to her. I watched only that. Then a bellow made me jerk my head.

Colonel Longstreth stood in the doorway in a magnificent rage. He had no weapon. Strange how he showed no fear!

He bellowed something again.

My shifting glance caught the robber's sudden movement. It was a kind of start. He seemed stricken. I expected him to shoot Longstreth. Instead, the hand that clutched Miss Longstreth's torn waist loosened its hold. The other hand, with its cocked weapon, slowly dropped till it pointed to the floor. That was my chance. Swift as a flash I drew my gun and fired.

Thud! went my bullet, and I could not tell on the instant whether it hit him or went into the ceiling. Then the robber's gun boomed harmlessly. He fell, with blood spurting over his face. I realized I had hit him, but the small bullet had glanced.

Miss Longstreth reeled and might have fallen had I not supported her. It was only a few steps to a couch, to which I half led, half carried her. Then I rushed out of the room, across the patio, through the bar to the yard. Nevertheless, I was cautious.

In the gloom stood a saddled horse, probably the one belonging to the fellow I had shot. His comrade had escaped. Returning to the sitting room, I found a condition approaching pandemonium.

The innkeeper rushed in, pitchfork in hands. Evidently he had been out at the barn. He was now shouting to find out what happened. Joel Harkness was trying to quiet the men who had been robbed. The woman, wife of one of the men, had come in, and she had hysterics. The girls were still and white.

Bill lay where he had fallen, and I guessed I had made a fair shot, after all. And, lastly, the thing that struck me strangest of all was Longstreth's rage. I never saw such passion. Like a caged lion he stalked and roared, and I saw him bestow a kick on the prostrate robber. I had no time then to think of his actions, but as was my habit I missed nothing that occurred.

There came a quieter moment in which the innkeeper shrilly protested. "Man! what'er you ravin' aboot? Nobody's hurt, an' that's lucky. I swear to God I hadn't nothin' to do with them fellers!"

"I ought to kill you, anyhow!" replied Longstreth, and his voice now astounded me. I saw that he had a gun, and I was about to remonstrate with him when he put it in his pocket.

When I turned, I realized that he was recovering from passion which had transformed him. Here I sensed a power incalculable at the moment.

"Russ, is this thug dead?" he asked.

Upon examination we found that my bullet had furrowed the robber's temple, torn a great piece out of his scalp, and, as I had guessed, had glanced. He was not seriously injured and already showed signs of returning consciousness.

"Drag him out of here," ordered Longstreth, and he turned to his daughter.

Before the innkeeper reached me, I had secured the money and gun taken from me. Presently we recovered the property of the other men. Joel helped the innkeeper carry the injured man somewhere outside.

Miss Longstreth was sitting, white but composed, upon the couch where lay Miss Ruth, who evidently had been carried there by the colonel. I did not believe she had wholly lost consciousness, and now she lay very still, with eyes dark and shadowy, her face pallid and wet. The colonel, now that he finally remembered his womenfolk, seemed to be gentle and kind. He talked soothingly to Miss Ruth, made light of the adventure, and said she must learn to have nerve out here where such things happened.

"Can I be of any service?" I asked solicitously.

"Thanks, Russ . . . guess there's nothing you can do," replied the colonel. "Talk to these frightened girls while I go see what's to be done with that thick-skulled robber." Then, telling the girls that there was no more danger, he went out.

Miss Longstreth sat with one hand holding her torn waist in place, while she extended the other to me. I took it awkwardly, I fear, but she was so wonderful then that I was embarrassed. She pressed my hand.

"You saved my life," she said in grave, sweet seriousness.

"No, no!" I exclaimed. "He might have struck you, hurt you . . . but no more."

"I saw murder in his eyes He thought I had jewels under my dress. I couldn't bear his touch. The beast! I'd have fought. Surely my life was in peril!"

"Did you kill him?" asked Miss Ruth who lay, listening.

"Oh, no. He's not badly hurt," I returned.

"I'm very glad he's alive," said Miss Longstreth, shuddering.

"My intention was bad enough," I went on. "It was a ticklish place for me. You see . . . he was half drunk, and I was afraid his gun might go off. Fool careless he was!"

"Yet you say you didn't save me!" Miss Longstreth returned quickly.

"Well, let it go at that," I responded. "I saved you something, and I'm proud."

"Tell me about it?" asked Miss Herbert, who was fast recovering.

So, happy to have a chance to talk to her, I told the incident from my point of view.

"Then you stood there all the time with your hands up, thinking of nothing . . . watching for nothing except a little moment when you might draw your gun?" asked Miss Ruth.

"I guess that's about it," I replied.

There was no occasion for me to regret that I had wanted to appear well in Miss Ruth's eyes.

"Ruth," said Miss Longstreth thoughtfully, "we're fortunate to have Mister Russ for a traveling companion on part of this wild journey. Papa scouts . . . laughs at danger. He seemed to think there was no danger. Yet he raved after it came."

"Go with us all the way to Fairdale . . . please?" asked Miss Ruth, sweetly offering her hand.

"Glad to go," I burst out, taking the proffered hand. What I lacked in speech I made up in pressure.

"But, Ruth, you should not ask so much," protested Miss Longstreth. "It may not suit Mister Russ. Did you not say he was . . . out of work?"

"Yes, out of a job. Poor . . . no money," she replied, and the demure little devil came back to her eyes. "I tell you what, Ray. Give Mister Russ a job! Your horses are coming. You'll buy more out here. Mister Russ is a cowboy. He knows horses. *I* can recommend him."

"Indeed, that's worth thinking of," replied Miss Longstreth. "Would you consider an offer from me, Mister Russ?"

"Consider it! Well, I think . . . I will," I replied, half bewildered by the idea and by Miss Ruth's little hand squeezing mine. "Wouldn't you need to consult your father?"

"Not at all. I've long had my own horses to take care of. And, when you see them, you'll understand why I am particular."

"What would be my duties?" I inquired, prolonging the pleasure of this startling new proposition.

"Merely to take care of my horses. Of course, you can have a boy or man to help you. Then I would expect you to ride with me and Ruth. We love riding. Papa made strenuous objections to the idea of taking my horses out to Fairdale. You know, he expects I'll last there only a few months. But I'm going for good."

"Miss Longstreth, I admire your pluck," I said. "Do you know . . . Fairdale is wild?"

"Yes, I've heard, but I don't pay much heed to warnings. I understand more . . . now . . . after tonight. I don't fear, but then it makes me a little sick. His home should be my home. I don't really know my father. I . . ." She broke off here and I respected her emotion.

"Shall you need references as to my character?" I asked.

"No," she replied.

"Well . . . let Miss Herbert decide it," I replied. "She made the suggestion. Let her say whether I go or not."

Miss Longstreth showed surprise.

"Yes," replied Miss Ruth instantly.

Colonel Longstreth returned then and, after bidding me what I thought a rather curt good night, which perhaps seemed so by contrast to the graciousness of the girls, he led them away.

Before going to bed I went outside to take a look at the injured robber, and perhaps to ask him a few questions. To my surprise he was gone and so was his horse. The innkeeper was dumbfounded. He said that he had left the fellow on the floor in the barroom.

"Had he come to?" I inquired.

"Sure. He asked me for whiskey."

"Did he say anything else?"

"Not to me. I heard him talkin' to the father of them girls."

"You mean Colonel Longstreth?"

"I reckon. He sure was some riled, wasn't he? Jest as if I was to blame fer thet two-bit hold-up!"

"What did you make of the old gent's rage?" I asked, watching the innkeeper.

He scratched his head dubiously. He was sincere, and I believed in his honesty. "Wal,

I'm dog-goned if I know what to make of it. But I reckon he's either crazy or got more nerve than most Texans."

"More nerve, maybe," I replied. "Show me a bed now, innkeeper."

Once in bed in the dark I composed myself to think over the several events of the evening. I called up the details of the hold-up and carefully revolved them in my mind. I approved of my own course of action — could not see how it could have been improved upon. The colonel's wrath, under circumstances where most any Texan would have been cool, nonplused me, and I put it down to a choleric temperament. I pondered long on the action of the robber when Longstreth's bellow of rage burst in upon us. This ruffian, as bold and mean a type as I had ever encountered, had for some reason or other been startled. From whatever point I viewed his strange indecision, I could come to only one conclusion — his start, his check, his fear had been that of recognition.

I compared this effect with the suddenly acquired sense I had gotten of Colonel Longstreth's powerful personality. Why had that desperate robber lowered his gun and stood paralyzed at sight and sound of the mayor of Fairdale? This was not answerable. There might have been a number of reasons, all to Colonel Longstreth's credit, but I could not harbor one of them in mind. Longstreth had not appeared to see danger for his daughter, even though she had been roughly handled and had struggled right in front of a cocked gun.

I probed deep into this singular fact, and I brought to bear on the thing all my knowledge and experience of violent Texas life. And I found that the instant Colonel Longstreth had appeared on the scene there *was* no further danger threatening his daughter. Why? That, likewise, I could not answer.

Then his rage, I concluded, had been solely at the idea of *his* daughter being assaulted by a robber. This deduction was indeed disturbing, but I put it aside to crystallize after far more careful consideration. I passed to thought of my relation to Miss Longstreth and her cousin. If my conscience had not begun to prick, I should have found the prospect most pleasant. But I was thrilled and fascinated even while I was ashamed.

Miss Longstreth was gracious, kind — too fine a woman to deceive. Miss Ruth was a most lovable little rogue, full of the devil, and perhaps, as I had imagined, a natural-born flirt, yet her trust should not have been requited with deceit. It often had been my business to sail under false colors, and the fact seldom disturbed me. Here, however, it was different.

Evidently I had, with my usual luck, made a favorable impression upon Miss Long-streth, and somehow I desired to be worthy of it. She was the kind of a woman to make a fellow want to be a man. In Miss Ruth's case I was all the deeper at sea because, if in one day I could so far fall victim to her charms, in a week I would be hopelessly in love. That was all the more reason why I needed to be myself. Thought of MacNeal came, then of Vaughn Steele, and the work cut out for me in Fairdale. They must be first because they had come first, and I kept my promises. I did not need to accept Miss Longstreth's kind offer — to have any relation with her at all. But to give up the prospects of riding with her, and especially with her cousin, to turn my back on something which beckoned smilingly and sweetly — that was hard.

It began to be so hard to consider that I thought there need be no hurry to tell them I could not accept the position. That was temptation assailing me — a rather new experience. Suddenly I conceived the idea that Steele might favor my working for Miss Longstreth. It might fall into line with his plans for my secret aid to him. Was I justified in being a liar for his sake and the ultimate good of Fairdale? Perhaps — but I hated the thought of being untrue to the beautiful woman who had looked straight into my eyes and said she needed no references as to my good character.

Finally I decided to put aside the tormenting problem until Steele had solved it for me. Then I went to sleep.

Evidently I had lain awake a long time thinking for, when I did fall asleep, I slept so soundly that I had to be called in the morning. I began the day in amusement with myself, for I found the new and natty suit distasteful, and I put on my rough clothes. Then I was late for breakfast and had to rush to catch the stage. Joel and Miss Ruth were up on the seat, and I received a hearty greeting from the one and a bright smile and appraising glance from the other. She liked me better — or she liked me — in the boots and corduroys and sombrero.

Miss Longstreth appeared no worse for the incident of the preceding night. She was glad to see me, and right then my conscience again awakened to what bade fair to be considerable activity. Her father, however, was gruff, and did not invite sociability. I wondered if she had told him and decided that she had. Then I climbed up in front.

Joel cracked his long whip and called cheerily to his horses. A smooth, open road strung out ahead as far as eye could see and then melted into a bright green haze. The morning was beautiful. We had a northeast wind at our backs with prospects of a cool day.

The horses struck out eagerly, and Joel had to hold them in. Song of lark and mockingbird filled the fresh morning air. There had been a little rain during the night, so now there was no dust, and the mesquite glistened in the sunlight.

Disquieting and sweet was the unmistakable fact that this morning I stood upon a different footing with Miss Ruth Herbert. The difference was impossible to describe, yet it was there. I saw a most enjoyable day before me, and with a feeling of shame I smothered the still, small voice that cried to be heard and prepared to enjoy myself.

"What became of the robber you shot?" was one of Miss Ruth's first questions.

"I remembered him as I came out," was my reply. "Haven't any idea. Of course, though, he rode away last night."

"Ray and I were . . . a little afraid you might have . . ."

"What?" I interrupted.

"Well, you see . . . Mister Harkness here told me you were such a terrible man with guns and things . . . and Ray and I feared . . ."

"Miss Herbert, Joel is an old liar," I declared. "And I never saw the robber after he was carried out. I'm glad I didn't hurt him much."

"Honest Injun?" she asked archly, but with thoughtful eyes.

"Yes," I answered, and returned her glance.

Then she besieged me with a thousand questions about horses, saddles, rides, about Fairdale and Pecos County and outlaws — every kind of question prompted by the alluring prospects of her visit to the wild ranges of Texas.

Not improbably I was a mine of information regarding all that pertained to the outdoors, ranges, and wildlife of the frontier, and I felt an unqualified pleasure in talking. The fact that my personal feelings of the moment did not lead me into any such rash speech as had offended her yesterday was further indication of how earnestly I desired to be liked by Miss Herbert. I could not help it. We were far on the road of acquaintance that morning.

At noon, Joel halted in a shady corner where, however, there was no water, and for that reason our midday rest was shorter than that of the day before. Colonel Longstreth's taciturnity made me rather avoid his presence, and, as I wandered aimlessly around under the mesquite, I did not give any chance to offer me lunch.

Again I was the last one to go aboard the stage. To my surprise, Miss Ruth drew a napkin from under her coat and gave it to me. It contained two sandwiches.

"Thank you. How good of you to think of me!" I said warmly.

"We'd have called you," she replied, "but Uncle's grouchy today. He isn't . . . just nice when he's that way."

"Grouchy? I hope it's not about . . . because Miss Longstreth offered me a job?"

"Oh, no. He didn't mind that. He said she could hire whom she likes. But I imagine he's put out or worried because Ray insists that she *will* make Fairdale her home. Uncle says he's happy to have her for a visit, but that the frontier is no place for a girl raised as Ray has been."

That afternoon I had deep insight into Miss Ruth Herbert's charming personality, and the deeper I saw, the more danger menaced my peace of mind. There had never been the real girl for me yet. Suppose Miss Ruth should be the one? I had a feeling of alarm before I persuaded myself that I was only caught for the moment.

One thing she did pleased Joel as much as it pleased me, and that was she drove his four horses at a bracing trot and did it beautifully. No small feat for a slip of a girl with those leaders pulling hard on the reins. I had always liked coy, roguish girls, but never until now had I met one who added to this doubtful charm the strength and spirit to do red-blooded things.

It was dark when we reached San Antonio, and I left the party at the inn where Joel hauled up. I said that I could continue the journey with them — they expected to stay a day in town — and would catch up with them by the time they reached Del Rio. Miss Ruth looked surprised, and, if my eyes did not deceive me in the dusk, she was disappointed.

A little thought after I had left her vicinity showed me that it would be an unwise move for me to be seen with Colonel Longstreth's party this side of Del Rio on the Rio Grande. I was well known in San Antonio and all along the stage route to the river. Fine predicament for me to have some outspoken Texan call me by name and ask what particular outlaw I was chasing. No, it would never do to risk so much. I spent the evening with friends and tried my best to appreciate their hospitable kindness, when all the time my mind was full of that hazel-eyed girl and the adventure which loomed strangely about her and Fairdale.

Next morning I took the stage for Uvalde where they were due to arrive the following night. The first day was wearisome, for a stage ride without any distraction was much harder on me than horseback, but the time passed quickly because I had much to think of. Similar was the next day — but, if anything, it passed even more quickly.

Upon reaching Uvalde, I wavered, wanting to wait there so as to see Miss Ruth all the sooner; and then somewhat in disgust at my vacillation I dismissed the temptation and next day continued on my journey to Del Rio. That day was long, and the next longer yet. At last, however, I reached the river town.

I passed the hours in a casual and unobtrusive questioning of ranchers and cowboys in regard to Fairdale, and I learned very little for my pains. It lay somewhere in the wilds of Pecos County, and from Sanderson could be reached by horseback or wagon.

The following evening I watched with

eager eyes for the stage to roll in from Uvalde. Finally it came. To my satisfaction I saw the Longstreth party alight and go into the little hotel. Perhaps it was imagination, but I thought Miss Ruth had peered around at the loungers lined up before the stage.

Next morning, when the Longstreth party came out to resume their journey, I was sitting on top of the stage. Ruth espied me, and her quick smile made me happy. Then Miss Longstreth bowed, as if right pleased to see me, and her father spoke civilly enough. I had forfeited my seat inside, and, before Miss Ruth expressed any desire to ride outside, a huge individual clambered up beside me, taking all the available room.

She laughed at something in my face and stepped into the stage with all the other passengers. Then we started on the long ride, this time traveling northwest. My state of mind was one of unprecedented content, while at the same time I had an unreasonable resentment toward the fat man beside me.

At midday we halted for a rest and lunch at a small village, where I at once joined Miss Longstreth and her cousin, and, if my usual hard-headed judgment had not succumbed to a softening vanity, both girls were glad to have me with them. Here, at this place, I discovered that Colonel Longstreth was addicted to drink, and under its influence his genial manner suffered.

When the stage driver made ready to start for the afternoon's travel, I outmaneuvered the stout gentleman and got Miss Ruth up on the front seat. Miss Longstreth said she would also like to ride outside, so we made room for her. Once the mountain of flesh came waddling toward the coach, Ruth giggled, and I endeavored to look grave. He did not see us at all. Laboriously he began to climb.

"Gracious!" whispered Ruth. "He's coming up. Where on earth will he sit?"

"Comrade, I'm afraid there's no room left," I said politely.

He looked up, saw us, and burst out with an *"Ah!"* like a huge puff, then he fell off clumsily. When he clambered inside, someone among the passengers uttered an audible groan, and then there came a squeezing kind of sound, followed by a growl, this last quite unmistakably from Colonel Longstreth.

Miss Longstreth did not succeed in suppressing a smile, and Miss Ruth's eyes clearly showed the little dancing devil. That incident started us off merrily, and straightway I found myself pleasantly engaged. The time sped by. I enjoyed that afternoon all the more because, despite the innumerable questions concerning myself I answered, I did not have to tell one lie.

With the passing of the afternoon, the sun set over the bleak low mountains in the west, and darkness came on. The air was cool at night, for we had climbed to a higher altitude that day. For hours we had not passed a house or shack or range — anything to indicate the nearness of a settlement. It was, indeed, wild country, and now in the darkness with the mesquite so gloomy and the road shadowy and mysterious ahead, the ride could no longer have been pleasant for the girls. No doubt their silence told of both weariness and anxiety.

When the moon came up over a dark broken line of hills, the wildness of the place seemed all the more notable. We were high on a slope from which the rolling land stretched away in night haze. Patches of dense mesquite seemed to be harboring robbers; shadows hanging over the road resembled waiting, hiding horsemen; rustlings in the brush made the girls start. Yet, there came a moment when this part of the ride was beautiful to me.

"I'm afraid," whispered Ruth.

"What of?" I asked.

"Nothing," she replied. That, perhaps, was the trouble — the feeling of nothingness roused by that weird moon and the vast, pale, barren land, stretching away under the sky.

Then an owl or a hawk tore out of a mesquite along the road. The sound startled Ruth. I caught the gleam of her eyes, now dark in the moonlight. The stage lurched a little and my hand touched hers, and then, but not from any action, her hand was in mine. I clasped it warmly. I understood. But I could scarcely believe. If it had not been a warm, soft, clinging hand, glad to be held, I never could have realized it was real.

So I sat there, tingling, afraid to look at her, with my gaze on the dark breaks in the slope and the moon-blanched ridges, wondering what on earth this adventure would lead to and conscious that with the clinging pressure of this little hand something strange and troublesome and sweet had birth within my breast. Sooner or later the coach swung around the slope and lights of a town twinkled below us, not far away. When Ruth slipped her hand from mine, the rest of the ride lacked something.

Sanderson was a much larger town than I had expected to see. The main street appeared to be one of stores and saloons, all ablaze with lights and busy. A good many Mexicans mingled in the crowd before the hotel where our driver brought us to a halt.

"It'd be jolly, if I wasn't scared," said Miss Ruth, looking down at the growing circle of curious bronzed faces. Miss Longstreth made no comment, but her look was scarcely flattering to Sanderson.

While I was assisting the girls to the ground, I distinctly heard Colonel Longstreth utter an exclamation. Then I saw him shake hands with a tall, dark, striking-looking fellow. Longstreth looked surprised and angry, and he spoke with force, but I could not hear what it was he said. The fellow laughed, yet somehow he struck me as sullen, until suddenly he spied Miss Longstreth. Then his face changed, and he removed his sombrero.

"Floyd, did you come with the teams?" asked Longstreth sharply.

"Not me. I rode a horse, good and hard," was the reply.

"*Humph!* I'll have a word to say to you later." Then Longstreth turned to his daughter. "Ray, here's the cousin I've told you about. You used to play with him ten years ago . . . Floyd Lawson. Floyd, my daughter . . . and my niece, Ruth Herbert."

' Straightway I seemed to be forgotten. Naturally I did not perceive this fact with any considerable degree of pleasure.

99

Taking my baggage, I turned away, entered the hotel, and asked for accommodations. I did not hurry to go in to supper, and, when I did, the Longstreth party had preceded me.

There were two tables, one large and one small. I seated myself at the smaller, because it was unoccupied. Miss Herbert was not so absorbed with the presence of this handsome cousin that she had not a smile for me, a fact for which I was grateful entirely beyond any reason. Miss Longstreth, however, did not see me at all. Her eyes were sparkling, and her cheeks were red.

Any man of my pursuits, who always scrutinizes everyone he meets, would have studied this stranger attentively, and I with a new and dangerous game to play, with a consciousness of Longstreth's unusual and significant personality, with a little jealousy sharpening my edge, assuredly bent a keen and searching glance upon this Floyd Lawson. He was under thirty, yet gray at his temples — dark, smooth-shaven, with lines left by wildness, dissipation, shadows under dark eyes, a mouth strong and bitter, and a square chin — a reckless, careless, handsome, sinister face, strangely losing the hardness when he smiled.

The grace of a gentleman clung around

him and seemed like an echo in his mellow voice. I did not doubt that he, like many a young man I had known, had drifted out to the frontier where rough and wild life had wrought sternly but had not quite effaced the mark of a good family. Colonel Longstreth apparently did not share the pleasure of his daughter and his niece in the advent of this cousin. I recalled what he had said to Lawson and pondered its import. Something hinged on this meeting.

After supper, they all went into the hall that did duty as parlor, office, and what not, and I imagined the girls, at Colonel Longstreth's suggestion, bade the newly found cousin a reluctant good night before they went to their room. The colonel and Lawson turned with voiceless but tacit intention toward the bar.

I followed, saw them seated at a table near an open door. It was dark outside. I went out the other exit and found my way around the corner to a porch upon which the door opened. I tiptoed as close as I dared, and, leaning against the wall in as careless a position as I could assume, I listened.

I heard the clink of glasses, the striking of a match, the scraping of a boot. I saw the red end of the burning match fall outside the door where it had been flung.

"Who's the little guy with the sharp eyes?" asked Lawson presently. "He was on the stage. I saw him help the girls off."

"Cowboy named Russ," replied Longstreth. "Ray hired him to come on. Wants him to handle her horses."

There was a long pause, fraught with more than interest for me. "Better drop him here," added Lawson.

"Easier said than done."

"Why?"

"Ray took a liking to him. She hired him. She'll want a good reason to fire him. The fellow's a cool hand. I'd just as lief let him go along. Ray and Ruth will need someone like him if they ride around much out here."

"I'll take care of them."

"Floyd, you've got work of mine to attend to, and, if you'd been doing it right, you wouldn't be here."

"Wait till you know why I'm here, will you?" replied Lawson impatiently. "As for this cowboy, Russ, I didn't like his sharp eye. I'll see that he goes in the morning."

"Have it your own way," replied Longstreth in a worried tone. "Now I want to know what you're doing here."

"I came to Sanderson to get Joe and Brick out of jail."

"What!" ejaculated Longstreth.

Lawson repeated his statement.

"What jail?"

"A jail put into use here in Sanderson," replied Lawson with grim, ironic humor. "You've been away for some time, Mayor Longstreth. Things have happened."

"What were my cowboys arrested for?"

"There's a difference of opinion. The boys say for nothing. The officer who made the arrest couldn't find anybody to appear against them. So I got them released. They're around town, wild and roaring for trouble."

"Officer? What officer?" Longstreth asked in amazement.

"Vaughn Steele, the ranger."

A blank silence ensued.

"Steele! Here in Pecos?"

"I should smile. About six feet four of him, and wide in proportion."

"Alone?"

"He always goes alone, they say. He certainly was alone when he collared Joe and Brick. And didn't need help."

"It happened here, then?"

"Yes. Nelson rode over to the ranch and hurried me here. The boys were drunk and deserved arrest, he said. The town's divided, half on Steele's side, half on the other side. Steele had the boys red-handed. But the rancher whom they fleeced . . . a fellow from El Paso . . . hadn't the nerve to appear against them, though he accused them to Steele."

"Law and order on the frontier! One ranger!" exclaimed Longstreth.

"It looks funny. But law and order and Steele went right into Sancho's saloon. The usual gang was there, a gang that ought to scare one ordinary man out of his skin. Steele didn't know Joe and Brick. He yelled at them . . . that they were wanted by law. Both boys rose to that. And Steele arrested them without even showing a gun."

There was another long pause.

"I'll speak to the boys," said Longstreth in a constrained voice. "Where is this Steele now?"

Chapter Five

VAUGHN STEELE

"Gone to Fairdale," replied Lawson with a short, expressive laugh.

"What?" roared Longstreth.

"Gone to Fairdale on extended ranger service . . . so I hear."

"He won't last a day!" bellowed the mayor.

"Wait till you see him," was the curt reply.

My burning curiosity was no further gratified. Both men left the bar, probably to go to bed, and I saw them no more. However, I had sufficient to think about for one night. So Vaughn Steele had passed through Sanderson, and already the frontier town was divided against itself. How glad that made me. How much I would have liked to get the news to MacNeal. *"Wait till you see him!"* That curt speech of Floyd Lawson's gave me a thrill. I had heard something of the kind before regarding Vaughn Steele. For my part, I could not curb my impatience to see the ranger.

Much as I had heard about Steele, he was

a stranger to me. I wanted to see him, judge him, form my own estimate of this singular man. It was just as well, perhaps, that Floyd Lawson intended to have Miss Longstreth let me go. But his disposal of me was the kind of bitter pill that was hard for me to swallow. If Lawson had otherwise impressed me favorably, this move would not have earned my resentment, but most assuredly I had not liked him. How much of this fact was owing to jealousy and how much to my instinct, I had no means to tell, but I gave him at least a benefit of my weakness. Conclusive estimate of Lawson must wait in all fairness till time proved what he was, and I had an intimation that this course would be just as fair in Colonel Longstreth's case.

I was a little off my balance, probably because I wanted to think well of Ray Longstreth's father and cousin. But without going any further and not in the least blindly, I knew there was something about these men that made me dubious. Naturally the mayor of Fairdale and his kin would resent any action that reflected upon Longstreth's ability to preserve what law and order were possible in the frontier town. If his honor were impeached, there would be a fight.

I tried to see the situation from the Longstreth side of the fence — tried not to be unduly influenced by the impression at that meeting in the adjutant general's office and by the significance of what had occurred at the road house. Moreover, I remembered two or three occasions in my service to the state where my suspicions proved to be unfounded and unjust.

Then I went to bed.

In the morning, after breakfasting early, I took a turn up and down the main street of Sanderson, made observations, got information likely to serve me at some future day, and then returned to the hotel ready for what might happen. The stagecoach was there and already full of passengers. This stage did not go to Fairdale, but I had found that another one left for that point three days in a week.

Several cowboy broncos stood hitched to a railing, and farther down were two buckboards with horses that took my eye. These probably were the teams Colonel Longstreth had spoken of to Lawson. As I strolled up, both men came out of the hotel. Lawson saw me, and, making an almost imperceptible sign to Longstreth, he walked toward me.

"You're the cowboy, Russ?" he asked.

I nodded and looked him over. By day he made as striking a figure as I had noted by night, but the light was not generous to his dark face.

"Here's pay," he said, handing me some bills. "Miss Longstreth won't need you out at the ranch."

I counted the money and with deliberation put it into my pocket.

"Is Miss Longstreth discharging me . . . or are you?" I asked coolly.

Perhaps at my tone, perhaps at my look, he gave me closer attention, as if meeting with something unexpected in a cowboy. Plainly he showed that he was intolerant of any opposition.

"She gave me the money . . . told me to pay you off," he replied coldly. "You needn't bother to speak with her."

He might as well have said, just as politely, that my seeing her, even to say good bye, was undesirable. As my luck would have it, the girls appeared at that moment, and I went directly up to them to be greeted in a manner I was glad Floyd Lawson could not help but see.

In Miss Longstreth's smile and "Good morning, Russ," there was not the slightest discoverable sign that I was not to serve her indefinitely. It was as I expected — she knew nothing of Lawson's discharging me in her name.

"Miss Longstreth," I said in dismay, "what have I done? Why did you let me go?"

She looked astonished. "Russ, I don't understand you."

"Why did you discharge me?" I went on, trying to look heart-broken. "I haven't had a chance yet. I wanted so much to work for you . . . Miss Ruth, what have I done? Why did she discharge me?"

"I did not," declared Miss Longstreth, her dark eyes lighting.

"But . . . look here . . . here's my pay," I went on, exhibiting the money. "Mister Lawson just came to me . . . said you sent this money . . . that you wouldn't need me out at the ranch."

It was Miss Ruth, then, who uttered a little exclamation. Miss Longstreth seemed scarcely to have believed what she had heard.

"My cousin . . . Mister Lawson . . . said that?"

I nodded vehemently.

At this juncture Lawson strode before me, practically thrusting me aside. "Come, girls, let's walk a little before we start," he said gaily. "I'll show you Sanderson."

"Wait, please," Miss Longstreth replied, looking directly at him. "Cousin Floyd, I think there's a misunderstanding. Here's the cowboy I've engaged . . . Mister Russ. He declares you gave him money . . . told him I discharged him."

"Yes, Cousin, I did," he replied, his voice rising a little. There was a tinge of red in his cheeks. "We . . . you don't need him out at the ranch. We've any number of boys. I just told him that . . . let him down easy . . . didn't want you to be bothered."

Certain it was that Floyd Lawson had made a poor reckoning. First she showed utter amaze, followed by distinct disappointment, and then she lifted her head with a kind of haughty grace. She would have addressed him again had not Colonel Longstreth come up.

"Papa, did you instruct Cousin Floyd to discharge Russ?" she asked.

"I sure didn't," declared the colonel with a laugh. "Floyd took that upon his own hands."

"Indeed! I'd like my cousin to understand that I'm my own mistress. I've been accustomed to attending to my own affairs and shall continue doing so. Russ, I'm sorry you've been treated this way. Please, in future, take your orders only from me."

"Then . . . I'm to go to Fairdale with you?" I asked.

"Assuredly. Ride with Ruth and me today, please."

She turned away with Ruth, and they walked toward the first buckboard.

Colonel Longstreth found a grim enjoyment in Lawson's discomfiture. "Ray's like her mother was, Floyd," he said. "You've made a bad start with the girl."

Here Lawson showed manifestation of the Longstreth temper, and I took him to be a dangerous man with unbridled passions. "Russ, here's my own talk to you," he said, hard and dark, leaning toward me. "Don't go to Fairdale."

"Say . . . Mister Lawson," I blustered, for all the world like a young and frightened cowboy, "if you threaten me, I'll have you put in jail."

Both men seemed to have encountered a slight shock.

Then Colonel Longstreth roared.

Lawson hardly knew what to make of my boyish speech. "Are you going to Fairdale?" he asked thickly.

I eyed him with an entirely different glance from my other fearful one. "I should smile" was my reply, as caustic as the most reckless cowboy's, and I saw him shake.

Colonel Longstreth laid a restraining hand on Lawson. Then they both regarded me with undisguised interest. I sauntered away.

"Floyd, your temper'll do for you some

111

day," I heard the colonel say. "You'll get in bad with the wrong man some time. Here are Joe and Brick."

Mention of these fellows engaged my attention once more. I saw two cowboys, one evidently getting his name from his brick-red hair. They were the roistering type, hard drinkers, devil-may-care fellows, packing guns and wearing bold fronts — a kind that the rangers always called four-flushes.

However, as the rangers' standard of nerve was high, there was room left for cowboys like these to be dangerous to ordinary men. The little one was Joe, and, directly Lawson spoke to him, he turned to look at me, and his thin mouth slanted down as he looked. Brick eyed me, too, and I saw that he was heavy, not a hard-riding cowboy. Here, right at the start, were three enemies for me — Lawson and his cowboys. But it did not matter. Under any circumstances there would have been friction between such men and me.

I believed there might have been friction right then had not Miss Longstreth called me.

"Get our baggage, Russ," she said.

I hurried to comply, and, when I had fetched it, Lawson and the cowboys had mounted their horses. Colonel Longstreth was in the one buckboard with two men I had not before observed, and the girls were in the other.

The driver of this one was a tall, lanky, tow-headed youth, growing like a Texas weed. We had not any too much room in the buckboard, but that fact was not going to spoil the ride for me. We followed the leaders through the main street, out into the open, onto a wide, hard-packed road, showing years of travel. It headed northwest.

To our left rose the range of low, bleak mountains I had noted yesterday, and to our right sloped the mesquite-patched sweep of ridge and flat. The driver pushed his team to a fast trot, which gait surely covered ground rapidly. We were close behind Colonel Longstreth who, from his vehement gestures, must have been engaged in very earnest colloquy with his companions.

The girls behind me, now that they were nearing the end of the journey, manifested less interest in the ride and were speculating upon Fairdale and what it would be like. Occasionally I asked the driver a question, and sometimes the girls did likewise, but to my disappointment the ride seemed not to be the same as that of yesterday.

Every half mile or so we passed a ranch house, and, as we traveled on, these ranches grew farther apart until, twelve or fifteen miles out of Sanderson, they were so widely separated that each appeared alone on the wild range. We came to a stream that ran north, and I was surprised to see a goodly volume of water. It evidently flowed down from the mountain far to the west. Tufts of grass were well scattered over the sandy ground, but it was high and thick, and, considering the immense area in sight, there was grazing for a million head of stock.

We made three stops in the forenoon, one at a likely place to water the horses, the second at a chuck wagon belonging to cowboys who were riding after stock, and the third at a small cluster of adobe and stone houses, constituting a hamlet the driver called Longstreth, named after the colonel. From that point on to Fairdale there were only a few ranches, each one controlling great acreage.

Early in the afternoon from a ridge top we sighted Fairdale, a green patch in the mass of gray. For the barrens of Texas it was indeed a fair sight. But I was more concerned with its remoteness from civilization than its beauty. At that time in the early 'Seventies, when the vast western third of Texas was a wilderness, perhaps the pioneer had done wonders to settle there and establish places like Fairdale.

As we rolled swiftly along, the whole sweeping range was dotted with cattle, and farther on, within a few miles of town, there were droves of horses that brought enthusiastic praise from Miss Longstreth and her cousin.

"Plenty of room here for the long rides," I said, waving a hand at the gray-green expanse. "Your horses won't suffer on this range."

"Isn't it glorious? The open is so different . . . there's no end. And the air!"

She was delighted, and her cousin for once seemed speechless.

"That's the ranch," said the driver, pointing with his whip.

It needed only a glance for me to see that Colonel Longstreth's ranch was on a scale fitting the country. The house was situated on the only elevation around Fairdale, and it was not high or more than a few minutes' walk from the edge of town. It was a low, flat-roofed structure made of red adobe bricks and covered what appeared to be fully an acre of ground. All was green about it except where the fenced corrals and numerous barns or sheds showed gray and red.

Lawson and the cowboys disappeared ahead of us in the cottonwood trees. Colonel

Longstreth got out of the buckboard and waited for us. His face wore the best expression I had seen upon it yet. There was warmth and love, and something that approached sorrow or regret.

His daughter was agitated, too. I got out and offered my seat, which Colonel Longstreth took. It was scarcely a time for me to be required, or even noticed at all, and I took advantage of it and turned toward the town. Ten minutes of leisurely walking brought me to the shady outskirts of Fairdale, and I entered the town with mingled feelings of curiosity, eagerness, and expectation.

The street I walked down was not a main one. There were small, red houses among oaks and cottonwoods. I went clear through to the other side, probably more than half a mile. I crossed a number of intersecting streets, met children, nice-looking women, and more than one dusty-booted man.

Half way back on this street I turned at right angles and walked up several blocks till I came to a tree-bordered plaza. On the far side opened a broad street which for all its horses and people had a sleepy look. I walked on, alert, trying to take in everything, wondering if I would meet Steele, wondering how I would know him if we did meet. But

I believed I could have picked that ranger out of a thousand strangers, though I had never seen him.

Presently the residences gave place to buildings, fronting right upon the stone sidewalk. I passed a grain store, a hardware store, a grocery store, then several unoccupied buildings and a vacant corner. The next block, aside from the rough fronts of the crude structures, would have done credit to a small town even in eastern Texas. Here was evidence of business consistent with any prosperous community of two thousand inhabitants.

The next block, on both sides of the street, was a solid row of saloons, resorts, hotels. Saddled horses stood hitched all along the sidewalk in two long lines with a buckboard and team here and there, breaking the continuity. This block was busy and noisy. From all outside appearances Fairdale was no different from other frontier towns, and my expectations were scarcely realized.

As the afternoon was waning, I retraced my steps and returned to the ranch. The driver boy, whom I had heard called Dick, was looking for me, evidently at Miss Longstreth's order, and he led me up to the house. It was even bigger than I had conceived from a distance, and so old that the adobe bricks were worn smooth by rain and wind. I had a glimpse in at several doors as we passed by. There was comfort here that spoke eloquently of many a freighter's trip from Del Rio. For the sake of the young ladies I was glad to see things little short of luxurious for that part of the country.

At the far end of the house Dick conducted me to a little room, very satisfactory, indeed, to me. I asked about bunkhouses for the cowboys, and he said they were full to overflowing.

"Colonel Longstreth has a big outfit, eh?"

"Reckon he has," replied Dick. "Doan' know how many cowboys. They're always comin' an' goin'. I ain't acquainted with half of them."

"Much movement of stock these days?"

"Stock's always movin'," he replied with a queer look.

"Rustlers?"

But he did not follow up that look with the affirmative I expected.

"Lively place, I hear . . . Fairdale is?"

"Ain't so lively as Sanderson, but it's bigger."

"Yes, I heard it was. Fellow down there was talking about two cowboys who were arrested."

"Sure. I heerd all about thet. Joe Bean an'

Brick Higgins . . . they belong heah, but they ain't heah much."

I did not want Dick to think me overly inquisitive, so I turned the talk into other channels. It appeared that Miss Longstreth had not left any instructions for me, so I was glad to go with Dick to supper, which we had in the kitchen.

Dick informed me that the cowboys prepared their own meals down at the bunkhouses. As I had been given a room at the ranch house, he supposed I would get my meals there, too.

After supper I walked all over the grounds, had a look at the horses in the corrals, and came to the conclusion that it would be strange if Miss Longstreth did not love her new home and if her cousin did not enjoy her sojourn there. From a distance I saw the girls approaching with Lawson, and, not wishing to meet them, I sheered off.

When the sun had set, I went down to the town with the intention of finding Steele. This task, considering I dare not make inquiries and must approach him secretly, might turn out to be anything but easy. While it was still light, I strolled up and down the main street. When darkness set in, I went into a hotel, bought cigars, sat around, and watched without any clue.

Then I left and went into the next place. This was of rough, crude exterior, but the inside was comparatively pretentious and ablaze with lights. It was full of men, coming and going — a dusty-booted crowd that smelled of horses and smoke. I sat down for a while with wide eyes and open ears. Then I hunted up the bar, where most of the guests had been or were going. I found a great square room lighted by six huge lamps, a bar at one side, and all the floor space taken up by tables and chairs.

This must have been the gambling resort mentioned in the ranger's letter to Captain MacNeal, and the one rumored to be owned by the mayor of Fairdale. This was the only gambling place of any size in southern Texas in which I had noted the absence of Mexicans. There was some card playing going on at this moment. I stayed in there for a spell and knew that strangers were too common in Fairdale to be conspicuous. But I saw no man whom I could have taken for Steele. Then I went out.

It had often been a boast of mine that I could not spend an hour in a strange town, or walk a block along a dark street, without having something happen out of the ordinary. Mine was an experiencing nature. MacNeal had always called this luck. But it was my private opinion that things gravitated my way because I looked and listened for them. However, upon the occasion of my first day and evening in Fairdale it appeared, despite my vigilance and inquisitiveness, that here was to be an exception.

This thought came to me just before I reached the last lighted place in the block, a little dingy restaurant out of which, at the moment, a tall, dark form passed. It disappeared in the gloom. I saw a man sitting on the low steps and another standing in the door.

"That was the fellow the whole town's talkin' about . . . the ranger," said one man.

Like a shot I halted in the shadow, where I had not been seen.

"Sho! ain't boardin' heah, is he?" said the other.

"Yes."

"Reckon he'll hurt your business, Jim."

The fellow called Jim emitted a mirthless laugh. "Wal, he's been all my business these two days. An' he's offered to rent that old 'dobe of mine just out of town. You know . . . where I lived before movin' in heah. He's goin' to look at it tomorrow."

"Lord! does he expect to *stay?*"

"Say so. An', if he ain't a stayer, I never see one. Nice, quiet, easy chap, but he looks deep. I don't know his game, but he says he was heah for a while. An' he impressed me some. Just now he says . . . 'Where does Longstreth live?' I asked him if he was goin' to make a call on our mayor, an' he says, yes. Then I told him how to go out to the ranch. He went out, headed that way."

"The hell he did!"

I gathered from this fellow's exclamation that he was divided between amaze and mirth. Then he got up from the steps, went into the restaurant, and was followed by the man called Jim. Before the door was closed, he made another remark, but it was unintelligible to me.

As I passed on, I decided I would scrape acquaintance with this restaurant keeper. The thing of most moment was that I had gotten track of Steele. I hurried ahead. While I had been listening back there, moments had elapsed, and evidently he had walked swiftly.

I came to the plaza, crossed it, and then did not know which direction to take. Concluding that it did not matter, I hurried on in an endeavor to reach the ranch before Steele. Although I was not sure, I believed I had succeeded.

The moon shone brightly. I heard a banjo in the distance and a cowboy song. There was not a person in sight in the wide courts or on the porch. I did not yet have a well defined idea about the inside of the house.

Peeping in at the first lighted window, I saw a large room. Miss Longstreth and Ruth were there alone. Evidently this was a parlor or a sitting room, and it had clean, white walls, a blanketed floor, an open fireplace with a cheery blazing log, and a large table upon which were lamp, books, papers. Backing away, I saw that this corner room had a door opening on the porch and two other windows.

I listened, hoping to hear Steele's footsteps coming up the road. But I heard only Ruth's merry laugh and her cousin's mellow voice. Then I saw lighted windows down at the other end of the front part of the house. I walked down. A door stood open, and through it I saw a room identical with that at the other corner. Here were Colonel Longstreth, Lawson, and several other men, all smoking and talking.

It might have been interesting to tarry there within earshot, but I wanted to get back to the road to intercept Steele. Scarcely had I retraced my steps and seated myself on the porch steps when a very tall, dark figure loomed up in the moonlit road.

Steele! I wanted to yell like a boy.

He came on slowly, looking all around, halted some twenty paces distant, surveyed the house, then evidently espying me, came on again. My first feeling was — *what a giant!* But his face was hidden in the shadow of a sombrero.

I had intended, of course, upon first sight to blurt out my identity. Yet I didn't. He affected me strangely, or perhaps it was my emotion at the thought that we rangers, with so much in common and at stake, had come together.

"Is Longstreth at home?" he asked abruptly.

I said yes.

"Ask him if he'll see Vaughn Steele, ranger."

"Wait here," I replied. I did not want to take up any time then, explaining my presence there.

Deliberately and noisily I strode down the porch and entered the room with the smoking men. I went in farther than was necessary for me to state my errand. But I wanted to see Longstreth's face, to see into his eyes. As I entered, the talking ceased. I saw no face except his, and that seemed blank.

"Vaughn Steele, ranger . . . come to see you, sir," I announced.

Did Longstreth start? — did his eyes show

a fleeting glint? — did his face almost imperceptibly blanch? I could not have sworn to any. But there was a change — maybe from surprise. The first sure effect of my announcement came in a quick exclamation from Lawson — a sibilant intake of breath that, strange to me, did not seem to denote surprise so much as certainty. Lawson might have emitted a curse with less force.

Longstreth moved his hand significantly, and the action was a voiceless command for silence as well as an assertion that he would attend to this matter. I read him clearly so far. He had authority, and again I felt his power.

"Steele to see me. Did he state his business?"

"No, sir," I replied.

"Russ, say I'm not at home," said Longstreth presently, bending over to relight his pipe.

I went out. Someone slammed the door behind me.

As I strode back across the porch, my mind worked swiftly. The machinery had been idle for a while and was now started.

"Mister Steele," I said, "Colonel Longstreth says he's not at home. Tell your business to his daughter."

Without waiting to see the effect of my

taking up so much upon myself, I knocked upon the parlor door. Miss Longstreth opened it. She wore white. Looking at her, I thought it would be strange if Steele's well-known indifference to women did not suffer an eclipse.

"Miss Longstreth, here is Vaughn Steele to see you," I said.

"Vaughn Steele?" she echoed. "The ranger! Why . . . ?"

Then she saw Steele, looming behind me, and in some degree hid her astonishment. "Won't . . . you come in?" she said graciously.

Steele had to bend his head to enter the door. I went in with him, an intrusion, perhaps, that in the interest of the moment she appeared not to notice. Steele seemed to fill the room with his giant form. His face was fine, stern, clear cut, with blue or gray eyes, strangely penetrating. He was coatless, vestless. He wore a gray flannel shirt, corduroys, a big gun swinging low, and top boots, reaching to his knees. He was the most stalwart son of Texas I had ever seen in many a day, but neither his great stature nor his striking face accounted for something I felt — something spiritual, vital, compelling that drew me.

"Mister Steele, I'm pleased to meet you,"

said Miss Longstreth. "This is my cousin, Ruth Herbert. We just arrived . . . I, to make this my home . . . she to visit me."

Steele smiled as he bowed to Ruth. He was easy with a kind of rude grace and showed no sign of embarrassment or that beautiful girls were unusual to him.

"Mister Steele, we heard of you in Austin," said Ruth with her eyes misbehaving.

I hoped I would not have to be jealous of Steele. But this girl was a little minx if not altogether a flirt.

"I did not expect to be received by ladies," replied Steele. "I called upon Mister Longstreth. He would not see me. I was to tell my business to his daughter. I'm glad to know you, Miss Longstreth, and your cousin, but sorry you've come to Fairdale now."

"Why?" queried both girls in unison.

"Because it's . . . oh, pretty rough . . . no place for girls to walk and ride."

"Ah! I see. And your business has to do with rough places," said Miss Longstreth. "Strange that Papa would not see you. Stranger that he should want me to hear your business. Either he's joking or wants to impress me. Papa tried to persuade me not to come. He tried to frighten me with tales

127

of this . . . this roughness out here. He knows I'm in earnest, how I'd like to help somehow . . . do some little good. Pray, tell me this business."

"I wished to get your father's co-operation in my work."

"Your work? You mean your ranger duty . . . the arresting of rough characters?"

"That, yes. But that's only a detail. Fairdale is bad internally. My job is to make it good."

"A splendid and worthy task," replied Miss Longstreth warmly. "I wish you success. But, Mister Steele, aren't you exaggerating Fairdale's wickedness?"

"No," he answered forcibly.

"Indeed! And Papa refused to see you . . . presumably refused to co-operate with you?" she asked thoughtfully.

"I take it that way."

"Mister Steele, pray tell me what is the matter with Fairdale and just what the work is you're called upon to do?" she asked seriously. "I heard Papa say that he was the law in Fairdale. Perhaps he resents interference. I know he'll not tolerate any opposition to his will. Please tell me. I may be able to influence him."

I listened to Steele's deep voice as he talked about Fairdale. What he said was old to me, and I gave heed only to its effect. Miss Longstreth's expression, that at first had been earnest and grave, turned into one of incredulous amaze. She, and Ruth, too, watched Steele's face in fascinated attention.

When it came to telling what he wanted to do, the ranger warmed with his subject. He talked beautifully, convincingly, with a certain strange, persuasive power that betrayed how he worked his way. His fine face, losing its stern, hard lines, seemed to glow and give forth a spirit austere, yet noble, almost gentle, assuredly something vastly different from what might have been expected in the expression of a gunfighting ranger. I sensed that Miss Longstreth felt this, just as I did.

"Papa said you were a hounder of outlaws . . . a man who'd rather kill than save!" she exclaimed.

The old stern cast returned to Steele's face. It was as if he had suddenly remembered himself. "My name is infamous, I am sorry to say," he replied.

"You *have* killed men?" she asked, her dark eyes dilating.

Had any one ever dared ask Steele that before? His face became a mask. It told the truth to me, but she could not see, and he did not answer.

"Oh, you are above that! Don't . . . don't kill anyone here!"

"Miss Longstreth, I hope I won't."

His voice seemed to check her. I had been right in my estimate of her character — young, untried, but all pride, fire, passion. She was white then, and certainly beautiful.

Steele watched her, could scarcely have failed to see the white gleam of her beauty, and all that evidence of a quick and noble heart.

"Pardon me, please, Mister Steele," she said, recovering her composure. "I am . . . just a little overexcited. I didn't mean to be inquisitive. Thank you for your confidence. I've enjoyed your call, though your news did distress me. You may rely on me to talk to Papa."

That appeared to be a dismissal, and, bowing to her and Ruth, the ranger went out. I followed, not having spoken.

At the end of the porch I caught up with Steele and walked out into the moonlight beside him. Just why I did not now reveal my identity, I could not say, for certainly I was bursting with the desire to surprise him, to earn his approval. He loomed dark above me, appearing not to be aware of my presence. What a cold, strange proposition this ranger was.

Still, remembering the earnestness of his talk to Miss Longstreth, I could not think him cold — but I thought him just that when it came to any attraction to those charming girls. Suddenly we passed under the shade of cottonwoods. He clamped a big hand on my shoulder.

"My God, Russ, isn't she lovely!"

In spite of my being dumbfounded I had to hug him. He knew me. "Thought you didn't swear!" I gasped.

Ridiculously those were my first words to Vaughn Steele.

"Old son, I saw you parading up and down the street, looking for me," he said. "I intended to help you find me tomorrow."

We gripped hands, and that strong feel and clasp meant much.

"Yes, she's lovely, Steele," I said. "But did you look at the cousin, the little girl with the eyes?"

Then we laughed and loosed hands.

"Come on," I said, "let's get out somewhere. I've a million things to tell you."

We went off into the open where some stones gleamed white in the sand. With our backs against a rest and all quiet about us, we settled down for a long conference. I began with MacNeal's urgent message to me, then told of my going to the capital —

what I had overheard when Governor Stone was in the adjutant's office — of my interview with them — of the spying on Colonel Longstreth — MacNeal's directions, advice, and command — the ride toward San Antonio — the hold-up, and my being engaged as a cowboy by Miss Longstreth — of the further ride on to Sanderson and the incident there — and finally how I had approached Longstreth and then had thought it well to get his daughter into the scheme of things. It was a long talk, even for me, and my voice sounded husky.

"I told MacNeal I'd be lucky to get you," said Steele, after a silence.

That was the only comment on my actions, the only praise, but the quiet way he spoke it made me feel like a boy, undeserving of so much.

"Here, I forgot the money MacNeal sent," I went on, glad to be rid of the huge roll of bills.

The ranger showed surprise, but he was also very pleased.

"The captain loves the service," said Steele. "He alone knows the worth of the rangers. And the work he's given his life to . . . the *good* that service really does . . . all depends on you and me, Russ."

I assented, gloomily enough. Then I

waited while he pondered.

The moon soared clear. There was a cool wind, rustling the greasewood. A dog bayed at a barking coyote. Lights twinkled down in the town. I looked back up at the dark hill and thought of Ruth Herbert. Getting here to Fairdale, meeting Steele, had not changed my feelings toward her, only somehow they had removed me far off in thought, out of possible touch, it seemed.

"Well, old son, listen," began Steele. His calling me that was a joke, yet I didn't feel it. "You've made a better start than I could have figured. MacNeal said you were lucky. Perhaps. But you've got brains.

"Now, here's your cue for the present. Work for Miss Longstreth. Do your best for her, as long as you last. I don't suppose you'll last long. You have got to get in with this gang in town. Be a flash cowboy. You don't need to get drunk, but you're to pretend it. Gamble. Be a good fellow. Hang round the barrooms. I don't care how you play the part, just so you make friends, learn the ropes. We can meet out here at night to talk and plan. You're to take sides with those who're against me. I'll furnish you the money. You'd better appear to be a winning gambler, even if you're not. How's this plan strike you?"

"Great . . . except for one thing," I replied. "I hate to lie to Miss Longstreth. She's true blue, Steele."

"Old son, you haven't gone soft on her?"

"Not a bit. Maybe I'm soft on the little cousin. But I just like Miss Longstreth . . . think she's fine . . . could look up to her. And I hate to be different from what she thinks."

"I understand, Russ," he replied in his deep voice that had such quality to influence a man. "It's no decent job. You'll be ashamed before her. So would I. But here's our work, the hardest ever cut out for rangers. Think of what depends upon it. And . . ."

"I hope Longstreth turns out to be on the square," I said. "He might be a lax mayor, too good-natured to uphold law in a wild country. And his Southern pride would fire at interference. I don't like him, but for his daughter's sake I hope we're wrong."

Steele's eyes, deep and gleaming in the moonlight, searched my face. "Old son, sure you're not in love with her . . . you'll not fall in love with her?"

"No. I'm positive. Why?"

"Because, in either case, I'd likely have need of a new man in your place," he said.

"Steele, you know something about Longstreth . . . something more!" I exclaimed swiftly.

"No more than you. When I meet Longstreth face to face, I may know more. Russ, when a fellow has been years at this game, he has a sixth sense. Mine seldom fails me. I never yet faced a criminal who didn't somehow betray fear . . . not so much fear of me, but fear of himself . . . his life . . . his deeds. That's conscience or, if not that, just realization of fate."

Had that been the thing I imagined I had seen in Longstreth's face?

"I'm sorry Ray Longstreth came out here," I said impulsively.

Steele did not say he shared that feeling. He was looking out upon the moon-blanched plain. Some subtle thing in his face made me divine that he was thinking of the beautiful girl to whom he might bring disgrace and unhappiness.

Chapter Six

A KISS AND AN ARREST

A month had passed, a swiftly flying time full of new life. Wonderful it was for me to think that I was still in Ray Longstreth's employ.

It was the early morning hour of a day in May. The sun had not yet grown hot. Dew like diamond drops sparkled on the leaves and grass. The gentle breeze was clear, sweet, with the song of larks upon it. And the range, a sea of gray-green growing greener, swept away westward in rolling ridges and hollows, like waves, to meet the dark low hills that notched the horizon line of blue.

I was sitting on the top bar of the corral fence, and before me stood three saddled horses that would have gladdened any eye. I was waiting to take the young ladies on their usual morning ride. Once upon a time, in what seemed the distant past to this eventful month, I had flattered myself that there had been occasions for thought, but scornfully I soliloquized that in those days I had no cue for thought such as I had now. This was one of the moments when my real self seemed to stand off and skeptically regard the fictitious cowboy. This gentleman of the range wore a huge sombrero with an ornamented silver band, a silken scarf of red, a black velvet shirt, much affected by the Indians, an embroidered buckskin vest, corduroys, and fringed chaps with silver buttons, a big blue gun swinging low, high heeled boots, and long spurs with silver rowels. A flash cowboy! Steele vowed I was a born actor, but I never divulged the fact that, had it not been for my infatuation with Ruth Herbert, I never could have carried on that part, not to save the ranger service or the whole state of Texas.

The hardest part had not been the establishing of a reputation. The scorn of cowboys, the ridicule of gamblers, the badinage of the young bucks of the settlement — these I had soon made dangerous procedures for anyone. I was quick with tongue and fist and gun. There had been fights and respect was quickly earned, though the constant advent of strangers in Fairdale always had me in hot water. Moreover, instead of being difficult, it was fun to spend all the time I could in the hotels and resorts, shamming a weakness for drink, gambling, lounging, making friends among the rough set, when all the time I was a cool, keenly registering machine. The hard thing was the lie I lived in the eyes of Ray Longstreth and Ruth Herbert.

I had, indeed, won the sincere regard of my employer. Her father, her cousin, Floyd, and new-made friends in town had come to her with tales of my reckless doings and had urged my dismissal. But she had kept me and all the time pleaded like a sister to have me mend my vicious ways. She believed what was told about me, but had faith in me despite that.

As for Ruth, I had fallen hopelessly in love with her. By turns, Ruth was indifferent to me, cold, friendly like a comrade, and dangerously sweet. Somehow she saw through me, knew I was not just what I pretended to be. But she never breathed her conviction. She championed me. I wanted to tell her the truth about myself, because I believed the doubt of me alone stood in the way of my winning her. Still, that might have been my vanity. She had never said she cared for me, although she had looked it.

This tangle of my personal life, however, had not in the least affected my loyalty and duty to Vaughn Steele. Day by day I had grown more attached to him, keener in the interest of our work. It had been a busy month — a month of foundation building. My vigilance and my stealthy efforts had not been rewarded by anything calculated to strengthen our suspicions of Longstreth. But, then, he had been absent from home very often and was difficult to watch even when he was at home.

Floyd Lawson came and went, too, presumably upon stock business. I could not yet see that he was anything but an honest rancher, deeply involved with Longstreth and other men in stock deals. Nevertheless, as a man he had earned my contempt. He was a hard drinker, cruel to horses, a gambler not above stacking the cards, a quick-tempered, passionate Southerner. He had fallen in love with Ray Longstreth, was like her shadow when at home. He hated me and treated me as if I were the scum of the earth. If he had to address me for something, which was seldom, he did it harshly, like ordering a dog. Whenever I saw his sinister, handsome face, with its dark eyes always half shut, my hand itched for my gun, and I would go my way with something thick and hot inside my breast.

In my talks with Steele we spent time studying Floyd Lawson's character and actions. He was Longstreth's partner and at the head of a small group of Fairdale ranchers who were rich in cattle and property, if not in money. Steele and I had seen fit to wait before we made any thorough investigation into their business methods. Ours was a waiting game, anyway.

Right at the start Fairdale had apparently risen in resentment at the presence of Vaughn Steele. But it was my opinion that there were men in Fairdale secretly glad of the ranger's presence. What he intended to do was food for great speculation. His fame, of course, had preceded him. A company of militia could not have had the effect upon the wild element of Fairdale that Steele's presence had. A thousand stories went from lip to lip, most of which were false. He was lightning swift on the draw. It was death to face him. He had killed thirty men — wildest rumor of all! He had the gun skill of Buck Duane, the craft of Cheseldine, the deviltry of King Fisher, these most notorious of Texas desperadoes. His nerve, his lack of fear — these made him stand out alone even among a horde of bold men.

At first there had not only been great conjecture among the vicious element, with which I had begun to affiliate myself, but also a very decided checking of all kinds of action calculated to attract a keen-eyed ranger. Steele did not hide, but, during these opening days of his stay in Fairdale, he was not often seen in town. At the tables, at the bars and lounging places remarks went the rounds: "Who's thet ranger after? What'll he do fust off? Is he waitin' fer somebody? Who's goin' to draw on him fust . . . an' go to hell? Jest about how soon will he be found somewhere full of lead?"

Those whom it was my interest to cultivate grew more curious, more speculative and impatient as time went by. When it leaked out somewhere that Steele was openly cultivating the honest stay-at-home citizens, to array them in time against the other element, then Fairdale showed those wolf teeth hinted at in the letters to Captain MacNeal.

Several times Steele was shot at in the dark and once slightly injured. Rumor had it that Jack Blome, the gunman of those parts, was coming in to meet Steele. Part of Fairdale awakened, and another part, much smaller, became quieter, more secluded. Strangers, upon whom we could get no line, mysteriously came and went. The drinking, gambling, fighting in the resorts seemed to gather renewed life. Abundance of money floated in circulation. And rumors, vague and unfounded, crept in from Sanderson and other points, rumors of a gang of rustlers off here, a hold-up of the stage off there, robbery of a rancher at this distant point, and murder done at another.

This was Texas and New Mexico life in these frontier days, but, strangely, neither Steele nor I had yet been able to associate any rumor or act with a possible gang of rustlers in Fairdale. Nevertheless, we had not been discouraged. After three weeks of waiting, we had become alive to activity around us, and, though it was unseen, we believed we would soon be on its track.

My task was the busier and the easier. Steele had to have a care for his life. I never failed to caution him of this. My long reflection on the month's happenings and possibilities was brought to any end by the appearance of Miss Longstreth and Ruth. My employer looked worried. Ruth was in regular cowgirl riding costume, in which her trim, shapely figure showed at its best, and her face was saucy, sparkling, daring.

"Good morning, Russ," said Miss Longstreth, and she gazed searchingly at me.

I had dropped off the fence, sombrero in hand. I knew I was in for a lecture, and I put on a brazen, innocent air.

"Did you break your promise to me?" she asked reproachfully.

"Which one?" I asked. It was Ruth's bright eyes upon me, rather than Miss Longstreth's reproach, that bothered me.

"About getting drunk again," she said.

"I didn't break that one."

"My cousin, Floyd, saw you in the Hope So gambling place last night . . . drunk, staggering, mixing with that riffraff, on the verge of a brawl."

"Miss Longstreth, with all due respect to Mister Lawson, I want to say that he has a strange wish to lower me in the eyes of you ladies," I protested with a fine show of spirit.

"Russ, were you drunk?" she demanded.

"No. I should think you needn't ask me that. Didn't you ever see a man the morning after a carouse?"

Evidently she had. And there I knew I stood, fresh, clean-shaven, clear-eyed as the morning.

Ruth's saucy face grew thoughtful, too. The only thing she had ever asked of me was not to drink. The habit had gone hard with the Longstreth family.

"Russ, you look just as . . . as nice as I'd want you to," Miss Longstreth replied. "I don't know what to think. They tell me things. You deny them. Whom shall I believe? Floyd swore he *saw* you."

"Miss Longstreth, did I ever lie to you?"

"Not to my knowledge."

143

Then I looked at her, and she understood what I meant.

"Floyd has lied to me. That day at Sanderson. And since, too, I fear. Do *you* say he lies?"

"Miss Longstreth, I would not call your cousin a liar."

Here Ruth edged closer, with the bridle rein of her horse over her arm. "Russ, Cousin Floyd isn't the only one who saw you. Burt Waters told me the same," she said nervously. I believe Ruth hoped I was telling the truth.

"Waters! So he runs me down behind my back. All right, I won't say a word about him. But do you believe I was drunk when I say no?"

"I'm afraid I do, Russ," she replied with reluctance. Was she testing me?

"See here, Miss Longstreth," I burst out. "Why don't you discharge me? Please let me go. I'm not claiming much for myself, but you don't believe even that. I'm pretty bad. I never denied the scraps, the gambling . . . all that. But I did do as Miss Ruth asked me . . . I did keep my promise to you. Now, discharge me. Then I'll be free to call on Mister Burt Waters."

Miss Longstreth looked alarmed, and Ruth, to my extreme joy, turned pale. Those girls believed I was a desperate devil of a cowboy, who had been held back from spilling blood solely through their kind relation to me.

"Oh, no!" exclaimed Ruth. "Ray, don't let him go."

"Russ . . . pray don't get angry," replied Miss Longstreth, and she put a soft hand on my arm that thrilled me, while it made me feel like a villain. "I won't discharge you. I need you. Ruth needs you. After all, it's none of my business what you do away from here. But, I hoped . . . I would be so happy to . . . to reclaim you from . . . Didn't you ever have a sister, Russ?"

I kept silent for fear that I would perjure myself anew. Yet this situation was delicious, and suddenly I conceived a wild idea. "Miss . . . Longstreth," I began haltingly, but with a brave front, "I've been wild in the past. But I've been tolerably straight here . . . trying to please you. Lately I *have* been going to the bad again. Not drunk, but leaning that way. Lord knows what I'll do soon if . . . if my trouble isn't cured."

"Russ! What trouble?"

"You know what's the matter with me," I went on hurriedly. "Anybody could see that."

Ruth turned a flaming scarlet. Miss Longstreth made it easier for me then by reason of her quick glance of divination.

"I've fallen in love with Miss Ruth. I'm crazy about her. Here I've got to see these fellows flirting with her. And it's killing me. I've . . ."

"If you *are* crazy about me, you don't have to tell!" cried Ruth, red and white by turns.

"I want to stop your flirting one way or another. I've been in earnest. I wasn't flirting. I begged you to . . . to . . ."

"You never did," interrupted Ruth furiously. That hint had been a spark.

"I couldn't have dreamed it," I protested in a passion to be earnest, yet tingling with the fun of it. "That day when I . . . didn't I ask . . . ?"

"If my memory serves me correctly, you didn't ask anything," she replied with anger and scorn now struggling with mirth.

"But, Ruth, I meant to. You understood me? Say, you don't believe I could take that liberty without honorable intentions."

That was too much for Ruth. She jumped at her horse, made the quickest kind of a mount, and was off like a flash. "Stop me if you can," she called back over her shoulder, her face alight and saucy.

"Russ, go after her," said Miss Longstreth. "In that mood she'll ride to Sanderson. My dear fellow, don't stare so. I understand many things now. Ruth *is* a flirt. She would drive any man mad. Russ, I've grown in a short time to like you. If you'll be a man . . . give up drinking and gambling . . . maybe you'll have a chance with Ruth. Hurry now . . . go after her."

I mounted and spurred my horse after Ruth's. She was down on the level now, out in the open, and giving her mount his head. Even had I wanted to overhaul her at once, the matter would have been difficult, well-nigh impossible under five miles. Ruth had as fast a horse as there was on the range. She made no weight in the saddle, and she could ride. From time to time she looked back over her shoulder.

I gained enough to make her think I was trying to catch her. Ruth loved a horse. She loved a race. She lived to win. My good fortune had given me more than one ride alone with Ruth. Miss Longstreth enjoyed riding, too, but she was not a madcap. When she accompanied us, there was never any race. If Ruth got out alone with me, she made me ride to keep her from disappearing somewhere on the horizon. This morning I wanted her to enjoy to the fullest her utter freedom and to feel that, for once, I could not catch her.

Perhaps my declaration to Miss Longstreth had liberated my strongest emotions. However that might be, the fact was that no ride before had ever been like this one — no sky so blue — no scene so open, free, and enchanting as that beautiful, gray-green range — no wind so sweet. The breeze that rushed at me might have been laden with the perfume of Ruth's hair.

I sailed along on what seemed a strange ride. Grazing horses pranced and whistled as I went by. Jackrabbits bounded away to hide in the longer clumps of grass. A prowling wolf trotted from his covert near a herd of cattle. Far to the west rose the low, dark lines of bleak mountains, always mysterious to me, as if holding a secret I needed to know.

It was a strange ride because in the back of my head worked a haunting consciousness of the deadly nature of my business here on the frontier — a business in such contrast with this dreaming and dallying, this longing for what surely was futile. Any moment I might be stripped of my disguise. Any moment I might have to be the ranger.

Ruth kept the lead across the wide plain and mounted to the top of a ridge where, tired out and satisfied with her victory, she awaited me. I was in no hurry to reach the summit of the long, slow-sloping ridge, and I let my horse walk.

Just how would Ruth Herbert meet me now, after my regretted exhibition before her cousin? There was no use to conjecture, but I was not hopeful. When I got there to find her in her sweetest mood, with some little difference never before noted — a touch of shyness — I concealed my surprise.

"Russ, I gave you a run that time," she said. "Ten miles and you never caught me!"

"But look at the start you had. I've had my troubles beating you with an even break." Ruth was susceptible to flattery in regard to her riding, a fact that I made subtle use of.

"But in a long race I was afraid you'd beat me. Russ, I've learned to ride out here. Back home, I never had room to ride a horse. Just look! Miles and miles of level, of green. Little hills with black bunches of trees. Not a soul in sight. Even the town hidden in the green. All wild and lonely. Isn't it glorious, Russ?"

"Lately it's been getting into me," I replied soberly.

We both gazed out over the sea of gray-green, at the undulating waves of ground in the distance. On these rides with her I had learned to appreciate the beauty of the lonely reaches of plain. But, when I could look at her, I seldom wasted time on scenery. Looking at her now, I tried to get again that impression of a difference in her. It eluded me.

Just now with the rose in her brown cheeks, her hair flying, her eyes with grave instead of mocking light, she seemed only prettier than usual. I got down, ostensibly to tighten the saddle girth on her horse, but I lingered over the task. Presently, when she looked down at me, I received that subtle impression of change and read it as her soft mood, the dangerous sweetness that came so seldom, mingled with something deeper, more of character and womanliness than I had ever sensed in her.

"Russ, it wasn't . . . nice to tell Ray," she said.

"Nice! It was . . . oh, I'd like to swear," I ejaculated. "But now I understand my miserable feeling. I was jealous, Ruth. I'm sorry. I apologize."

She had drawn off her gloves, and one little hand, brown, shapely, rested upon her knee very near to me. I took it in mine. She let it stay, though she looked away from me, the color richer in her cheeks.

"I can forgive that," she murmured. "But the lie. Jealousy doesn't excuse a lie."

"You mean . . . what I intimated to your

cousin," I said, trying to make her look at me. "That was the devil in me. Only it's true, Ruth."

"How can it be true when you never asked . . . said . . . a word you hinted of?" she queried. "Ray believed what you said. I know she thinks me horrid."

"No, she doesn't. As for what I said, or meant to say, which's the same thing, how'd you take my actions? I hope not the same as you take Lawson's or the other fellows'."

Ruth was silent, a little pale now, and I saw that I did not need to say any more about the other fellows. The change, the difference was now marked. It drove me to give in wholly to this earnest and passionate side of myself.

"Ruth, I do love you. I don't know how you took my actions. Anyway, now I'll make them plain. I was beside myself with love and jealousy. Will you marry me?"

She did not answer. But the old willful Ruth was not in evidence. Watching her face, I gave her a slow and gentle pull, one she could easily resist if she cared to, and she leaned from her saddle into my arms.

Then there was one wildly sweet moment in which I had the blissful certainty that she kissed me of her own accord. She was abashed, yet yielding. She let herself go, yet seemed not utterly unstrung. Perhaps I was rough, held her too hard, for she cried out a little.

"Russ! Let me go. Help me . . . back."

I righted her in the saddle, although not entirely releasing her. "But, Ruth, you haven't told me anything," I remonstrated tenderly. "Do you love me?"

"I think so," she whispered.

"Ruth, will you marry me?"

She disengaged herself then, sat erect, and faced away from me, with her breast heaving. "No, Russ," she presently said, once more calm.

"But Ruth . . . if you love me . . . ?" I burst out, and then stopped, stilled by something in her face.

"I can't help . . . loving you, Russ," she said. "But to promise to marry you, that's different. Why, Russ, I know nothing about you, not even your first name. You're not a . . . a steady fellow. You drink, gamble, fight. You'll kill somebody yet, I fear. *Then* I'll not love you. Besides, I've always felt you're not just what you seemed. I can't trust you. There's something wrong about you."

I knew my face darkened, and perhaps hope and happiness died in it. Swiftly she placed a kind hand on my shoulder.

"Now I've hurt you. Oh, I'm sorry! Your asking me makes such a difference. The *others* are not in earnest. But, Russ, I had to tell you why I couldn't be engaged to you."

"I'm not good enough for you. I'd no right to ask you to marry me," I replied abjectly.

"Russ, don't think me . . . proud," she faltered. "I wouldn't care who you were if I could only . . . only respect you. Some things about you are splendid . . . you're such a man . . . that's why I cared. But you gamble. You drink . . . and I *hate* that. You're dangerous, they say . . . and I'd be . . . I am in constant dread you'll kill somebody. Remember, Russ, I'm no Texan."

This regret of Ruth's, this faltering distress at giving me pain, was such sweet assurance that she did love me better than she knew, that I was divided between extremes of emotion.

"Will you wait? Will you trust me a little? Will you give me a chance? After all . . . maybe I'm not so bad as I seem."

"Oh, if you weren't! Russ, are you asking me to trust you?"

"I beg you to . . . dearest. Trust me, and wait."

"Wait? What for? Are you really on the square, Russ? Or are you what Floyd calls you . . . a drunken cowboy, a gambler, sharp with the cards, a gunfighter?"

My face grew cold as I felt the blood leave it. At that moment mention of Floyd Lawson fixed once for all my hate of him. Bitter, indeed, was it that I dared not give him the lie. But what could I do? The character Lawson gave me was scarcely worse than what I had chosen to represent. I had to acknowledge the justice of his claim, but, nevertheless, I hated him.

"Ruth, I ask you to trust me . . . in spite of my reputation."

"You ask a great deal," she replied.

"Yes, it's too much. Let it be only this, then . . . you'll wait. And, while you wait, promise not to flirt with Lawson and Waters."

"Russ, I'll not let Floyd or any of them as much as dare touch me," she declared in girlish earnestness, her voice rising. "I'll promise, if you'll promise me not to go into those saloons any more."

One word would have brought her into my arms for good and all. The better side of Ruth Herbert showed then in her appeal. That appeal was as strong as the drawing power of her little face, all eloquent with its light, eyes dark with tears, and lips wanting to smile.

My response should have been instantaneous. How I yearned to give it and win the reward I imagined I saw on her tremulous lips! But I was bound. The grim, dark nature of my enterprise there in Fairdale returned to stultify my eagerness, dispel my illusion, shatter my dream. For one moment it flashed through my mind to tell Ruth who I was, what my errand was, all the truth, but the secret was not mine to tell. And I kept my pledge.

The hopeful glow left Ruth's face. Her disappointment seemed keen. Then a little scorn of certainty was the bitterest of all for me to bear.

"That's too much to promise all at once," I protested lamely, and I knew I would have done better to keep silent.

"Russ, a promise like that is nothing if a man loves a girl," she retorted. "Don't make any more love to me, please, unless you want me to laugh at you. And don't feel so terribly hurt if you happen to see me flirting occasionally."

She ended with a little mocking laugh. That was the perverse side of her, the cat using her claws. I tried not to be angry, but failed.

"All right, I'll take my medicine," I replied bitterly. "I'll certainly never make love to you again. And I'll stand it, if I happen to see Waters kiss you, or any other decent fellow. But look out how you let that damned backbiter Lawson fool around you!"

I spoke to her as I had never spoken before, in quick, fierce meaning, with eyes holding hers. She paled. But even my scarcely veiled hint did not chill her anger. Tossing her head, she wheeled and rode away.

I followed at a little distance, and thus we traveled the ten miles back to the ranch. When we reached the corrals, she dismounted, and, turning her horse over to Dick, she went off toward the house without so much as a nod or good-bye to me.

I went down to town for once in a mood to live up to what had been heretofore only a sham character. But, turning a corner into the main street, I instantly forgot myself at sight of a crowd congregated before the town hall. There was a babel of voices and an air of excitement that I immediately associated with Longstreth who, as mayor of Fairdale, once in a month of moons held court in this hall.

It took slipping and elbowing to get through the crowd. Once inside the door I saw that the crowd was mostly outside and evidently not so desirous as I was to enter. The first man I saw was Steele, looming up.

The next was Longstreth, chewing his mustache — the third, Lawson, whose dark and sinister face told much. Something was up in Fairdale. Steele had opened the ball.

There were other men in the hall, a dozen or more, and all seemed shouting excitedly in unison with the crowd outside. I did not try to hear what was said. I edged closer in among the men to the front.

Longstreth sat at a table up on a platform. Near him sat a thick-set grizzled man, with deep eyes. This was Hanford Owens, county judge. To the right stood a tall, angular, yellow-faced fellow with a drooping sandy mustache. Conspicuous on his vest was a huge silver shield. This was Gorsech, one of Longstreth's sheriffs. There were four other men whom I knew, several whose faces were familiar, and half a dozen strangers, all dusty horsemen.

Steele stood apart from them, a little to one side, so that he faced them all. His hair was disheveled, and his shirt open at the neck. He looked cool and hard. When I caught his eye, I realized in an instant that the long-deferred action — the beginning of our real fight in Fairdale — was at hand.

Longstreth pounded hard on the table to be heard. Mayor or not, he was unable at once to quell the excitement. Gradually, however, it subsided. From the last few utterances before quiet was restored, I gathered that Steele had intruded upon some kind of a meeting in the hall.

"Steele, what'd you break in here for?" demanded Longstreth.

"Isn't this the court? Aren't you the mayor of Fairdale?" interrogated Steele. His voice was so clear and loud, almost piercing, that I saw at once that he wanted all those outside to hear.

"Yes," replied Longstreth. Like flint he seemed, yet I felt his intense interest.

I had no doubt then that Steele intended to make him stand out before the crowd as the real mayor of Fairdale, or as a man whose office was a sham.

"I've arrested a criminal," said Steele. "Bud Snell. I charge him with assault on Laramie and attempted robbery . . . if not murder. Snell has a shady past here, as the court will know if it keeps a record."

Then I saw Snell, hunching down on a bench, a nerveless and shaken man if there ever was one. He had been a hanger-on around the gambling dens — the kind of sneak I never turned my back to.

Jim Laramie, the restaurant keeper, was present also, and on second glance I saw that he was pale. There was blood on his face. I knew Jim, liked him, had tried to make a friend of him.

I was not dead to the stinging interrogation in the concluding sentence of Steele's speech. Then I felt sure I had correctly judged Steele's motive. I began to warm to the situation.

"What's this I hear about you, Bud? Get up and speak for yourself," said Longstreth gruffly.

Snell got up, not without a furtive glance at Steele, and he shuffled forward a few steps toward the mayor. He had an evil front, but not the boldness even of a rustler.

"It ain't so, Longstreth," he began loudly. "I went in Laramie's place fer grub. Some feller I never seen before come in from the hall . . . an' hit Laramie an' wrastled him on the floor. Then this big ranger grabbed me an' fetched me here. I didn't do nothin'. This ranger's hankerin' to arrest somebody. Thet's my hunch, Longstreth."

"What do you have to say about this, Laramie?" sharply queried Longstreth. "I call to your mind the fact that you once testified falsely in court, and got punished for it."

Why did my sharpened and experienced wits interpret a hint of threat or menace in Longstreth's reminder? Laramie rose from the bench and with an unsteady hand reached down to support himself. He was no longer young, and he seemed broken in health and spirit. He had been hurt somewhat about the head.

"I haven't much to say," he replied. "The ranger dragged me here. I told him I didn't take my troubles to court. Besides, I can't swear it was Snell who hit me."

Longstreth said something in an undertone to Judge Owens, and that worthy nodded his great, bushy head.

"Bud, you're discharged," said Longstreth bluntly. "Now, the rest of you clear out of here."

He absolutely ignored the ranger. That was his rebuff to Steele's advances — his slap in the face to an interfering ranger service.

If Longstreth was crooked, he certainly had magnificent nerve. I almost decided he was above suspicion. But his nonchalance, his air of finality, his authoritative assurance — these to my keen and practiced eyes were in significant contrast to a certain tenseness of line about his mouth and a slow paling of his olive skin. He had crossed the path of Vaughn Steele. He had blocked the way of this Lone Star ranger. If he had intelligence, which surely he had, and remembered

160

Steele's fame, then he had some appreciation of what he had undertaken.

In that momentary lull my scrutiny of Longstreth gathered an impression of the man's intense curiosity. Then the prisoner, Bud Snell, with a cough that broke the spell of silence, shuffled a couple of steps toward the door.

"Hold on!" called Steele.

It was a bugle call. It halted Snell as if it had been a bullet. He seemed to shrink.

"Longstreth, I saw Snell attack Laramie," said Steele, his voice still ringing. "What has the court to say to that?"

The moment for open rupture between ranger service and Longstreth's idea of law was at hand. Longstreth showed not the slightest hesitation.

"The court has this to say . . . west of the Pecos we'll not aid or abet or accept any ranger service. Steele, we don't want you out here. Fairdale doesn't need you."

"That's a lie, Longstreth," retorted Steele. "I've a pocket full of letters from Fairdale citizens, all begging for ranger service."

Longstreth turned white. The veins corded at his temples. He appeared about to burst into rage. He was at a loss for a quick reply.

Steele shook a long arm at the mayor. "I

asked your help. You refuse. Now, I'll work alone. This man, Snell, goes to Del Rio in irons."

Floyd Lawson rushed up to the table. The blood showed black and thick in his face. His utterance was incoherent, and his uncontrollable outbreak of temper seemed out of all proportion to any cause he should reasonably have had for anger. Longstreth shoved him back with a curse and a warning glare.

"Where's your warrant to arrest Snell?" shouted Longstreth to Vaughn. "I won't give you one. You can't take him without a warrant."

"I don't need warrants to make arrests. Longstreth, you're ignorant of the power of the Texas Rangers."

"You'll take Snell without papers?" bellowed Longstreth.

"He goes to Del Rio to jail," answered Steele grimly.

"He won't. You'll pull none of your damned ranger stunts out here. I'll block you, Steele."

That passionate reply of Longstreth's appeared to be the signal Steele had been waiting for. He had helped on the crisis. I believe I saw how he wanted to force Longstreth's hand and show the town his stand.

Steele backed clear of everybody, and like two swift flashes of light his guns leaped forth. He was transformed. My wish was fulfilled. Here was Steele, the ranger, in one of his lone lion stands. Not exactly alone, either, for my hand itched for my gun.

"Men! I call on you all!" cried Steele piercingly. "I call on you to witness the arrest of a criminal opposed by Longstreth, mayor of Fairdale. It will be recorded in the report sent to the adjutant general at Austin. Longstreth, I warn you . . . don't follow up your threat."

Longstreth sat white with working jaw.

"Snell, come here," ordered Steele. The man went, as if drawn, and appeared to slink out of line with the guns. Steele's cold gray glance held every eye in the hall. "Take the handcuffs out of my pocket. This side. Go over to Gorsech with them. Gorsech, snap those irons on Snell's wrists. Now, Snell, back here to the right of me."

No wonder was it to me to see how instantly Steele was obeyed. He might have seen more danger in that moment than was manifest to me. On the other hand, he might have wanted to drive home hard what he meant.

It was a critical moment for those who opposed him. There was death in the balance. This ranger, whose last resort was gun play, had instantly taken the initiative, and his nerve chilled even me. Perhaps, though, he read this crowd differently from me and saw that intimidation was his cue. I forgot I was not a spectator, but an ally.

"Longstreth, you've shown your hand," said Steele in the deep voice that carried so far and held those who heard. "Any honest citizen of Fairdale can now see what's plain . . . yours is a damn' poor hand! You're going to hear me call a spade a spade. Your office is a farce. In the two years you've been mayor you've never arrested one rustler. Strange . . . when Fairdale's a nest for rustlers! You've never sent a prisoner to Del Rio, let alone to Austin. You have no jail. There have been nine murders during your office . . . innumerable street fights and hold-ups. Not one arrest! But you have ordered arrests for trivial offenses and have punished these out of all proportion.

"There have been lawsuits in your court . . . suits over water rights, cattle deals, property lines. Strange how in these lawsuits you or Lawson or other men close to you were always involved . . . stranger how it seems the law was stretched to favor your interests."

Steele paused in his cold, ringing speech.

164

In the silence, both outside and inside the hall, could be heard the deep breathing of agitated men. I did not need to fear that any man might draw on Steele. Never had I seen a crowd so cold, so stiff, so held. I would have liked to search for possible satisfaction on the faces of any present, but I was concerned only with Longstreth, and Longstreth was indeed a study. Yet, did he betray anything but rage at this interloper?

"Longstreth, here's plain talk for you and Fairdale to digest," went on Steele. "I don't accuse you and your court of dishonesty. I say . . . *strange!* Law here has been a farce. The motive behind all this laxity isn't plain to me . . . yet. But I call your hand."

Chapter Seven

SOUNDING THE TIMBER

When Steele left the hall, pushing Snell before him, making a lane through the crowd, it was not any longer possible to watch everybody. Yet, now, he seemed to ignore the men behind him. Any friend of Snell's among the vicious element might have pulled a gun. I wondered if Steele knew how I watched those men at his back — how fatal it would have been for any of them to make a significant move. No. I decided that Steele trusted to the effect his boldness had created. It was this power to cow ordinary men that explained so many of his feats — just the same as it was his keenness to read desperate men, his nerve to confront them, that made him great.

The crowd followed Steele and his captive down the middle of the main street, watched him secure a team and buckboard, and drive off on the road to Sanderson. Only then did the crowd appear to realize what had happened.

Then my long-awaited opportunity arrived. In the expression of silent men I found something which I had sought. From the hurried departure of others homeward I gathered import. On the husky, whispering lips of yet others I read words I needed to hear. The other part of that crowd — to my surprise, the smaller part — was the roaring, threatening, complaining one. Thus, I segregated those in Fairdale who were lawless from those in Fairdale who wanted law, but for some reason not yet clear the latter did not dare to voice their choice. How could Steele and I win them openly to our cause? If that could be done long before the year was up, Fairdale would be free of violence and Captain MacNeal's ranger service saved in the state.

I went from place to place, corner to corner, bar to bar, watching, listening, recording. It was not until long after sunset that I went back out to the ranch. The excitement had preceded me and speculation was rife. Hurrying through my supper, to get away from questions and to go on with my spying, I went out to the front of the house.

The evening was warm. The doors were open, and in the twilight the only lamps that had been lit were in Longstreth's big sitting room at the far end of the house. Neither Longstreth nor Lawson had come home to supper. I would have given much to hear their talk right then and certainly intended to try to hear it when they did come home. When the buckboard drove up, and they alighted, I was well hidden in the bushes, so well screened that I could get but a fleeting glimpse of Longstreth as he went in. For all I could see, he appeared to be a calm and quiet man, intense beneath the surface, with an air of dignity under insult. My chance to observe Lawson was lost. They went into the house without speaking, and closed the door.

At the other end of the porch, close under a window, was an offset between step and wall, and there in the shadow I hid. If Longstreth or Lawson visited the girls that evening, I wanted to hear what was said about Steele. It seemed to me that it might be a good clue for me — the circumstance whether or not Ray Longstreth was told the truth. So I waited there in the darkness with patience born of many hours of similar watches.

Presently the small lamp was lit — I could tell the difference in light when the big one was burning — and I heard the swish of skirts.

"Something's happened surely, Ruth," I heard Miss Longstreth say anxiously. "Papa just met me in the hall and didn't speak. He seemed pale, worried."

"Cousin Floyd looked like a thunder-cloud," said Ruth. "For once, he didn't try to kiss me. Something's happened. Well, Ray . . . this has been a bad day for me, too."

Plainly I heard Ruth sigh, and the little pathetic sound brought me vividly out of my sordid business of suspicion and speculation. So she was sorry.

"Bad for you, too?" replied Ray in amused surprise. "Oh, I see . . . I forgot. You and Russ had it out."

"Out? We fought like the very deuce. I'll never speak to him again."

"So your little . . . affair with Russ is all over?"

"Yes." Here she sighed again.

"Well, Ruth, it began swiftly and it's just as well short," said Ray earnestly. "We know nothing at all of Russ . . ."

"Ray, after today I respect him in . . . in spite of things . . . even though he seems no good. I . . . I cared a lot, too."

"My dear, your loves are like the summer flowers. I thought maybe your flirting with Russ might amount to something. Yet, he seems so different now from what he was at first. It's only occasionally I get the impression I had of him after that night he saved

169

me from violence. He's strange. Perhaps it all comes of his infatuation with you. He *is* in love with you. I'm afraid of what may come of it."

"Ray, he'll do something dreadful to Floyd, mark my words," whispered Ruth. "He swore he would if Floyd fooled around me any more."

"Oh, dear! Ruth, what can we do? These are wild men. Floyd makes life miserable for me. And he teases you unmer . . ."

"I don't call it teasing. Floyd wants to spoon," declared Ruth emphatically. "He'd run after any woman."

"A fine compliment to me, Cousin Ruth," laughed Ray.

"I don't care," replied Ruth stubbornly. "It's so. He's spoony. And when he's been drinking and tries to kiss me . . . I hate him!"

"Ruth, you look as if you'd rather like Russ to do something dreadful to Floyd," said Ray with a laugh that this time was only half mirth.

"Half of me would and half of me wouldn't," returned Ruth. "But all of me would if I weren't afraid of Russ. I've got a feeling . . . I don't know what . . . something will happen between Floyd and Russ some day."

There were quick steps on the hall floor,

steps I thought I recognized.

"Hello, girls!" sounded Lawson's voice, minus its usual gaiety.

Then ensued a pause that made me bring to mind a picture of Lawson's glum face.

"Floyd, what's the matter?" asked Ray presently. "I never saw Papa as he is tonight, nor you so . . . so worried. Tell me . . . what has happened?"

"Well, Ray, we had a jar today," replied Lawson with a blunt, expressive laugh.

"Jar?" echoed the girls curiously.

"Jar? We had to submit to a damnable outrage," added Lawson passionately, as if the sound of his voice augmented his feeling. "Listen, girls. I'll tell you all about it."

He coughed, clearing his throat in a way that betrayed he had been drinking. I sank deeper in the shadow of my covert and, stiffening my muscles for a protracted spell of rigidity, prepared to listen with all acuteness and intensity. Just one word from this Lawson, inadvertently uttered in a moment of passion, might be the word Steele needed to provide his clue.

"It happened at the town hall," began Lawson rapidly. "Your father and Judge Owens and I were there in consultation with three ranchers from out of town. First we were disturbed by gunshots from somewhere, but not close at hand. Then we heard the loud voices outside.

"A crowd was coming down the street It stopped before the hall, Men came running in, yelling. We thought there was a fire. Then that damned ranger, Vaughn Steele, stalked in, dragging a fellow by the name of Snell. We couldn't tell what was wanted because of the uproar. Finally your father restored order.

"Steele had arrested Snell for alleged assault on a restaurant keeper named Laramie. It developed that Laramie didn't accuse anybody, didn't know who attacked him. Snell, being obviously innocent, was discharged. Then this . . . this gunfighting ranger pulled his guns on the court and halted the proceedings."

When Lawson paused, I plainly heard his intake of breath. Far, indeed, was he from calm.

"Steele held everybody in that hall in fear of death, and he began shouting his insults. Law was a farce in Fairdale. The court was a farce. There was no law. Your father's office as mayor should be impeached. He made arrests only for petty offenses. He was afraid of the rustlers, highwaymen, murderers. He was afraid or . . . he just let them alone. He used his office to cheat ranchers and cattlemen in lawsuits. All this Steele yelled for everyone to hear. A damnable outrage! Your father, Ray, insulted in his own court by a rowdy ranger! Not only insulted, but threatened with death . . . two big guns thrust almost in his face."

"Oh, how horrible!" cried Ray Longstreth in mingled distress and anger.

"Steele's a ranger. The ranger service wants to rule western Texas," went on Lawson. "These rangers are all a low set, many of them worse than the outlaws they hunt. Some of them were outlaws and gunfighters before they became rangers. This Steele is one of the worst of the lot. He's keen, intelligent, smooth, and that makes him more to be feared. For he is to be feared. He wanted to kill. He meant to kill. If your father had made the least move, Steele would have shot him. He's a cold-nerved devil . . . the born gunman. My God, any instant I expected to see your father fall dead at my feet!"

"Oh, Floyd! The . . . the unspeakable ruffian!" cried Ray Longstreth passionately.

"You see, Ray, this fellow Steele has failed here in Fairdale. He's been here weeks and done nothing. He must have got desperate. He's infamous, and he loves his name. He seeks notoriety. He made that play with

Snell just for a chance to rant against your father. He tried to inflame all Fairdale against him. That about lawsuits was the worst. Damn him. He'll make us enemies "

"What do you care for the insinuations of such a man?" said Ray Longstreth, her voice now deep and rich with feeling. "After a moment's thought no one will be influenced by them. Do not worry, Floyd. Tell Papa not to worry. Surely, after all these years he can't be injured in reputation by . . . by an adventurer."

"Yes, he can be injured," replied Floyd quickly. "The frontier is a queer place. There are many bitter men here . . . men who have failed at ranching. And your father has been wonderfully successful. Steele has dropped some poison, and it'll spread."

Then followed a silence during which, evidently, the worried Lawson bestrode the floor.

"Cousin Floyd, what became of Steele and his prisoner?" asked Ruth suddenly.

How like her it was, with her inquisitive bent of mind and shifting points of view, to ask a question of which the answering would be gall and wormwood to Lawson. It amused while it thrilled me. Ruth might be a flirt, but she was no fool.

"What became of them? Ha! Steele bluffed

the whole town . . . at least all of it who had heard the mayor's order to discharge Snell," growled Lawson. "He took Snell . . . rode off for Del Rio to jail him there."

"Floyd!" exclaimed Ray. "Then, after all, this ranger was able to arrest Snell, the innocent man father discharged, and take him off to jail?"

"Exactly. That's the toughest part . . ." — Lawson stopped abruptly, and then broke out fiercely — "but, by God, he'll never come back!"

Lawson's slow pacing quickened, and he strode from the parlor, leaving behind him a silence eloquent of the effect of his sinister prediction.

"Ruth, what did he mean?" asked Ray in a low voice.

"Steele will be killed," replied Ruth, just as low-pitched.

"Killed! That magnificent fellow! Ah, I forgot. Ruth, my wits are sadly mixed. I ought to be glad if somebody kills my father's defamer. But, oh, I can't be. This bloody frontier makes me sick. Papa doesn't want me to stay for good. And no wonder! Shall I go back? I hate to show a white feather. Do you know, Ruth, I was . . . a little taken with this Lone Star ranger. Miserably, I confess. He seemed so like in spirit to the good stature of him. How can so splendid a man be so bloody, so base at heart? It's hideous. How little we know of men. I had my dream about Vaughn Steele. I confess because it shames me . . . because I hate myself."

Next morning I awakened with a feeling that I was more like my old self. In the experience of activity of body and mind, with a prospect that this was merely the forerunner of great events, I came around to my own again. Ruth was not forgotten. She just had become a sorrow. So, perhaps, my downfall as a lover was a precursor of better results as an officer.

I held in abeyance my last conclusion regarding Longstreth and Lawson, and only awaited Steele's return to have fixed in mind what these men were. Lawson's remark about Steele's not returning did not worry me. I had heard many such dark sayings in reference to rangers. Rangers had a trick of coming back. I did not see any man or men on the present horizon of Fairdale equal to the killing of Vaughn Steele.

As Miss Longstreth and Ruth had no inclination to ride, I had even more freedom. I went down to the town and burst, cheerily whistling, into Jim Laramie's place. Jim always made me welcome there, as much for my society as for the money I spent, and I never neglected being free with both. I bought a handful of cigars and shoved some of them in Jim's pocket.

"How's tricks, Jim?" I asked.

"Reckon I'm feelin' as well as could be expected," replied Jim. His head was circled by a bandage that did not conceal the lump where he had been struck. He looked a little pale, but he was bright enough.

"That was a hell of a biff Snell gave you, the skunk!" I remarked with nonchalant assurance.

"Russ, I ain't accusin' Snell," remonstrated Laramie with eyes that made me thoughtful.

"Sure, I know you're too good a sport to send a fellow up. But Snell deserved what he got. I saw his face when he made his talk to Longstreth. Snell lied. And I'll tell you what, Jim, if it'd been me instead of that ranger, Bud Snell would have got settled."

Laramie appeared to be agitated by my forcible intimation of friendship.

"Jim, that's between ourselves," I went on. "I'm no fool. And much as I blab when I'm hunky, it's all air. Maybe you've noticed that about me. In some parts of Texas it's policy to be close-mouthed. Policy and health-preserving! Between ourselves, as friends, I want you to know I lean some on Steele's side of the fence."

As I lighted a cigar, I saw, out of the corner of my eye, how Laramie gave a quick start. I expected some kind of a startling idea to flash into his mind. Presently I turned and frankly met his gaze. I had startled him out of his habitual set taciturnity, but, even as I looked, the light that might have been amaze and joy faded out of his face, leaving it the same old mask. Still I had seen enough. Like a bloodhound, I had a scent.

"Thet's funny, Russ, seein' as you drift with the gang Steele's bound to fight," remarked Laramie.

"Sure. I'm a sport. If I can't gamble with gentlemen, I'll gamble with . . . rustlers."

Again he gave a slight start, and this time he hid his eyes. "Wal, Russ, I've heard you was slick," he said.

"You tumble, Jim. I'm a little better on the draw."

"On the draw? With cards, an' gun, too, eh?"

"Now, Jim, that last follows natural. I haven't had much chance to show how good I am on the draw with a gun. But that'll come soon."

"Reckon thet talk's a little air," said

Laramie with his dry laugh. "Same as you leanin' a little on the ranger's side of the fence."

"But Jim, wasn't he game? What'd you think of that stand? Bluffed the whole gang! The way he called Longstreth . . . why, it was great. The justice of that call doesn't bother me. It was Steele's nerve that got me. That'd warm any man's blood."

There was a little red in Laramie's pale cheeks, and I saw him swallow hard. I had struck deeply again.

"Say, don't you work for Longstreth?" he queried.

"Me? I *guess* not. I'm Miss Longstreth's man. He and Lawson have tried to fire me many a time."

"Thet so?" he said curiously. "What for?"

"Too many silver trimmings on me, Jim. And . . . I pack my gun low down."

"Wal, them two don't go much together out here," replied Laramie. "But I ain't seen thet anybody has shot off the trimmin's."

"Maybe it'll commence, Jim, as soon as I stop buying drinks. Talking about work . . . who'd you say Snell worked for?"

"When he works at all, which sure ain't often, he rides for Longstreth."

"*Humph!* Seems to me, Jim, that Longstreth's the whole circus 'round Fairdale. I was some sore the other day to find I was losing good money at Longstreth's faro game. Sure, if I'd won, I wouldn't have been sore, eh? But I was surprised to hear some cully say Longstreth owned the Hope So dive."

"I've heard he owned considerable property hereabouts," replied Jim constrainedly.

"*Humph* again! Why, Jim, you know it . . . only like every other cully I meet in this town, you're afraid to open your mug about Longstreth. Get me straight, Jim Laramie. I don't care a damn for Colonel Mayor Longstreth. And for cause I'd throw a gun on him just as quick as on any rustler in Pecos."

"Talk's cheap, my boy," replied Laramie, making light of my bluster, but the red was deeper in his face.

"Sure. I know that," I said, calming down. "My temper gets up, Jim. Then it's not well known that Longstreth owns the Hope So?"

"Reckon it's known in Pecos, all right. But Longstreth's name isn't connected with the Hope So. Blandy runs the place."

"That Blandy . . . I've no use for him. His faro game's crooked, or I'm a locoed bronc'. Not that we don't have lots of crooked faro dealers. A fellow can stand for them. But Blandy's mean, back-handed, never looks you in the eyes. That Hope So place ought to be run by a good fellow like you, Laramie."

"Thanks, Russ," he replied, and I imagined his voice a little husky. "Didn't you ever hear I used to . . . run it?"

"No. Did you?" I said quickly.

"I reckon. I built the place, made additions twice, owned it for eleven years."

"Well, I'll be dog-goned." It was indeed my turn to be surprised, and with the surprise came a glimmering. "I'm sorry you're not there now. Jim, did you sell out?"

"No. Just lost the place."

Laramie was bursting for relief now — to talk — to tell. Sympathy had made him soft. I did not need to ask another question.

"It was two years ago . . . two years last March," he went on. "I was in a big cattle deal with Longstreth. We got the stock . . . an' my share . . . eighteen hundred head . . . was rustled off. I owed Longstreth. He pressed me. It come to a lawsuit . . . an' I . . . was ruined."

It hurt me to look at Laramie. He was white, and tears rolled down his cheeks. I saw the bitterness, the defeat, the agony of the man. He had failed to meet his obligation because he had been swindled. All that he suppressed, all that would have been passion, had the man's spirit not been broken, lay bare for me to see. I had now the secret of his bitterness. But the reason he did not openly accuse Longstreth, the secret of his reticence and fear — these I thought best to try to learn at some later time, after I had consulted with Steele.

"Hard luck. Jim, it certainly was tough," I said. "But you're a good loser. And the wheel turns. Now, Jim, here's what I come particular to see you for. I need your advice. I've got a little money. Between you and me, as friends, I've been adding some to that roll all the time. But, before I lose it, I want to invest some. Buy some stock or buy an interest in some rancher's herd. What I want you to steer me on is a good, square rancher. Or maybe a couple of ranchers, if there happen to be two honest ones in Pecos. Eh? No deals with ranchers who ride in the dark with rustlers. I've got a hunch Fairdale is full of them. Now, Jim, you've been here for years. Sure you must know a couple of men above suspicion."

"Thank God I do, Russ," he replied feelingly. "Frank Morton an' Si Zimmer, my friends an' neighbors all my prosperous days. An' friends still. You can gamble on Frank an' Si. But, Russ, if you want advice from me, don't invest money in stock now."

"Why?"

"Because any new feller buyin' stock in Pecos these days will be rustled faster an' quicker'n he can say Jack Robinson. The pioneers, the cattlemen . . . these are easy enough pickin'. But the new fellers have to learn the ropes. They don't know anythin' or anybody. An' the old ranchers are wise an' sore. They'd fight if they . . ."

"What?" I put in as he paused. "If they knew who was rustling the stock?"

"Nope."

"If they had the nerve?"

"Not that so much."

"What then? What'd make them fight?"

"A leader."

I went out of Laramie's with that word ringing in my ears. A leader. In my mind's eye I saw a horde of dark-faced, dusty-booted cattlemen, riding grim and armed behind Vaughn Steele. More thoughtful than usual I walked on, passing some of my old haunts, and was about to turn in front of a feed and grain store when a hearty slap on my back disturbed my reflection.

"Howdy thar, cowboy," boomed a big voice.

It was Morton, the rancher whom Jim had mentioned and whose acquaintance I had made. He was a man of great bulk with a ruddy, merry face.

"Hello, Morton. Let's have a drink," I suggested.

"Gotta rustle home," he said. "Young feller, I've a ranch to work."

"Sell it to me, Morton."

He laughed and said he wished he could. His buckboard stood at the rail, the horses stamping impatiently. "Cards must be runnin' lucky," he went on with another hearty laugh.

"Can't kick on the luck. But I'm afraid it will change. Morton, my friend, Laramie, gave me a hunch you'd be a good man to tie to. Now, I've a little money, and, before I lose it, I'd like to invest it in stock."

He smiled broadly, but for all his doubt of me he took definite interest.

"I'm not drunk, and I'm on the square," I continued bluntly. "You've taken me for a no-good cowpuncher without any brains. Wake up, Morton. If you never size up your neighbors any better than you have me . . . well, you won't get any richer."

It was sheer enjoyment for me to make my remarks to this man pregnant with meaning. Morton showed his pleasure, his interest, but his faith remained aloof.

"I've got some money. I had some. The cards have run lucky. Will you let me in on some kind of deal? Will you start me up as a stockman with a little herd all my own?"

"Russ, this's durn strange, comin' from Longstreth's cowboy," he said bluntly.

"I'm not in his outfit. My job's with Miss Longstreth. She's fine. But the old man? Nit! He's been after me for weeks. I won't last long. That's one reason why I want to start up for myself."

"Laramie sent you to me, did he? Poor ole Jim! Wal, Russ, to come out flat-footed, you'd be foolish to buy cattle now. I don't want to take your money an' see you lose out. Better go back across the Pecos where the rustlers ain't so strong. I haven't had more'n twenty-five hundred head of stock for ten years. The rustlers let me hang on to a breedin' herd. Kind of them, ain't it?"

"Sort of kind. All I hear is rustlers, Morton," I replied with impatience. "You see, I haven't ever lived long in a rustler-run county. Who heads the gang, anyway?"

Frank Morton looked at me with a curiously amused smile.

"I hear a lot about Jack Blome and Snecker," I continued. "Everybody calls them out-and-out bad. Do they head this mysterious gang?"

"Russ, I opine Blome an' Snecker parade themselves as boss rustlers, same as gun-throwers. But thet's the love such men have

185

for bein' thought hell. Thar's brains headin' the rustler gang hereabouts."

"Maybe Blome and Snecker are blinds. Savvy what I mean, Morton? Maybe there's more in the parade than just the fame of it."

Morton snapped his big jaw as if to shut in impulsive words.

"Look here, Morton. I'm not so young in years even if I am young west of the Pecos. I can figure ahead. It stands to reason, no matter how damn' strong these rustlers are, how hidden their work, however involved with supposedly honest men . . . they can't last."

"They come with the pioneers, an' they'll last while thar's a single steer left," he declared.

"Well, if you take that view of circumstances, I just figure you as one of the rustlers."

Morton looked as if he were about to brain me with the butt of his whip. His anger flashed by then as unworthy of him, and something striking him as funny caused him to boom out a laugh.

"It's not so amusin'," I went on. "If you're not going to pretend a yellow streak, what else will I think?"

"Pretend?" he repeated.

"Sure. You can't fool me, Morton. I know

men of nerve. And here in Pecos they're not any different from those in other places. I say, if you show anything like a lack of sand, it's all bluff. By nature, you've got nerve. There are a lot of men round Fairdale who're afraid of their shadows . . . afraid to open their mouths. But you're not one. So I say, if you claim these rustlers will last, you're pretending lack of nerve just to help the popular side along. For they can't last. Morton, I don't want to be a hard-riding cowboy all my days. Do you think I'd let fear of a gang of rustlers keep me from going in business with a rancher? Nit. What you need out here in Pecos is some new blood . . . a few youngsters like me to get you old guys started. Savvy what I mean?"

"Wal, I reckon I do," he replied, looking as if a storm had blown over him. I gauged the hold the rustler gang had on Fairdale by the difficult job it was to stir this really courageous old cattleman. He had grown up with the evil. To him it must have been a necessary one, the same as dry seasons and cyclones. "Russ, I'll look you up the next time I come to town," he said soberly.

We parted, and I, more than content with the meeting, retraced my steps downstreet to the Hope So saloon. Here I entered, bent on tasks as sincere as the ones just finished, but displeasing, because I had to mix with a low, profane set to cultivate them, to drink occasionally despite my deftness at emptying glasses on the floor, to gamble with them and strangers, always playing the part of a flush and flashy cowboy, half drunk, ready to laugh or fight.

On the night of the fifth day after Steele's departure I went, as was my habit, to the rendezvous we maintained at the pile of rocks out in the open. The night was clear, with bright starlight but no moon, and for this latter fact safer to be abroad. Often from my covert I had seen dark figures, skulking in and out of Fairdale. It would have been interesting to hold up these mysterious travelers. So far, however, this had not been our game. I had enough to keep my own tracks hidden, and my own comings and goings.

I liked to be out in the night, with the darkness close down to the earth, and the feeling of a limitless open all around. Not only did I listen for Steele's soft step, but for any sound — the yelp of coyote or mourn of wolf, the creak of wind in the dead brush, the distant clatter of hoofs, a woman's singing voice, faintly from the town.

This time, just when I was about to give up for that evening, Steele came looming like a black giant long before I heard his soft step. It was good to feel his grip, even if it hurt, because after five days I had begun to worry. We sat down close together, he, facing one direction, and I, the other.

"Well, boy, how've you been?" he asked easily.

"Well, old man, did you land that son-of-a-gun in jail?" I mimicked.

"You bet I did. And he'll stay there for a while. Del Rio rather liked the idea, Russ. All right there. I sidestepped Sanderson on the way back. But over here at the little village . . . Longstreth they call it . . . I was held up. Couldn't help it, because there wasn't any road around."

"Held up?" I queried.

"That is, the buckboard was held up. I got into the brush in time to save my bacon. They began to shoot too soon."

"Did you get any of them?"

"Didn't stay to see," he chuckled. "Had to hoof it to Fairdale, and it's a good long walk."

"Been to your 'dobe yet tonight?"

"I slipped in at the back. Russ, it bothered me some to make sure no one was laying for me in the dark."

"You'll have to get a safer place. Why not take to the open every night?"

"Russ, that's well enough on a trail. But I need grub, and I've got to have a few comforts. I'll risk the 'dobe yet a little."

Then I narrated all that I had seen, done, and heard during his absence, holding back one thing. What I did tell him sobered him at once, brought the quiet, somber mood, the thoughtful air.

"So that's all. Well, it's enough."

"All pertaining to our job, Vaughn," I replied. "The rest is sentiment, perhaps. I had a pretty bad case of moons over the little Herbert girl. But we quarreled. And it's ended now. Just as well, too, because if she'd . . ."

"Russ, did you honestly care for her? The real thing, I mean?"

"I . . . I'm afraid so, Vaughn. I'm sort of hurt inside. But, hell! There's one thing sure, a love affair might have hindered me, made me soft. I'm glad it's over."

He said no more, but his big hand pressing on my knee told me of his sympathy — another indication that there was nothing wanting in this ranger.

"The other thing concerns you," I went on, somehow reluctant now to tell this. "You remember how I heard Lawson making you out as vile to Miss Longstreth. Swore you'd never come back? Well, after he'd gone, when Ruth said he'd meant you'd be killed, Miss Longstreth felt bad about it. She said she ought to be glad if someone killed you, but she couldn't be. She called you a bloody ruffian, yet she didn't want you shot. She said some things about the difference between your hideous character and your splendid stature. Called you a magnificent fellow . . . that was it. Well, then she choked up and confessed to Ruth in shame and disgrace."

"Shame . . . disgrace?" he echoed, greatly interested. "What was it?"

"She confessed she had been taken with you . . . had her little dream about you. And she hated herself for it."

Never, I thought, would I forget Vaughn Steele's eyes. It did not matter that it was dark. I saw the fixed gleam, then the leaping, shadowy light.

"Did she . . . say that?" His voice was not quite steady. "Wonderful! Even if it only . . . lasted a minute. She might . . . we might . . . if it wasn't for this hellish job! Russ, has it dawned on you yet . . . what I've got to do to Ray Longstreth?"

"Yes," I replied. "Vaughn, you haven't . . . gone sweet on her?"

What else could I make of that terrible thing in his eyes? He did not reply to that at all. I thought my arm would break in his clutch.

"You said you knew what I've got to do to Ray Longstreth," he repeated hoarsely.

"Yes. You've got to ruin her happiness, if not her life."

"Why? Speak out, Russ. All this comes like a blow. There, for a little, I hoped you had worked out things . . . differently from me. No hope. Ruin her life. Why?"

I could explain this strange agitation in Steele in no other way except that realization had brought keen suffering as incomprehensible as it was painful. I could not tell if it came from suddenly divined love for Ray Longstreth equally with a poignant conviction that his fate was to wreck her. But I did see that he needed me to speak the brutal truth.

"Steele, old man, you'll ruin Ray Longstreth because . . . as arrest looks improbable to me . . . you'll have to kill her father."

"My God! Why, why? Say it."

"Because Longstreth is the leader of the Fairdale gang of rustlers."

That night, before we parted, we had gone rather deeply into the plan of action for the immediate future. First I gave Steele my earnest counsel and then as stiff an argument

I knew how to put up, all anent the absolute necessity of his eternal vigilance. If he got shot in a fair encounter with his enemies — well, that was a ranger's risk and no disgrace. But to be massacred in bed, knifed in the dark, shot in the back, ambushed in any manner — not one of these miserable ends must be the last record of Vaughn Steele.

He promised me to remain vigilant in a way that made me wonder if he would ever sleep or turn his back on anyone — made me wonder, too, at the menace in his voice. Steele seemed likely to be torn in two ways, and already there was a hint of future desperation.

It was agreed that I make cautious advances to Laramie and Morton and, when I could satisfy myself of their trustworthiness, reveal my identity to them. Through this I was to cultivate Zimmer, and then other ranchers whom we should decide could be let into the secret. It was not only imperative that we learn from them clues by which we might eventually fix guilt on the rustler gang, but also just as imperative that we develop a band of deputies to help us when the fight began.

Steele, now that he was back in Fairdale, would have the center of the stage, with all eyes upon him. We agreed, moreover, that the bolder the front now, the better chance of ultimate success. The more nerve he showed, the less danger of being ambushed, the less peril in facing vicious men.

But we needed a jail. Prisoners had to be corralled after arrest, or the work would be useless, almost a farce, and there was no possibility of repeated trips to Del Rio. We could not use an adobe house for a jail because that could be easily cut out of or torn down. Finally I remembered an old stone house near the end of the main street. It had one window and one door, and had been long in disuse. Steele would rent it, hire men to guard and feed his prisoners. If these prisoners bribed or fought their way to freedom, that would not injure the great principle for which he stood.

Both Steele and I simultaneously, from different angles of reasoning, had arrived at a conviction of Longstreth's guilt. It was not so strong as realization, rather a divination. Long experience in detecting, in feeling the sudden guilt of men, had sharpened our senses for that particular thing. Steele acknowledged a few mistakes in his day, but I, allowing for the same strength of conviction, had never made a single mistake. But conviction was one thing — and proof vastly another. Furthermore, when proof was secured, then came the crowning task — that of taking desperate men in a wild country they dominated.

Verily, Steele and I had our work cut out for us. However, we were prepared to go at it with infinite patience and implacable reserve. Steele and I differed only in the driving incentive, of course, outside of that one binding vow to save the ranger service. He had a strange passion, almost an obsession, to represent the law of Texas, and by so doing render something of safety and happiness to the honest pioneers. Beside Steele, I knew, I shrunk to a shadow. I was not exactly a heathen, and certainly I wanted to help harassed people, especially women and children, but mainly with me it was the zest, the thrill, the hazard, the matching of wits — in a word, the adventure of the game.

᛭ Next morning I rode with the young ladies. In the light of Ruth's persistently flagrant advances, to which I was apparently blind, I saw that my hard-won victory over self was likely to be short-lived. That possibility made me outwardly like ice. I was an attentive, careful, reliable, and respectful attendant, seeing to the safety of my charges, but the one-time gay and debonair cowboy was a thing of the past.

Ruth, womanlike, had been a little — a

very little — repentant. She had showed it. My indifference had piqued her. She made advances, and then my coldness aroused her spirit. She was the kind of girl to value most what she had lost, and to throw conse-quences to the winds in winning it back.

When I divined this, I saw my revenge. To be sure, when I thought of it, I had no reason to want revenge. She had been most gracious to me. But there was the catty thing she had said about being kissed again by her admirers. Then, in all seriousness, sentiment aside, I dared not make up with her.

We halted out on the ridge and dis-mounted for the usual little rest. Mine I took in the shade of a scrubby mesquite. The girls strolled away out of sight. It was a drowsy day, and I nearly fell asleep.

Something roused me — a patter of foot-steps or a rustle of skirts. Then a soft thud behind me gave me at once a start and a thrill. First, I saw Ruth's little brown hands on my shoulders. Then her head, with hair all shiny and flying and fragrant, came around over my shoulder, softly smoothing my cheek, until her sweet, saucy, heated face was right under my eyes.

"Russ, don't you love me any more?" she whispered.

Chapter Eight

HE LOVES YOU

The little devil! She did not have the grace to wear a blush of shame. She was brazenly sure — and all the prettier for it. Some latent dignity gave me power to regard her with silent scorn.

"Russ, no one has kissed me for seven days . . . seven long days."

She sighed. Her implied faithfulness to me was balm to wounded love and vanity, even if it were only a hinted ruse to soften me.

My great trial, however, lay in the dewy, red, coaxing lips so near my own. How I ever held back from them was strange, indeed. Perhaps I could not have held back a moment longer had not Miss Longstreth's steps alarmed Ruth.

Like a bent branch she sprang erect. Her eyes darted clear flames down at me. Under them I preserved a melancholy dignity that was not all pretense. Miss Longstreth returned and said we had better be starting for home.

All the way Ruth seemed to become more

and more thoughtful, as if the significance of the repulse to her presented varying aspects, each of which mitigated her anger. Assuredly she was over her temper by the time we reached the ranch, and, when she turned over her horse to me, it was with a sweet, appealing smile.

Longstreth remained at home, invisible most of the time. When I did get a glimpse of him, it was to see him moody, irascible, and altogether out of sorts. I heard a scrap of conversation between him and his daughter, in which he was urging her to go back to Louisiana, and she was replying with a will of her own. For my part, I hoped she would go away, and Ruth, too, before the trouble began.

In view of Longstreth's state of mind, I was somewhat surprised to learn that he had consented to allow his daughter to give a party, to which all Fairdale was to be invited. Miss Longstreth was delighted, immediately fixed the date, and put us all to various tasks. As I had imagined, a party was Ruth Herbert's especial weakness, and she appeared quite beside herself with rapture. Ruth's emotion was always sincere while it lasted. She waylaid me at my work and might have hugged me, I dare say, if someone had not been near.

"Russ, I've a dress you never saw. All white . . . low neck . . . short sleeves."

It was impossible not to respond to her pleasure, but I did not let show any outward satisfaction. "Fine feathers make fine birds," I said.

"Russ, will you dance with me?" she whispered, undaunted.

"Miss Herbert, I'll dance at your wedding . . . soon, I hope."

"My wedding with whom, Mister Russ?" she replied with tilted chin and fire beginning to kindle in her eyes.

"Oh, I suppose one of these fortunate young bucks . . . the one who has the most wool pulled over his eyes . . . and who doesn't drink."

She gazed down upon me, suddenly furious, and I was ready to dodge to save my ears. "Very well, my one-time cowboy cavalier," she said with more force than elegance. "I'll bet I make you sick Thursday night."

Then she flounced away, as if my presence breathed contagion. I had not the slightest doubt that she would succeed in her threat, but I did not intend to let her find that out. My lack of responsiveness to her friendly and then more intimate advances had discovered to me the fact that of all routes to Miss Herbert's affections this one was likely to be the surest. She simply could not stand indifference. She was like a spoiled child.

Then, perhaps, my iron and callous front, so suddenly following upon my abject adoration, was something calculated to rouse even a less coquettish girl than she. Although the situation for me began to be vexatiously irresistible, the possibilities it opened up were bewildering.

Up to Wednesday I was so busily engaged helping with a multiplicity of tasks that I found no time to get away to go to town. That night, however, I saw Steele at our meeting place. We compared notes and pondered details of our problem.

Steele had rented the stone house to be used as a jail. While the blacksmith was putting up a door and window calculated to withstand many onslaughts, all the idlers and strangers in town had gone to see the sight. Manifestly it was an occasion for Fairdale. When Steele had let it be known that he wanted to hire a jailer and a guard, this caustically humorous element had offered itself *en masse*. The men had made a joke out of it. Steele said dryly that it would not be much of a joke after a week.

When Steele and I were about to separate, I remembered the party to be given by Miss Longstreth, and I told him about it. He shook his head sadly, almost doubtfully. Was it possible that Longstreth could be a deep-eyed, cunning scoundrel, yet keep that beautiful and innocent girl out on the frontier and let her give parties to sons and daughters of a community he had robbed? To any but remorseless rangers the idea was incredible.

Thursday evening came in spite of what the girls must have regarded as an interminably dragging day. It was easy to differentiate their attitudes toward this party. Ruth wanted to look beautiful, to excel all the young ladies who were to attend, to attach to her train all the young men and have them fighting to dance with her. Miss Longstreth had an earnest desire to open her father's house to the people of Fairdale, to show that a daughter had come into his long-cheerless home, to make the evening one of pleasure and entertainment.

I happened to be present in the parlor and was carrying in some flowers for final decoration when Miss Longstreth learned that her father had just ridden off with three horsemen Dick, who brought the news, had not recognized. In her keen disappointment she scarcely heard Dick's concluding remark about the hurry of the colonel. My sharp ears, however, took this in, and it was thought-provoking. Longstreth was known to ride off at all hours, yet this incident seemed unusual.

At eight o'clock the house and porch and patio were ablaze with lights. Every lantern and lamp on the place, together with all that could be bought and borrowed, had been brought into requisition. The cowboys arrived first, all dressed in their best, clean-shaven, red-faced, bright-eyed, eager for the fun to commence. Then the young people from town, and a good sprinkling of older people, came in a steady stream. Miss Longstreth received them graciously, excused her father's absence, and bade them be at home.

The music, or the discordance that went by the name, was furnished by two cowboys with banjos and an antediluvian gentleman with a fiddle. Nevertheless, it was music that could be danced to, and there was no lack of enthusiasm.

I went from porch to parlor and thence to patio, watching and amused. The lights and the decorations of flowers, the bright dresses and the flashy scarves of the cowboys furnished a gay enough scene to a man of lonesome and stern life like mine. During the dance there was a steady, continuous shuffling of boots and, during the interval following, a steady low hum of merry talk and laughter.

My wandering from place to place, apart from my usual careful observation, was an unobtrusive but, to me, a sneaking pursuit of Ruth Herbert. She had on the white dress I had never seen, with the low neck and the short sleeves, and she looked so sweet, so dainty, so altogether desirable, that I groaned a hundred times in my jealousy — because, manifestly, Ruth did not intend to run any risk of my not seeing her in her glory, no matter where my eyes looked. A couple of times, in promenading, I passed her on the arm of some proud cowboy or gallant young buck from town, and on these occasions she favored her escort with a languishing glance that probably did as much damage to him as to me.

Presently she caught me red-handed in my careless, sauntering pursuit of her, and then, whether by intent or from indifference, she apparently deigned me no more notice. But, quick to feel a difference in her, I marked that from that moment her gaiety gradually merged into coquettishness and soon into flirtation. Then, just to see how far she would go, perhaps desperately hoping she would make me hate her, I followed her shamelessly from patio to parlor, porch to court, even into the waltz.

To her credit, she always weakened when

some young fellow got her in a corner and tried to push the flirting to extremes. Young Waters was the only one lucky enough to kiss her, and there was more of strength in his conquest of her than any decent fellow could be proud of.

When Floyd Lawson sought Ruth out, there was added to my jealousy a real anxiety. I had brushed against Lawson more than once that evening. He was not drunk, yet under the influence of liquor. Ruth, however, evidently did not discover this, because, knowing her abhorrence of drink, I believe she would not have walked out with him had she known. Anyway, I followed them, close in the shadow.

Lawson was unusually gay. I saw him put his arm around her without remonstrance. When the music recommenced, they went back to the house. Lawson danced with Ruth, not ungracefully for a man who rode a horse as much as he. After the dance he waved aside Ruth's many partners, not so gaily as would have been consistent with good feeling, and led her away. I followed. They ended that walk at the extreme corner of the patio, where, under gaily colored lights, a little arbor had been made among the flowers and vines.

Ruth seemed to have lost something of

her vivacity. They had not been out of my sight for a moment before Ruth cried out. It was a cry of impatience or remonstrance, rather than alarm, but I decided that it would serve me an excuse. I dashed back, leaped to the door of the arbor, my hand on my gun.

Lawson was holding Ruth. When he heard me, he let her go. Then she uttered a cry that was one of alarm. Her face blanched; her eyes grew strained. One hand went to her breast. She thought I meant to kill Lawson.

"Excuse *me*," I burst out frankly, turning to Lawson. I never saw a hyena, but he looked like one. "I heard a squeal. Thought a girl was hurt . . . or something. Miss Longstreth gave me orders to watch out for accident, fire, anything. So, excuse me, Lawson."

As I stepped back, to my amaze, Ruth, excusing herself to the scowling Lawson, hurriedly joined me.

"Oh, it's our dance, Russ!" She took my arm, and we walked through the patio. "I'm afraid of him, Russ," she whispered. "You frightened me worse, though. You didn't mean to . . . to . . . ?"

"I made a bluff. Saw he'd been drinking, so I kept near you."

"You return good for evil," she replied, squeezing my arm. "Russ, let me tell you . . . whenever anything frightens me, since we got here, I think of you. If you're only near, I feel safe."

We paused at the door, leading into the big parlor. Couples were passing. Here I could scarcely distinguish the last words she said. She stood before me, eyes downcast, face flushed, as sweet and pretty a lass as any man could want to see, and with her hand she twisted around and around a silver button on my buckskin vest.

"Dance with me . . . the rest of this," she said. "Floyd shooed away my partners. I'm glad for the chance. Dance with me, Russ . . . not gallantly or dutifully, because I ask you, but because you *want* to. Else not at all."

There was a limit to my endurance. There would hardly be another evening like this — at least, for me — in that country. I capitulated with what grace I could express.

We went into the parlor, and, as we joined the dancers, despite all that confusion I heard her whisper, "I've been a little beast to you."

That dance, seemingly, lasted only a moment — a moment while she was all airy grace, radiant, and alluring, floating close to me, with our hands clasped. Then it appeared the music had ceased, the couples were passing out and finding seats, and Ruth and I were laughingly accosted by Miss Longstreth. She said we made a graceful couple in the dance. And Ruth said she did not have to reach up a mile to me — I was not so awfully tall. And I, tongue-tied for once, said nothing.

Lawson had returned and was now standing, cigarette between lips, in the door leading out to the patio. At the same moment that I heard a heavy tramp of boots from the porch side, I saw Lawson's face change remarkably, expressing amaze, consternation, then fear. I wheeled in time to see Vaughn Steele bend his head to enter the door on that side. The dancers fell back.

At sight of him I was again the ranger — his ally. Steele was pale, yet heated. He panted. He wore no hat. He had his coat turned up, and with left hand he held the lapels together.

In a quick ensuing silence Miss Longstreth rose, white as her dress. The young women present stared in astonishment, and their partners showed excitement.

"Miss Longstreth . . . I came to search . . . your house!" panted Steele, courteous yet with authority.

I disengaged myself from Ruth, who was clinging to my hands, and stepped forward out of the corner. Steele had been running. Why did he hold his coat like that? I sensed action, and the cold thrill animated me.

Miss Longstreth's astonishment was succeeded by anger difficult to control. "In the absence of my father I am mistress here. I will not permit you to search my house."

"Then . . . I regret to say . . . I must do so without your permission," he said sternly.

"Do not dare!" she flashed. She stood erect, her bosom swelling, her eyes magnificently black with passion. "How dare you intrude here? Have you not insulted us enough? To search my house tonight . . . to break up my party . . . oh, it's worse than outrage. Why on earth do you want to search here? Ah, for the same reason you dragged a poor innocent man into my father's court. Sir, I forbid you to take another step into this house."

Steele's face was bloodless now, and I wondered if it had to do with her scathing scorn — or with something having to do with his hand, closing his coat that way.

"Miss Longstreth, I don't need warrants to search houses," he said. "But this time I'll respect your command. It would be . . . too bad . . . to spoil your party. Let me add

. . . perhaps you do me a . . . little wrong. God knows, I hope so. I was shot by a rustler. He fled. I chased him here. He has taken refuge here . . . in your father's house. He's hidden somewhere."

Steele spread wide his coat lapel. He wore a light shirt, the color of which in places was white. The rest was all a bloody mass — from which dark red drops fell to the floor.

"Oh!" cried Miss Longstreth.

Scorn and passion vanished in the horror, the pity of a woman who imagined she saw a man mortally wounded. It was a hard sight for a woman's eyes — that crimson, heaving breast.

"Surely I didn't seek that," went on Steele, closing his coat. "You used unforgettable words, Miss Longstreth. From you . . . they hurt. For I stand alone. My fight is to make Fairdale safer, cleaner, a better home for women and children. Some day you will remember what you just said."

How splendid he looked — how strong against odds — how simple a dignity fitted his words — and a woman, far blinder than Ray Longstreth was, could have seen that here stood a man. Steele bowed, turned on his heel, and strode out to vanish in the dark.

Then, while she stood bewildered, still shocked, I elected to do some rapid thinking.

How seriously was Steele injured? An instant's thought was enough to tell me that, if he had sustained any more than a flesh wound, he would not have chased his assailant — not with so much at stake in the future. I concerned myself with a cold grip of desire to get near the rustler who had wounded Steele. As I started forward, however, Miss Longstreth detained me, Ruth once more clung to my hands, and directly we were surrounded by an excited circle. It took a moment or two to calm them.

"Then there's a rustler . . . here . . . hiding?" repeated Miss Longstreth. "What shall I do? We can't go on with the dance."

"Miss Longstreth, I'll find him . . . I'll rout him out," I said.

"Yes, yes, find him Russ, but don't use violence," she replied. "Send him away . . . no, give him over to . . ."

"Nothing of the kind," interrupted Floyd Lawson, loud-voiced. "Cousin, go on with your dance. I'll take a couple of cowboys. I'll find this . . . this rustler, if there's one here. But I think it's only another bluff of Steele's."

This from Lawson angered me deeply, and I strode right for the door.

"Where are you going?" he demanded.

"I've Miss Longstreth's orders. She wants

me to find this hidden man. She trusts me not to allow any violence."

"Didn't I say I'd see to that?" he snarled.

"Lawson, I don't care what you say," I retorted. "But I'm thinking you might not want me to find this . . . rustler."

Lawson turned black in the face. Verily, if he had worn a gun, he would have pulled it on me. As it was, Miss Longstreth's interference probably prevented more words, if no worse.

"Don't quarrel," she said. "Floyd, you go with Russ. Please hurry. I'll be nervous till . . . the rustler's found or you're sure there's not one."

We started with several cowboys to ransack the house. We went through the rooms, searching, calling out, flashing our lanterns in dark places. It struck me more than forcibly that Lawson did all the calling. He was hurried, too, trying to keep in the lead. I wondered if he knew his voice would be recognized by the hiding man.

Be that as it might, it was I who peered into a dark corner — and then, with a cocked gun leveled, I said: "Come out!"

He came forth into the flare of lanterns, a tall, slim, dark-faced youth, wearing dark sombrero, blouse, and trousers. I collared him before any of the others could move, and I held the gun close enough to make him shrink. He did not impress me as being frightened just then. Nevertheless, he had a clammy face, the pallid look of a man who had just gotten over a shock. He peered into my face, then into that of the cowboy next to me, then into Lawson's, and, if ever in my life I beheld relief, I saw it then. That was all I needed to know, but I meant to find out more, if I could.

"Who're you?" I asked quietly.

He gazed rather arrogantly down at me. It always irritated me to be looked down at that way.

"Say, don't be smart with me, or you'll get it good," I yelled, prodding him in the side with the cocked gun. "Who are you? Quick!"

"Bo Snecker," he said.

"Any relation . . . what relation to Bill Snecker?"

"His son."

"What'd you hide here for?"

He appeared to grow sullen. "Reckoned I'd be as safe in Longstreth's as anywhere."

"Uh-huh. You're taking a long chance," I replied, and he never knew, or did any of the others, just how long a chance that was.

Sight of Steele's bloody breast remained with me, and I had something sinister to

212

combat. This was no time for me to reveal myself or to show unusual feeling or interest for Steele. Since Steele had abandoned his search, I had nothing to do now but let the others decide what disposition was to be made of Snecker.

"Lawson, what'll you do with him?" I queried, as if uncertain now that the capture was made. I let Snecker go and sheathed my weapon.

That seemed a signal for Lawson to come to life. I guessed he had not much fancied the wide and somewhat variable sweep of the cocked gun.

"I'll see to that," replied Lawson gruffly, and he pushed Snecker in front of him into the hall. I followed them out into the court. This was at the back of the house.

As I had very little further curiosity, I did not wait to see where they went, but hurried back to relieve Miss Longstreth and Ruth. I found them as I had left them — Ruth quiet and pale, Miss Longstreth nervous and distressed. I soon calmed their fears of any further trouble or possible disturbance. Miss Longstreth then became curious and wanted to know who the rustler was.

"How strange he should come here," she said several times.

"Probably he'd run this way or thought

he had a better chance where there was dancing and confusion," I replied, lying glibly.

I wondered how much longer I would find myself keen to shunt her mind from any channel leading to suspicion.

"Would Papa have arrested him?" she asked.

"Colonel Longstreth might have made it hot for him," I replied frankly, feeling that, if what I said had a double meaning, it still was no lie.

"Oh, I forgot . . . the ranger!" she exclaimed suddenly. "That awful sight . . . the whole front of him bloody . . . wet. Russ, how could he stand up under such a wound? Do you think it'll . . . kill him?"

"That's hard to say. A man like Steele can stand a lot."

"Russ, please go find him. See . . . how it is with him," she said, almost pleadingly.

I started, glad of the chance, and hurried toward the town.

There was a light in the little adobe house where he lived and, proceeding cautiously so as to be sure no one saw me, I went close and whistled low in a way he would recognize. Then he opened the door, and I went in.

"Hello, old son," he said. "You needn't

look worried. Sling a blanket over that window so no one can see in."

He had his shirt off and had been in the act of bandaging a wound that the bullet had cut in the tip of his shoulder.

"Let me tie that up," I said, taking the strip of linen. "Uh-huh, shot you from behind, didn't he?"

"How else, you locoed lady charmer? It's a wonder I didn't have to tell you that."

"Tell me about it, anyway."

Steele related a circumstance, differing but little from other attempts at his life, and concluded by saying that Snecker was a good runner, if he was not a good shot. I finished the bandaging and stood off, admiring Steele's magnificent shoulders. I noted, too, on the fine white skin more than one scar made by bullets. I got an impression that his strength and vitality were like his spirit — unconquerable.

"So you knew it was Bill Snecker's son?" I asked when I had told him about finding the rustler.

"Sure. Laramie pointed him out to me yesterday. Both the Sneckers are in town. From now on we're going to be busy, Russ."

"It can't come too soon for me," I replied. "Shall I chuck my job? Come out from behind these cowboy togs?"

215

"Not yet. We need proof, Russ. We've got to be able to prove things. Hang on at the ranch yet a while."

"This Bo Snecker was scared stiff till he recognized Lawson. Isn't that proof?"

"No, that's nothing. We've got to catch Longstreth and Lawson red-handed."

"I don't like the idea of you trailing along alone," I protested. "Remember what Mac-Neal told me. I'm to kick. It's time for me to hang 'round with a couple of guns. You'll never use one."

"The hell I won't!" he retorted with a dark glance of passion. I was surprised that my remark had angered him. "You fellows are all wrong. I know *when* to throw a gun. You ought to remember that rangers have a bad name for wanting to shoot. And I'm afraid it's deserved."

"Did you shoot at Snecker?" I queried.

"I could have got him in the back. But that wouldn't do. I shot three times at his legs . . . tried to let him down. I'd have made him tell everything he knew. Say, but he ran. He was too fast for me."

"Shooting at his legs! No wonder he ran. He savvied your game, all right. It's funny, Vaughn, how these rustlers and gunmen don't mind being killed. But to cripple them . . . rope them . . . jail them . . . that is hell to them. Well, I'm to go on, up at the ranch . . . falling further in love with that sweet kid . . . instead of coming out straight to face things with you?"

Steele had to laugh, yet he was more thoughtful at my insistence. "Russ, you think you have patience, but you don't know what patience is. I won't be hurried on this job. But I'll tell you what . . . I'll hang under cover most of the time when you're not close to me. See? That can be managed. I'll watch for you when you come in town. We'll go in the same places. And in case I get busy, you can stand by and trail along after me. That satisfy you?"

"Fine," I said, both delighted and relieved. "Well, I'll have to rustle back now to tell Miss Longstreth you're all right."

Steele had about finished pulling on a clean shirt, exercising care not to disarrange the bandages, when he stopped short to turn squarely and look at me with hungry eyes.

"Russ, did she . . . show sympathy?"

"She was all broken up about it. Thought you were going to die."

"Did she send you?"

"Sure. And she said hurry," I replied.

I was not a little gleeful over the apparent possibility of Steele being in the same boat with me.

"Do you think she would have cared if . . . if I had been shot up badly?"

The great giant of a ranger asked this like a boy, hesitatingly, with color in his face.

"Care! Vaughn, you're as thick headed as you say I'm locoed. Ray Longstreth has fallen in love with you. That's all. Love at first sight. She doesn't realize it. But I know."

There he stood, as if another bullet had struck him, this time straight through the heart. Perhaps one had — and I repented a little of my over-confident declaration. Still, I would not go back on it. I believed it.

"Russ! For God's sake! What a terrible thing to say," he ejaculated hoarsely.

"No. It's not terrible to say it . . . only the fact is terrible," I went on. "I may be wrong. But I swear I'm right. When you opened your coat . . . showed that bloody breast . . . well, I'll never forget her eyes. She had been furious. She showed passion . . . hate. Then, all in a second, something wonderful, beautiful broke through. Pity . . . fear . . . agonized thought of your death. If that's not love . . . if . . . if she did not betray love, then I never saw it. She thinks she hates you. But she loves you."

"Get out of here," he ordered thickly.

I went, not forgetting to peep out at the door and to listen a moment, then I hurried into the open, toward the ranch. The stars were very big and bright, so calm, so cold, that it somehow hurt me to look at them. Not like men's lives surely.

What had fate done to Vaughn Steele and to me? I had a moment of bitterness — an emotion rare with me. Most rangers put love behind them when they entered the service and seldom found it after that. But love had certainly met me on the way, and I now had confirmation of my fear that Vaughn was hard hit.

Then the wildness, the adventurer in me stirred to the wonder of it all. It was in me to exult even in the face of fate. Steele and I, while balancing our lives on the hair-trigger of a gun, had certainly fallen into a tangled web of circumstances not calculated in the rôle of rangers.

I went back to the ranch with regret, remorse, sorrow knocking at my heart but, notwithstanding, that tingling alive to the devilish excitement of the game. I knew not what it was that prompted me to sow the same seed in Ray Longstreth's breast that I had sown in Steele's. Probably it was just a propensity for sheer mischief — and just as probably a certainty of the truth, a strange foreshadowing of a coming event.

If Ray Longstreth did love him, perhaps

through her this event might be made to seem less tragic. Somehow love might save us all. That was the shadowy portent, flitting in the dark maze of my mind.

At the ranch dancing had been resumed. There might never have been any interruption of the gaiety. I found Miss Longstreth on the look-out for me, and she searched my face with eyes that silenced my one last qualm of conscience.

"Let's go out in the patio," I suggested. "I don't want anyone to hear what I say."

Outside in the starlight she looked white and very beautiful. I felt her tremble. Perhaps my gravity presaged the worst. It did presage one thing — about Vaughn.

"I went down to Steele's 'dobe, the little place where he lives," I began, weighing my words. "He let me in . . . was surprised. He had been shot high in the shoulder, not a dangerous wound. I bandaged it for him. He was grateful . . . said he had no friends."

"Poor fellow. Oh, I'm glad it isn't bad," said Miss Longstreth. Something glistened in her eyes.

"He looked strange . . . sort of forlorn. I think your words . . . what you said . . . hurt him more than the bullet. I'm sure of that, Miss Longstreth."

"Oh, I saw that myself. I was furious. But

I . . . I meant what I said."

"You wronged Steele. I happen to know. I know his record along the Rio Grande. It's scarcely my place, Miss Longstreth, to tell you what you'll find out for yourself, sooner or later."

"What shall I find out?" she demanded.

"I've said enough."

"No. You mean my father and Cousin Floyd are misinformed or wrong about Steele? I've feared it this last hour. It was his look. That pierced me. Oh, I'd hate to be unjust. *You* say I wronged him, Russ? Then you take sides with him against my father?"

"Yes," I replied in a very low tone.

She was keenly hurt and seemed defiant, despite an effort to shrink from me.

"It's only natural you should fight for your father," I went on. "Perhaps you don't understand. He has ruled here for so long. He's been . . . well, let's say, easy with evil-doers. But times are changing. He opposes the ranger idea, which is also natural, I suppose. Still, he's wrong about Steele . . . terribly wrong, and it means trouble."

"Oh, I don't know what to believe!"

"It might be well for you to *think* things out for yourself."

"Russ, I feel as if I couldn't. I can't make

head or tail of life out here. My father seems so strange . . . though, of course, I've only seen him twice a year since I was a little girl. He has two sides to him. When I come upon that strange side . . . the one I never saw . . . he's like a man I never knew. I want to be a good and loving daughter. I want to help him fight his battles. But he doesn't . . . he doesn't satisfy me. He grows impatient and wants me to go back to Louisiana. That gives me a feeling of mystery. Oh, it's all a mystery!"

"True, you're right," I replied, my heart aching for her. "It's all a mystery . . . and trouble, too, for you. Perhaps you'll do well to go home."

"Russ, you suggest I leave here . . . leave my father?" she asked.

"I advise it. You've struck a . . . a rather troublesome time. Later, you might return, if . . ."

"Never. I came to stay, and I'll stay," she declared, and there her temper spoke.

"Miss Longstreth," I began again, after taking a long, deep breath, "I ought to tell you one thing once more about Steele."

"Well, go on."

"Doesn't he strike you now as being the farthest removed from a ranting, brutal ranger?"

"I confess he was at least a gentleman."

"Rangers don't allow anything to interfere with the discharge of their duty. He was courteous after you defamed him. He respected your wish. He did not break up the dance. This may not strike you particularly. But let me explain that Steele was chasing an outlaw who had shot him. Under ordinary circumstances he would have searched your house. He would have been like a lion. He would have torn the place down around our ears to get that rustler. But his action was so different from what I had expected, it amazed me. Just now, when I was with him, I learned . . . I guessed . . . what stayed his hand. I believe you ought to know."

"Know what?" she asked. How starry and magnetic her eyes! A woman's divining intuition made them wonderful with swift-varying emotion.

They drew me on to the fatal plunge. What was I doing to her — to Vaughn? Something bound my throat, making speech difficult.

"He's fallen in love with you," I hurried on in a husky whisper. "Love at first sight! Terrible! Hopeless! I saw it . . . felt it. I can't explain how I know, but I do know. That's what stayed his hand here. And that's why I'm on his side. He's alone. He has a terrible task here without any handicaps. Every man is against him. If he fails . . . you might be the force that weakened him. So you ought to be kinder in your thoughts of him. Wait before you judge him further If he isn't killed, time will prove him noble instead of vile. If he is killed, which is more than likely, you'll feel the happier for a generous doubt in favor of the man who loved you."

Like one stricken blind, she stood an instant, then, with her hands at her breast, she walked straight across the patio into the dark, open door of her room.

Chapter Nine

CLEANING OUT FAIRDALE

Not much sleep visited me that night. In the morning — the young ladies not stirring and no prospects of duty — I rode to town.

Sight of the wide street, lined by its hitching-posts and saddled horses, the square buildings with their ugly signs, the something unfinished yet old, the lounging, dust-gray men at every corner — these awoke in me a significance that had gone into oblivion overnight.

That last talk with Miss Longstreth had unnerved and wrought strangely upon me. Afterward, waking and dozing, I had dreamed, lived in a warm, golden place where there were music and flowers and Ruth's sprite-like form leading me on after two tall, beautiful lovers, Ray and Vaughn, walking hand in hand. Fine employment of mind for a ranger whose single glance down a quiet street pictured it with dark-garbed men in grim action, guns spouting red, horses plunging.

In front of Laramie's restaurant I dismounted and threw my bridle. Jim was unmistakably glad to see me.

"Where've you been? Morton was in an' powerful set on seein' you. I steered him from goin' up to Longstreth's. What kind of a game was you givin' Frank?"

"Jim, I just wanted to see if he was a safe rancher to make a stock deal for me."

"He says you told him he didn't have no yellow streak an' that he was a rustler. Frank can't git over them two hunches. When he sees you, he's goin' to swear he's no rustler, but he *has* got a yellow streak, unless . . ."

This little, broken-down Texan had eyes like flint striking fire.

"Unless?" I queried sharply.

Jim breathed a deep breath and looked around the room before his gaze fixed again on mine. "Wal," he replied, speaking low, "me an' Frank allows you've picked the right men. It was me that sent them letters to the ranger captain at Austin. Now who in hell are you?"

It was my turn to draw a deep breath. I had taken six weeks to strike fire from a Texan whom I instinctively felt had been a prey to the power that shadowed Fairdale. There was no one in the room except us, no one passing or near. Reaching into the inside pocket of my buckskin vest, I turned the lining out. A star-shaped, bright, silver object flashed as I shoved it, pocket and all, under Jim's hard eyes. He could not help but read: United States Deputy Marshal.

"Son of a bitch," he whispered, cracking the table with his fist. "Russ, you sure run true to me. But never as a cowboy."

"Jim, the woods is full of us."

Heavy footsteps sounded on the walk. Presently Steele's bulk darkened the door.

"Hello," I greeted. "Steele, shake hands with Jim Laramie."

"Hello," replied Steele slowly. "Say, I reckon I know Laramie."

"Nit. Not this one. He's the old Laramie. He used to own the Hope So saloon. It was on the square when he ran it. Maybe he'll get it back . . . pretty soon. Hope so."

I laughed at my execrable pun. Steele leaned against the counter, his gray glance studying the man I had so oddly introduced. Laramie in one flash associated the ranger with me — a relation he had not dreamed of. Then, whether from shock or hope or fear I know not, he appeared about to faint.

"Laramie, do you know who's boss of this secret gang of rustlers hereabouts?" asked Steele bluntly.

It was characteristic of him to come sharp to the point. His voice — something deep, easy, cool about him — seemed to steady Laramie.

"No," replied Laramie.

"Does anybody know?" went on Steele.

"Wal, I reckon there's not one honest native of Pecos who *knows*."

"But you have your suspicions?"

"We have."

"You can keep your suspicions to yourself. But you can give me your idea about this crowd that hangs round the saloons . . . the regulars."

"Jest a bad lot," replied Laramie with the quick assurance of knowledge. "Most of them have been here years. Others have drifted in. Some of them work odd times. They rustle a few steers . . . steal . . . rob . . . anythin' for a little money to drink an' gamble. Jest a bad lot. But the strangers as are always comin' an' goin' . . . strangers thet never git acquainted . . . some of them are likely to be *the* rustlers. Bill an' Bo Snecker are in town now. Bill's a known cattle thief. Bo's no good, the makin' of a gunfighter. He heads thet way. They might be rustlers. But the boy, he's hardly careful enough for this gang. Then there's Jack Blome. He comes to town often. He lives up in the hills. He always has three or four strangers with him. Blome's the fancy gunfighter. He shot a gambler here last fall. Then he was in a fight in Sanderson lately. Got two cowboys then. Blome's killed a dozen Pecos men. He's a rustler, too, but I reckon he's not the brains of thet secret outfit, if he's in it at all."

Steele appeared pleased with Laramie's idea. Probably it coincided with the one he had arrived at himself.

"Now, I'm puzzled over this," said Steele. "Why do men . . . apparently honest men . . . seem to be so close-mouthed here? Is that a fact or only my impression?"

"It's a sure fact," replied Laramie darkly. "Men have lost cattle an' property in Fairdale . . . lost them honestly or otherwise, as hasn't been proved. An' in some cases when they talked . . . hinted a little . . . they was found dead. Apparently held up an' robbed. But dead. Dead men don't talk! Thet's why we're close-mouthed."

Steele's face wore a dark, somber sternness. Rustling cattle was not intolerable. Western Texas had gone on prospering, growing in spite of the horde of rustlers ranging its vast stretches, but this cold, secret, murderous hold on a little struggling community was something too strange, too terrible for them to stand long. It had waited for a leader like Steele, and now it could not last. Laramie's revivified spirit showed that.

The ranger was about to speak again when the clatter of hoofs interrupted him. Horses halted out in front.

A motion of Steele's hand caused me to dive through a curtained door back of Laramie's counter. I turned to peep out and was in time to see Floyd Lawson enter with the red-headed cowboy called Brick. This was the first time I had ever seen Lawson come into Laramie's. He called for tobacco.

If his visit surprised Jim, he did not show any evidence of it. But Lawson did show astonishment as he saw the ranger, and then a dark glint flitted from eyes that shifted from Steele to Laramie and back again.

Steele leaned easily against the counter, and he said good morning pleasantly. Lawson deigned him no reply, although he bent a curious and hard scrutiny upon Steele. In fact, Lawson evinced nothing that would lead one to think he had any respect for Steele as a man or as a ranger.

"Steele, that was the second break of yours last night," he said finally. "If you come fooling 'round the ranch again, there'll be hell."

It seemed strange that a man who had lived west of the Pecos for ten years could not see in Steele something which forbade that kind of talk. It certainly was not nerve Lawson showed. Men of courage are seldom intolerant, and with the matchless nerve that characterized Steele or the great gunmen of the day there went a cool unobtrusive manner, a speech brief, almost gentle, certainly courteous. Lawson was a hot-head Louisianian of French extraction, a man evidently who had never been crossed in anything, and who was strong, brutal, passionate, qualities that in the face of a situation like this made him simply a fool.

The way Steele looked at Lawson was a joy to me. I hated this smooth, dark-skinned Southerner. But, of course, an ordinary affront like Lawson's only earned silence from Steele.

"I'm thinking you used your ranger bluff just to get near Ray Longstreth," Lawson sneered. "Mind you, if you come up there again, there'll be hell!"

"You're damned right, there'll be hell!" retorted Steele, a kind of high ring in his voice. I saw thick, dark red creep into his face.

Had Lawson's incomprehensible mention of Ray Longstreth been an instinct of love — of jealousy? Verily, it had pierced the depths of the ranger, probably as no other threat could have.

"Ray Longstreth wouldn't stoop to know a dirty blood-tracker like you," continued Lawson hotly. His was not a deliberate intention to rouse Steele. The man was simply being rancorous. "I'll call you right . . . you cheap blutter! Your four-flush! You damned interfering, conceited ranger!"

Long before Lawson ended his tirade, Steele's face had lost the tinge of color, so foreign to it in moments like this, and the cool shade, the steady eyes like ice on fire, the ruthless lips had warned me, if they had not Lawson.

"Lawson, I'll not take offense, because you seem to be championing your beautiful cousin," replied Steele in slow, biting speech. "But let me return your compliment. You're a fine Southerner! Why, you're only a cheap four-flush . . . damned . . . bull-headed . . . *rustler!*"

Steele hissed the last word. Then for him — for me — for Laramie — there was the truth in Lawson's working, passion-blackened face. Lawson jerked, moved, meant to draw. But how slow! Steele lunged forward. His long arm swept up. Lawson staggered backward, knocking a table and chairs, to fall hard in a half-sitting position against the wall.

"Don't draw," warned Steele.

"Lawson, git away from your gun!" yelled the cowboy, Brick.

But Lawson was crazed by fury. He tugged at his hip, his face corded with purple welts, malignant, murderous, while he got to his feet. I was about to leap through the door when Steele shot. Lawson's gun went ringing to the floor. Like a beast in pain Lawson screamed. Frantically he waved a limp arm, flinging blood over the white tablecloths. Steele had crippled him.

"Here, you cowboy," ordered Steele, "take him out. Quick!"

Brick saw the need of expediency, if Lawson did not realize it, and he pulled the raving man out of the place. He hurried Lawson down the street, leaving the horses behind.

Steele calmly sheathed his gun. "Well, I guess that opens the ball," he said as I came out.

Laramie seemed fascinated by the spots of blood on the tablecloths. It was horrible to see him rubbing his hands there like a ghoul.

"I tell you what, fellows," said Steele, "we've just had a few pleasant moments with the man who has made it healthy to keep close-mouthed in Fairdale."

Laramie lifted his shaking hands. "What'd you wing him for?" he wailed. "He was drawin' on you. Shootin' arms off men like him won't do out here."

I was inclined to agree with Laramie.

"That bull-headed fool will roar and butt himself with all his gang right into our hands," Steele rejoined. "He's just the man I've needed to meet. Besides, shooting him would have been murder for me."

"Murder!" exclaimed Laramie.

"He was a fool, and slow at that. Under such circumstances could *I* kill him . . . when I didn't have to?"

"Sure, it'd been the trick," declared Jim positively. "I'm not allowin' for whether he's really a rustler or not. It just won't do, because these fellers out here ain't goin' to be afraid of you."

"See here, Laramie. If a man's going to be afraid of me at all, that trick will make him more afraid of me. I know it. It works out. When Lawson cools down, he'll remember, he'll begin to think, he'll realize that I could snap a shot at more than his arm. I'll bet you he goes pale to the gills next time he even sees me."

"That may be true, Steele. But, if Lawson's the man you think he is, he'll begin that secret underground bizness. It's been tolerable healthy these last six months. You can gamble on this. If thet secret work does commence, you'll have more reason to suspect Lawson. I won't feel very safe from now on. I heard you call him a rustler. He knows thet. Why, Lawson won't sleep o' nights now. He an' Longstreth have always been after me."

"Laramie, what are your eyes for?" demanded Steele. "Watch out. And now here, see your friend, Morton. Tell him this game grows hot. Together you approach four or five men you know well and can absolutely trust. Say, there's somebody coming. You meet Russ and me tonight out in the open, a quarter of a mile straight from the end of this street. You'll find a pile of stones. Meet us there tonight at ten o'clock."

The next few days, for the several hours each day that I was in town, I had Steele in sight all the time or knew that he was safe. Nothing happened. His presence in the saloons or any place where men congregated was marked by a certain uneasy watchfulness on the part of almost everybody, and some amusement on the part of a few.

It was natural to suppose that the lawless element would rise up in a mass and slay Steele on sight. But this sort of thing never happened. It was not so much that these enemies of the law awaited his next move, but just a slowness peculiar to the frontier. The ranger was in their midst. He was interesting, if formidable. He would have been welcomed at card tables, at the bars, to play and drink with the men who knew they were under suspicion. There was a rude kind of good humor even in their open hostility. Besides, one ranger or a company of rangers could not have held the undivided attention of these men from their games and drinks and quarrels, except by some decided move. Excitement, greed, appetite were rife in them.

I marked, however, a striking exception to the usual run of strangers I had been in the habit of seeing. The Sneckers had gone or were undercover. Again I caught a vague rumor of the coming of Jack Blome, yet he never seemed to arrive. Moreover, the goings-on among the habitués of the resorts and the cowboys who came in to drink and gamble were unusually mild in comparison with former conduct. This lull, however, did not deceive Steele and me. It could not last. The wonder was that it had lasted so long.

There was, of course, no post office in Fairdale. A stage arrived twice a week from Sanderson, if it did not get held up on the way, and the driver usually had letters, which he turned over to the keeper of a little store.

This man's name was Jones, and everybody liked him. On the evenings the stage arrived, there was always a crowd at his store, which fact was a source of no little revenue to him.

One night, so we ascertained, after the crowd had dispersed, two thugs entered his store, beat the old man, and robbed him. He made no complaint. However, when Steele called upon him, he rather reluctantly gave not only descriptions of his assailants, but their names. Steele straightway went in search of the men and came across them in Lerett's place. I was around when it happened. Steele strode up to a table which was surrounded by seven or eight men, and he tapped Sim Bass on the shoulder.

"Get up. I want you," he said.

Bass looked up lazily to see who had accosted him.

"The hell you say!" he replied impudently.

Steele's big hand shifted to the fellow's collar. One jerk, seemingly no effort at all, sent Bass sliding, chair and all, to crash into the bar and fall in a heap. He lay there, wondering what had struck him.

"Miller, I want you. Get up," said Steele.

Miller complied with alacrity. A sharp kick put more life and understanding into Bass.

Then Steele searched these men right before the eyes of their comrades, took what money and weapons they had, and marched them out, followed by a crowd that gathered more and more to it as they went down the street. Steele took his prisoners into Jones's store, had them identified, returned the money they had stolen, and then, pushing the two through the gaping crowd, he marched them down to his stone jail and locked them up.

Obviously the serious side of this incident was entirely lost upon the highly entertained audience. Many and loud were the coarse jokes cracked at the expense of Bass and Miller and, after the rude door had closed upon them, similar remarks were addressed to Steele's jailer and guard who, in truth, were just as disreputable-looking as their prisoners. Then the jocose crowd returned to their pastimes, leaving their erstwhile comrades to taste the sweetness of prison life.

When I got a chance, I asked Steele if he could rely on his hired help, and, with a twinkle in his eye that surprised me as much as his reply, he said Miller and Bass would have flown the coop before morning.

He was right. When I reached the lower end of town next morning, the same old crowd, enlarged by other curious men and youths, had come down to pay their respects to the new institution. Jailer and guard were on hand, loud in their proclamations and explanations. Naturally they had fallen asleep, as all other hard-working citizens had, and, while they slept, the prisoners made a hole somewhere and escaped.

Steele examined the hole, and then engaged a stripling of a youth to see if he could crawl through. The youngster essayed the job, stuck in the middle, and was with difficulty extricated. Whereupon the crowd evinced its delight. Steele, without more ado, shoved his jailer and guard inside the jail, deliberately closed, barred, and chained the iron-bolted door, and put the key in his pocket. Then he remained there all day without giving heed to his prisoners' derision and threats. Toward evening, having gone without drink infinitely longer than was customary, they made appeals to which Steele was deaf.

He left the jail, however, just before dark. When we met, he told me to be on hand to help him watch that night. We went around the outskirts of town, carrying two heavy double-barreled shotguns Steele had gotten somewhere. Taking up a position behind bushes in the lot adjoining the jail, we awaited developments. Steele was not above paying back these fellows in their own coin.

All the early part of the evening gangs of

half a dozen men or more came down the street and had their last treat at the expense of the jailed guard and jailer. These worthies yelled for drink — not water — but drink, and the more they yelled, the more merri ment was loosened upon the night air.

About ten o'clock the last gang left to the despair of the hungry and thirsty prisoners. Steele and I had hugely enjoyed the fun and thought the best part of the joke for us was yet to come. The moon had arisen and, though somewhat hazed by clouds, had lightened the night. We were hidden about sixty paces from the jail, a little above it, and we had a fine command of the door.

About eleven o'clock, when all was still, we heard soft steps back of the jail and soon two dark forms stole around in front. They laid down something that gave forth a metallic clink — likely a crowbar. We heard whisperings and then low, coarse laughs. Then the two rescuers, who undoubtedly were Miller and Bass, set to work to open the door. Softly they worked at first, but, as that door had been put there to stay, and they were not fond of hard work, they began to swear and make noises.

Steele whispered to me to wait until the door had been opened and then, when all four presented a good target, to fire both barrels. We could easily have slipped down and captured the rescuers, but that was not Steele's game. A trick met by trick, cunning matching craft, would be surest of all ways to command respect.

Four times the workers had to rest, and once they were so enraged at the insistence of the prisoners, who wanted to delay proceedings to send one of them after a bottle, that they swore they would go away and quit the job altogether. But they were prevailed upon to stay and attack the stout door once more. Finally it yielded, with enough noise to have awakened sleepers a block distant, and, forth into the moonlight, came rescuers and rescued with low, satisfied grunts of laughter.

Just then Steele and I each discharged both barrels, and the reports blended as one in a tremendous boom. That little compact bunch disintegrated like quicksilver. Two tumbled over. The others leaped out, and all yelled in pain and terror. Then the fallen ones scrambled up and began to hobble and limp and jerk along after their comrades.

Before the four of them got out of sight they had ceased their yells but were moving slowly, hanging on to one another in a way that satisfied us they would be lame for many a day.

The next morning at breakfast Dick re-galed me with an elaborate story about how the ranger had turned the tables on the jok-ers. Evidently in a night the whole town knew it. Probably a desperate stand of Steele's, even to the extreme of killing men, could not have educated these crude natives so quickly into the realization that the ranger was not to be fooled with.

That morning I went for a ride with the girls, and both had heard something and wanted to know everything. I had become a news carrier, and Miss Longstreth never thought of questioning me in regard to my fund of information. She showed more than curiosity. The account I gave of the jail affair amused her and made Ruth laugh heartily.

Ray questioned me also about a rumor that had come to her, concerning Floyd Lawson. He had wounded himself with a gun, it seemed, and though not seriously injured was not able to go about. He had not been up to the ranch for days.

"I asked Papa about him," said Ray, "and Papa laughed like . . . well, like a regular hyena. I was dumbfounded. Papa's so queer. He looked thunderclouds at me. When I insisted, for I wanted to know, he ripped out . . . 'Yes, the damn' fool got himself shot, and I'm sorry it's not worse.' Now, Russ, what do you make of my dad? Cheerful and kind, isn't he?"

I laughed with Ruth, but I disclaimed any knowledge of Floyd's accident. I hated the thought of Lawson, let alone anything concerning the fatal certainty that sooner or later these cousins of his were to suffer through him.

Ruth did not make these rides easy for me, for she was sweeter than anything that has a name. Since the evening of the dance I had tried to avoid her. Either she was sincerely sorry for her tantrum or she was bent upon utterly destroying my peace. I took good care we were never alone, for in that case, if she ever got into my arms again, I would find the ground slipping from under me. Despite, however, the wear and constant strain of resisting Ruth, I enjoyed the ride. There was a charm about being with these girls.

Then perhaps Miss Longstreth's growing curiosity in regard to Steele was no little satisfaction to me. I pretended a reluctance to speak of the ranger, but, when I did, it was to drop a subtle word or briefly tell of an action that suggested much. I never again hinted the thing that had been such a shock to her. What was in her mind, I could not guess. Nevertheless, I divined that some of her curiosity, perhaps the greater part, was due to a generous nature not entirely satisfied with itself. She probably had not abandoned her father's estimate of the ranger, but absolute assurance that this was truly just did not abide with her. For the rest she was like any other girl, a worshiper of the lion in a man, a weaver of romance, ignorant of her own heart.

Not the least talked about and speculated upon of all the details of the jail incident was the part played by the storekeeper, Jones, who had informed upon his assailants. Steele and I both awaited results of this significant fact. When would the town wake up — not only to a little nerve, but to the usefulness of a ranger?

Three days afterward Steele told me a woman accosted him in the street. She seemed a poor, hard-working person, plain-spoken and honest. Her husband did not drink enough to complain of, but he liked to gamble, and he had been fleeced by a crooked game in Jack Martin's saloon. Other wives could make the same complaints. It was a God's blessing for such women that Ranger Steele had come to Fairdale. Of course, he could not get back the lost money, but would it be possible to close Martin's place, or at least break up the crooked game?

Steele had asked this woman, whose name was Price, how much her husband had lost, and, being told, he assured her that, if he found evidence of cheating, not only would he get back the money, but also he would shut up Martin's place. Steele instructed me to go that night to the saloon in question and get in the game. I complied, and, in order not to be too carefully sized up by the dealer, I pretended to be well under the influence of liquor. By nine o'clock, when Steele strolled in, I had the game well studied, and a more flagrantly crooked one I had never sat in. It was barefaced robbery.

Steele and I had agreed upon a sign from me, because he was not so adept in the intricacies of gambling as I was. I was not in a hurry, however, for there was a little freckle-faced cattleman in the game, and he had been losing, too. He had sold a bunch of stock that day and had considerable money, which evidently he was to be deprived of before he got started for Del Rio. Steele stood at our backs, and I could feel his presence. He thrilled me. He had some kind of effect on the others, especially the dealer, who was honest enough while the stranger looked on.

When, however, Steele shifted his attention to other tables and players, our dealer reverted to his crooked work. I was about to make a disturbance, when the little cattleman, leaning over, fire in his eye and gun in hand, made it for me. Evidently he was a keener and nervier gambler than he had been taken for. There might have been gun play right then if Steele had not interfered.

"Hold on!" he yelled, leaping for our table. "Put up your gun!"

"Who're you?" demanded the cattleman, never moving. "Better keep out of this."

"I'm Steele. Put up your gun."

"You're thet ranger, hey?" replied the other. "All right! But just a minute. I want this dealer to sit quiet. I've been robbed. And I want my money back."

Certainly the dealer and everyone else around the table sat quietly while the cattleman coolly held his gun leveled.

"Crooked game?" asked Steele, bending over the table. "Show me."

It did not take the aggrieved gambler more than a moment to prove his assertion. Steele, however, desired corroboration from others beside the cattleman, and one by one he questioned them. To my surprise, one of the players admitted his conviction that the game was not straight.

"What do you say?" demanded Steele of me.

"Worse'n a hold-up, Mister Ranger," I burst out. "Let me show you."

Deftly I made the dealer's guilt plain to all, and then I seconded the cattleman's angry claim for lost money. The players from other tables gathered around, curious, muttering. And just then Martin strolled in. His appearance was not prepossessing.

"What's this holler?" he asked, and halted as he saw the cattleman's gun still in line with the dealer.

"Martin, you know what it's for," replied Steele. "Take your dealer and dig . . . unless you want to see me clean out your place."

Sullen and fierce, Martin stood, looking from Steele to the cattleman and then the dealer. Some men in the crowd muttered, and that was a signal for Steele to shove the circle apart and get out, back to the wall.

The cattleman rose slowly in the center, pulling another gun, and he certainly looked all business to me.

"Wal, ranger, I reckon I'll hang 'round an' see you ain't bothered none," he said. "Friend," he went on, indicating me with a slight wave of one extended gun, "jest rustle the money in sight. We'll square up . . . after the show."

I reached out and swept the considerable sum toward me, and, pocketing it, I, too, rose, ready for what might come.

"You-all give me elbow room!" yelled Steele at Martin and his cowed contingent.

Steele looked around, evidently for some kind of implement, and, espying a heavy axe in a corner, he grasped it, and, sweeping it to and fro as if it had been a buggy whip, he advanced on the faro layout. The crowd fell back, edging toward the door. One crashing blow wrecked the dealer's box and table, sending them splintering among the tumbled chairs. Then the giant ranger began to spread further ruin about him.

Martin's place was rough and bare, of the most primitive order, and, like a thousand other dens of its kind, consisted of a large room with adobe walls, a rude bar of boards, piles of kegs in a corner, a stove, and a few tables with chairs. Steele required only one blow for each article he struck, and he demolished it. He stove in the head of each keg. When the dark liquor gurgled out, Martin cursed, and the crowd followed suit. That was a loss!

The little cattleman, holding the men covered, backed them out of the room, Martin needing a plain, stern word to put him out entirely. I went out, too, for I did not want to miss any moves on the part of that gang. Close behind me came the cattleman — the kind of cool, nervy Texan I liked. He had Martin well judged, too, for there was no evidence of any bold resistance. But there were shouts and loud acclamation, and these, with the crushing blows of Steele's axe, brought a curious and growing addition to the crowd.

Soon sodden thuds from inside the saloon and red dust pouring out the door told that Steele was attacking the walls of Martin's place. These adobe bricks, old and crumbly, were easily demolished. Steele made short work of the back wall, and then he smashed out half the front of the building. That seemed to satisfy him.

When he stepped out of the dust, he was wet with sweat, dirty, and disheveled, hot with his exertion — a man whose great stature and muscular development expressed a wonderful physical strength and energy. And his somber face, with the big gray eyes like open furnaces, expressed a passion equal to his strength.

Perhaps only then did wild and lawless Fairdale grasp the real significance of this ranger. Steele threw the axe at Martin's feet.

"Martin, don't re-open here," he said curtly. "Don't start another place in Fairdale. If you do . . . jail at Austin for you."

Martin, livid and scowling, yet seemingly

dazed with what had occurred, slunk away, accompanied by his cronies. Steele took the money I had appropriated, returned to me what I had lost, did likewise with the cattleman, and then, taking out the sum named by Mrs. Price, he divided the balance with the other players who had been in the game. Then he stalked off through the crowd, as if he knew that men who slunk from facing him would not have nerve enough to attack him even from behind.

"Wal, damn me!" ejaculated the little cattleman in mingled admiration and satisfaction. "So thet's Lone Star Steele, hey? Never seen him before. All Texas, thet ranger!"

I lingered downtown as much to enjoy the sensation as to gain the different points of view. No doubt about the sensation. In one hour every male resident of Fairdale and almost every female had viewed the wreck of Martin's place. A fire could not have created half the excitement. And in that excitement both men and women gave vent to speech they might not have voiced at a calmer moment. The women, at least, were not afraid to talk, and I made mental note of the things they said.

"Did he do it all alone?"

"Thank God a man's come to Fairdale."

It almost seemed that all the women were

glad, and this was in itself a vindication of the ranger's idea of law. The men, however — Blandy, proprietor of the Hope So, and others of his ilk, together with the whole brood of idle gaming loungers, and in fact even storekeepers, ranchers, cowboys — all shook their heads sullenly or doubtfully. Striking, indeed, was the absence of any joking. Steele had showed his hand, and as one gambler said: "It's a hard hand to call."

The truth was this ranger service was hateful to the free and easy Texan who lived by anything except hard and honest work, and it was damnably hateful to the lawless class. Steele's authority, now obvious to all, was unlimited. It could go as far as he had power to carry it.

From present indications that power might be considerable. The work of native sheriffs and constables in western Texas had been an honest farce, an utter failure. If an honest native of a community undertook to be a sheriff, he became immediately a target for the rowdy cowboys and other vicious element. Many a town south and west of San Antonio owed its peace and prosperity to rangers, and only to them. They had killed or driven out the criminals. They interpreted the law for themselves, and it was only such an attitude toward law — the stern, uncompromising, implacable extermination of the lawless — that was going to do for all Texas what it had done for part.

Steele was the driving wedge that had begun to split Fairdale — split the honest from dominance by the dishonest. To be sure, Steele might be killed at any moment, and that contingency was voiced in the growl of one sullen man who said: "Wot the hell are we up against? Ain't somebody goin' to plug this ranger?"

It was then that the thing for which Steele stood — the ranger service, to help, to save, to defend, to punish with such somber menace of death as seemed embodied in his cold attitude toward resistance — took hold of Fairdale and sank deeply into both black and honest hearts. It was what was behind Steele that seemed to make him more than an officer — a man.

I could feel how he began to loom up, the embodiment of a powerful force — the ranger service — the fame of which, long known to this lawless Pecos gang, but scouted as a vague and distant thing, now became invested in a clearer light, that of a ranger in the flesh whose surprising attributes included both the law and the enforcement of it.

When I reached the ranch, the excitement

had preceded me. Miss Longstreth and Ruth, both talking at once, acquainted me with the fact that they had been in a store on the main street a block or more from Martin's place. They had seen the crowd, heard the uproar, and, as they had been hurriedly started home by the attendant Dick, they had encountered Steele, stalking past.

"He looked grand!" exclaimed Ruth.

Then I told the girls the whole story in detail.

"Russ, is it true just as you tell it?" inquired Ray earnestly.

"Absolutely. I know Missus Price went to Steele with her trouble. I was in Martin's place when he entered. Also I was playing in the crooked game. And I saw him wreck Martin's place. Also, I heard him forbid Martin to start another place in Fairdale."

"Then he does do splendid things," she said softly, as if affirming it to herself.

I walked on, having gotten a glimpse of Colonel Longstreth in the background. Before I reached the corrals, Ruth came running after me, quite flushed and excited.

"Russ, Uncle wants to see you," she said. "He's in a bad temper. Don't . . . don't lose yours, please."

She actually shook my hand. What a child

she was — in all ways except that fatal propensity to flirt. Her statement startled me out of any further thought of her. Why did Longstreth want to see me? He never noticed me. I dreaded facing him — not from fear, but because I must see more and more the signs of the guilt of Ray Longstreth's father.

He awaited me on the porch. As usual, he wore riding garb, but evidently he had not been out so far this day. He looked worn. There was a hinted, furtive shadow in his eyes. The haughty, imperious temper, despite Ruth's conviction, seemed to be in abeyance.

"Russ, what's this I hear about Martin's saloon being cleaned out?" he asked. "Dick can't give particulars."

Briefly and concisely I told the colonel exactly what had happened. He chewed his cigar, then spat it out with an unintelligible exclamation.

"Martin's no worse than the others," he said. "Blandy leans to crooked faro. I can't stop it. I've tried to stop that, anyway. If Steele can . . . more power to him!"

Longstreth turned on his heel then and left me with a queer feeling of surprise and pity. He had surprised me before, but he had never roused the least sympathy. How probable was it that Longstreth was, indeed, powerless, no matter what his position? I had known men before then who had become involved in crime, yet were too manly to sanction a crookedness they could not help.

Miss Longstreth had been standing in the door. I could tell that she had heard. She looked agitated. I knew she had been talking to her father.

"Russ, he hates the ranger," she said. "That's what I fear. It'll bring trouble on us. Besides, like everybody here, he's biased. He can't see anything good in Steele. Yet he says . . . 'More power to him!' I'm mystified, and, oh, I'm between two fires."

Steele's next noteworthy achievement was as new to me as it was strange to Fairdale. I heard a good deal about it from my acquaintances, some little from Steele, and the concluding incident I saw and heard myself. Andy McVey was a broken-down rustler whose activity had ceased and who spent his time hanging on at the places frequented by younger and better men of his kind. As he was a parasite, he was often thrown out of the dens. Moreover, it was an open secret that he had been a rustler, and the men with whom he associated had not yet, to most of

Fairdale, become known as such.

One night McVey had been badly beaten in some back room of a saloon and carried out into a vacant lot and left there. He lay there all that night and all the next day. Probably he would have died there had not Steele happened along.

The ranger gathered up the crippled rustler, took him home, attended to his wounds, nursed him, and in fact spent days in the little adobe house with him. During this time I saw Steele twice at night, out at our rendezvous. He had little to communicate but was eager to hear when I had seen Laramie, Morton, Lawson, Longstreth, and all I could tell him about them, and the significance of things in town.

Andy McVey recovered, and it was my good fortune to be in the Hope So when he came in and addressed a crowd of gamesters there.

"Fellers," he said, "I'm biddin' good bye to them as was once my friends. I'm leavin' Fairdale. An' I'm askin' some of you to take thet good bye an' a partin' word to them as did me dirt.

"I ain't a-goin' to say if I'd crossed the trail of this ranger years ago thet I'd turned 'round an' gone straight. But mebbe I would . . . mebbe. There's a hell of a lot a man doesn't know till too late. I'm old now, ready fer the bone pile, an' it doesn't matter. But I've got a head on me yet, an' I want to give a hunch to thet gang who done me. An' that hunch wants to go around an' up to the big guns of Pecos.

"This Lone Star ranger was the feller who took me in. I'd died like a poisoned coyote but fer him. An' he talked to me. He gave me money to git out of Pecos. Mebbe everybody'll think he helped me because he wanted me to squeal. To squeal who's who 'round these rustler diggin's! Wal, he *never* asked me. Mebbe he seen I wasn't a squealer. But I'm thinkin' he wouldn't ask a feller thet, nohow.

"An' here's my hunch. Steele has spotted the outfit. Thet ain't so much, mebbe. But I've been with him, an' I'm old, figgerin' men. Jest as sure as God made little apples, he's a-goin' to stop thet outfit . . . or he's a-goin' to kill 'em."

Chapter Ten

ENTER JACK BLOME

Strange that the narrating of this incident made Ray Longstreth unhappy. When I told her, she exhibited one flash of gladness, such as any woman might have shown for a noble deed, and then she became thoughtful, almost gloomy, sad. I could not understand her complex emotions. Perhaps she contrasted Steele with her father; perhaps she wanted to believe in Steele and dared not; perhaps she had, all at once, seen the ranger in his true light and to her undoing. She bade me take Ruth for a ride and sought her room. I had my misgivings when I saw Ruth come out in that trim cowgirl suit and look at me as if to say, this day would be my Waterloo.

She rode hard and long ahead of me before she put any machinations into effect. The first one found me with a respectful demeanor but an internal conflict.

"Russ, tighten my cinch," she said when I caught up with her.

Dismounting, I drew the cinch up another hole and fastened it.

"My boot's unlaced, too," she added, slipping a shapely foot out of the stirrup.

To be sure, it was very much unlaced. I had to take off my gloves to lace it up, and I did it heroically, with bent head and outward calm, when all the time I was mad to snatch the girl out of the saddle and hold her tight or run off with her or do some like fool thing.

"Russ, I believe Ray's in love with Steele," she said soberly, with the sweet confidence she sometimes manifested in me.

"Small wonder! It's in the air," I replied.

She regarded me doubtfully. "It *was*," she retorted demurely.

"The fickleness of women is no new thing to me. I didn't expect Waters to last long."

"Certainly not when there are nicer fellows around. *One*, anyway, when he cares." A little brown hand slid out of its glove and dropped to my shoulder. "Make up. You've been hateful to me lately. Make up with me."

It was not so much what she said as the sweet tone of her voice and the nearness of her that made a tumult within me. I felt the blood tingle to my face.

"Why should I make up with you?" I queried in self-defense. "You're only flirting. You won't . . . you can't ever be anything to me . . . really."

Ruth bent over me, and I had not the nerve to look up.

"Never mind things . . . really," she replied. "The future's far off. Let it alone. We're together. I . . . I like you, Russ. And I've got to be . . . to be loved. There! I never confessed that to any other man. You've been hateful when we might have had such fun. The rides in the sun . . . in the open with the wind in our faces. The walks at night in the moonlight. Russ, haven't you missed something?"

The sweetness and seductiveness of her, the little luring devil of her, were no more irresistible than were her naturalness, the truth of her. I trembled even before I looked up into her flushed face and arch eyes. After that I knew, if I could not frighten her out of this daring mood, I would have to yield despite my conviction that she only trifled. As my manhood, as well as duty to Steele, forced me to be unyielding, all that was left to me seemed to be to frighten her.

The instant this was decided, a wave of emotion — love, regret, bitterness, anger — surged over me, making me shake. I felt the skin on my face tighten and chill. I grasped her with strength that might have been needed to hold a plunging, unruly horse. I hurt her. I held her as in a vise. The action, the feel of her, her suddenly uttered cry wrought against all pretense, hurt me as my brutality hurt her, and then I spoke what was hard, passionate truth.

"Girl, you're playing with fire!" I cried out hoarsely. "I love you . . . love you as I'd want my sister loved. I asked you to marry me. That was proof, if it was foolish. Even if you were on the square, which you're not, we couldn't ever be anything to each other. Understand. There's a reason, besides your being above me. Now listen. Stop playing with me. I can't stand it. If you don't, I'll . . . I'll . . ."

Whatever I meant to say was not spoken, for Ruth turned deathly white, probably from my grasp and my looks as well as my threat. I let go of her and, stepping back to my horse, choked down my emotion.

"Russ!" she faltered, and there was womanliness and regret trembling with the fear in her voice. "I . . . I am on the square."

That had touched the real heart of the girl.

"If you are, then play the game square," I replied darkly.

"I will, Russ . . . I promise. I'll never tease or coax you again. If I do, then I'll deserve what you . . . what I get. But, Russ, don't think me a . . . a four-flush."

All the long ride home we did not exchange another word. The traveling gait of Ruth's horse was a lope, that of mine a trot, and, therefore, to my relief she was always out in front.

As we neared the ranch, however, Ruth slowed down until I caught up with her. Side by side we rode the remainder of the way. At the corrals, while I unsaddled, she lingered.

"Russ, you didn't tell me if you agreed with me about Ray," she said finally.

"Maybe you're right. I hope she's fallen in love with Steele. Lord knows, I hope so," I blurted out.

"Why?" she asked curiously.

I bit my tongue. There was no use in my trying to be as shrewd with women as I was with men. I made no reply.

"Misery loves company. Maybe that's why," she added. "You told me Steele lost his head over Ray at first sight. Well, we . . . all have company. Good night, Russ."

That night I told Steele about the singular effect the story of his treatment of McVey had had upon Miss Longstreth. He could not conceal his feelings. I read him like an open book. If she was unhappy because he did something really good, then she was unhappy because she was realizing she had wronged him. Steele never asked questions, but the hungry look in his big eyes was enough to make even a truthful fellow exaggerate things.

I told him how Ray was dressed, how her face had changed with each emotion, how her eyes had burned and softened and shadowed, how her voice had been deep and full when she admitted her father hated him, how much she must have meant when she said she was between two fires. I divined how he felt, and I tried to satisfy in some little measure his craving for news of her. When I had exhausted my fund and stretched my imagination, I was rewarded by being told that I was a regular old woman for gossip.

Much taken back by this remarkable statement, I could but gape at my comrade. Irritation had followed shortly upon his curiosity and pleasure, and then the old sane mind reasserted itself, the old stern look, a little sad now, replaced the glow, the strange eagerness of youth on his face.

"Son, I beg your pardon," he said, with his hand on my shoulder. "We're rangers, but we can't help being human. To speak right out, it seems two sweet and lovable girls have come, unfortunately for us all, across the dark trail we're on. Let us find what solace we can in the hope that some-how . . . God only knows how . . . in doing our duty as rangers we may yet be doing right by these two innocent girls. I ask you, as my friend, please do not speak again to me of . . . of Miss Longstreth."

I left him and went up the quiet trail with the thick shadows all around me and the cold stars overhead. I was sober in thought, sick at heart for him as much as for myself, and I tortured my mind in fruitless conjecture as to what the end of this strange and fateful adventure would be. I discovered that less and less the old wild spirit abided with me, and I became conscious of a dull, deep-seated ache in my breast, a pang in the bone.

From that day there was a change in Ray Longstreth. She became feverishly active. She wanted to ride, to see for herself what was going on in Fairdale, to learn of that wild Pecos country life at first hand. She made such demands on my time now that I scarcely ever found an hour to be with or near Steele until after dark. However, as he was playing a waiting game with the rustlers, keeping out of the resorts for the present, I had no great cause to worry. Laramie was slowly gathering together a band of trustworthy men, and, until this organization was complete and ready, Steele thought it better to go slow.

It was of little use for me to remonstrate with Miss Longstreth when she refused to obey a distracted and angry father. I began to feel sorry for the colonel. He was an unscrupulous man, but he loved this daughter who belonged to another and better past side of his life. I heard him appeal to her to go back to Louisiana, to let him take her home, giving as urgent reason the probability of trouble for him. She could not help, would only handicap him. She agreed to go, provided he sold his property, took the best of his horses, and went with her back to the old home to live there the rest of their lives. He replied with considerable feeling that he wished he could go, but it was impossible. Then that settled the matter for her, she averred.

Failing to persuade her to leave Fairdale, he told her to keep to the ranch. Naturally, in spite of his anger, Miss Longstreth refused to obey. She frankly told him that it was the free, unfettered life of the country, the riding here and there, that appealed so much to her.

Longstreth came to me a little later, and his worn face showed traces of internal storm. "Russ, for a while there I wanted to get rid of you," he said. "I've changed. Ray always was a spoiled kid. Now she's a woman. Something's fired her blood. Maybe it's this damned wild country. Anyway, she's got the bit between her teeth. She'll run till she's run herself out.

"Now, it seems the safety of Ray, and Ruth, too, has fallen into your hands. The girls won't have one of my cowboys near them. Lately they've gotten shy of Floyd, too. Between you and me I want to tell you that conditions here in Pecos are worse than they've seemed since you-all reached the ranch. And bad work will break out again . . . it's coming soon. I can't stop it. The town will be full of the hardest gang in western Texas. My daughter and Ruth would not be safe if left alone to go anywhere. With you, perhaps, they'll be safe. Can I rely on you?"

"Yes, Colonel Longstreth, you sure can," I replied. "I'm on pretty good terms with 'most everybody in town. I think I can say none of the tough set who hang out down there would ever make any move while I'm with the girls. But I'll be pretty careful to avoid that bunch and particularly strange fellows who may come riding in. And if any of them do meet us and get gay, I'm going for my gun, that's all. There won't be any talk."

"Good! I'll back you," Longstreth replied. "Understand, Russ, I didn't want you here, but I always had you sized up as a pretty hard nut . . . a man not to be trifled with. You've got a bad name. Ray insists the name's not deserved. She'd trust you with herself under any circumstances. And the kid, Ruth, she'd be fond of you if it wasn't for the drink. Have you been drunk a good deal? Straight, now, between you and me."

"Not once," I replied.

"Floyd's a liar then. He's had it in for you since that day at Sanderson. Look out you two don't clash. He's got a temper, and, when he's drinking, he's a devil. Keep out of his way."

"I've stood a great deal from Lawson, and guess I can stand more."

"All right, Russ," he continued, as if relieved. "Chuck the drink and cards for a while and keep an eye on these girls. When my affairs straighten out, maybe I'll make you a proposition."

Longstreth left me material for thought. It must have been more than the presence of a ranger in town that gave him concern, or the willfulness of his daughter. There must be internal strife in the rustler gang

267

with which we had associated him. Perhaps a menace of publicity, rather than risk, was the cause of the wearing strain on him. I began to get a closer insight into Longstreth, and in the absence of any conclusive evidence of his personal baseness I felt pity for him.

In the beginning he had opposed me just because I did not happen to be a cowboy he had selected. This latest interview with me, amounting in some instances to confidence, proved absolutely that he had not the slightest suspicion that I was otherwise than the cowboy I pretended to be. Another interesting deduction was that he appeared to be out of patience with Lawson. In fact, I imagined I sensed something of fear and distrust in this spoken attitude toward his relative. Not improbably here was the internal strife — between Longstreth and Lawson — and there flashed into my mind, absolutely with good reason, the idea that the clash was over Ray Longstreth.

I scouted this intuitive idea as absurd, but, just the same, it refused to be dismissed. As I turned my back on the coarse and exciting life in the saloons and gambling hells, and spent all my time, except when sleeping, out in the windy open, under blue sky and starry heaven, my spirit had an uplift. I was glad to be free of that job. It was bad enough to have to go into those dens to arrest men, let alone living with them, almost being one.

Ray Longstreth noted a change in me, attributed it to the absence of the influence of drink, and was glad. Ruth made no attempt to conceal her happiness, and, to my dismay, she utterly failed to keep her promise not to tease or tempt me further. She was adorable, distracting. We rode every day and almost all day. We took our dinner and went clear to the foothills, to return as the sun set. We visited outlying ranches, water holes, old adobe houses famous in one way or another as scenes of past fights between rustlers and ranchers.

We rode to the little village, Longstreth, and half way to Sanderson, and all over the country. There was no satisfying Miss Longstreth with rides, new places, new faces, new adventures. And every time we rode out, she insisted on first riding through Fairdale. And every time we rode home, she insisted on going back that way. We visited all the stores, the blacksmith, the wagon shop, the feed and grain houses — everywhere that she could find excuse for visiting. I had to point out to her all the infamous dens in town and all the lawless and lounging men we met.

She insisted upon being shown the inside of the Hope So, to the extreme confusion of that bewildered resort. I pretended to be blind to this restless curiosity. Ruth understood the cause, too, and it divided her between a sweet gravity and a naughty humor. The last, however, she never evinced in sight or hearing of Ray.

It seemed that we were indeed fated to cross the path of Vaughn Steele. We saw him, working around his adobe house. Then we saw him on horseback. Once we met him face to face in a store. He gazed steadily into Ray Longstreth's eyes and went his way without any sign of recognition. There was red in her face when he passed and white when he had gone. That day she rode as I had never seen her, risking her life, unmindful of her horse. Another day we met Steele down in the valley, where, inquiry discovered to us, he had gone to the home of an old cattleman who lived alone and was ill. Last, and perhaps most significant of all these meetings, was the one when we were walking tired horses home through the main street of Fairdale, and we came upon Steele just in time to see him in action.

It happened at a corner where the usual slouchy, shirt-sleeved loungers were congregated. They were in high glee over the predicament of one ruffian who had purchased or been given a poor, emaciated little burro that was on his last legs. The burro evidently did not want to go with its new owner who pulled on a halter and then viciously swung the end of the rope to make welts on the worn and scarred back. If there was one thing that Ray Longstreth could not bear, it was to see an animal in pain. She passionately loved horses and hated the sight of a spur or whip.

When we saw the man beating the little burro, she cried out to me: "Make the brute stop!"

I might have made a move had I not on the instant seen Steele heaving into sight around the corner. Just then the fellow, whom I now recognized to be a despicable character named Andrews, began to bestow heavy and brutal kicks upon the body of the little burro. These kicks sounded deep, hollow, almost like the boom of a drum. The burro uttered the strangest sound I ever heard issue from any beast, and it dropped in its tracks with jerking legs that told any horseman what had happened.

Steele saw the last swings of Andrews's heavy foot. He yelled. It was a sharp yell that would have made anyone start. But it came too late, for the burro had dropped.

Steele knocked over several of the jeering men to get to Andrews. He kicked the fellow's feet from under him, sending him hard to the ground. Then Steele picked up the end of the halter and began to swing it powerfully. Resounding smacks mingled with hoarse bellows of fury and pain. Andrews flopped here and there, trying to rise, but every time the heavy knotted halter beat him down.

Presently Steele stopped. Andrews rose right in front of the ranger, and there, like the madman he was, he went for his gun. But it scarcely leaped from its holster when Steele's swift hand intercepted it. Steele clutched Andrews's arm. Then came a wrench, a cracking of bones, a scream of agony. The gun dropped into the dust, and in a moment of wrestling fury Andrews, broken, beaten down, just able to moan, lay beside it. Steele — so cool and dark for a man who had acted with such passionate swiftness — faced the others as if to dare them to move. They neither moved nor spoke, and then he strode away.

Miss Longstreth did not speak a word while we were riding the rest of the way home, but she was strangely white of face and dark of eye. Ruth could not speak fast enough to say all she felt. I, of course, had my measure of feelings. One of them was that, as sure as the sun rose and set, it was written that Ray Longstreth was to love Vaughn Steele.

I could not read her mind, but I had a mind of my own. How could any woman, seeing this maligned and menaced ranger, whose life was in danger every moment he spent on the streets, in the light of his action on behalf of a poor little beast help but wonder and brood over the magnificent height he might reach if he had love — passion — a woman for his inspiration?

It was the day after this incident that, as Ray, Ruth, and I were riding homeward on the road from Longstreth, I caught sight of a group of dark horses and riders swiftly catching up with us. We were on the main road in plain sight of town and passing by ranches. Nevertheless, I did not like the looks of the horsemen and grew uneasy. Still, I scarcely thought it needful to race our horses just to reach town a little ahead of these strangers. Accordingly, they soon caught up with us.

They were five in number, all dark-faced except one, dark-clad, and superbly mounted on dark bays and blacks. They had no pack animals, and, for that matter, carried no packs at all. Four of them at a swinging canter passed us, and the fifth pulled his horse to suit our pace and fell in behind Ruth and me.

"Good day," he said pleasantly to me. "Don't mind my ridin' in with you-all, I hope?"

Considering his pleasant approach, I could not but be civil. He was a singularly handsome fellow, at a quick glance under forty years, with curly, blond hair, almost gold, a skin very fair for that country, and the keenest, clearest, boldest blue eyes I had ever seen in a man.

"You're Russ, I reckon," he said. "Some of my men have seen you ridin' 'round with Longstreth's girls. I'm Jack Blome."

He did not speak that name with any flaunt or flourish. He merely stated it. Blome, the rustler! I grew tight all over.

Still, manifestly there was nothing for me to do but return his pleasantry. I really felt less uneasiness after he had made himself known to me. And without any awkwardness I introduced him to the girls. He took off his sombrero and made gallant bows to both.

Miss Longstreth had heard of him and his record, and she could not help a paleness, a shrinking, which, however, he did not appear to notice. Ruth had been dying to meet a real rustler, and here he was, a very prince of rascals. But I gathered that she would require a little time before she could be natural. Blome seemed to have more of an eye for Ruth than for Ray.

"Do you like Pecos?" he asked Ruth.

"Out here? Oh, yes, indeed!" she replied.

"Like ridin'?"

"I love horses."

Like almost every man who made Ruth's acquaintance, he hit upon the subject best calculated to make her interesting to free-riding, outdoor Western men. That he loved a Thoroughbred horse himself was plain. He spoke naturally to Ruth with interest, just as I had upon first meeting her, and he might not have been Jack Blome for all the indication he gave of the fact in his talk. But the look of the man was different. He was a desperado — one of the dashing, reckless kind — more famous along the Pecos and Rio Grande than really more desperate men. His attire proclaimed a vanity seldom seen in any Westerner except of that unusual brand, yet it was neither gaudy or showy.

One had to be close to Blome to see the silk, the velvet, the gold, the fine leather. When I envied a man's spurs, then they were indeed worth coveting. Blome had a short rifle and a gun in saddle sheaths. My sharp eye, running over him, caught a row of notches on the bone handle of the big Colt he packed. It was then that the marshal, the ranger in me, went hot under the collar. The custom that desperadoes and gunfighters had of cutting a notch on their guns for every man killed was one of which the mere mention made my gorge rise.

At the edge of town Blome doffed his sombrero again, said *"Adios,"* and rode on ahead of us. It was then I was hard put to keep track of the queries, exclamations, and other wild talk of two very much excited young ladies. I wanted to think. I needed to think.

"Wasn't he lovely? Oh, I could adore him!" rapturously uttered Miss Ruth Herbert several times, to my ultimate disgust.

Also, after Blome had ridden out of sight, Miss Longstreth lost the evident effect of his sinister presence, and she joined Miss Herbert in paying the rustler compliments, too. Perhaps my irritation was an indication of the quick and subtle shifting of my mind to harsher thoughts.

"Jack Blome!" I broke in upon their adulations. "Rustler and gunman. Did you see the notches on his gun? Every notch for a man he killed! For weeks reports have come to Fairdale that soon as he could get around to it he'd ride down and rid the community of that bothersome fellow . . . that Lone Star ranger. He's come to kill Vaughn Steele."

Chapter Eleven

RAY AND VAUGHN

Then, as gloom descended on me with my uttered thought, my heart smote me at Ruth's broken: "Oh, Russ. No. No!"

Ray Longstreth bent dark, shocked eyes upon the hill and ranch in front of her, but they were sightless. They looked into space and eternity, and in them I read a truth suddenly and cruelly revealed to her — she loved Steele.

I found it impossible to leave Miss Longstreth with the impression I had given. My own mood fitted a kind of ruthless pleasure in seeing her suffer through love as I had intimation I was to suffer. But now, when my strange desire that she should love Steele had its fulfillment, and my fiendish subtleties to that end had been crowned with success, I was confounded in pity and the enormity of my crime. For it had been a crime to make, or help to make, this noble and beautiful woman love a ranger, the enemy of her father, and surely the author of her coming misery. I felt shocked at my work. I tried to hang excuse on my old motive that through her love we might all be saved. When it was too late, however, I found that this motive was wrong and perhaps without warrant.

We rode home in silence. Miss Long-streth, contrary to her usual custom of riding to the corrals or the porch, dismounted at a path leading in among the trees and flowers.

"I want to rest . . . to think before I go in," she said.

Ruth accompanied me to the corrals. As our horses stopped at the gate, I turned to find confirmation of my fears in Ruth's wet eyes.

"Archie," she said — I had told her my middle name which she had since abbreviated to her taste and now tended to use it all the time — "it's worse than we thought."

"Worse? I should say so," I replied.

"It'll about kill her. She never cared that way for any man. When the Longstreth women love, they love."

"Well, you're lucky to be a Herbert," I retorted bitterly.

"I'm Longstreth enough to be unhappy," she flashed back at me, "and I'm Herbert enough to have some sense. You haven't any sense or kindness, either. Why'd you want to blurt out that Jack Blome was here to kill Steele?"

"I'm ashamed, Ruth," I returned with

279

hanging head. "I've been a brute. I've wanted her to love Steele. I thought I had a reason, but now it seems silly. Just now I wanted to see how much she did care. Ruth, the other day you said misery loved company. That's my trouble. I'm sore . . . bitter. I'm like a sick coyote that snaps at everything. I've wanted you to go into the very depths of despair. But I couldn't send *you*. So I took out my spite on poor Miss Longstreth. It was a damn' unmanly thing for me to have done."

"Oh, it's not so bad as all that. But you might have been less abrupt. Archie, you seem to take an . . . an awful tragic view of your . . . your own case."

"Tragic? Hah!" I cried like the villain in a play. "What other way could I look at it? I tell you I love you so I can't sleep . . . or do anything."

"*That's* not tragic. When you've no chance . . . then . . . that's tragic."

Ruth, as swiftly as she had blushed, could change into that deadly sweet mood. She did both now. She seemed warm, softened, agitated. How could this be anything but sincere? I felt myself slipping, so I laughed harshly.

"Chance! I've no chance on earth."

"Try!" she whispered.

But I caught myself in time. Then the shock of bitter renunciation made it easy for me to simulate anger.

"You promised not to . . . not to . . . ," I choked. My voice was hoarse, and it broke — a state surely far removed from pretense.

I had seen Ruth Herbert in varying degrees of emotion, but never as she appeared now. She was pale, and she trembled a little. If it was not fright, then I could not tell what it was. But there were contrition and earnestness about her, too.

"Archie, I know. I promised not to . . . to tease . . . to tempt you any more," she faltered. "I've broken it. I'm ashamed. I haven't played the game squarely. But I couldn't . . . I can't help myself . . . I've got sense enough not to engage myself to you, but I can't keep from loving you. I can't let you alone. There . . . if you want it on the square! What's more, I'll go on . . . as I have done . . . unless you keep away from me. I don't care what I deserve . . . what you do . . . I will . . . I *will!*"

She had begun falteringly, and she ended passionately. Somehow I kept my head, even though my heart pounded like a hammer, and the blood drummed in my ears. It was the thought of Steele that saved me. But I felt cold at the narrow margin. I had reached a point, I feared, where a kiss, one touch from this bewildering creature of fire and change and sweetness would make me put her before Steele and my duty.

"Ruth, if you dare break your promise again, you'll wish you never had been born," I said with all the fierceness at my command.

"I wish that now. And you can't bluff *me*, Mister Gambler. I may have no hand to play, but you can't make me lay it down," she replied.

Something told me Ruth Herbert was finding herself, that presently I could not frighten her, and then . . . then I would be doomed. "Why, if I got drunk, I might do anything," I said, cool and hard now. "Cut off your beautiful chestnut hair for bracelets for my arms."

Ruth laughed, but she was still white. She was indeed finding herself. "If you ever get drunk again, you can't kiss me any more. And if you don't . . . you *can*."

I felt myself shake. With all of the iron will I could assert, I hid from her the sweetness of this thing that was my weakness and her strength. "I might lasso you from my horse, drag you through the cactus," I added with the implacability of an Apache.

"Archie!" she cried. Something in that last ridiculous threat had found a vital mark.

"After all, maybe those awful stories Joel Harkness told about you were true."

"They sure were," I declared with great relief. "And now to forget ourselves . . . I'm more than sorry I distressed Miss Longstreth, more than sorry because what I said wasn't on the square. Blome, no doubt, has come to Fairdale after Steele. His intention is to kill him. I said that . . . let Miss Longstreth think it all meant fatality to the ranger. But, Ruth, I don't believe that Blome can kill Steele any more than . . . than *you* can."

"Why?" she asked, and she seemed eager, glad.

"Because he's not man enough. That's all, without details. You need not worry, and I wish you'd go tell Miss Longstreth . . ."

"Go yourself," interrupted Ruth. "I think she's afraid of my eyes. But she won't fear you've guessed her secret. Go to her, Archie. Find some excuse to tell her. Say you thought it over . . . believed she'd be distressed about what might never happen. Go . . . and afterward pray for your sins, you strange, good-natured, love-meddling cowboy devil, you!"

For once I had no retort ready for Ruth. I hurried off as quickly as I could walk in chaps and spurs. I found Miss Longstreth sitting on a bench in the shade of a tree.

Her pallor and quiet composure told of the conquering and passing of the storm. Always she had a smile for me, and now it smote me, for I, in a sense, had betrayed her.

"Miss Longstreth," I began awkwardly yet swiftly, "I . . . I got to thinking it over, and the idea struck me . . . maybe you felt bad about this gunfighter, Blome, coming down here to kill Steele. At first I imagined you felt sick just because there might be blood spilled. Then I thought you've showed interest in Steele . . . naturally *his* kind of ranger work is bound to appeal to women . . . you might be sorry it couldn't go on . . . you might care."

"Russ, don't beat about the bush," she said, interrupting my foundering. "You know I care."

How wonderful her eyes were then — great, dark, sad gulfs with the soul of a woman at the bottom. Almost I loved her myself — I did love her truth, the woman of her that scorned any subterfuge. Instantly she inspired me to take command over myself.

"Listen," I said, "Jack Blome has come here to meet Steele. There will be a fight. But Blome *can't* kill Steele."

"How is that? Why can't he? You said this Blome was a killer of men. You spoke of notches on his gun. I've heard my father and my cousin, too, speak of Blome's record. He must be a terrible ruffian. If his intent is evil, *why* will he fail in it?"

"Because, Miss Longstreth, when it comes to the last word, Steele will be on the lookout, and Blome won't be quick enough on the draw to kill him. That's all."

"Quick enough on the draw? I understand, but I want to know more."

"I doubt if there's a man on the frontier today quick enough to kill Steele in an even break. That means a fair fight. This Blome is conceited. He'll make the meeting fair enough. It'll come off about like this, Miss Longstreth. Blome will send out his bluff . . . he'll begin to blow . . . to look for Steele. But Steele will avoid him as long as possible, perhaps altogether, though that's improbable. If they do meet, then Blome must force the issue. It's interesting to figure on that.

"Steele affects men strangely. It's all very well for this Blome to rant about himself and to hunt Steele up. But the test'll come when he faces the ranger. He never saw Steele. He doesn't know what he's up against. He knows Steele's reputation, but I don't mean that. I mean Steele in the flesh, his nerve, the something that's in his eyes. Now, when it comes to handling a gun, the man doesn't breathe who has anything on Steele. There was an outlaw . . . Duane . . . who might have killed Steele, had they ever met. I'll tell you Buck Duane's story some day. A girl saved him, made a ranger of him, then got him to go far away from Texas."

"That was wise. Indeed, I'd like to hear the story," she replied. "Then, after all, Russ, in this dreadful part of Texas life, when man faces man, it's all in the quickness of hand?"

"Absolutely. It's the draw. And Steele's a wonder. See here. Look at this."

I stepped back and drew my gun.

"I didn't see how you did that," she said curiously. "Try it again."

I complied, and still she was not quick enough of eye to see my draw. Then I did it slowly, explaining to her the action of hand and then of finger. She seemed fascinated, as a woman might have been by the striking power of a rattlesnake.

"So men's lives depend on that! How horrible for me to be interested . . . to ask about it . . . to watch you. But I'm out here on the frontier now, caught somehow in its wildness, and I feel a relief, a gladness to know Vaughn Steele has the skill you claim. Thank you, Russ."

She seemed about to dismiss me then, for

she rose and half turned away. Then she hesitated. She had one hand at her breast, the other on the bench.

"Have you been with him . . . talked to him lately?" she asked, and a faint rose tint came into her cheeks. But her eyes were steady, dark, and deep, and peered through and far beyond me.

"Yes, I've met him a few times . . . around places."

"Did he ever speak of . . . of me?"

"Once or twice, and then as if he couldn't help it."

"What did he say?"

"Well, the last time he seemed hungry to hear something about you. He didn't exactly ask, but, all the same, he was begging. So I told him."

"What?"

"Oh, how you were dressed, how you looked, what you said, what you did . . . all about you. Don't be offended with me, Miss Longstreth. It was real charity. I talk too much. It's my weakness. Please don't be offended."

She never heard my apology or my entreaty. There was a kind of glory in her eyes. Looking at her, I found a dimness hazing my sight, and, when I rubbed it away, it came back.

"Then . . . what did he say?" This was whispered, almost shyly, and I could scarcely believe the proud Miss Longstreth stood before me.

"Why, he flew into a fury, called me an . . ." Hastily I caught myself. "Well, he said if I wanted to talk to him any more not to speak of you. Sure he was unreasonable."

"Russ . . . you think . . . you told me once . . . he . . . you think he still . . . ?"

She was not facing me at all now. She had her head bent. Both hands were at her breast, and I saw it heave. Her check was white as a flower — her neck darkly, richly red with mounting blood.

I understood. And I pitied her, hated myself, and marveled at this thing, love. It made another woman out of Ray Longstreth. I could scarcely comprehend that she was asking me, almost beseechingly, for further assurance of Steele's love. I knew nothing of women, but this seemed strange. Then a thought sent the blood, chilling, back to my heart. Had Ray Longstreth guessed the guilt of her father? Was it more for his sake than for her own that she hoped — for surely she hoped — that Steele loved her?

Here was more mystery, more food for reflection. Only a powerful motive or a self-leveling love could have made a woman of

Ray Longstreth's pride ask such a question. Whatever her reason, I determined to assure her, once and forever, what I knew to be true. Accordingly I told her in unforgettable words, with my own regard for her and love for Ruth filling my voice with emotion, how I could see that Steele loved her, how madly he was destined to love her, how terribly hard that was going to make his work in Fairdale.

There was a stillness about her then, a light on her face which brought to my mind thought of Ruth when I had asked her to marry me. "Russ, I beg you . . . bring us together," said Miss Longstreth, "bring about a meeting. You are my friend."

Then she went swiftly away through the flowers, leaving me there, thrilled to my soul at her betrayal of herself, ready to die in her service, yet cursing the fatal day Vaughn Steele had chosen me for his comrade in this tragic game.

That evening in the girls' sitting room, where they invited me, I was led into a discourse upon the gunfighters, outlaws, desperadoes, and badmen of the frontier. Miss Longstreth and Ruth had been, before their arrival in Texas, as ignorant of such characters as any girls in the North or East. They were now peculiarly interested, fascinated, and at the same time repelled. Miss Longstreth must have placed the rangers in one of those classes, somewhat as Governor Stone had and her father, too. Ruth thought she was in love with a cowboy whom she had been led to believe had as bad a record as any. They were certainly a most persuasive and appreciative audience.

So, as it was in regard to horses, if I knew any subject well, it was this one of dangerous and bad men. Texas, and the whole developing Southwest, was full of such characters. It was a very difficult thing to distinguish between fighters who were badmen and fighters who were good men. However, it was no difficult thing for one of my calling to tell the difference between a real badman and the imitation four-flush. I told the girls the story of Buck Duane, the famous outlaw and ranger. And I narrated the histories of Murrell, most terrible of blood-spillers ever known to Texas; of Hardin, whose long career of crime ended in the main street in Huntsville when he faced Buck Duane; of Sandobal, the Mexican terror; of Cheseldine, Bland, Alloway, and other outlaws of the Rio Grande; of King Fisher and Thompson and Sterrett, all still living and still busy, adding notches to their guns.

I ended my little talk by telling the story

of Amos Clark, a criminal of a higher type than most badmen, yet infinitely more dangerous because of that. He was a Southerner of good family. After the war he went to Dimmick County and there developed and prospered with the country. He became the most influential citizen of his town and the richest in that section. He held offices. He was energetic in his opposition to rustlers and outlaws. He was held in high esteem by his countrymen. But this Amos Clark was the leader of a band of rustlers, highwaymen, and murderers. Captain MacNeal and some of his rangers ferreted out Clark's relation to this lawless gang and in the end caught him red-handed. He was arrested and eventually hanged. His case was unusual, and it furnished an example of what was possible in this wild country. Clark had a son who was honest and a wife whom he dearly loved, both of whom had been utterly ignorant of the other and wicked side of his life.

I told this last story deliberately, yet with some misgivings. I wanted to see — I convinced myself it was needful for me to see — if Miss Longstreth had any suspicion of her father. To look into her face then was no easy task. But, when I did, I experienced a shock, though not exactly the kind I had prepared myself for. She knew something.

Maybe she knew actually more than Steele or I. Still, if it were crime, she had a marvelous control over her true feelings.

Jack Blome and his men had been in Fairdale for several days. Old Snecker and his son, Bo, had reappeared, and other hardlooking customers, new to me if not to Fairdale — these helped to create a charged and waiting atmosphere. The saloons did unusual business and were never closed. Respectable citizens of the town were awakened in the early dawn by rowdies, carousing in the streets.

Steele kept pretty closely undercover. He did not entertain the opinion, nor did I, that the first time he walked down street he would be a target for Blome and his gang. Things seldom happened that way, and, when they did happen so, it was more accident than design. Blome was setting the stage for his little drama.

Meanwhile Steele was not idle. He told me he had met Laramie, Morton, Zimmer, and that these men had approached others of like character. A secret club had been formed, and all the members were ready for action.

Steele also told me that he had spent hours at night, watching the house where Floyd Lawson stayed when he was not up at Longstreth's. Lawson had almost recovered from the injury to his arm, but he still remained for the most of the time indoors. At night he was visited, or at least the house was, by strange men who were swift, stealthy, mysterious — all that merely kindly disposed friends or neighbors would not have been. Steele had not been able to recognize any of these night visitors, and he did not think the time was ripe for a bold holding up of one of them. Nevertheless, he was sure such an event would discover Lawson, or someone in that house, to be in touch with crooked men.

Laramie had forcibly declared and repeated that some deviltry was afoot — something vastly different from Jack Blome's open intention of meeting the ranger. Laramie was right. Not twenty-four hours after his last talk with Steele, in which he advised quick action, he was found behind the little bar of his restaurant with a bullet hole in his breast, dead. No one could be found who had heard a shot.

It had been deliberate murder, for upon the bar had been left a piece of paper rudely scrawled with a pencil:

**All friends of Ranger Steele
look for the same.**

293

Later that day I met Steele at Laramie's and was with him when he looked at the body and the written message which spoke so tersely of the deadly enmity toward him. We left there together, and I hoped Steele would let me stay with him from that moment.

"Russ, it's all in the dark," he said, "but I feel Lawson's hand in this."

"I thought of him first," I replied.

"Why?"

"Hard to say. Because I remember his face at Laramie's that day you winged him. Because Jim swore you were wrong not to kill instead of cripple him. You *were* wrong."

"No, Russ, I never let feeling run away with my head. We can't prove anything on Lawson."

"Come on, let's hunt him up. I'll bet you I can accuse him and make him show his hand. Come on."

That Steele found me hard to resist was all the satisfaction I got for the anger and desire to avenge Laramie that consumed me.

"Old son, you'll have your belly full of trouble soon enough," replied Steele. "Hold yourself in. Wait. Try to keep your eye on Longstreth at night. See if anyone visits him. Spy on him. I'll watch Lawson."

"Don't you think you'd do well to keep out of town, especially when you sleep?"

"Sure. I've got blankets out in the brush, and I go there every night late and leave before daylight. But I keep a light burning in the 'dobe house and make it look as if I were there."

"Good. That worried me. Now, what's this murder of Laramie going to do to Morton, Zimmer, and their crowd?"

"Russ, they've all got blood in their eyes. This'll make them see red. I've only to say the word, and we'll have all the backing we need."

"Have you run into Blome?"

"Once. I was across the street. He came out of the Hope So with some of his gang. They lined up and watched me. But I went right on."

"He's looking for trouble, Steele."

"Yes, and he'd have found it before this, if I just knew his relation to Longstreth and Lawson."

"Do you think Blome a dangerous man to meet?"

"Hardly. He's a genuine badman, but for all that he's not much to be feared. If he were quietly keeping away from trouble, then that'd be different. Blome will probably die in his boots, thinking he's the worst man and the quicker one on the draw in the West."

That was conclusive enough for me. The little shadow of worry that had haunted me in spite of my confidence vanished entirely.

"Russ, for the present, help me do something for Laramie's family," Steele went on. "His wife's in bad shape. She's not a strong woman. There are a lot of kids, and you know Laramie was poor. She told me her neighbors would keep shy of her now. They'd be afraid. Oh, it's tough! But we can put Jim away decently and help his family."

Several hours after this talk with Steele I took Miss Longstreth and Ruth out to see Laramie's wife and children. I knew Steele would be there that afternoon, but I did not mention this fact to Miss Longstreth.

We rode down to the little adobe house, which belonged to Mrs. Laramie's people and where Steele and I had moved her and the children after Laramie's funeral. The house was small, but comfortable, and the yard green and shady. If this poor wife and mother had not been utterly forsaken by neighbors and friends, it certainly appeared so, for to my knowledge no one besides Steele and me visited her.

Miss Longstreth had packed a big basket

full of good things to eat, and I carried this in front of me on the pommel as we rode. We hitched our horses to the fence and went around to the back of the house. There was a little porch with a stone flooring, and here several children were playing.

The door stood open. At my knock Mrs. Laramie bade me come in. Evidently Steele was not there. So I went in with the girls.

"Missus Laramie, I've brought Miss Longstreth and her cousin to see you," I said cheerfully.

The little room was not very light, there being only one window and the door, but Mrs. Laramie could be seen plainly enough as she lay, hollow-cheeked and haggard, on a bed. Once she had evidently been a woman of some comeliness. The ravages of trouble and grief were there to read in her worn face. She had not, however, any of the hard and bitter lines that had characterized her husband. I wondered, considering that Longstreth had ruined Laramie, how Mrs. Laramie was going to regard the daughter of an enemy.

"So you're Granger Longstreth's girl?" queried the woman, with her bright black eyes fixed on her visitor.

"Yes," replied Miss Longstreth simply. "This is my cousin, Ruth Herbert. We've come to nurse you, take care of the children, help you in any way you'll let us."

There was a long silence.

"Well, you look a little like Longstreth," said Mrs. Laramie finally, "but you're not *at all* like him. You must take after your mother. . . . Miss Longstreth, I don't know if I can . . . if I ought to accept anything from you. Your father ruined my husband."

"Yes, I know," replied the girl sadly. "That's all the more reason you should let me help you. Pray don't refuse. It will . . . mean so much to me."

If this poor, stricken woman had any resentment, it speedily melted in the warmth and sweetness of Miss Longstreth's manner. My idea was that the impression of Ray Longstreth's beauty was always swiftly succeeded by that of her generosity and nobility.

At any rate, she had started well with Mrs. Laramie, and, no sooner had she begun to talk to the children, than both they and the mother were won. The opening of that big basket was an event. Poor, starved little beggars. I went out on the porch to get away from them. My feelings seemed too easily aroused.

Hard, indeed, would it have gone with Jim Laramie's slayer, if I could have laid my eyes on him then. However, Miss Longstreth and

Ruth, after the nature of tender and practical girls, did not appear to take the sad situation to heart. The havoc was wrought in that household. The needs now were cheerfulness, kindness, help, action — and these the girls furnished with a spirit that did me good.

"Missus Laramie, who dressed this baby?" Miss Longstreth asked presently.

I peeped in to see a dilapidated youngster on her knees. That sight, if any other was needed, completed my full and splendid estimate of Ray Longstreth.

"Mister Steele," replied Mrs. Laramie.

"Mister Steele!" exclaimed Miss Longstreth.

"Yes, he's taken care of us all since . . . since . . ." Mrs. Laramie choked.

"Oh, so you've had no help but his," replied Miss Longstreth hastily. "No women? Too bad. I'll send someone, Missus Laramie, and I'll come myself."

"It'll be good of you," went on the older woman. "You see, Jim had few friends . . . that is, right in town. And they've been afraid to help us . . . afraid they'd get what poor Jim . . ."

"That's awful!" burst out Miss Longstreth passionately. "A brave lot of friends! Missus Laramie, don't you worry any more. We'll take care of you. Here, Ruth, help me.

Whatever is the matter with baby's dress?"

Manifestly Miss Longstreth had some difficulty in subduing her emotion.

"Why, it's on hind side before," declared Ruth. "I guess Mister Steele hasn't dressed many babies."

"He did the best he could," said Mrs. Laramie. "Lord only knows what would have become of us. He brought your cowboy, Russ, who's been very good, too."

"Mister Steele, then, is . . . is something more than a ranger?" queried Miss Longstreth with a little break in her voice.

"He's more than I can tell," replied Mrs. Laramie. "He buried Jim. He paid our debts. He fetched us here. He bought food for us. He cooked for us and fed us. He washed and dressed the baby. He sat with me the first two nights after Jim's death, when I thought I'd die myself. He's so kind, so gentle, so patient. He has kept me up just by being near. Sometimes I'd wake from a doze an', seeing him there, I'd know how false were all these tales Jim heard about him and believed at first. Why, he plays with the children just . . . just like any good man might. When he has the baby up, I just can't believe he's a bloody gunman, as they say.

"He's good, but he isn't happy. He has

300

such sad eyes. He looks far off sometimes when the children climb 'round him. They love him. I think he must have loved some woman. His life is sad. Nobody need tell me . . . he sees the good in things. Once he said somebody had to be a ranger. Well, I say, thank God for a ranger like him!"

After that, there was a long silence in the little room, broken only by the cooing of the baby. I did not dare to peep in at Miss Longstreth then.

Somehow I expected Steele to arrive at that moment, and his step did not surprise me. He came around the corner as he always turned any corner, quick, alert, with his hand down. If I had been an enemy, waiting there with a gun, I would have needed to hurry. Steele was instinctively and habitually on the defense.

"Hello, old son! How are Missus Laramie and the youngsters today?" he asked.

"Hello yourself! Why, they're doing fine!" I stepped into the room after him. "I brought the girls down . . ."

Then in the semi-shadow of the room, across Mrs. Laramie's bed, Ray Longstreth and Steele faced each other. That was a moment! Having seen her face then I would not have missed sight of it for anything I could name. Never so long as memory remained with me would I forget. She did not speak.

Ruth, however, bowed and spoke to the ranger. Steele, after the first start, showed no unusual feeling. He greeted both girls pleasantly.

"Russ, that was thoughtful of you," he said. "It was womankind needed here. I could do so little . . . Missus Laramie, you look better today. I'm glad. . . . And here's baby, all clean and white. Baby, what a time I had trying to puzzle out the way your clothes went on! Well, Missus Laramie, didn't I tell you . . . friends would come? So will the brighter side."

"Yes, I've more faith than I had," replied Mrs. Laramie. "Granger Longstreth's daughter has come to me. There for a while after Jim's death I thought I'd sink. We have nothing. How could I ever take care of my little ones? But I'm gaining courage to . . ."

"Missus Laramie, do not distress yourself any more," said Miss Longstreth. "I shall see . . . you are well cared for. I promise you."

"Miss Longstreth, that's fine!" exclaimed Steele with a ring in his voice. "It's what I'd have hoped . . . expected of you."

It must have been sweet praise to her, for the whiteness of her face burned out in a beautiful blush.

"And it's good of you, too, Miss Herbert, to come," added Steele. "Let me thank you both. I'm glad to have you girls as allies in part of my lonely task here. More than glad for the sake of this good woman and the little ones. But both of you be careful. Don't stir without Russ. There's risk. And now I'll be going. Good bye. Missus Laramie, I'll drop in again tonight. Good bye."

Steele backed to the door, and I slipped out beside him.

"Mister Steele . . . wait!" called Miss Longstreth as he stepped out.

He uttered a little sound like a hiss, or a gasp, or an intake of breath, I did not know what, and then the incomprehensible fellow bestowed a kick upon me that I thought about broke my leg. But I understood and gamely endured the pain.

Then we were looking at Ray Longstreth. She was white and wonderful. She stepped out of the door, close to Steele. She did not see me. She cared nothing for my presence. All the world would not have mattered to her then.

"I have wronged you," she said impulsively.

Looking on, I seemed to see or feel some slow, mighty force gathering in Steele to meet this ordeal. Then he appeared to me

303

as always — yet, to me, how different!

"Miss Longstreth, how can you say that?" he returned.

"I believed what my father and Floyd Lawson said about you . . . that bloody, despicable record! Now I do not believe. I see . . . I wronged you."

"You make me very glad when you tell me. It was hard to have you think so ill of me. But, Miss Longstreth, please don't speak of wronging me. I *am* a ranger . . . and much said of me is true. My duty is hard on others . . . sometimes on those who are innocent, alas. But God knows that duty is hard, too, on me."

"I *did* wrong you. In thought . . . in word. I ordered you from my home as if you were, indeed, what they called you. But I was deceived. I see my error. If you entered my home again, I would think it an honor. I . . ."

"Please . . . please don't, Miss Long-streth," interrupted poor Steele. I could see that gray beneath his bronze and something that was like gold deep in his eyes.

"But, sir, my conscience flays me," she went on.

There was no other sound like her voice. If I was all distraught with emotion, what must Steele have been?

"I make amends. Will you take my hand? Will you forgive me?"

She gave it royally, while the other was there pressing at her breast.

Steele took the proffered hand and held it, and did not release it. What else could he have done? But he could not speak.

Then it seemed to dawn upon Steele that there was more behind this white, sweet, noble intensity of her than just the making amends for a fancied or real wrong. For myself, I thought the man did not live on earth who could have resisted her then. And there was resistance. I felt it. She must have felt it. It was poor Steele's hard fate, to fight the charm and eloquence and sweetness of this woman when, for some reason unknown to him, and only guessed at by me, she was burning with all the fire and passion of her soul.

"Mister Steele, I honor you for your goodness to this unfortunate woman," she said, and now her speech came swiftly. "When she was all alone and helpless, you were her friend. It was the deed of a man. But Missus Laramie isn't the only unfortunate woman in the world. I, too, am unfortunate. Ah, how *I* may soon need a friend!

"Vaughn Steele, the man whom I need most to be my friend . . . *want* most to lean upon . . . he is the one whose duty is to stab me to the heart, to ruin me. *You!* Will *you* be my friend? If you knew Ray Longstreth, you would know she would never ask you to be false to your duty. Be true to us both! I'm so alone . . . no one but Ruth loves me. I'll need a friend soon . . . soon.

"Oh, I know . . . I know what you'll find out sooner or later. I know *now!* I want to help you. Let us save life, if not honor. Must I stand alone . . . all alone? Will you . . . will you be . . . ?"

Her voice failed. She was swaying toward Steele. I expected to see his arms spread wide and enfold her in their embrace.

"Ray Longstreth, I love you!" whispered Steele hoarsely, white now to his lips. "I must be true to my duty. But if I can't be true to you . . . then, by God, I want no more of life!"

He kissed her hand and rushed away.

She stood a moment, as if blindly watching the place where he had vanished, and then, as a sister might have turned to a brother, she reached for me.

Chapter Twelve

THE EAVESDROPPER

We silently rode home in the gathering dusk. Miss Longstreth dismounted at the porch, but Ruth went on with me to the corrals. I felt heavy and somber, as if a catastrophe was near at hand.

"Help me down," said Ruth. Her voice was low and tremulous.

"Ruth, did you hear what Miss Longstreth said to Steele?" I asked.

"A little . . . here and there. I heard Steele tell her he loved her. Isn't this a terrible mess?"

"It sure is. Did you hear . . . do you understand why she appealed to Steele, asked him to be her friend?"

"Did she? No, I didn't hear that. I heard her say she had wronged him. Then I tried not to hear any more. Tell me."

"No, Ruth. It's not my secret. I wish I could do something . . . help them somehow. Yes, it's sure a terrible mix. I don't care so much about myself."

"Nor me," Ruth retorted.

"You. Oh, you're only a shallow, spoiled child! You'd cease to love anything the moment you won it. And I . . . well, I'm no good, you say. But their love. My God, what a tragedy. You've no idea, Ruth. They've hardly spoken to each other, yet are ready to be overwhelmed."

Ruth sat so still and silent that I thought I had angered or offended her. But I did not care much, one way or another. Her coquettish fancy for me and my own trouble had sunk into insignificance.

I did not look up at her, though she was so close I could feel her little restless foot touching me. The horses in the corrals were trooping up to the bars. Dusk had about given place to night, although in the west a broad flare of golden sky showed bright behind dark mountains.

"So *I* say you're no good?" asked Ruth after a long silence.

Then her voice and the way her hand stole to my shoulder should have been warning for me. But it was not, and I did not care.

"Yes, you said that, didn't you?" I replied absently.

"I can change my mind, can't I? Maybe you're only wild and reckless when you drink. Missus Laramie said such nice things about you. They made me feel so good."

I had no reply for that and still did not look up at her. I heard her swing herself in the saddle.

"Lift me down," she said.

Perhaps at any other time I would have remarked that this request was rather unusual, considering the fact that she was very light and sure of action, extremely proud of it, and likely to be insulted by an offer of assistance. But my spirit was dead. I reached for her hands, but they eluded mine, slipped up my arms as she came sliding out of the saddle — and then her face was very close to mine.

"Archie," she whispered.

It was torment, wistfulness, uncertainty, and yet tenderness all in one little whisper. It caught me off my guard or indifferent to consequences. So I kissed her, without passion, with all regret and sadness. She uttered a little cry that might have been mingled exultation and remorse for her victory and her broken faith. Certainly the instant I kissed her she remembered the latter.

She trembled against me, and, leaving unsaid something she had meant to say, she slipped out of my arms and ran. She assuredly was frightened, and I thought it just as well that she was.

Presently she disappeared in the darkness,

and then the swift little clink of her spurs ceased. I laughed somewhat ruefully and hoped she would not be satisfied. Then I put away the horses and went in for my supper.

After supper, I noisily bustled around my room and soon stole out for my usual evening's spying. The night was dark, without starlight, and a stiff wind rustled the leaves and tore through the vines on the old house. The fact that I had seen and heard so little during my constant vigilance did not make me careless or the task monotonous. I had so much to think about that sometimes I sat in one place for hours and never knew where the time went.

This night, the very first thing, I heard Lawson's well-known footsteps, and I saw Longstreth's door open, flashing a broad bar of light into the darkness. Lawson crossed the threshold, the door closed, and all was dark again outside. Not a ray of light escaped from the window.

This was the first visit from Lawson for a considerable stretch of time. Little doubt there was that his talk with Longstreth would be interesting to me. I tiptoed to the door and listened, but I could hear only a murmur of voices. Besides, that position was too risky. I went around the corner of the house.

Some time before I had made a discovery that I imagined would be valuable to me. This side of the big adobe house was of much older construction than the back and larger part. There was a narrow passage about a foot wide between the old and new walls, and this ran from the outside through to the patio. I had discovered the entrance by accident, as it was concealed by vines and shrubbery. I crawled in there, upon an opportune occasion, with the intention of boring a small hole through the adobe bricks. But it was not necessary to do that, for the wall was cracked, and in one place I could see into Longstreth's room.

This passage now afforded me my opportunity, and I decided to avail myself of it in spite of the very great danger. Crawling on my hands and knees very stealthily, I got under the shrubbery to the entrance of the passage. In the blackness a faint streak of light showed the location of the crack in the wall. I had to slip in sidewise. It was a tight squeeze, but I entered without the slightest noise. If my position were to be betrayed, it would not be from noise.

As I progressed, the passage grew a very little wider in that direction, and this fact gave rise to the thought that in case of a necessary and hurried exit I would do my best by working toward the patio. It seemed a good deal of time was consumed in reaching my vantage point. When I did get there, the crack was a foot over my head. If I had only been tall like Steele. There was nothing to do but find toe-holes in the crumbling walls and, by bracing knees on one side, back against the other, hold myself up to the crack.

Once with my eye there I did not care what risk I ran. Longstreth appeared disturbed. He sat, stroking his mustache. His brow was clouded. Lawson's face seemed darker, more sullen, yet lighted by some indomitable resolve.

"We'll settle both deals tonight," Lawson was saying. "That's what I came for. That's why I've asked Snecker and Blome to be here."

"But suppose I don't choose to talk here?" protested Longstreth impatiently. "I never before made my house a place to . . ."

"We've waited long enough. This place's as good as any. You've lost your nerve since that ranger hit the town. First, now, will you give Ray to me?"

"Floyd, you talk like a spoiled boy. Give Ray to you! Why, she's a woman, and I'm finding out that she's got a mind of her own. I told you I was willing for her to marry you.

I tried to persuade her. But Ray hasn't any use for you now. She liked you at first, but now she doesn't. So what can I do?"

"You can make her marry me," replied Lawson.

"Make that girl do what she doesn't want to? It couldn't be done, even if I tried. I haven't the highest opinion of you as a prospective son-in-law, Floyd. But, if Ray loved you, I would consent. We'd all go away together before this damned miserable business is out. Then she'd never know. And maybe you might be more like you used to be before the West ruined you. But, as matters stand, you fight your own game with her, and I'll tell you now, you'll lose."

"What'd you want to let her come out here for?" demanded Lawson hotly. "It was a dead mistake. I've lost my head over her. I'll have her or die. Don't you think, if she was my wife, I'd soon pull myself together? Since she came, we've none of us been right. And the gang has put up a holler. No, Longstreth, we've got to settle things tonight."

"Well, we can settle what Ray's concerned in right now," replied Longstreth, rising. "Come on. We'll go ask her. See where you stand."

They went out, leaving the door open. I dropped down to rest myself and to wait. I would have liked to hear Miss Longstreth's answer to him. But I could guess what it would be.

Lawson appeared to be all I had thought him, and I believed I was going to find out presently that he was worse. Just then I wanted Steele as never before. Still, he was too big to worm his way into this place.

The men seemed to be absent a good while, though that feeling might have been occasioned by my thrilling interest and anxiety. Finally I heard heavy steps. Lawson came in alone. He was leaden-faced, humiliated. Then something abject in him gave place to rage. He strode the room. He cursed.

When Longstreth returned, he was now appreciably calmer. I could not but decide that he felt relief at the evident rejection of Lawson's proposal.

"Don't fume about it, Floyd," he said. "You see I can't help it. We're pretty wild out here, but I can't rope my daughter and give her to you as I would an unruly steer."

"Longstreth, I can *make* her marry me," declared Lawson thickly.

"How?"

"You know the hold I got on you . . . the deal that made you boss of this rustler gang?"

"It isn't likely I'd forget," replied Long-streth grimly.

"I can go to Ray . . . tell her that . . . make her believe I'd tell it broadcast . . . tell this Ranger Steele, unless she'd marry me."

Lawson spoke breathlessly, with haggard face and shadowed eyes. He had no shame. He was simply in the grip of passion. Long-streth gazed with dark, uncontrolled fury at his relative. In that look I saw a strong, unscrupulous man fallen into evil ways, but still a man. It betrayed Lawson to be a wild and passionate weakling.

I seemed to see also how, during all the years of association, this strong man had upheld the weak one. But that time had gone forever, both in intent on Longstreth's part and in possibility. Lawson, like the great majority of evil and unrestrained men on the border, had reached a point where influence was futile. Reason had degenerated. He saw only himself.

"But, Floyd, Ray's the one person on earth who must never know I'm a rustler, a thief, a red-handed ruler of the worst gang on the border," replied Longstreth impressively.

Floyd bowed his head at that, as if the significance had just occurred to him. But he was not long at a loss.

"She's going to find it out sooner or later.

315

I tell you, she knows now there's something wrong out here. She's got eyes. And that meddling cowboy of hers is smarter than you give him credit for. They're always together. You'll regret the day Russ ever straddled a horse on this ranch. Mark what I say."

"Ray's changed, I know, but she hasn't any idea yet that her daddy's a boss rustler. Ray's concerned about what she calls my duty as mayor. Also I think she's not satisfied with my explanations in regard to certain property."

Lawson halted in his restless walk and leaned against the stone mantelpiece. He squared himself as if this was his last stand. He looked desperate, but at the moment showed an absence of his usual nervous excitement.

"Longstreth, that may well be true," he said. "No doubt all you say is true. But it doesn't help me. I want the girl. If I don't get her, I reckon we'll all go to hell."

He might have meant anything, probably meant the worst. He certainly had something more in mind. Longstreth gave a slight start, barely perceptible, like the switch of an awakening tiger. He sat there, head down, stroking his mustache.

I almost saw his thought. I had long experience in reading men under stress of such emotion. I had no means to vindicate my judgment, but my conviction was that Longstreth right then and there decided that the thing to do was to kill Lawson. For my part, I wondered that he'd not come to such a conclusion before. Not improbably the advent of his daughter had put Longstreth in conflict with himself.

Suddenly he threw off a somber cast of countenance, and he began to talk. He talked swiftly, persuasively, yet I imagined he was talking to smooth Lawson's passion for the moment. Lawson no more caught the fateful significance of a line crossed, a limit reached, a decree decided, than if he had not been present. He was obsessed with himself. How, I wondered, had a man of his mind ever lived so long and gone so far among the exacting conditions of Pecos County? The answer was, perhaps, that Longstreth had guided him, upheld him, protected him. The coming of Ray Longstreth had been the entering wedge of dissension.

"You're too impatient," concluded Longstreth. "You'll ruin any chance of happiness if you rush Ray. She might be won. If you told her who I am, she'd hate you forever. She might marry you to save me, but she'd hate you. That isn't the way. Wait. Play for time. Be different with her. Cut out your drinking. She despises that. Let's plan to sell out here, stock, ranch, property, and leave the country. Then you'd have a show with her."

"I told you we've got to stick," growled Lawson. "The gang won't stand for our going. It can't be done unless you want to sacrifice everything."

"You mean double-cross the men? Go without their knowing? Leave them here to face whatever comes?"

"I mean just that."

"I'm bad enough, but not that bad," returned Longstreth. "If I can't get the gang to let me off, I'll stay and face the music. All the same, Lawson, did it ever strike you that most of the deals the last few years have been *yours?*"

"Yes. If I hadn't rung them in, there wouldn't have been any. You've had cold feet, Owens says, especially since this Ranger Steele, has been here."

"Well, call it cold feet if you like. But I call it sense. We reached our limit long ago. We began by rustling a few cattle at a time . . . when rustling was laughed at. But as our greed grew, so did our boldness. Then came the gang, the regular trips, the one thing and another till, before we knew it . . .

before *I* knew it, we had shady deals, hold-ups, and *murders* on our record. Then we *had* to go on. Too late to turn back."

"I reckon we've all said that. None of the gang wants to quit. They all think, and I think, we can't be touched. We may be blamed, but nothing can be proved. We're too strong."

"There's where you're dead wrong," rejoined Longstreth emphatically. "I imagined once, not long ago . . . I was bull-headed . . . who would ever connect Granger Longstreth with a rustler gang? I've changed my mind. I've begun to think. I've reasoned out things. We're crooked, and we can't last. It's the nature of life, even in wild Pecos, for conditions to grow better. The wise deal for us would be to divide equally and leave the country, all of us."

"But you and I have all the stock . . . all the gain," protested Lawson.

"I'll split mine."

"I won't . . . that settles that," added Lawson instantly.

Longstreth spread wide his hands, as if it was useless to try to convince this man. Talking had not increased his calmness, and he now showed more than impatience. A dull glint gleamed deep in his eyes.

"Your stock and property will last a long

time . . . do you lots of good when Steele . . ."

"Bah!" croaked Lawson hoarsely. The ranger's name was a match applied to powder. "Haven't I told you he'd be dead soon . . . any time . . . same as Laramie is?"

"Yes, you mentioned the . . . the supposition," replied Longstreth sarcastically. "I inquired, too, just how that very desired event was to be brought about."

"Blome's here to kill Steele."

"Bah!" retorted Longstreth in turn. "Blome can't kill this ranger. He can't face him with a ghost of a show . . . he'll never get a chance at Steele's back. The man don't live on this border who's quick and smart enough to kill Steele."

"I'd like to know why?" demanded Lawson sullenly.

"You ought to know. You've seen the ranger pull a gun."

"Who told you?" queried Lawson, his face working.

"Oh, I guessed it, if that'll do you."

"If Jack doesn't kill this damned ranger, I will," replied Lawson, pounding the table.

Longstreth laughed contemptuously. "Floyd, don't make so much noise. And don't be a fool. You've been on the border for ten years. You've packed a gun and you've used it. You've been with Blome and Snecker when they killed their men. You've been present at many fights. But you never saw a man like Steele. You haven't got sense enough to see him right if you had a chance. Neither has Blome. The only way to get rid of Steele is for the gang to draw on him, all at once. Then he's going to drop some of them."

"Longstreth, you say that like a man who wouldn't care much if Steele did drop some of them," declared Lawson, and now he was sarcastic.

"To tell you the truth, I wouldn't," returned the other bluntly. "I'm pretty sick of this mess."

Lawson cursed in amaze. His emotions were all out of proportion to his intelligence. He was not at all quick-witted. I had never seen a vainer or more arrogant man.

"Longstreth, I don't like your talk," he said.

"If you don't like the way I talk, you know what you can do," replied Longstreth quickly.

He stood up then, cool and quiet, with flash of eyes and set of lips that told me he was dangerous.

"Well, after all, that's neither here nor there," went on Lawson, unconsciously cowed by the other. "The thing is, do I get the girl?"

"Not by any means . . . *except* her consent."

"You'll not make her marry me?"

"No. *No,*" replied Longstreth, his voice still cold, low-pitched.

"All right. Then *I'll* make her."

Evidently Longstreth understood the man before him so well that he wasted no more words. I knew what Lawson never dreamed of, and that was that Longstreth had a gun somewhere within reach and meant to use it.

Then heavy footsteps sounded outside, tramping upon the porch. I might have been mistaken, but I believed those footsteps saved Lawson's life.

"There they are," said Lawson, and he opened the door.

Five masked men entered. About two of them I could not recognize anything familiar. I thought one had old Snecker's burly shoulders and another Bo Snecker's stripling shape. I did recognize Blome in spite of his mask, because his fair skin and hair, his garb and air of distinction made plain his identity. They all wore coats, hiding any weapons. The big man with the burly shoulders shook hands with Longstreth, and the others stood back.

The atmosphere of the room had changed. Lawson might have been a nonentity for all he counted. Longstreth was another man — a stranger to me. If he had entertained a hope of freeing himself from this band, of getting away to a safer country, he abandoned it at the very sight of these men. There was power here, and he was bound.

The big man spoke in low, hoarse whispers, and, at this, all the others gathered around him, close to the table. There were evidently some signs of membership not plain to me.

Then all the heads were bent over the table. Low voices spoke, queried, answered, argued. By straining my ears, I caught a word here and there. They were planning. I did not attempt to get at the meaning of the few words and phrases I distinguished, but held them in mind so to piece all together afterward. Before the plotters finished conferring, I had an involuntary flashed knowledge of much, and my whirling, excited mind made reception difficult. When these rustlers finished whispering, I was in a cold sweat.

Steele was to be killed as soon as possible by Blome, or by the gang going to Steele's house at night. Morton had been with the ranger. He was to meet the same fate as

Laramie, dealt by Bo Snecker, who evidently worked in the dark like a ferret. Any other person known to be communing with Steele, or interested in him, or suspect of either, was to be silenced. Then the town was to suffer a short deadly spell of violence, directed anywhere, for the purpose of intimidating those people who had begun to be restless under the influence of the ranger. After that, the big herds of stock were to be rustled off the ranches to the north and driven to El Paso.

The big man, who evidently was the leader of the present convention, got up to depart. He went as swiftly as he had come and was followed by the slender fellow. As far as it was possible for me to be sure, I identified these two as Snecker and son. The others, however, remained.

Blome removed his mask, which action was duplicated by the two rustlers who had stayed with him. They were both young, bronzed, hard of countenance, not unlike cowboys. Evidently this was now a social call on Longstreth. He set out cigars and liquors for his guests, and a general conversation ensued, differing little from what might have been indulged in by neighborly ranchers. There was not a word spoken that would have caused suspicion.

Blome was genial, gay, and he talked the most. Lawson alone seemed uncommunicative and unsociable. He smoked fiercely and drank continually. All at once he straightened up as if listening.

"What's that?" he called suddenly.

The talking and laughter ceased. My own strained ears were pervaded by a slight rustling sound.

"Must be a rat," replied Longstreth in relief.

Strange how any sudden or unknown thing weighed upon him. The rustling became a rattle.

"Sounds like a rattlesnake to me," said Blome.

Longstreth got up from the table and peered round the room. Just at that instant I felt an almost inappreciable movement of the adobe wall which supported me. I could scarcely credit my senses. But the rattle inside Longstreth's room was mingling with little dull thuds of falling dirt. The adobe wall, merely dried mud, was crumbling. I distinctly felt a tremor pass through it. Then the blood gushed with sickening coldness back to my heart and seemingly clogged it.

"What in the hell!" exclaimed Longstreth.

"I smell dust," said Blome sharply.

That was the signal for me to drop down from my perch, yet despite my care I made a noise.

"Did you hear a step?" queried Longstreth.

No one answered. But a heavy piece of adobe wall fell with a thud.

"There's somebody between the walls!" thundered Longstreth.

Then a section of the wall fell inward with a crash. I began to squeeze my body through the narrow passage toward the patio.

"Hear him!" yelled Lawson. "This side!"

"No, he's going that way," yelled someone else.

The tramp of heavy boots lent me the strength and speed of desperation. I was not shirking a fight, but to be cornered like a trapped coyote was another matter. I almost tore my clothes off in that passage. The dust nearly stifled me.

When I burst into the patio, it was not one single instant too soon. But one deep gasp of breath revived me, and I was up, gun in hand, running for the outlet into the court. Thumping footsteps turned me back. While there was a chance to get away, I did not want to meet odds in a fight. I thought I heard someone running into the patio from the other end.

I stole along, and, coming to a door without any idea of where it might lead, I softly pushed it open a little way and slipped in.

Chapter Thirteen

IN FLAGRANTE DELICTO

A low cry greeted me. The room was light. I saw Ruth Herbert, sitting on her bed in her dressing gown. Shaking my gun at her with a fierce, warning gesture to be silent, I turned to close the door. It was a heavy door, without bolt or bar, and, when I had shut it, I felt safe only for the moment.

I gazed around the room. There was one window with blind closely drawn. I listened and seemed to hear footsteps retreating, dying away. Then I turned to Ruth. She had slipped off the bed to her knees and was holding out trembling hands, as if both to supplicate mercy and to ward me off. She was as white as the pillow on her bed and terribly frightened.

Again with a warning hand commanding silence, I stepped softly forward, meaning to reassure her.

"Archie. Archie," she whispered wildly.

I thought she was going to faint. When I got close and looked into her eyes, I understood the strange dark expression in them.

She was terrified because she believed I meant to kill her, or do worse — probably worse. She had believed many a hard story about me and had cared for me in spite of them.

I remembered, then, that she had broken her promise, she had tempted me, led me to kiss her, made a fool out of me. I remembered, also, how I had threatened her. This intrusion of mine was the wild cowboy's vengeance. I verily believed she thought I was drunk. I must have looked pretty hard and fierce, bursting into her room with that big gun in hand. My first action then was to lay the gun down on her bureau.

"You poor kid!" I whispered, taking her hands and trying to raise her.

But she stayed on her knees and clung to me. "Archie! It was vile of me," she whispered. "I know it. I deserve anything . . . anything! But I am only a kid. Archie, I didn't . . . break my word . . . I didn't make you kiss me just for vanity's sake. I swear I didn't. I wanted you to. For I care . . . Archie . . . I can't help it. Please, forgive me. Please let me off this time. Don't . . . don't . . ."

"Will you shut up!" I interrupted, half beside myself. And I used force in another way than speech. I shook her and sat her on the bed. "You little fool, I didn't come in here to kill you or do some other awful thing, as you think. For God's sake, Ruth, what do you take me for?"

"Archie, you swore . . . you'd do something terrible if I . . . tempted you . . . any more," she faltered.

The way she searched my face with doubtful, fearful eyes hurt me.

"Listen," and with the word I seemed to be pervaded by peace. "I didn't know this was your room. I came in here to get away . . . to save my life. I was pursued. I was spying on Longstreth and his men. They heard me, but did not see me. They don't know who was listening. They're after me now. I'm Special United States Deputy Marshal Sittell . . . Russell Archibald Sittell. I'm a ranger. I'm here as secret aid to Steele."

Ruth's eyes changed from blank gulfs to dilating, shadowing, quickening windows of thought. "Russ-ell Archi-bald Sittell," she echoed. "Ranger. Secret aid to Steele."

"Yes."

"Then you're no cowboy?"

"No."

"Only a make-believe one?"

"Yes."

"And the drinking, the gambling, the association with those low men . . . that was all put on?"

"Part of the game, Ruth. I'm not a drinking man. And I sure hate those places I had to go in, and all that pertains to them."

"Oh, so that's it. I knew there was something. How glad . . . how glad I am. Archie. Archie."

Then Ruth threw her arms around my neck, and without reserve or restraint began to kiss me. It must have been a moment of sheer gladness to feel that I was not disreputable — a moment when something deep and womanly in her was vindicated. Assuredly she was entirely different from what she had ever been before.

There was a little space of time — a sweet confusion of senses — when I could but meet her half way in tenderness. Quite as suddenly, then, she began to cry. I whispered in her ear, cautioning her to be careful, that my life was at stake. After that she cried silently, with one of her arms around my neck, her head on my breast, and her hand clasping mine.

So I held her for what seemed a long time. Indistinct voices came to me and footsteps seemingly a long way off. I heard the wind in the rosebush outside. Someone walked down the stony court.

Then a shrill neigh of a horse pierced the silence. A rider was mounting out there for some reason. With my life at stake I grasped all the sweetness of that situation. Ruth stirred in my arms, raised a red, tear-stained yet happy face, and tried to smile.

"It isn't any time to cry," she whispered. "But I had to. You can't understand what it made me feel to learn you're no drunkard, no desperado, but a man . . . a man like that ranger."

Very sweetly and seriously she kissed me again.

"Archie, if I didn't honestly and truly love you before, I do now." She stood up and faced me with the fire and intelligence of a woman in her eyes. "Tell me. You were spying on my uncle?"

Briefly I told her what had happened before I entered her room, not omitting a terse word as to the character of the men I had watched.

"My God! So it's Uncle Granger! I knew something was very wrong here . . . with him . . . with the place . . . the people. And right off I hated Floyd Lawson. Archie, does Ray know?"

"She knows something. I haven't any idea how much."

"This explains her appeal to Steele. Oh, it'll kill her. You don't know how proud . . . how good Ray is. Oh, it'll kill her."

"Ruth, she's no baby. She's got sand, that girl . . ."

The sound of soft steps somewhere near distracted my attention, reminded me of my peril and now, what counted more with me, made clear the probability of being discovered in Ruth's room.

"I'll have to get out of here," I whispered.

"Wait," she replied, detaining me. "Didn't you say they were hunting for you?"

"They sure are," I returned grimly.

"Oh, then you mustn't go. They might shoot you before you got away. Stay. If we hear them, you can hide under my bed. I'll turn out the light. I'll meet them at the door. You can trust me. Stay, Archie. Wait till all quiets down, if we have to wait till morning. Then you can slip out."

"Ruth, I oughtn't to stay. I don't want to . . . I won't," I replied, perplexed and stubborn.

"But you must. It's the only safe way. They won't come here."

"Suppose they should? It's an even chance Longstreth'll search every room and corner in this old house. If they found me here, I couldn't start a fight. You might be hurt. Then . . . the fact of my being here . . ." I did not finish what I meant, but instead made a step toward the door.

Ruth was on me like a little whirlwind, white of face and dark of eye, with a resoluteness I could have not have deemed her capable of. She was as strong and supple as a panther, too. But she need not have been either resolute or strong, for the clasp of her arms, the feel of her warm breast as she pressed me back — these were enough to make me weak as water.

My knees buckled as I touched the chair, and I was glad to sit down. My face was wet with perspiration and a kind of cold ripple shot over me. I imagined I was losing my nerve then. Proof beyond doubt that Ruth loved me was so sweet, so overwhelming a thing, that I could not resist, even to save her disgrace.

"Archie, the fact of your being here is the very thing to save you . . . if they come," Ruth whispered softly. "What do I care what they think?"

She put her arms around my neck. I gave up then and held her as if she indeed were my only hope. A noise, a stealthy sound, a step froze that embrace into stone.

"Up yet, Ruth?" came Longstreth's clear voice, too strained, too eager to be natural.

"No, I'm in bed, reading. Good night, Uncle," replied Ruth instantly, so calmly and naturally that I marveled at the difference between man and woman. Perhaps that was the difference between love and hate.

"Are you alone?" went on Longstreth's penetrating voice, colder now.

"Yes," replied Ruth.

The door swung inward with a swift scrape and jar. Longstreth half entered, haggard, flaming-eyed. His leveled gun did not have to move an inch to cover me. Behind him I saw Lawson and, indistinctly, another man.

"Well, I'll be damned!" cursed Longstreth. He showed amaze. "Hands up, Russ."

I put up my hands quickly, but all the time I was calculating what chance I had to leap for my gun or dash out the light. Risk was too great for Ruth.

I was trapped. And fury, like the hot teeth of a wolf, bit into me. That leveled gun — the menace in Longstreth's puzzled eyes — Lawson's dark and hateful face — these loosened the spirit of fight in me. If Ruth had not been there, I would have made some desperate move.

Longstreth barred Lawson from entering, which action showed control as well as distrust. "You lied!" he said to Ruth. He was hard as flint, yet doubtful and curious, too.

"Certainly I lied," snapped Ruth in reply. She was cool, almost flippant. I awakened to the knowledge that she was to be reckoned with in this situation. Suddenly she stepped squarely between Longstreth and me.

"Move aside," ordered Longstreth sternly.

"I won't! What do I care for your old gun? You sha'n't shoot Russ or do anything else to him. It's my fault he's here in my room. I coaxed him to come."

"You little hussy!" exclaimed Longstreth, and he lowered the gun.

If I ever before had occasion to glory in Ruth, I had it then. She betrayed not the slightest fear. She looked as if she could fight like a little tigress. She was white, composed, defiant.

"How long has Russ been in here?" demanded Longstreth.

"All evening. I left Ray at eight o'clock. Russ came right after that."

"But you're undressed for bed!" ejaculated the angry and perplexed uncle.

"Yes." That simple answer was so noncommittal, so above subterfuge, so innocent, and yet so confounding in its provocation of thought that Longstreth just stared his astonishment.

I started as if I had been struck. "See here, Longstreth . . . ," I began passionately.

Like a flash Ruth whirled into my arms,

and one hand crossed my lips.

"It's my fault. I *will* take the blame!" she cried, and now the agony of fear in her voice quieted me. I realized I would be wise to be silent. "Uncle," began Ruth, turning her head, yet still clinging to me, "I've tormented Russ into loving me. I've flirted with him . . . teased him . . . tempted him. We love each other now. We're engaged. Please . . . please don't . . ."

She began to falter, and I felt her weight sag a little against me.

"Well, let go of him," said Longstreth. "I won't hurt him. Ruth, how long has this affair been going on?"

"For weeks . . . I don't know . . . how long."

"Does Ray know?"

"She knows we love each other, but not that we met . . . did this . . ."

"I should hope not. I . . ."

Light, swift steps — the rustle of silk — interrupted Longstreth and made my heart sink like lead.

"Is that you, Floyd?" came Miss Longstreth's deep voice, nervous, hurried. "What's all this commotion I hear . . . ?"

"Ray, go on back," ordered Longstreth.

Just then Miss Longstreth's beautiful agitated face appeared beside Lawson. He failed to prevent her from seeing all of us.

"Papa! Ruth!" she exclaimed in consternation. Then she swept into the room. "What has happened?"

Longstreth, like the devil he was, laughed when it was too late. He had good impulses, but they never interfered with his sardonic humor. He paced the little room, shrugging his shoulders, offering no explanation. Ruth appeared about ready to collapse, and I could not have told Ruth's lie to Miss Longstreth to save my life.

"Ray, your father and I broke in on a little Romeo and Juliet scene," said Floyd Lawson with a leer.

Then Miss Longstreth's dark gaze swept from Floyd to her father, then to Ruth's attire and her shamed face, and finally to me. What effect the magnificent wrath and outraged trust in her eyes had upon me.

"Russ, do they dare insinuate you came to Ruth's room?"

For myself I could keep silent, but for Ruth I began to feel a hot clamoring outburst swelling my throat.

"Ruth confessed it, Ray," replied Lawson.

"*Ruth!*" A shrinking, shuddering disbelief filled Miss Longstreth's voice.

"Ray . . . I told you . . . I loved him . . . didn't I?" replied Ruth.

She managed to hold up her head with a ghost of her former defiant spirit.

"Miss Longstreth, it's a . . . ," I burst out.

Then Ruth fainted. It was I who caught her. Miss Longstreth hurried to her side with a little cry of distress.

"Russ, your hand's called," said Longstreth. "Of course, you'll swear the moon's green cheese. And I like you the better for it. But we know now, and you can save your breath. If Ruth hadn't stuck up so gamely for you, I'd have shot you. But . . . at that I wasn't looking for you. Now clear out of here."

I picked up my gun from the bureau and dropped it in its sheath. For the life of me I could not leave without another look at Miss Longstreth. The scorn in her eyes did not wholly hide the sadness. She who needed friends was experiencing the bitterness of misplaced trust. That came out in the scorn, but the sadness — I knew what hurt her most was her sorrow. I dropped my head and stalked out.

Chapter Fourteen

A SLAP IN THE FACE

When I got out into the dark, where my hot face cooled in the wind, my relief equaled my other feelings. Longstreth had told me to clear out, and, although I did not take that as a dismissal, I considered I would be wise to leave the ranch at once. Daylight might disclose my footprints between the walls, but, even if it did not, my work there was finished. So I went to my room and packed my few belongings.

The night was dark, windy, stormy, yet there was no rain. I hoped as soon as I got clear of the ranch to lose something of the pain I felt. But long after I had tramped out into the open, there was a lump in my throat and an ache in my breast. And all my thoughts centered round Ruth. What a game and loyal little girl she had turned out to be. I was absolutely at a loss concerning what the future held in store for us. I had a vague, but clinging, hope that after the trouble was over, there might be — there *must* be — something between us.

Steele was not at our rendezvous among the rocks. The hour was late. Among the few dim lights flickering on the outskirts of town I picked out the one of his little adobe house, but I knew almost to a certainty that he was not there. So I turned my way into the darkness, not with any great hope of finding Steele out there, but with the intention of seeking a covert for myself until morning.

There was no trail, and the night was so black that I could see only the lighter sandy patches of ground. I stumbled over the little clumps of brush, fell into washes, and pricked myself on cactus. By and by mesquite and rocks began to make progress still harder for me. I wandered around, at last getting on higher ground, and here in spite of the darkness felt some sense of familiarity with things. I was probably near Steele's hiding place.

I went on till rocks and brush barred further progress, and then I ventured to whistle. But no answer came. Whereupon I spread my blanket in as sheltered a place as I could find and lay down. The coyotes were on noisy duty; the wind moaned and rushed through the mesquite. But, despite these sounds and worry about Steele and the never-absent haunting thought of

Ruth, I went to sleep.

A little rain fell during the night, as I discovered upon waking, but it had not been enough to cause me any discomfort. The morning was bright and beautiful, yet somehow I hated it. I had work to do that did not go well with that golden wave of grass and brush on the windy open. I climbed to the highest rock of that ridge and looked about. It was a wild spot, some three miles from town.

Presently I recognized landmarks given to me by Steele, and I knew I was near his place. I whistled, then hallooed, but got no reply. Then, by working back and forth across the ridge, I found what appeared to be a faint trail. This I followed, lost, and found again, and eventually still higher up on another ridge, with a commanding outlook, I found Steele's hiding place. He had not been there for perhaps forty-eight hours. I wondered where he had slept.

Under a shelving rock I found a pack of food, carefully protected by a heavy slab. There was also a canteen full of water. I lost no time getting myself some breakfast, and then, hiding my own pack, I set off at a rapid pace, heading for town. I had scarcely gone a quarter of a mile, had, in fact, just reached a level, when sight of two horsemen halted me and made me take to cover. They appeared to be cowboys, hunting for a horse or a steer. Under the circumstances, however, I was suspicious, and I watched them closely and followed them a mile or so around the base of the ridges, until I had thoroughly satisfied myself they were not tracking Steele. They were a long time working out of sight, which further retarded my venturing forth into the open.

Finally I did get started. Then, about half way to town, more horsemen in the flat caused me to lie low for a while and make a wide detour to avoid being seen. Somewhat to my consternation it was afternoon before I arrived in town. For my life I could not have told why I knew something had happened since my last visit, but I certainly felt it and was proportionately curious and anxious.

The first person I saw whom I recognized was Dick, and he handed me a note from Ruth. She seemed to take it for granted that I had been wise to leave the ranch. Miss Longstreth had softened somewhat when she learned Ruth and I were engaged, and she had forgiven my deceit. Ruth asked me to come that night after eight, down among the trees and shrubbery, to a secluded spot we knew. It was a brief note and all to the point.

But there was something in it that affected me strangely.

I had imagined the engagement an invention for the moment. But after danger to me was past Ruth would not have carried on a pretense, not even to win back Miss Longstreth's respect. The fact was, Ruth meant that engagement. If I did the right thing now, I would not lose her. But what was the right thing?

I was sorely perplexed and deeply touched. Never had I a harder task than that of the hour — to put her out of my mind. I went boldly to Steele's house. He was not there. There was nothing by which I could tell when he had been there. The lamp might have been turned out or might have burned out. The oil was low. I saw a good many tracks around in the sandy walks. I did not recognize Steele's. As I hurried away, I detected more than one of Steele's nearest neighbors peering at me from windows and doors.

I went to Mrs. Laramie's. She was up and about and cheerful. The children were playing, manifestly well cared for and content. Mrs. Laramie had not seen Steele since I had. Miss Longstreth had sent her servant. There was a very decided change in the atmosphere of Mrs. Laramie's home, and I saw that for her the worst was past, and she was bravely, hopefully facing the future.

From there I hurried to the main street of Fairdale and to that section where violence brooded, ready at any chance moment to lift its hydra head. For that time of day the street seemed unusually quiet. Few pedestrians were abroad and few loungers. There was a row of saddled horses on each side of the street, the full extent of the block. I went into the big barroom of the Hope So.

I had never seen the place so full, nor had it ever seemed so quiet. The whole long bar was lined by shirt-sleeved men, with hats slouched back and vests flapping wide. Those who were not drinking were talking low. Half a dozen tables held as many groups of dusty, motley men, some silent, others speaking and gesticulating, all earnest. At first glance I did not see anyone in whom I had especial interest. The principal actors of my drama did not appear to be present. However, there were rough characters more in evidence than at any other time I had visited the saloon.

Voices were too low for me to catch, but I followed the direction of some of the significant gestures. Then I saw that these half dozen tables were rather closely grouped and drawn back from the center of the big room.

Next my quick sight took in a smashed table and chairs, some broken bottles on the floor, and then a dark sinister splotch of blood. I had not time to make inquiries, for my roving eye caught Frank Morton in the doorway, and evidently he wanted to attract my attention.

He turned away, and I followed. When I got outside, he was leaning against the hitching rail. One look at this rancher was enough for me to see that he had been told my part in Steele's game and that he himself had roused to the Texas fighting temper. He had a clouded brow and looked somber and thick. He also seemed slow, heavy, guarded.

"Howdy, Russ," he said. "We've been wantin' you. There's ten of us in town, all scattered 'round, ready. It's goin' to start today."

"Where's Steele?" was my first query.

"Saw him less'n an hour ago. He's somewhere's close. He may show up any time."

"Is he all right?"

"Wal, he was pretty fit a little while back," replied Morton significantly.

"What's come off? Tell me all."

"Wal, the ball opened last night, I reckon. Jack Blome came swaggerin' in here, askin' for Steele. We all knew what he was in town for. But last night he came out with it. Every man in the saloons, every man on the streets heard Blome's loud an' longin' call for the ranger. Blome's pals took it up, an' they all enjoyed themselves some."

"Drinking hard?"

"Nope . . . they didn't hit it up very hard. But they laid foundations. Of course, Steele was not to be seen last night. This mornin' Blome an' his gang were out pretty early. But they traveled alone. Blome just strolled up an' down by himself. I watched him walk up this street on one side an' then down the other just a matter of thirty-one times. I counted 'em. For all I could see, maybe Blome didn't take a drink. But his gang, especially Bo Snecker, sure looked on the red liquor.

"By eleven o'clock everybody in town knew what was comin' off. There was no work or business, 'cept in the saloons. Zimmer an' I were together, an' the rest of our crowd in pairs at different places. I reckon it was about noon when Blome got tired, paradin' up an' down. He went in the Hope So, an' the crowd followed. Zimmer stayed outside so to give Steele a hunch in case he came along. I went in to see the show.

"Wal, it was some curious to me. I've lived all my life in Texas, but I never before saw a gunman on the job, so to say. Blome's a handsome fellow, an' he seemed different from what I expected. Sure, I thought he'd yell an' prance 'round like a drunken fool. But he was cool an' quiet enough. The blowin' and drinkin' was done by his pals. After n while it got to me that Blome gloried in this situation. I've seen a man dead set to kill another all dark, sullen, restless, but Blome wasn't that way. He wasn't thinkin' about Steele. He didn't seem at all like a bloody devil. He was vain, cock-sure. He was revelin' in the effect he made. I had him figured all right.

"Blome sat on the edge of a table, an' he faced the door. Of course, there was a pard outside, ready to pop in an' tell him if Steele was comin'. But Steele didn't come in that way. He wasn't on the street just before that time, because Zimmer told me afterward. Steele must have been in the Hope So somewhere. Anyway, just like he dropped from the clouds, he came through the door near the bar. Blome didn't see him come. But most of the gang did, an' I want to tell you that big room went pretty quiet.

" 'Hello, Blome, I hear you're lookin' for me,' called out Steele.

"I don't know if he spoke ordinary or not, but his voice drew me up same as it did the rest, an' . . . damn me! . . . Blome seemed

348

to turn to stone. He didn't start or jump. He turned gray. An' I could see that he was tryin' to think in a moment when thinkin' was hard. Then he turned his head. Sure Blome expected to look into a six-shooter. But Steele was standin' back there in his shirt sleeves, his hands on his hips, an' he looked more man than anyone I ever saw. It's easy to remember the look of him, but how he made me feel, that isn't easy.

"Blome was at a disadvantage. He was half sittin' on a table, an' Steele was behind an' to the left of him. For Blome to make a move then would have been a fool play. He saw that. So did everybody. The crowd slid back without noise, but Bo Snecker an' a rustler named March stuck near Blome. I figured this Bo Snecker as dangerous as Blome, an' results proved I was right. Steele didn't choose to keep his advantage, so far as position in regard to Blome went. He just walked 'round in front of the rustler. But this put all the crowd in front of Steele, an' perhaps he had an eye for that.

" 'I hear you've been looking for me,' repeated the ranger.

"Blome never moved a muscle, but he seemed to come to life. It struck me that Steele's presence had made an impression on Blome which was new to the rustler.

" 'Yes, I have,' replied Blome.

" 'Well, here I am. What do you want?'

"When everybody knew what Blome wanted and had intended, this question of Steele's seemed strange, on one hand. An' yet, on the other, now that the ranger stood there, it struck me as natural enough.

" 'If you heard I was lookin' for you . . . you sure heard what for,' replied Blome.

" 'Blome, my experience with such men as you is that you'll brag one thing behind my back an' you mean different when I show up. I've called you now. What do *you* mean?'

" 'I reckon you know what Jack Blome means.'

" 'Jack Blome! That name means nothin' to me. Blome, you've been braggin' around that you'd meet me . . . kill me! You thought you meant it, didn't you?'

" 'Yes . . . I did mean it.'

" 'All right. Go ahead!'

"The barroom became perfectly still, except for the slow breaths I heard. There wasn't any movement anywhere. That queer gray came to Blome's face again. He might again have been stone, I thought, an' I'll gamble everyone else watchin' thought Blome would draw an' get killed in the act. But he never moved. Steele had cowed him. If Blome had been heated by drink or mad or anythin' but what he was just then, maybe he might have throwed a gun. But he didn't. I've heard of really brave men gettin' panic like that, an', after seein' Steele, I didn't wonder at Blome.

" 'You see, Blome, you don't want to meet me, for all your talk,' went on the ranger. 'You thought you did, but that was before you faced the man you intended to kill. Blome, you're one of these dandy, cock-of-the-walk four-flushers. I'll tell you how I know. Because I've met *real* gunfighters, an' there never was one of them yet who bragged or talked. Now don't you go 'round blowin' any more.'

"Then Steele deliberately stepped forward an' slapped Blome on one side of his face an' again on the other.

" 'Keep out of my way after this, or I'm liable to spoil some of your dandy looks.'

"Blome got up an' walked straight out of the place. I had my eyes on him, which kept me from seein' Steele. But on hearin' somethin', I don't know what, I turned back an' there Steele had got a long arm on Bo Snecker, who was tryin' to throw a gun. But he wasn't quick enough. The gun banged in the air, an' then it went spinnin' away, while Snecker dropped in a heap on the floor. The table was overturned, an' March, the other rustler, who was on that side, got up, pullin' his gun.

"But somebody in the crowd killed him before he could get goin'. I didn't see who fired that shot, an' neither did anybody else. But the crowd broke an' run. Steele drugged Bo Snecker down to jail an' locked him up."

Morton, having concluded his narrative, was evidently somewhat dry of tongue, since he produced knife and tobacco and cut himself a huge quid.

"That's all so far today, Russ, but I reckon you'll agree with me on the main issue . . . Steele's game's opened."

I had felt the rush of excitement, the old exultation at the prospect of danger, but this time there was something lacking in them. The wildness of the boy that had persisted in me was gone now.

"Yes, Steele has opened it, and I'm ready to boost the game along. Wait till I see him! But, Morton, you say someone you don't know played a hand in here and killed March."

"I sure do. It wasn't any of our men. Zimmer was outside. The others were at different places."

"The fact is, then, Steele has more friends than we know, perhaps more than he knew himself."

"Right. An' it's got the gang in the air. There'll be hell tonight."

"Steele hardly expects to keep Snecker in jail, does he?"

"I can't say. Probably not. I wish Steele had put both Blome and Snecker out of the way. We'd have less to fight."

"Maybe. I'm for the elimination method myself. But Steele doesn't follow out the gun method. He will use one only when he's driven. It's hard to make him draw. You know these desperate men aren't afraid of guns or fights, yet they're afraid of Steele. Perhaps it's his nerve, the way he faces them, the things he says, the fact that he has mysterious allies."

"Russ, we're all with him, an' I'll gamble that the honest citizens of Fairdale will flock to him in another day. I can see signs of that. There were twenty or more men on Laramie's list, but Steele didn't want so many."

"We don't need any more. Morton, can you give me any idea where Steele is?"

"Not the slightest."

"All right. I'll hunt for him. If you see him, tell him to hole up, and then you come after me. Tell him I've got our men spotted."

"Russ, if you ranger fellows ain't wonders!" exclaimed Morton, with shining eyes.

★ ★ ★

Steele did not show himself in town again
that day. Here his cunning was manifest. By
four o'clock that afternoon Blome was
drunk, and he and his rustlers went roaring
up and down the street. There was some
shooting, but I did not see or hear that
anyone was hurt. The lawless element, both
native to Fairdale and those visiting, followed in Blome's tracks from saloon to saloon. How often had I seen this sort of
procession, though not on so large a scale,
in many towns of wild Texas. The two great
and dangerous things in Fairdale at the hour
were whiskey and guns. Under such conditions the rustlers were capable of any mad
act or folly.

Morton and his men sent word flying
around town that a fight was imminent and
all citizens should be prepared to defend
their homes against possible violence. But
despite his warning I saw many respectable
citizens abroad whose quiet, unobtrusive
manner and watchful eyes and hard faces
told me that, when trouble began, they
wanted to be there. Verily Ranger Steele had
built his house of service upon a rock. It did
not seem too much to say that the next few
days, perhaps hours, would see a great
change in the character and a proportionate

decrease in number of the inhabitants of this corner of Pecos County.

Morton and I were in the crowd that watched Blome, Snecker, and a dozen other rustlers march down to Steele's jail. They had crowbars, and they had cans of giant powder which they had appropriated from a hardware store. If Steele had a jailer, he was not in evidence.

The door was wrenched off, and Bo Snecker, evidently not wholly recovered, was brought forth to his cheering comrades. Then some of the rustlers began to urge back the pressing circle, and the word given out acted as a spur to haste. The jail was to be blown up. The crowd split, and some men ran one way, some another. Morton and I were among those who hurried over the vacant ground to a little ridge that marked the edge of the open country. From this vantage point we heard several rustlers yell in warning, then they fled for their lives.

It developed that they might have spared themselves such headlong flight. The explosion appeared to be long in coming. At length we saw the lifting of the roof in a cloud of red dust, and then heard an exceedingly heavy but low detonation. When the pall of dust drifted away, all that was left of Steele's jail was a part of the stone walls.

The building that stood nearest, being constructed of adobe, had been badly damaged.

However, this wreck of the jail did not seem to satisfy Blome and his followers, for amid wild yells and huzzahs they set to work with crowbars and soon laid low every stone. Then with young Snecker in the fore they set off uptown. If this was not a gang in fit mood for any evil or any ridiculous celebration, I greatly missed my guess. It was a remarkable fact, however, and one that convinced me of deviltry afoot, that the crowd broke up, dispersed, and actually disappeared off the streets of Fairdale.

The impression given was that they were satisfied. But this impression did not remain with me. Morton was scarcely deceived, either. I told him that I would almost certainly see Steele early in the evening and that we would be out of harm's way. He told me that we could trust him and his men to keep sharp watch on the night's doings of Blome's gang. Then we parted.

It was almost dark. By the time I had gotten something to eat and drink at the Hope So, the hour for my meeting with Ruth was about due. On the way out I did not pass a lighted house until I got to the end of the street and then, strange to say, that one was Steele's. I walked down past the place, and, though I was positive he would not be there, I whistled low.

I halted and waited. He had two lights lit, one in the kitchen and one in the big room. The blinds were drawn. They were light-colored blinds and transparent. I saw a long dark shadow cross one window and then, a little later, cross the other. This would have deceived me had I not remembered Steele's device for casting the shadow. He had expected to have his house attacked at night, presumably while he was at home, but he had felt that it was not necessary for him to stay there to make sure. Lawless men of this class were sometimes exceedingly simple and gullible.

I bent my steps across the open, avoiding road and path, to the foot of the hill upon which Longstreth's house stood. It was dark enough under the trees. I could hardly find my way to the secluded nook and bench where I had been directed to come. I wondered if Ruth would be able to find it. Trust that girl! She might have a few qualms and come shaking a little, but she would be there on the minute.

I had hardly seated myself to wait when my keen ears detected something, then slight rustlings, then soft steps, and a dark form emerged from the blackness into the little starlit glade. Ruth came swiftly toward me and right into my arms.

That was sure a sweet moment. Through the excitement and dark boding thoughts of the day, I had forgotten that she would do just this thing. And now I anticipated tears, clingings, fears. But I was agreeably surprised.

"Archie, are you all right?" she whispered.

"Just at this moment I am," I replied.

Ruth gave me another little hug, and then, disengaging herself from my arms, she sat down beside me. "I can only stay a minute. Oh, it's safe enough. But I told Ray I was to meet you, and she's waiting to hear if Steele is . . . is . . ."

"Steele's safe so far," I interrupted.

"There were men coming and going all day. Uncle Granger never appeared at meals. He didn't eat, Ray said. Floyd tramped up and down, smoking, biting his nails, listening for these messengers. When they'd leave, he'd go in for another drink. We heard him roar someone had been shot, and we feared it might be Steele."

"No," I replied steadily.

"Did Steele shoot anybody?"

"No. A rustler named March tried to draw on Steele, and someone in the crowd killed March."

"Someone? Archie, was it you?"

"It sure wasn't. I didn't happen to be there."

"Ah! Then Steele has other men like you around him. I might have guessed that."

"Ruth, Steele makes men his friends. It's because he's on the side of justice."

"Ray will be glad to hear that. Archie, she doesn't think only of Steele's life. I believe she has a secret pride in his work. And I've an idea what she fears most is some kind of a clash between Steele and her father."

"I shouldn't wonder. Ruth, what does Ray know about her father?"

"Oh, she's in the dark. She got hold of papers that made her ask him questions. And his answers made her suspicious. She realizes he's not what he pretended to be all these years. But she never dreams her father is a rustler chief. When she finds that out . . ."

Ruth broke off, and I finished the sentence in thought. "Listen, Ruth," I said then, "I've an idea that Steele's house will be attacked by the gang tonight, and destroyed same as the jail was this afternoon. These rustlers are crazy. They'll expect to kill him while he's there. But he won't be there. If you and Ray hear shooting and yelling tonight, don't be frightened. Steele and I will be safe."

"Oh, I hope so. Archie, I must hurry back.

But, first, can't you arrange a meeting between Ray and Steele? It's her wish. She begged me to. She must see him."

"I'll try," I promised, knowing that promise would be hard to keep.

"We could ride out from the ranch somewhere. You remember we used to rest on the high ridge where there was a shady place . . . such a beautiful outlook? It was there I . . . I . . ."

"My dear, you needn't bring up painful memories. I remember where."

Ruth laughed softly. She could laugh in the face of the gloomiest prospects.

"Well, tomorrow morning, or the next, or any morning soon, you tie your red scarf on the dead branch of that high mesquite. I'll look every morning with the glass. If I see the scarf, Ray and I will ride out."

"That's fine. Ruth, you have ideas in your pretty little head. And once I thought it held nothing but . . ."

She put a hand on my mouth. "I must go now," she said, and rose. She stood close to me and put her arms around my neck. "One thing more, Archie. It . . . it was dif . . . ferent telling Ray we . . . we were engaged. I lied to Uncle. But *what else* could I have told Ray? I . . . I . . . Oh . . . was it . . . ?" She faltered.

"Ruth, you lied to Longstreth to save me. But you must have accepted me before you could have told Ray the *truth*."

"Oh, Archie, I had . . . in my heart! But it has been a long time since you asked me . . . and . . ."

"You imagined my offer might have been withdrawn. Well, it stands."

She slipped closer to me then, with that soft sinuousness of a woman, and I believed she might have kissed me had I not held back, toying with my happiness.

"Ruth, do you love me?"

"Ever so much. Since the very first."

"I'm a marshal, a ranger like Steele, a hunter of criminals. It's a hard life. There's spilling of blood. And any time I . . . I might . . . All the same, Ruth . . . will you be my wife?"

"Oh, Archie! Yes. But let me tell you, when your duty's done here, that *I* will have a word to say about your future. Archie, it'll be news to you to learn I'm an orphan. And I'm not a poor one. I own a plantation in Louisiana. I'll make a planter out of you. There!"

"Ruth! You're rich?" I exclaimed.

"I'm afraid I am. But nobody can ever say *you* married me for my money."

"Well, no, not if you tell of my abject

courtship when I thought you a poor relation on a visit. My God, Ruth, if I *only* could see this ranger job through safely and to success."

"You will," she said softly.

Then I took a ring from my little finger and slipped it on hers.

"That was my sister's. She's dead now. No other girl ever wore it. Let it be your engagement ring. Ruth, I pray I may somehow get through this awful ranger deal to make you happy . . . to become worthy of you."

"Archie, I fear only one thing," she whispered.

"And what's that?"

"There will be fighting. And you . . . Oh, I saw into your eyes the other night when you stood with your hands up. You would kill anybody, Archie. It's awful. But don't think me a baby. I can conceive what your work is . . . what a man you must be. I can love you and stick to you, too. But, if you killed a blood relative of mine, I would have to give you up. . . . I'm a Southerner, Archie, and blood is thick. I scorn my uncle, and I hate my cousin. And I love you. But don't you kill one of my family. I . . . Oh, I beg of you, go as far as you dare to avoid that."

I could find no voice to answer her, and for a long moment we were locked in an embrace, breast to breast and lips to lips — an embrace of sweet pain. Then she broke away, called a low, hurried good bye, and stole like a shadow into the darkness.

An hour later I lay in the open starlight among the stones and brush, out where Steele and I always met. He lay there with me, but, while I looked up at the stars, he had his face covered with his hands. For I had given him my proofs of the guilt of Ray Longstreth's father.

Steele had made one comment: "I wish to God I'd sent for some fool who'd have bungled the job!"

This was a compliment to me, but it showed what a sad pass Steele had come to. My regret was that I had no sympathy to offer him. I failed him there. I had trouble of my own. The feel of Ruth's clinging arms around my neck, the warm, sweet touch of her lips remained on mine. What Steele was enduring I did not know, but I felt that it was agony.

Meanwhile time passed. The blue, velvety sky darkened as the stars grew brighter. The wind grew stronger and colder. I heard sand blowing against the stones like the rustle of silk. Otherwise it was a singularly quiet night.

I wondered where the coyotes were and longed for their chorus. By and by a prairie wolf sent up his lonely lament from the distant ridges. That mourn was worse than the silence. It made the cold shudders creep up and down my back. It was just the cry that seemed to be the one to express my own trouble. No one hearing that long-drawn, quivering wail could ever dissociate it from tragedy. Finally it ceased, and then I wished it would come again.

Steele lay like the stone beside him. Was he ever going to speak? Among the vagaries of my mood was a petulant desire to have him sympathize with me. I had just looked at my watch, making out in the starlight that the hour was eleven, when the report of a gun broke the silence. I jumped up to peer over the stones. Steele lumbered up beside me, and I heard him draw his breath hard.

Chapter Fifteen

THE FIGHT IN THE HOPE SO

I could plainly see the lights of his adobe house, but, of course, nothing else was visible. There were no other lighted houses nearby. Several flashes gleamed, faded swiftly, to be followed by reports, and then the unmistakable jingle of glass.

"I guess the fools have opened up, Steele," I said.

His response was an angry grunt.

It was just as well, I concluded, that things had begun to stir. Steele needed to be roused. Suddenly a single sharp yell pealed out. Following it, came a huge flare of light, a sheet of flame in which a great cloud of smoke or dust shot up — then, with accompanying darkness, burst a low, deep, thunderous boom. The lights of the house went out — then came a crash.

Points of light flashed in a half-circle, and the reports of guns blended with the yells of furious men, and all these were swallowed up in the roar of a mob. Another and a heavier explosion momentarily lightened the darkness and then rent the air. It was succeeded by a continuous volley and a steady sound that, though composed of yells, screams, cheers, was not anything but a hideous roar of hate. It kept up long after there could have been any possibility of life under the ruins of that house. It was more than hate of Steele. All that was wild and lawless and violent hurled this deed at the ranger service.

Such events had happened before in Texas and other states, but, strangely, they never happened more than once in one locality. They were expressions, perhaps, that could never come but once. I watched Steele through all that hideous din, that manifestation of insane rage at his life and joy at his death, and, when silence once more reigned, and he turned his white face to mine, I had a sensation of dread. And dread was something particularly foreign to my nature.

"So Blome and the Sneckers think they've done for me," he muttered.

"Pleasant surprise for them tomorrow, eh, old man?" I queried.

"Tomorrow? Look, Russ, what's left of my old 'dobe house is on fire. The ruins can't be searched soon. And I was particular to fix things so it'd look like I was home. I just wanted to give them a chance. It's incomprehensible how easy men like them can be duped. Whiskey-soaked. Yes, they'll be surprised."

He lingered a while, watching the smoldering fire and the dim columns of smoke curling up against the dark blue.

"Russ, do you suppose they hear up at the ranch and think I'm . . . ?"

"They heard, of course," I replied. "But the girls know you're safe with me."

"Safe? I almost wish to God I was there under that heap of ruins, where the rustlers think they've left me."

"Well, Steele, old fellow, *almost* is not quite. Come on. We need some sleep."

Then, with Steele in the lead, we stalked away into the open.

Two days later, about the middle of the forenoon, I sat upon a great flat rock in the shade of a bushy mesquite, and, besides enjoying the vast clear sweep of gold and gray plain below, I was otherwise pleasantly engaged. Ruth sat as close to me as she could get, holding to my arm as if she never intended to let go. On the other side Miss Longstreth leaned against me, and she was white and breathless, partly from the quick ride out from the ranch, partly from agitation. She had grown thinner, and there were dark shadows under her eyes, yet she seemed only more beautiful.

The red scarf with which I had signaled the girls waved from a branch of the mesquite. At the foot of the ridge their horses were halted in a shady spot.

"Take off your sombrero," I said to Ruth. "You look hot. Besides, you're prettier with your hair flying."

As she made no move, I took it off for her. Then I made bold to perform the same office for Miss Longstreth. She faintly smiled her thanks. Assuredly she had forgotten all her resentment. There were little beads of perspiration upon her white brow. What a beautiful mass of black-brown hair, with strands of red or gold. Pretty soon she would be bending that exquisite head and face over poor Steele, and I, who had schemed this meeting, did not care what he might do to me. Pretty soon, also, there was likely to be an interview that would shake us all to our depths, and, naturally, I was somber at heart. But, though my outward mood of good humor may have been pretense, it certainly was a pleasure to be with the girls again way out in the open.

Both girls were quiet, and this made my task harder, and perhaps in my anxiety to ward off questions and appear happy for their own sakes I made an ass of myself with my silly talk and familiarity. Had ever a ranger such a job as mine?

"Ray, did Ruth show you her engagement ring?" I went on, bound to talk.

Miss Longstreth either did not notice my use of her first name, or she did not object. She seemed so friendly, so helplessly wistful.

"Yes. It's very pretty. An antique. I've seen a few of them," she replied.

"I hope you'll let Ruth marry me soon."

"Let her? Ruth Herbert! You haven't become acquainted with your fiancée. When . . . ?"

"Oh, next week, just as soon . . ."

"Archie!" cried Ruth, blushing furiously.

"What's the matter?" I queried innocently.

"You're a little previous."

"Well, Ruth, I don't presume to split hairs over dates. But, you see . . . you've become extremely more desirable . . . in the light of certain revelations. Ray, wasn't Ruth the deceitful thing? An heiress all the time. And I'm to be a planter and smoke fine cigars and drink mint juleps. No, there won't be any juleps."

"Archie, you're talking nonsense," reproved Ruth. "Surely it's no time to be funny."

"All right," I replied with resignation.

It was no task to discard that hollow mask of humor. A silence ensued, and I waited for it to be broken.

"Is Steele badly hurt?" asked Miss Longstreth presently.

"No. Not what he or I'd call hurt at all. He's got a scalp wound, where a bullet bounced off his skull. It's only a scratch. Then he's got another in the shoulder, but it's not bad, either."

"Where is he now?"

"Look across on the other ridge. See the big white stone? There, down under the trees, is our camp. He's there."

"When may . . . I see him?" There was a catch in her low voice.

"He's asleep now. After what happened yesterday, he was exhausted, and the pain in his head kept him awake till late. Let him sleep a while yet. Then you can see him."

"Did he know we were coming?"

"He hadn't the slightest idea. He'll be overjoyed to see you. He can't help *that*. But he'll about fall upon me with harmful intent."

"Why?"

"Well, I know he's afraid to see you."

"Why?"

"Because it only makes his duty harder."

"Ah," she breathed.

It seemed to me that my intelligence confirmed a hope of hers and gave her relief. I felt something terrible in the balance for Steele. And I was glad to be able to throw them together. The catastrophe must fall, and now the sooner it fell, the better. But I experienced a tightening of my lips and a tugging at my heart-strings.

"Ruth, what do you and Ray know about the goings-on in town yesterday?" I asked.

"Not much. Floyd was like an insane man. I was afraid to go near him. Uncle wore a sardonic smile. I heard him curse Floyd . . . oh, terribly! I believe he hates Floyd. Same as day before yesterday, there were men riding in and out. But Ray and I heard very little and conflicting statements at that. We knew there was fighting. Dick and the servants, the cowboys, all brought rumors. Steele was killed at least ten times and came to life just as many. I can't recall . . . don't want to recall . . . all we heard. But this morning, when I saw the red scarf flying in the wind . . . well, Archie, I was so glad I could not see through the glass any more. We knew then Steele was all right, or you wouldn't have put up the signal."

"Reckon few people in Fairdale realize just what *did* come off," I replied with a grim chuckle.

"Russ, I want you to tell me," said Miss Longstreth earnestly.

"What?" I queried sharply.

"About yesterday . . . what Steele did . . . what happened."

"Miss Longstreth, I could tell you in a few short statements of fact . . . or I could take two hours in the telling. Which do you prefer?"

"I prefer the long telling. I want to know all . . . all about him."

"But why, Miss Longstreth? Consider. This is hardly a story for a sensitive woman's ears."

"I am no coward," she replied, turning eyes to me that flashed like dark fire.

"But why?" I persisted.

I wanted a good reason for calling up all the details of the most strenuous and terrible day in my border experience. She was silent a moment. I saw her gaze turn to the spot where Steele lay asleep, and it was a pity he could not see her eyes then.

"Frankly, I don't want to tell you," I added, and I surely would have been glad to get out of the job.

"I want to hear . . . because I glory in his work," she replied deliberately.

I gathered as much from the expression on her face as from the deep ring of her voice, the clear content of her statement. She loved the ranger, but that was not all of her reason.

"His work?" I echoed. "Do you want him to succeed in it?"

"With all my heart," she said with a white glow on her face.

"My God!" I ejaculated.

I just could not help it. I felt Ruth's small fingers clutching my arm like sharp pincers. I bit my lips to keep them shut. What if Steele had heard her say that? Poor, noble, justice-loving, blind girl! She knew even less than I hoped.

I forced my thought on the question immediately at hand. She gloried in the ranger's work. She wanted with all her heart to see him succeed at it. She had a woman's pride in his manliness. Perhaps, with a woman's complex, incomprehensible motive, she wanted Steele to be shown to her in all the power that made him hated and feared by lawless men. She had finally accepted the wild life of this border as something terrible and inevitable, but passing. Steele was one of the strange and great and misunderstood men who were making that wild life pass.

For the first time I realized that Miss Longstreth, through sharpened eyes of love, saw Steele as he really was — a wonderful and necessary violence. Her intelligence and sympathy had enabled her to see through defamation and the false records following a ranger. She had had no choice but to love him, and then a woman's glory in work that freed men, saved women, and made children happy effaced forever the horror of a few dark deeds of blood.

"Miss Longstreth, I must tell you first that" — I began, and hesitated — "that I'm not a cowboy. My wild stunts, my drinking and gaming . . . these were all pretense."

"Indeed! I am very glad to hear it. And was Ruth in your confidence?"

"Only lately. I am a United States deputy marshal in the service of Steele."

She gave a slight start but did not raise her head.

"I have deceived you. But all the same, I've been your friend. I ask you to respect my secret a little while. I'm telling you because otherwise my relation to Steele yesterday would not be plain. Now, if you and Ruth will use this blanket, make yourselves more comfortable seats, I'll begin my story."

Miss Longstreth allowed me to arrange a place for her where she could rest at ease, but Ruth returned to my side and stayed there. She was an enigma today — pale, brooding, silent — and she never looked at me, except when my face was half averted.

"Well," I began, "night before last Steele and I lay hidden among the rocks near the edge of town, and we listened to and watched the destruction of Steele's house. It had served his purpose to leave lights burning, to have shadows blow across the window blinds, and to have a dummy in his bed. Also, he arranged guns to go off inside the house at the least jar. Steele wanted evidence against his enemies.

"It was not the pleasantest kind of thing to wait there, listening to that drunken mob. There must have been a hundred men. The disturbance and the intent worked strangely upon Steele. It made him different. In the dark I couldn't tell how he looked, but I felt a mood coming in him that fairly made me dread the next day.

"About midnight we started for our camp here. Steele got in some sleep, but I couldn't. I was cold and hot by turns, eager and backward, furious and thoughtful. You see, the deal was such a complicated one, and tomorrow certainly was nearing the climax. By morning I was sick, distraught, gloomy, and uncertain.

"I had breakfast ready when Steele awoke. I hated to look at him, but, when I did, it was like being revived.

"He said, 'Russ, you'll trail alongside me today and through the rest of this mess.'

"That gave me another shock. I want to explain to you girls that this was the first time in my life I was backward at the prospect of a fight. The shock was the jump of my pulse. My nerve came back. To line up with Steele against Blome and his gang . . . that would be great!

" 'All right, old man,' I replied. 'We're going after them, then?'

"He only nodded.

"After breakfast I watched him clean, oil, and reload his guns. I didn't need to ask him if he expected to use them. I didn't need to urge upon him Captain MacNeal's command.

" 'Russ,' said Steele, 'we'll go in together. But, before we get to town, I'll leave you, circle, and come in at the back of the Hope So. You hurry on ahead, post Morton and his men, get the lay of the gang, if possible, and then be at the Hope So when I come in.'

"I didn't ask him if I had a free hand with my gun. I intended to have that. We left camp together and hurried toward town. It was near noon when we separated.

"I came down the road, apparently from

Longstreth's ranch. There was a crowd around the ruins of Steele's house. It was one heap of crumbled 'dobe bricks and burned logs. It was still hot and smoking. No attempt had been made to dig into the ruins. The curious crowd was certain that Steele lay buried under all that stuff. I walked around with a busy tongue.

"One feature of that night assault made me ponder. Daylight discovered the bodies of three dead men, rustlers, who had been killed, the report went out, by random shots. Other participants in that affair had been wounded. I believed Morton and his men, under cover of the darkness and in the mêlée had sent in some shots not calculated upon in the program.

"From there I hurried to town. Just as I had expected, Morton and Zimmer were lounging in front of the Hope So. They had company, disreputable and otherwise. As yet Morton's crowd had not come under suspicion. He was wild for news of Steele, and, when I gave it and outlined the plan, he became as cool and dark and grim as any man of my kind could have wished.

"He sent Zimmer to get the others of their clique. Then he acquainted me with a few facts, although he was non-committal in regard to my suspicion as to the strange killing of the three rustlers. Blome, Bo Snecker, Hilliard, and Pickens, the ring-leaders, had painted the town in celebration of Steele's death. They all got gloriously drunk except old man Snecker. He had cold feet, they said. They were too happy to do any more shooting or mind what the old rustler cautioned. It was two o'clock before they went to bed.

"This morning, after eleven, one by one they appeared with their followers. The excitement had died down. Ranger Steele was out of the way, and Fairdale was once more wide open, free and easy. Blome alone seemed sullen and spiritless, unresponsive to his comrades and their admirers. And now, at the time of my arrival, the whole gang, with the exception of old Snecker, were assembled in the Hope So.

" 'Zimmer will be smart enough to drift his outfit along one or two at a time?' I asked Morton, and he reassured me. Then we went into the saloon.

"There were perhaps sixty or seventy men in the place, more than half of whom were in open accord with Blome's gang. Of the rest, there were many of doubtful repute, and a few that might have been apparently neutral yet all the time were secretly burning to help any cause against these rustlers. At all events, I gathered that impression from the shadowed faces, the tense bodies, the too-evident indication of anything but careless presence there.

"The windows were open. The light was clear. Few men smoked, but all had a drink before them. There was the ordinary subdued hum of conversation. I surveyed the scene, picked out my position so as to be close to Steele, when he entered, and sauntered around to it. Morton aimlessly leaned against a post. Presently Zimmer came in with a man, and they advanced to the bar. Other men entered as others went out.

"Blome, Bo Snecker, Hilliard, and Pickens had a table full in the light of the open windows. I recognized the faces of the two last-named, but I had not, until Morton informed me, known who they were. Pickens was little, scrubby, dusty, sandy, mottled, and he resembled a rattlesnake. Hilliard was big, gaunt, bronzed, with a huge mustache and hollow, fierce eyes. I never have seen a grave-robber, but I imagine one would look like Hilliard. Bo Snecker was a sleek, slim, slender, hard-looking boy, marked dangerous, because he was too young and too wild to have caution or fear.

"Blome, the last of the bunch, showed the effects of a bad night. You girls remember how handsome he was, but he didn't look it now. His face was swollen, dark red, and, as it had been bright, now it was dark. Indeed, he looked sullen, shamed, sore. He was sober now. Thought written on his clouded brow. He was awakening now to the truth that the day before had branded him a coward and that had sent him out to bolster up his courage with drink. His vanity had begun to bleed. He knew, if his faithful comrades had not awakened to it yet, that his prestige had been ruined. For a gunman, he had suffered the last degradation. He had been bidden to draw, and he had failed of nerve. He breathed heavily. His eyes were not clear. His hands were shaky. I almost pitied this rustler who very soon must face an incredibly swift and mercilessly fatal ranger . . . face him, too, suddenly, as if the grave had opened to give up its dead.

"Friends and comrades of this center group passed to and fro, and there was much lazy, merry, talk, though not very loud. The whole crowd was still half asleep. It certainly was an auspicious hour for Steele to confront them. No man knew the stunning, paralyzing effect of surprise better than Steele. I, of course, must take my cue from him or from the sudden development of events. But Jack Blome did not enter into my calculations. I gave him, at most, about a minute to live after Steele entered the place.

"I meant to keep sharp eyes all around. I knew, once with a gun out, Steele could kill Blome's comrades at the table as quick as lightning, if he chose. I rather thought my game was to watch his outside partners. This was right and, as it turned out, enabled me to save Steele's life.

"Moments passed, and still the ranger did not come. I began to get nervous. Had he been stopped? I scouted the idea. Who could have stopped him, then? Probably the time seemed longer than it really was. Morton showed the strain, also. Other men looked drawn, haggard, waiting, as if expecting a thunderbolt. Once in my roving gaze I caught Blandy's glinty eye on me. I didn't like the gleam. I said to myself I'd watch him, if I had to do it out of the back of my head. Blandy, by the way, is . . . *was* I should say . . . the Hope So bartender."

I stopped to clear my throat and got my breath.

"*Was,*" whispered Ruth. She quivered with excitement.

Miss Longstreth bent eyes upon me that would have stirred a stone man.

"Yes, he was once," I replied ambiguously, but mayhap my grimness betrayed the truth. "Don't hurry me, Ruth. I guarantee you'll be sick enough presently.

"Well, I kept my eyes shifty. And I reckon I'll never forget that room. Likely I saw what wasn't really there. In the excitement, the suspense, I must have made shadows into real substance. Anyway, there was the half-circle of bearded, swarthy men around Blome's table. There were the four rustlers . . . Blome, brooding, perhaps vaguely, spiritually, listening to a knock . . . there was Bo Snecker, reckless youth, fondling a flower he had, putting the stem in his glass, then to his lips, and lastly into the button-hole of Blome's vest . . . there was Hilliard, big, gloomy, maybe with his cavernous eyes seeing the hell where I expected he'd soon be . . . and last, the little dusty, scaly Pickens, who looked about to leap and sting someone.

"In a lull of the general conversation, I heard Pickens say, 'Jack, drink up an' come out of it. Every man has an off day. You've gambled long enough to know every feller gits called. An', as Steele has cashed, what the hell do you care?'

"Hilliard nodded his ghoul's head and blinked his dead eyes. Bo Snecker laughed. It wasn't a different laugh from any other boy's. I remembered then that he killed

Laramie. I began to sweat fire. Would Steele ever come?

" 'Jim, the ole man hed cold feet, an' he's give 'em to Jack,' said Bo. 'It ain't nothin' to lose your nerve once. Didn't I run like a scared jackrabbit from Steele? Watch me, if he comes to life, as the old man hinted.'

" 'Mebbe Steele wasn't in the 'dobe at all. Aw, thet's a joke! I seen him in bed. I seen his shoulder. I heard his shots comin' from the room. Jack, you seen an' heerd same as me.'

" 'Sure. I *know* the ranger's cashed,' replied Blome. 'It's not that. I'm sore, boys.'

" 'Deader'n a doornail in hell,' replied Pickens, louder, as he lifted his glass. 'Here's to Lone Star Steele's ghost! An', if I seen it this minnit, I'd ask it to waltz with me.'

"The back door swung violently, and Steele, huge as a giant, plunged through and leaped square in front of that table. Someone among them let out a strange, harsh cry. It wasn't Blome or Snecker . . . probably Pickens. He dropped the glass he had lifted. The cry had stilled the room, so the breaking of the glass was plainly heard.

"For a space that must have been short, yet seemed long, everybody stood tight. Steele, with both hands out and down, leaned a little, in a way I had never seen him

383

do. It was the position of a greyhound, but that was merely the body of him. Steele's nerve, his spirit, his meaning was there, like lightning about to strike. Blome maintained a ghastly, stricken silence. Then the instant was plain when he realized this was no ghost of Steele, but the ranger in the flesh. Blome's whole frame rippled as thought jerked him out of his trance. His comrades sat stone-still. Then Hilliard and Pickens dived without rising from the table. Their haste broke the spell.

"I wish I could tell it as quick as it happened. But Bo Snecker, turning white as a sheet, stuck to Blome. And the others failed him, as he had guessed they would fail. Low curses and exclamations were uttered by men, sliding and pressing back, but the principals were mute. I was thinking hard, yet I had no time to get to Steele's side. I, like the rest, was held fast. But I kept my eyes sweeping around, then back again to that center pair.

"Blome slowly rose. I think he did it instinctively because, if he had expected his first movement to start the action, he never would have moved. Snecker sat partly on the rail of his chair, with both feet square on the floor, and he never twitched a muscle. There was a striking difference in the looks of these two rustlers . . . Snecker had burning holes for eyes in his white face. At the last he was stanch, defiant, game to the core. He didn't think. But Blome faced death and knew it. It was infinitely more than the facing of foes, the taking of stock, preliminary to the even break. Blome's attitude was that of a trapped wolf about to start into savage action . . . nevertheless, it was also the pitifully weak stand of a ruffian against ruthless and powerful law.

"The border of Pecos County could have had no greater lesson than this . . . Blome face-to-face with the ranger. That part of the border present saw its most noted exponent of lawlessness a coward, almost powerless to go for his gun, fatally sure of his own doom. But that moment . . . seeming so long, and really so short . . . had to end. Blome made a spasmodic upheaval of shoulder and arm. Snecker a second later flashed into movement.

"Steele blurred in my sight. His action couldn't be followed. But I saw his gun, waving up, flame red, once . . . twice . . . and the reports almost boomed together.

"Blome bent forward, arm down, doubled up, and fell over the table and slid to the floor. But Snecker's gun cracked with Steele's last shot. I heard the bullet strike

Steele. It made me sick as if it had hit me. Steele never budged. Snecker leaped up, screaming. His gun went clattering to the floor. His left hand swept to his right arm, which had been shattered by Steele's bullet. Blood streamed everywhere. His screams were curses, and then ended, choking him in rage hardly human. Leaping, he went down on his knees after the gun.

" 'Don't pick it up!' called Steele, and his command would have checked anyone save an insanely maddened youth. For an instant it even held Snecker. On his knees, right arm hanging limp, left extended, and face ghastly with agony and fiendish fury, he certainly was an appalling sight.

" 'Bo, you're courtin' death!' called a hard voice from the crowd.

" 'Snecker, wait! Don't make me kill you!' cried Steele swiftly. 'You're only a boy. Surrender! You'll outlive your sentence many years. I promise clemency. Hold, you fool . . . !'

"But Snecker was not to be denied his last game move. He scrabbled for his gun. Just then something, a breath perhaps, or intuition . . . I'll never know what . . . made me turn my head. I saw Blandy, the bartender, deliberately aiming a huge gun at Steele. If he had not been so slow, so sure, I would

386

have been too late. I whirled and shot. Talk about nick of time! Blandy pulled trigger just as my bullet smashed into his head. He dropped dead behind the bar, and his gun dropped in front. But he had hit Steele.

"The ranger staggered, almost fell. I thought he was done, and, yelling, I leaped to him. But he righted himself. Then, as I wheeled again, someone in the crowd killed Bo Snecker as he wobbled up with his gun. That was the signal for a wild break for outdoors, for cover. I heard the crack of guns and whistle of lead. I shoved Steele back of the bar, falling over Blandy as I did so.

"When I got up, Steele was leaning over the bar with a gun in each hand. There was a hot fight, then, for a minute or so, but I didn't fire a shot. Morton and his crowd were busy.

"Men ran everywhere, shooting, ducking, cursing. The room got blue with smoke till you couldn't see, and then the fight changed to the street. Steele and I ran out. There was shooting everywhere. Morton's crowd appeared to be in pursuit of rustlers in all directions. I ran with Steele and did not observe his condition until suddenly he fell down in the street. He looked so white and so bloody I thought he'd stopped another bullet and . . ."

Here Miss Longstreth's agitation made it necessary for me to halt my story, and I hoped she had heard enough. But she was not sick, as Ruth appeared to be. She simply had been overcome by emotion. And presently, with a blaze in her eyes that showed how her soul was aflame with righteous wrath at these rustlers and ruffians, and how, whether she knew it or not, the woman in her loved a fight, she bade me go on.

So I persevered, and, with poor little Ruth sagging against me, I went on with the details of that fight. I told how Steele rebounded from his weakness and could no more have been stopped than an avalanche. For all I saw, he did not use his guns again.

Here, there, everywhere, as Morton and his squad cornered a rustler, Steele would go in, ordering surrender, promising protection. He seemed to have no thought of bullets. I could not hold him back, and it was hard to keep pace with him. How many times he was shot at, I had no idea, but it was many. He dragged forth this and that rustler and turned them all over to Morton to be guarded. More than once he protected a craven rustler from the summary dealing Morton wanted.

I told Miss Longstreth particularly how Steele appeared to me, what his effect was on these men, how toward the end of the fight rustlers were appealing to him to save them from these new-born vigilantes. I believe I drew a picture of the ranger that would live forever in her heart of hearts. If she were a hero-worshiper, she would have her fill.

One thing that was strange to me — leaving fight, action, blood, peril out of the story — was the singular exultation, for want of some better term, that I experienced in recalling Steele's look, his wonderful, cold, resistless, inexplicable presence, his unquenchable spirit that was at once deadly and merciful. Other men would have killed where he saved. I recalled this magnificent spiritual something about him, remembered it strongest in the ring of his voice as he appealed to Bo Snecker not to force him to kill.

Then I told how we left a dozen prisoners under guard and went back to the Hope So to find Blome where he had fallen. Steele's bullet had cut one of the petals of the rose Snecker had playfully put in the rustler's buttonhole. Bright and fatal target for an eye like Steele's.

Bo Snecker lay clutching his gun, his face set rigidly in that last fierce expression of his savage nature. There were five other dead men on the floor, and, significant of the work of Steele's unknown allies, Hilliard and Pickens were among them.

"Steele and I made for camp then," I concluded. "We didn't speak a word on the way out. When we reached camp, all Steele said was for me to go off and leave him alone. He looked sick.

"I went off, only not very far. I knew what was wrong with him, and it wasn't bullet wounds. I was near when he had his spell and fought it out. Strange how spilling blood effects some men. It never bothered me much. I hope I'm human, too. I certainly felt like a . . . an awful joy when I sent that bullet into Blandy's bloated head in time. And I'll always feel that way about it. But Steele's different."

Chapter Sixteen

TORN TWO WAYS

Steele lay in a shady little glade, partly walled by masses of uprearing rocks that we used as a look-out point. He was asleep, yet far from comfortable. The bandage I had put around his head had been made from strips of soiled towel, and, having collected sundry bloody spots, it was an unsightly affair. There was a blotch of dried blood down one side of Steele's face. His shirt bore more dark stains and in one place was pasted fast to his shoulder where a bandage marked the location of his other wound.

A number of green flies were crawling over him and buzzing around his head. He looked helpless, despite his giant size, and certainly a great deal worse off than I had intimated and, in fact, than he really was. Miss Longstreth gasped when she saw him, and both her hands flew to her breast.

"Girls, don't make any noise," I whispered. "I'd rather he didn't wake suddenly to find you here. Go 'round behind the rocks there. I'll wake him and call you presently."

They complied with my wish, and I stepped down to Steele and gave him a little shake. He awoke instantly.

"Howdy, old son. Want a drink?"

"Water or champagne?" he inquired.

I stared at him. "I've some champagne behind the rocks."

"Water, you locoed son of a gun!"

He looked about as thirsty as a desert coyote; he also looked flighty. I was reaching for the canteen when I happened to think what a pleasure it would be to Miss Longstreth to minister to him, and I drew back.

"Wait a little." Then with an effort I plunged. "Vaughn, listen. Miss Longstreth and Ruth are here."

I thought he was going to jump up he started so violently. I pressed him back.

"*She* . . . ? Why, has she been here all the time? Russ, you haven't double-crossed me?"

"Steele!" I exclaimed. He was certainly out of his head. "Pure accident, old man."

He appeared to be half stunned, yet an eager, strange, haunting look shone in his eyes.

"Fool!" he exclaimed.

"Can't you make the ordeal easier for her?" I asked. "This'll be hard on Ray. She's got to be told things."

"Ah," breathed Steele, sinking back. "Make it easier for her . . . Russ, you're a damned schemer. You *have* given me the double-cross. You have, and she's going to."

"We're in bad, both of us," I replied thickly. "I've ideas, crazy enough maybe. I'm between the devil and the deep sea, I tell you. I'm about ready to show yellow. . . . All the same, I say, see Miss Longstreth and talk to her, even if you can't talk straight."

"All right, Russ," he replied hurriedly. "But God, man, don't I look a sight . . . ? All this dirt and blood!"

"Well, old man, if she takes that bungled mug of yours in her lap, you can be sure you're loved. You needn't jump out of your boots. Brace up, now, for I'm going to bring the girls."

As I got up to go, I heard him groan. I went around behind the stones and found them.

"Come on," I said. "He's awake now, but a little queer. Feverish. He gets that way sometimes. It won't last long."

I led Miss Longstreth and Ruth back into the shade of our little camp glade. Steele had gotten worse all in a moment. Also the fool had pulled the bandage off his head. His wound had begun to bleed anew, and the flies were paying no attention to his weak efforts to brush them away. His head rolled as we reached his side, and his eyes were certainly wild and wonderful and devouring enough.

"Who's that?" he demanded.

"Easy there, old man," I replied. "I've brought the girls."

Miss Longstreth shook like a leaf in the wind.

"So you've come to see me die?" asked Steele in a deep and hollow voice.

Miss Longstreth gave me a lightning glance of terror.

"He's only off his head," I said. "Soon as we wash and bathe his head . . . cool his temperature, he'll be all right."

Miss Longstreth dropped to her knees, flinging her gloves aside. She lifted Steele's head into her lap. When I saw her tears falling upon his face, I felt worse than a villain. She bent over him for a moment, and one of the tender hands at his cheeks met the flow of fresh blood and did not shrink. "Ruth," she said, "bring the scarf out of my coat. There's a veil, too. Bring that. Russ, you get me some water . . . pour some in the pan there."

"Water," whispered Steele.

She gave him a drink.

Ruth came with the scarf and veil, and

then she backed away to a large stone and sat there. The sight of blood had made her a little pale and weak. Miss Longstreth's hands trembled, and her tears still fell, but neither interfered with her tender and skillful dressing of that bullet wound. Steele certainly said a lot of crazy things.

"But why'd you come . . . why're you so good . . . when you don't love me?"

"Oh, but . . . I do . . . love you," whispered Miss Longstreth brokenly.

"How do I know?"

"I'm here. I tell you."

There was a silence, during which she kept on bathing his head, and he kept on watching her. "Ray!" he broke out suddenly.

"Yes . . . yes."

"That won't stop the pain in my head."

"Oh, I hope so."

"Kiss me . . . that will," he whispered.

She obeyed, as a child might have, and kissed his damp forehead close to the red furrow where the bullet had cut.

"Not there," Steele whispered.

Then blindly, as if drawn by a magnet, she bent to his lips. I could not turn away my head, though my instincts were delicate enough. I believe that kiss was the first kiss of love for both Ray Longstreth and Vaughn Steele. It was so strange, so long, and somehow beautiful.

Steele looked rapt. I could only see the side of her face and that was white, like snow. After she raised her head, she seemed unable, for a moment, to take up her task where it had been broken off, and Steele lay as if he really were dead. Here I got up, and, seating myself beside Ruth, I put an arm around her.

"Dear Ruth, there are others," I said.

"Oh . . . Archie . . . what's to come of it all?" she faltered, and then she broke down and began to cry softly.

I would have been only too glad to tell her what hung in the balance, one way or another, had I known — but, surely, catastrophe. Then I heard Steele's voice again, and its huskiness, its different tone, made me fearful, made me strain my ears when I tried, or thought I tried, not to listen.

"Ray, you know how hard my duty is, don't you?"

"Yes . . . I know . . . I *think* I know."

"You've guessed . . . about your father?"

"I've seen all along you must clash. But it needn't be . . . so bad. If I can only bring you two together . . . ? Ah, please don't speak any more. You're excited now, not just yourself."

"No, listen. We *must* clash, your father

and I. Ray, he's not . . ."

"Not what he seems! Oh, I know, to my sorrow."

"*What* do you know?"

She seemed drawn by a will stronger than her own. "To my shame I know. He has been greedy, crafty, unscrupulous . . . dishonest."

"Ray, if he were only that. That wouldn't make my duty torture. That wouldn't ruin your life. . . . Dear, sweet girl . . . forgive me . . . your father's . . ."

"Hush, Vaughn. You're growing excited. It will not do. Please . . . please . . . !"

"Ray, your father's . . . chief of this . . . gang that I came to break up."

"My God, hear him . . . ! How dare you . . . ? Oh, Vaughn, poor, poor boy, you're out of your mind. Ruth, Russ, what shall we do? He's worse. He's saying the most dreadful things. I . . . I can't bear to hear him."

Steele heaved a sigh and closed his eyes. I walked away with Ruth, led her to and fro in a shady aisle beyond the rocks, and tried to comfort her as best I could. After a while, when we returned to the glade, Miss Longstreth had considerable color in her cheeks, and Steele was leaning against the rock, grave and sad. I saw that he had recovered, and he had reached the critical point.

"Hello, Russ," he said. "Sprung a little

surprise on me, didn't you? Miss Longstreth says I've been a little flighty while she bandaged me up. I hope I wasn't bad. I certainly feel better now. I seemed to . . . to have dreamed."

Miss Longstreth flushed at his concluding words. Then silence ensued. I could not think of anything to say, and Ruth was silent.

"You all seem very strange," said Miss Longstreth.

When Steele's face turned gray to his lips, I knew the moment had come.

"No doubt. We all feel so deeply for you," he said.

"Me? Why?"

"Because the truth must no longer be concealed."

It was her turn to blanch, and her eyes, strained, dark as night, flashed from one of us to the other.

"The truth. Tell it, then." She had more courage than any of us.

"Miss Longstreth, your father is the leader of this gang of rustlers I have been tracing. Your cousin, Floyd Lawson, is his right-hand man."

Miss Longstreth heard, but she did not believe.

"Tell her, Russ," Steele added huskily, turning away.

398

Wildly she turned to me. I would have given anything to have been able to lie to her. As it was, I could not speak. But she read the truth in my face. And she collapsed as if she had been shot.

I caught her and laid her on the grass. Ruth, murmuring and crying, worked over her. I helped. But Steele stood aloof, dark and silent, as if he hoped she would never return to consciousness. When she did come to and began to cry, to moan, to talk frantically, Steele swaggered away, while Ruth and I made futile efforts to calm her. All we could do was to prevent her doing herself violence.

Presently, when her fury of emotion subsided, and she began to show a hopeless, stricken shame, I left Ruth with her and went off a little way myself. How long I remained absent, I had no idea, but it was no inconsiderable length of time.

Upon my return, to my surprise and relief, Miss Longstreth had recovered her composure or, at least, self-control. She stood, leaning against the rock where Steele had been, and at this moment, beyond any doubt, she was supremely more beautiful than I had ever seen her. She was white, tragic, wonderful.

"Where is Mister Steele?" she asked.

Her tone and her look did not seem at all suggestive of the mood I expected to find her in — one of beseeching agony — of passionate appeal to Steele not to ruin her father.

"I'll find him," I replied, turning away.

Steele was readily found and came back with me. He was as unlike himself as she was strange. But, when they again faced each other, then they were indeed new to me.

"I want to know . . . what you must do," she said.

Steele told her briefly, and his voice was stern.

"Those . . . those criminals outside of my own family don't concern me now," she said then. "But can my father and cousin be taken without bloodshed? I want to know the absolute truth."

Steele knew that they could not be, but he could not tell her so. Again she appealed to me. Thus my part in the situation grew harder. It hurt me so that it made me angry, and my anger made me cruelly frank.

"No. It can't be done. Longstreth and Lawson will be desperately hard to approach, which'll make the chances even. So, if you must know the truth, it'll be your father and cousin who'll go under . . . or it'll be Steele or me . . . or any combination,

400

as luck would have it . . . perhaps all of us."

Her self-control seemed to fly to the four winds. Swift as light she flung herself down before Steele, against his knees, clasping her arms around him.

"Good God! Ray, you mustn't do that," implored Steele. He tried to break her hold with shaking hands, but he could not.

"Listen! Listen!" she cried, and her voice made Steele, and Ruth and me also, still as the rocks behind us. "Hear me! Do you think I beg you to let my father go, for his sake? No! No! I have glorified in your ranger duty. I have loved you because of it. But some awful tragedy threatens here. Listen, Vaughn Steele. Do not you deny me, as I kneel here. I love you. I never loved any other man. But not for my love do I beseech you. There is no help here unless you forswear your duty. Forswear it! Do not kill my father . . . the father of the woman who loves you. Worse and more horrible it would be to let my father kill you! It's I who make this situation unnatural, impossible. You must forswear your duty. I can live . . . no longer if you don't. I pray you. . . ."

Her voice had sunk to a whisper, and now it failed. Then she seemed to get into his arms, to wind herself around him, her hair loosened, her face upturned white and spent, her arms blindly circling his neck. She was all love, all surrender, all supreme appeal, and these alone, without her beauty, would have made her wonderful. But her beauty! Would not Steele have been less than a man, or more than a man, had he been impervious to it? She was like some snow-white exquisite flower, broken, and suddenly blighted. She was a woman then in all that made a woman helpless — in all that made her mysterious, sacred, absolutely and unutterably more than any other thing in life.

All this time my gaze had been riveted on her only. But, when she lifted her white face, tried to lift it, rather, and he drew her up — and then, when both white faces met and seemed to blend in something rapt, awesome, tragic as life — then I saw Steele. I saw a god, a man as beautiful as she was. They might have stood — indeed, they did stand — alone in the heart of a desert — alone in the world — alone with their love and their agony.

It was a solemn and profound moment for me. I faintly realized how great it must have been for them, yet all the while there hammered at my mind the vital thing at stake. Had they forgotten, while I remembered?

It might have been only a moment that he held her. It might have been my own agitation that conjured up such swift and whirling thoughts. But, if my mind sometimes played me false, my eyes never had. I thought I saw Ray Longstreth die in Steele's arms. I could have sworn his heart was breaking, and mine was on the point of breaking, too.

How beautiful they were together. How strong, how mercifully strong, yet shaken he seemed. How tenderly, hopelessly, fatally appealing she was in that hour of her broken life. If I had been Steele, I would have forsworn my duty, honor, name, service for her sake. Did I even have mind enough to divine his torture, his temptation, his narrow escape? I seemed to feel them, at any rate, and, while I saw him with a beautiful light on his face, I saw him also ghastly, ashen, with hands that shook as they groped around her, loosing her only to draw her convulsively back again.

It was the saddest sight I had ever seen. Death was nothing to it. Here was the death of happiness. He must wreck the life of the woman who loved him and whom he loved.

I was becoming half frantic, almost ready to cry out at the uselessness of this scene, almost on the point of pulling them apart, when Ruth dragged me away. Her clinging hold then made me feel perhaps a little of what Miss Longstreth's must have been to Steele. Yet, how different the feeling when it was mine! I could have thrust them apart, after all my schemes and tricks to throw them together, in vague, undefined fear of their embrace. Still, when love beat at my own pulses, when Ruth's soft hand held me tight, and she leaned to me — that was different. I was glad to be led away — glad to have a chance to pull myself together.

But was I to have that chance? Ruth, who in the strife of emotion had been forgotten, might have to be reckoned with. Deep within me some motive, some purpose, was being born in travail. I did not know what, but instinctively I feared Ruth. I feared her because I loved her.

My wits came back to combat my passion. This hazel-eyed girl, soft, fragile creature, might be harder to move than the ranger. But could she divine a motive scarcely yet formed in my brain? Suddenly I became cool, with craft to conceal.

"Oh, Archie! What's the matter with you?" she queried quickly. "Can't Ray and Steele, you and I ride away from this bloody, bad country? Our own lives, our happiness, come first, don't they?"

"They ought to, I suppose," I muttered, fighting against the insidious sweetness of her. I knew then I must keep my lips shut or betray myself.

"You look so strange. Archie, I wouldn't want you to kiss me with that mouth. Thin, shut lips . . . smile! Soften and kiss me. Oh, you're so cold, strange. You chill me."

"Dear child, I'm badly shaken," I said. "Don't expect me to be natural yet. There are things you can't guess. So much depended upon . . . Oh, never mind! I'll go now. I want to be alone . . . to think things out. Let me go, Ruth."

She held me only the tighter — tried to pull my face around. How intuitively keen women are. She felt my distress and that growing, stern, and powerful thing I scarcely dared acknowledge to myself.

Strangely, then, I relaxed and faced her. There was no use trying to fool these feminine creatures. Every second I seemed to grow farther from her. The swiftness of this mood of mine was my only hope. I realized I had to get away quickly and make up my mind after that what I intended to do.

It was an earnest, soulful, and loving pair of eyes that I met. What did she read in mine? Her hands left mine to slide to my shoulders, to slip behind my neck, to lock there like steel bands. Here was my ordeal. Was it to be as terrible as Steele's had been?

I thought it would be, and I swore by all that was rising grim and cold in me that I would be strong. Ruth gave a little cry that cut like a blade in my heart, and then she was pressed close against me, her quivering breast beating against mine, her eyes, dark as night now, searching my soul.

She saw more than I knew and with her convulsive clasp of me confirmed my half-formed fears. Then she kissed me — kisses that had no more of girlhood or coquetry or joy or anything but woman's passion to blind and hold and tame. By their very intensity I sensed the tiger in me. And it was the tiger that made her new and alluring sweetness fail of its intent. I did not return one of her kisses. Just one kiss given back — and I would be lost.

"Oh, Archie, I'm your promised wife," she whispered at my lips. "Soon, you said. I want it to be . . . soon. *Tomorrow!*"

All the subtlety, the intelligence, the cunning, the charm, the love that made up the whole of woman's power breathed in her pleading. What speech known to the tongue could have given me more torture? She chose the strongest weapon nature afforded her. And had the calamity to consider been mine alone, I would have laughed at it and taken Ruth at her word.

Then I told her in short, husky sentences what had depended on Steele — that I loved the ranger service, but loved him more; that his character, his life, embodied this service I loved; that I had ruined him; and now I would forestall him, do his work, force the issue myself or die in the attempt.

"Dearest, it's great of you," she cried. "But the cost. If you kill one of my kin, I'll . . . I'll shrink from you! If you're killed . . . ? Oh, the thought is dreadful. You've done your share. Let Steele . . . or some other ranger . . . finish it. I swear I don't plead for my uncle or my cousin, for their sakes. If they are vile, let them suffer. Archie, it's *you* I think of. Oh, my pitiful little dreams. I wanted so to surprise you with my beautiful home . . . the oranges, the mossy trees, the mockingbirds. Now you'll never . . . never come."

"But Ruth, there's a chance . . . a mere chance I can do the job without . . ."

Then she let go of me. She had given up. I thought she was going to drop and drew her toward the stone. I cursed the day I ever saw MacNeal and the service.

Where, now, was the arch prettiness, the gay, sweet charm of Ruth Herbert? She looked as if she were suffering from a desperate physical injury. And her final breakdown showed how, one way or another, I was lost to her. As she sank on the stone, I had my supreme wrench, and it left me numb, hard, in a cold sweat.

"Don't betray me. I'll forestall him. He's planned nothing for today," I whispered hoarsely. "Ruth . . . you dearest, gamest little girl in the world. Remember, I loved you . . . even if I couldn't prove it . . . your way. It's for his sake. I'm to blame for their love. Some day my act will look different to you. Good-bye."

Chapter Seventeen

RUSS SITTELL IN ACTION

I ran like one possessed of devils down that rough slope, hurdling the stones and crashing through the brush, with a sound in my ears that was not all the rush of the wind. When I reached a level, I kept running, but something dragged at me.

I slowed down to a walk. Never in my life had I been victim of such sensations. I must flee from something that was drawing me back. Apparently one side of my mind was unalterably fixed, while the other was a hurrying conglomeration of flashes of thought, receiving of sensations. I could not get calmness.

By and by, almost involuntarily, with a fleeting look backward as if in expectation of pursuit, I hurried on faster. Action seemed to make my state less oppressive. It eased the weight upon me. But the farther I went on, the harder it was to continue. I was turning my back upon love, happiness, success in life, perhaps on life itself. I was doing that, but my decision had not been absolute.

There seemed no use to go on farther until I was absolutely sure of myself. I received a clear warning thought that such work as seemed haunting and driving me could never be carried out in the mood under which I labored. I clung onto that thought. Several times I slowed up, then stopped, only to tramp on again.

At length, as I mounted a low ridge, Fairdale lay bright and green before me, not far away, and the sight was a conclusive check. There were mesquites on the ridge, and I sought the shade beneath them. It was the noon hour, with hot, glaring sunlight, and no wind. Here I had to fight it out.

If ever in my varied life of exciting adventure I strove to think, to understand myself, to see through difficulties, I assuredly strove then. I was utterly unlike myself. I could not bring the old self back. I was not the same man I once had been. But I could understand why. It was because of Ruth Herbert — the gay and roguish girl who had bewitched me — the girl whom love had made a woman — the kind of woman meant to make life beautiful for me.

I saw her changing through all these weeks, holding many of the old traits and graces, acquiring new character of mind and body, to become what I had just fled from

410

— a woman sweet, fair, loyal, loving, passionate. Temptation assailed me. To have her tomorrow — my wife! She had said it. Just one little twenty-four hours, and she would be mine — the only woman I ever really coveted — the only one who had ever found the good in me. The thought was alluring.

I followed it out — a long, happy stage ride back to Austin, and then by train to her home where, as she had said, the oranges grew, and the trees waved with streamers of gray moss, and the mockingbirds made melody. I pictured that home. I wondered that long before I had not associated wealth and luxury with her family. Always I had owned a weakness for plantations, for the agricultural life with its open air and freedom from towns. I saw myself, riding through the cotton and rice and cane, at home in a stately old mansion, where long-eared hounds bayed me welcome, and a woman looked for me and met me with happy and beautiful smiles.

There might — there would be children. And something new, strange, confounding with its emotion came to life deep in my heart. There would be children! Ruth, their mother, I, their father. The kind of life a lonely ranger always yearned for and never had. I saw it all, felt it keenly, lived its sweetness in an hour of temptation that made me weak physically and my spirit faint and low.

For what had I turned my back on this beautiful, all-satisfying prospect? Was it to arrest and jail a few rustlers? Was it to meet that mocking Longstreth face to face and show him my shield and reach for my gun? Was it to kill that hated Lawson? Was it to save the people of Fairdale from further greed, raid, murder? Was it to please and aid my old captain, MacNeal of the Texas Rangers? Was it to save the service to the state? No — a thousand times no. It was for the sake of Steele. Because he was a wonderful man. Because I had been his undoing. Because I had thrown Ray Longstreth into his arms.

That had been my great error. This ranger had always been the wonder and despair of his fellow officers — so magnificent a machine — so sober, temperate, chaste — so unremittingly loyal to the service — so strangely stern and faithful to his conception of law — so perfect in his fidelity to duty. He was the model, the inspiration which fighting Texas had developed to oppose wildness and disorder and crime. He would carry through this Fairdale case, but even so, if he were not killed, his life would be ruined. He might save the service, yet at the cost of his happiness. He was not a machine. He was a man. He might be a perfect ranger, still he was a human being.

The loveliness, the passion, the tragedy of a woman, great as they were, had not power to shake him from his duty. Futile, hopeless, vain her love had been to influence him. But there had flashed over me with subtle, overwhelming suggestion that not futile, not vain was my love to save him. Therefore, beyond and above all other claims, and by reason of my wrong to him, his claim came first.

It was then there was something cold and death-like in my soul. It was then I bade farewell to Ruth Herbert. For I knew, whatever happened, that of one thing I was sure — I would have to kill either Longstreth or Lawson. Snecker could be managed. Longstreth might be trapped into arrest, but Lawson had no sense, no control, no fear. He would snarl like a panther and go for his gun, and he would have to be killed. This, of all consummations, was the one to be calculated upon.

And, of course, by Ruth's own words, that contingency would put me forever outside the pale for her. I did not deceive myself. I did not accept the slightest intimation of hope. I gave her up. And then for a time

413

regret, remorse, pain, darkness worked their will with me.

I came out of it all bitter and callous and sore — in the most fitting of moods to undertake a difficult and deadly enterprise. Miss Longstreth completely slipped my mind. Ruth became a wraith as of someone dead. Steele began to fade. In their places came the bushy-bearded Snecker, the olive-skinned Longstreth with his sharp eyes, and the dark, evil-faced Lawson. Their possibilities began to loom up, and with my speculation returned tenfold more thrilling and sinister the old strange zest of the manhunt.

It was about one o'clock when I strode into Fairdale. The streets for the most part were deserted. I went directly to the hall where Morton and Zimmer, with their men, had been left by Steele to guard the prisoners. I found them camping out in the place, restless, somber, anxious. The fact that only about half the original number of prisoners were left struck me as further indication of Morton's summary dealings. But, when I questioned him as to the decrease in number, he said bluntly that they had escaped.

I did not know whether or not to believe him. But that didn't matter. I tried to get in some more questions, only I found that

Morton and Zimmer meant to be heard first.

"Where's Steele?" they demanded.

"He's out of town, in a safe place," I replied. "Too badly hurt for action. I'm to rush through with the rest of the deal."

"That's good," Morton said. "We've waited long enough. This gang has been split, and, if we hurry, they'll never get together again. Old man Snecker showed up today. He's drawin' the outfit in ag'in. Reckon he's waitin' for orders. Sure he's ragin' since Bo was killed. The old fox will be dangerous if he gets goin'."

"Where is he now?" I queried.

"Over at the Hope So. Must be a dozen of the gang there. But he's the only leader left we know of. If we get him, the rustler gang will be broke for good. He's sent word down here for me to let our prisoners go or there'll be a damn' bloody fight. We haven't sent our answer yet. Was hoping Steele would show up. An' now we're sure glad you're back."

"Morton, I'll take the answer," I replied quickly. "Now there're two things. Do you know if Longstreth and Lawson are at the ranch?"

"They were an hour ago. We have word. Zimmer saw Dick."

"All right. Have you any horses handy?"

"Sure. Those hitched outside belong to us."

"I want you to take a man with you, in a few moments, and ride 'round the back roads and up to Longstreth's house. Get off and wait under the trees till you hear me shoot or yell, then come fast."

Morton's breast heaved. He whistled as he breathed. His neck churned. "God Almighty! So there the scent leads. We always wondered . . . half believed. But no one spoke . . . no one had any nerve." Morton moistened his lips. His face was livid; his big hands shook. "Russ, you can gamble on me."

"Good. Well, that's all. Come out and get me a horse."

When I had mounted and was half way to the Hope So, my plan as far as Snecker was concerned had been formed. It was to go boldly into the saloon, ask for the rustler, first pretend I had a reply from Morton, and then, when I had Snecker's ear, whisper a message supposedly from Longstreth. If Snecker was too keen to be decoyed, I could at least surprise him, then run for my horse.

The plan seemed clever to me. I had only one thing to fear, and that was a possibility of the rustlers having seen my part in Steele's defense the other day. That had to be risked.

There were always some kind of risks to be faced.

It was scarcely a block and a half to the Hope So. Before I arrived, I knew I had been observed. When I dismounted before the door, I felt cold, yet there was an exhilaration in the moment. I never stepped more naturally and carelessly into the saloon.

It was full of men. There were men behind the bar, helping themselves. Evidently Blandy's job had not been filled. Every face near the door was turned toward me, dark, intent, scowling, malignant they were, and made me stiffen my resolve.

"Say, boys, I've a word for Snecker," I called, quite loudly. Nobody stirred. I swept my glance over the crowd but did not see Snecker. "I'm in some hurry," I added.

"Bill ain't here," said a man at the table nearest me. "Air you comin' from Morton?"

"Nit. But I'm not yellin' this message."

The rustler rose and in a few long strides confronted me.

"Word from Longstreth," I whispered, and the rustler stared. "I'm in his confidence. He's got to see Bill at once. Longstreth sends word he's quit . . . he's done . . . he's through. The jig is up, and he means to hit the road out of Fairdale."

"Bill'll kill him, surer'n hell," muttered

the rustler. "But we all said it'd come to thet. An' what'd Lawson say?"

"Lawson? Why, he's cashed in. Didn't you'all hear? Reckon Longstreth shot him."

The rustler cursed his amaze and swung his right arm with fist clenched tight. "When did Lawson git it?"

"A little while ago. I don't know how long. Anyway, I saw him lyin' dead on the porch. An' say, pard, I've got to rustle. Send Bill up quick as he comes. Tell him Longstreth wants to turn over all his stock an' then light out."

I backed to the door, and the last I saw of the rustler he was standing there in a scowling amaze. I had fooled him all right. If only I had the luck to have Snecker come along soon. . . . Mounting, I trotted the horse leisurely up the street.

Business and everything else was at a standstill in Fairdale these days. The doors of the stores were barricaded. Down side streets, however, I saw a few people, a buckboard, and stray cattle. When I reached the edge of town, I turned aside a little and took a look at the ruins of Steele's adobe house. The walls and débris had all been flattened, scattered about, and, if anything of value had escaped destruction, it had disappeared. Steele, however, had left very little that would have been of further use to him.

Turning again, I continued on my way to the ranch. It seemed that, though I was eager rather than backward, my mind seized avidly upon suggestion or attraction, as if to escape the burden of grim pondering. When about half way across the flat, and perhaps just out of gunshot sound of Longstreth's house, I heard a rapid clatter of hoofs on the hard road. I wheeled, expecting to see Morton and his man, and was ready to be chagrined at their coming openly instead of by the back way. But this was only one man, and it was not Morton.

He seemed of big build, and he bestrode a fine bay horse. There evidently was reason for hurry, too. At about one hundred yards, when I recognized Snecker, complete astonishment possessed me.

Well, as it was, I had ample time to get on my guard. In wheeling my horse I booted him so hard that he reared. As I had been warm, I had my sombrero over the pommel of the saddle. And, when the head of my horse blocked any possible sight of movement of my hand, I pulled my gun and held it concealed under my sombrero.

This rustler had bothered me in my calculations. And here he came galloping alone. Exultation would have been involuntary then but for the sudden shock, and then the cold settling of temper, the breathless suspense. Snecker pulled his huge bay and pounded to halt abreast of me. Luck favored me. Had I ever had anything but luck in these dangerous deals?

Snecker seemed to fume. Internally there was a volcano. His wide sombrero and bushy beard hid all of his face except his eyes, which were deep-set furnaces. He, too, like his lieutenant, had been carried completely off his balance by the strange message, apparently from Longstreth. "Hey! You're the feller who jest left word fer someone at the Hope So?" he asked.

"Yes," I replied, while with my left hand I patted the neck of my horse, holding him still.

"Longstreth wants me bad, eh?"

"Reckon there's only one man who wants you more."

Steadily, I met his piercing gaze. This was a rustler not to be long victim to any ruse. I waited in cold surety.

"You thet cowboy, Russ?" he asked.

"I was . . . and I'm not!" I replied significantly.

The violent start of this violent outlaw was a rippling jerk of passion. "What'n hell!" he ejaculated.

"Bill, you're easy."

"Who're you?" he uttered hoarsely.

I watched Snecker with hawk-like keenness. "United States deputy marshal . . . Bill, you're under arrest."

He roared a mad curse as his hand clapped down to his gun. Then I fired through my sombrero. Snecker's big horse plunged. The rustler fell back, and one of his legs pitched high as he slid off the lunging steed. His other foot caught in the stirrup. This fact terribly frightened the horse. He bolted, dragging the rustler for a dozen jumps. Then Snecker's foot slipped loose. He lay limp and still and shapeless in the road. I did not need to go back to look him over. But to make assurance doubly sure, I dismounted and went back to where he lay. My bullet had gone where it had been aimed.

As I rode up into Longstreth's courtyard and turned in to the porch, I heard loud and angry voices. Longstreth and Lawson were quarreling again. How my lucky star guided me! I had no plan of action, but my brain was equal to a hundred lightning-swift evolutions. The voices ceased. The men had heard the horse. Both of them came out on the porch.

In an instant I was again the lolling, impudent cowboy, half under the influence of liquor.

"It's only Russ, and he's drunk," said Floyd Lawson contemptuously.

"I heard horses trotting off there," replied Longstreth. "Maybe the girls are coming. I bet I teach them not to run off again. . . . Hello, Russ."

He looked haggard, thin, but seemed amiable enough. He was in his shirtsleeves, and he had come out with a gun in his hand. This he laid on a table near the wall. He wore no belt.

I rode right up to the porch and, greeting them laconically, made a show of a somewhat tangle-footed cowboy dismounting. The moment I got off and straightened up, I asked no more. The game was mine. It was the great hour of my life, and I met it as I had never met another.

I looked and acted what I pretended to be, though a deep and intense passion, an almost ungovernable suspense, an icy sickening nausea abided within me. All I needed, all I wanted was to get Longstreth and Lawson together or, failing that, to maneuver into such a position that I had any kind of chance. Longstreth's gun on the table made three distinct objects for me to watch and two of them could change position.

"What do you want here?" demanded Lawson.

He was red, bloated, thick-lipped, all fiery and sweaty from drink, though sober at the moment, and he had the expression of a desperate man in his last stand. It *was* his last stand, though he was ignorant of that.

"Me . . . ? Say, Lawson, I ain't fired yet," I replied in slow-rising resentment.

"Well, you're fired now," he replied insolently.

"Who fires me, I'd like to know?"

I walked up to the porch, and I had a cigarette in one hand, a match in the other. I struck the match.

"I do," said Lawson.

I studied him with apparent amusement. It had taken only one glance around for me to divine that Longstreth would enjoy any kind of a clash between Lawson and me.

"Huh! You fired me once before, an' it didn't go. Lawson, I reckon you don't stack up here as strong as you think."

He was facing the porch, moody, preoccupied, somber, all at the same time. Only a little of his mind was concerned with me. Manifestly there were strong forces at work. Both men were strained to the last degree, and Lawson could be made to break at almost a word. Longstreth laughed mockingly at this sally of mine, and that stung Lawson. He stopped his pacing and turned his handsome, fiery eyes on me.

"Longstreth, I won't stand this man's impudence."

"Aw, Lawson, cut that talk. I'm not impudent. Longstreth knows I'm a good fellow, on the square, and I have you sized up about OK."

"All the same, Russ, you'd better dig out," said Longstreth. "Don't kick up any fuss. We're busy with deals today. And I expect visitors."

"Sure. I won't stay around where I ain't wanted," I replied.

Then I lit my cigarette and did not move an inch out of my tracks. Longstreth sat in a chair near the door. The table upon which lay his gun stood between him and Lawson. This position did not invite me to start anything. But the tension had begun to be felt. Longstreth had his sharp gaze on me.

"What'd you come for, anyway?" he asked suddenly.

"Well, I had some news I was asked to fetch in."

"Get it out of you, then."

"See here now, Mister Longstreth, the fact is I'm a tender-hearted fellow. I hate to hurt people's feelin's. And, if I was to spring this

424

news in Mister Lawson's hearin', why, such a sensitive, high-tempered gentleman as he would go plumb off his nut."

Unconcealed sarcasm was the dominant note in that speech. Lawson flared up, yet he was eagerly curious. Longstreth probably thought I was only a little worse for drink, and, but for the way I rubbed Lawson, he would not have tolerated me at all.

"What's this news? You needn't be afraid of my feelings," said Lawson.

"Ain't so sure of that," I drawled. "It concerns the lady you're sweet on . . . an' the ranger . . . you ain't sweet on."

Longstreth jumped up. "Russ, has Ray gone out to meet Steele?" he asked angrily.

"Sure she has," I replied.

I thought Lawson would choke. He was thick-headed anyway, and the rush of blood made him tear at the soft collar of his shirt. Both men were excited now, moving about, beginning to rouse. I waited my chance, patient, cold, all my feelings shut in the vise of my will.

"How do you know she met Steele?" demanded Longstreth.

"I was there. I met Ruth at the same time."

"But *why* should my daughter meet this ranger?"

"She's in love with him, and he's in love with her."

The simple statement might have had the force of a juggernaut. I reveled in Lawson's state, but I felt sorry for Longstreth. He had not outlived his pride. Then I saw the leaping thought — would this daughter side against him? He seemed to shrivel up, to grow old while I watched him. Lawson, finding his voice, cursed Ray, cursed the ranger, then Longstreth, then me.

"You damned, selfish fool!" cried Longstreth in deep, bitter scorn. "All you think of is yourself. Your loss of the girl. Think once of me . . . my home . . . my life."

Then the connection subtly put out by Longstreth apparently dawned upon the other. Somehow, through this girl, her father and cousin were to be betrayed. I got that impression, though I could not tell how true it was. Certainly Lawson's jealousy was his paramount emotion.

Longstreth thrust me sidewise off the porch. "Go away," he ordered. He did not look around to see if I came back.

Quickly I leaped to my former position. He confronted Lawson. He was beyond the table where the gun lay. They were close together. My moment had come — the game was mine — and a ball of fire burst in my brain to race all over me.

"To hell with you!" burst out Lawson incoherently. He was frenzied. "I'll have her or nobody else will!"

"You never will," returned Longstreth stridently. "So help me God. I'd rather see her Ranger Steele's wife than yours."

Absorbing that shock, Lawson leaned toward him, all hate and menace in his mien. They had forgotten the half-drunken cowboy.

"Lawson, you made me what I am," continued Longstreth. "I backed you . . . protected you, finally went in with you. Now it's ended. I quit you. I'm done."

Their gray, passion-corded faces were still as stones.

"Gentlemen," I called in clear, high, far-reaching voice with the intonation of authority, "you're both done!"

They wheeled to confront me, to see my leveled gun.

"Don't move! Not a muscle! Not a finger!" I warned.

Longstreth read what Lawson had not the mind to read. His face turned paler gray, to ashen.

"What d'ye mean?" yelled Lawson fiercely, shrilly.

It was not in him to obey my command,

to see impending death. All quivering and strung, yet with perfect control, I raised my left hand to turn back a lapel of my open vest. The silver shield flashed brightly.

"United States deputy marshal in service of Ranger Steele."

Lawson howled like a dog. With barbarous and instant fury, with sheer, impotent folly, he swept a clawing hand for his gun. My shot broke his action as it cut short his life.

Before Lawson even tottered, before he loosed the gun, Longstreth leaped behind him, clasped him with left arm, quick as lightning jerked the gun from both clutching fingers and sheath. I shot at Longstreth — then again — then a third time.

All my bullets sped into the upheld, nodding Lawson. Longstreth had protected himself with the body of the dead man. I had seen red flashes, puffs of smoke, had heard quick reports. Something stung my left arm. Then a blow like wind, light of sound yet shocking in impact, struck me, knocked me flat. The hot rend of lead followed the blow. My heart seemed to explode, yet my mind kept extraordinarily clear and rapid.

I raised myself, felt a post at my shoulder, leaned on it. I heard Longstreth work the action of Lawson's gun. I heard the hammer click, fall upon empty shells. He had used up all the loads in Lawson's gun. I heard him curse as a man curses at defeat.

I waited, cool and sure now for him to show his head or other vital part from behind his bolster. He tried to lift the dead man, to edge him closer toward the table where his gun lay. But, considering the peril of exposing himself, he found that task beyond him. He bent, peering at me under Lawson's arm.

Longstreth's eyes were the eyes of a man who meant to kill me. There was never any mistaking the strange and terrible light of eyes like those. More than once I had a chance to aim at them, at the tip of Longstreth's head, at a strip of his side. I wanted to make sure. Suddenly I remembered Morton and his men. Then I pealed out a cry — hoarse, strange, yet far-reaching.

It was answered by a shout.

Longstreth heard it. It called forth all that was in the man. He flung Lawson's body off. But, even as it dropped, before Longstreth could recover to leap as he surely intended for the gun, I covered him, called piercingly to him. I could kill him there or as he moved. But one chance I gave him.

"Don't jump for the gun! Don't! I'll kill you! I've got two shells left! Sure as God, I'll kill you!"

He stood perhaps ten feet from the table

where his gun lay. I saw him calculating his chances. He was game. He had courage that forced me to respect him. I saw him measure the distance to that gun. He was magnificent. He meant to do it. I would have to kill him

"Longstreth, listen!" I cried, very swiftly. "The game's up. You're done. But think of your daughter. I'll spare your life . . . I'll give you freedom on one condition. For her sake. I've got you nailed . . . all the proofs. It was I behind the wall the other night. Blome, Hilliard, Pickens, Bo Snecker are dead. I killed Bill Snecker on the way up here. There lies Lawson. You're alone. And here come Morton and another to my aid. Give up! Surrender! Consent to demands, and I'll spare you. You can go free back to your old country. It's for Ray's sake. Her life, perhaps her happiness, can be saved. Hurry, man. Your answer."

"Suppose I refuse?" he queried with a dark and terrible earnestness.

"Then I'll kill you in your tracks. You can't move a hand. Your word or death. Hurry, Longstreth. I can't last much longer. But I can kill you before I drop. Be a man. For her sake. Quick. Another second now. . . . By God, I'll kill you."

"All right, Russ. I give my word," he said,

and deliberately walked to the chair and fell into it, just as Morton came running up with his man.

"Put away your guns," I ordered them. "The game's up. Snecker and Lawson are dead. Longstreth is my prisoner. He has my word he'll be protected. It's for you to draw up the papers with him. He'll divide all his property, every last acre, every herd of stock as you and Zimmer dictate. He gives up all. Then he's free to leave the country, and he's never to return."

Chapter Eighteen

THROUGH THE VALLEY

Longstreth looked strangely at the great bloody blot on my breast, and his look made me conscious of a dark hurrying of my mind. Morton came stamping up the steps with blunt queries, with anxious mien. When he saw the front of me, he halted, threw wide his arms.

"There come the girls!" suddenly exclaimed Longstreth. "Morton, help me drag Lawson inside. They mustn't see him."

I was facing down the porch toward the court and corrals. Miss Longstreth and Ruth had come in sight, were swiftly approaching, evidently alarmed. Steele, no doubt, had remained out at the camp. I was watching them, wondering what they would do and say presently, and then Longstreth and Morton came to carry me indoors. They laid me on the couch in the parlor where the girls used to be so often.

"Russ, you're pretty hard hit," said Longstreth, bending over me with his hands at my breast.

The room was bright with sunshine, yet the light seemed to be fading.

"Reckon I am," I replied.

"I'm sorry. If only you could have told me sooner. Lawson, damn him! Always I've split over him."

"But the last time, Longstreth."

"Yes, and I came near driving you to kill me, too. Russ, you talked me out of it. For Ray's sake! She'll be here in a minute. This'll be harder than facing a gun."

"Hard now. But it'll . . . turn out OK."

"Russ, will you do me a favor?" he asked, and he seemed shamefaced.

"Sure."

"Let Ray and Ruth think Lawson shot you. He's dead. It can't matter. And you're hard hit. The girls are fond of you. If . . . if you go under . . . Russ, the old side of my life is coming back. It's been coming. It'll be here just about when she enters this room. And by God, I'd change places with you if I could."

"Glad you . . . said that, Longstreth," I replied. "And sure . . . Lawson plugged me. It's our secret. I've reason, too, not . . . that . . . it . . . matters . . . much . . . now."

The light was failing. I could not talk very well. I felt dumb, strange, locked in ice, with dull little prickings of my flesh, with dim rushing sounds in my ears. But my mind was clear. Evidently there was little to be done.

Morton came in, looked at me, and went out. I heard the quick, light steps of the girls on the porch and murmuring voices.

"Where'm I hit?" I whispered.

"Three places," Longstreth said. "Arm, shoulder, and a bad one in the breast. It got your lung, I'm afraid. But if you don't go quick, you've got a chance."

"Sure I've a chance."

"Russ, I'll tell the girls, do what I can for you, settle with Morton, and clear out."

Just then Ray and Ruth entered the room. I heard two low cries, so different in tone, and I saw two dim white faces. Ruth flew to my side and dropped to her knees. Both hands went to my face, then to my breast. She lifted them, shaking. They were red. White and mute she gazed from them to me. But some woman's intuition kept her from fainting.

"Papa!" cried Ray, wringing her hands.

"Don't give way," he replied. "Both you girls will need your nerve. Russ is badly hurt. There's little hope for him."

Ruth moaned and dropped her face against me, clasping me convulsively. I tried to reach a hand out to touch her, but I could not move. I felt her hair against my face. Ray uttered a low, heart-rending cry, which both Longstreth and I understood.

"Listen, let me tell it quick," he said huskily. "There's been a fight. Russ killed Snecker and Lawson. They resisted arrest. It . . . it was Lawson . . . it was Lawson's gun that put Russ down. Russ let me off. In fact, Ray, he saved me. I'm to divide my property . . . return so far as possible what I've stolen . . . leave Texas at once and forever. You'll find me back in old Louisiana . . . if . . . if you ever want to come home."

As she stood there, realizing her deliverance, with the dark and tragic glory of her eyes passing from her father to me, my own sight shadowed, and I thought, *if I were dying, then it was not in vain.*

"Send . . . for . . . Steele," I whispered.

Silently, swiftly, breathlessly, they worked over me. I was exquisitely sensitive to touch, to sound, but I could not see anything. By and by all was quiet, and I slipped into a black void.

Familiar heavy, swift footsteps, the thump of heels of a powerful and striding man, jarred into the blackness that held me, seemed to split it to let me out. I opened my eyes in a sunlit room to see Ruth's face all lined and haggard, to see Miss Longstreth fly to the door, and the stalwart ranger bow his lofty head to enter.

However far life had ebbed from me, then it came rushing back, keen-sighted, memorable, with agonizing pain in every nerve. I saw him start. I heard him cry, but I could not speak.

He bent over me, and I tried to smile. He stood silent, his hand on me, while Ray Longstreth told swiftly, brokenly what had happened. How she told it! I tried to whisper a protest. To anyone on earth, except Steele, I might have wished to appear a hero. Still, at that moment I had more dread of him than any other feeling. She finished the story with her head on his shoulder, with tears that certainly were in part for me.

Once in my life, then, I saw him stunned. But, when he recovered, it was not Ray that he thought of first, nor of the end of Longstreth's power. He turned to me.

"Little hope?" he cried out with the deep ring in his voice. "No! There's every hope. No bullet hole like that could ever kill this ranger. Russ!"

I could not answer him. But this time I did achieve a smile.

There was no shadow, no pain in his face such as had haunted me in Ruth's and Ray's.

He could fight death the same as he could fight evil. He vitalized the girls. Ray began to hope. Ruth lost her woe. He changed the atmosphere of that room. Something filled it — something like himself, big, virile, strong. The very look of him made me suddenly want to live; and all at once it seemed I felt alive. And that was like taking the deadened ends of nerves, to cut them raw, and quicken them with fiery current. From stupor I had leaped to pain, and that tossed me into fever.

There were spaces, darkened mercifully, shutting me in. There were others of light, where I burned and burned in my heated blood. Ruth, like the wraith she had become in my mind, passed in and out. Ray watched and helped in those hours when sight was clear. The fever passed, and with the first nourishing drink given me I seemed to find my tongue, to gain something.

"Hello, old man," I whispered to Steele.

"Oh, Lord, Russ, to think you would double-cross me the way you did."

That was his first speech to me after I had appeared to face around from the grave. His good-humored reproach told me more than any other thing how far from his mind was the thought of my death. Then he talked a little to me, cheerfully, with that directness and force characteristic of him always, showing me that the danger was past, and that I would now be rapidly on the mend. I discovered that I cared little whether I was on the mend or not.

When I had passed the state of somber unrealities, then the hours of pain, and then that first inspiring flush of renewed desire to live, an entirely different mood came over me. But I kept it to myself. I never even asked, for three days, why Ruth never entered the room where I lay. I associated this fact, however, with what I had imagined, her shrinking from me, her intent and pale face, her singular manner when occasion made it necessary or unavoidable for her to be near me. No difficulty was there in associating my change of mood with her absence. I brooded. Steele's keen insight betrayed me to him, but all his power and his spirit availed nothing to cheer me.

I pretended to be cheerful. I drank and ate anything given me. I was patient and quiet. But I ceased to mend. Then, one day, she came back, and Steele, who was watching me as she entered, quietly got up and without a word took Ray out of the room and left me alone with Ruth.

"Archie, I've been sick myself . . . in bed for three days," she said. "I'm better now.

I hope you are. You look so pale. . . . Do you still think . . . brood about that fight?"

"Yes, I can't forget. I'm afraid it cost me more than life."

Ruth was somber, gloomy, thoughtful. "You weren't driven to kill Floyd?" she asked.

"How do you mean?"

"By that awful instinct, that hankering to kill, you once told me gunmen have."

"No. I can swear it wasn't that. I didn't want to kill him. But he forced me. As I had to go after these two men, it was a foregone conclusion about Lawson. It was premeditated. I have no excuse."

"Hush. Tell me, if you confronted them, drew on them, then you had a chance to kill my uncle?"

"Yes. I could have done it easily."

"*Why*, then, didn't you?"

"It was for Ray's sake. I'm afraid I didn't think of you. I had put you out of my mind."

"Well, if a man can be noble at the same time he's terrible, you've been. . . . Archie . . . I don't know how I feel. I'm sick, and I can't think. I see, though, that you saved Ray and Steele. Why, she's touching happiness again, fearfully yet really. Think of that. God only knows what you did for Steele. If I judged it by his suffering, as you lay there about to die, it would be beyond words to tell. But, Archie, you're pale and shaky now. Hush! No more talk!"

With all my eyes and mind and heart and soul I watched to see if she shrank from me. She was passive, yet tender, as she smoothed my pillow and moved my head. A dark abstraction hung over her, and it was so strange, so foreign to her nature. No sensitiveness on earth could have equaled mine at that moment. And I saw and felt and knew that she did not shrink from me.

Thought and feeling escaped me for a while. I dozed. The old shadows floated to and fro. When I awoke, Steele and Ray had just come in. As he bent over me, I looked up into his keen gray eyes, and there was no mask over mine when I looked up at him.

"Son, the thing that was needed was a change of nurses," he said gently. "I intend to make up some sleep now and leave you in better care."

From that hour I improved. I slept. I lay quietly awake. I partook of nourishing food. I listened and watched, and all the time I gained. But I spoke very little, and, though I tried to brighten when Steele was in the room, I made only indifferent success of it.

Days passed. Ruth was almost always with me, yet seldom alone. She was grave where once she had been gay. How I watched her face, praying for that shade to lift. How I listened for a note of the old music in her voice.

Ruth Herbert had sustained a shock to her soul almost as dangerous as had been the blow at my life. Still I hoped. I had seen other women's deadened and darkened spirits rebound and glow once more. It began to dawn upon me, however, that more than time was imperative if she were ever to become her old self again.

Studying her closer, with less thought of myself and her reaction to my presence, I discovered that she trembled at shadows, seemed like a frightened deer with a step always on its trail, was afraid of the dark. Then I wondered why I had not long before divined one cause of her strangeness. The house where I had killed one of her kin would ever be haunted for her. She had said she was a Southerner and that blood was thick.

When I had thought out the matter a little further, I deliberately sat up in bed, scaring the wits out of all my kind nurses. "Steele, I'll never get well in this house. I want to go home. When can you take me?"

They remonstrated with me, and pleaded, and scolded, all to little avail. Then they were persuaded to take me seriously, to plan, providing I improved, to start in a few days. We were to ride out of Pecos County together, back along the stage trail to civilization.

The look in Ruth's eyes decided my measure of improvement. I could have started that very day and have borne up under any pain or distress. Strange to see, too, how Steele and Ray responded to the stimulus of my idea, to the promise of what lay beyond the wild and barren hills.

Steele told me that day about the headlong flight of every lawless character out of Fairdale, the very hour that Snecker and Lawson and Longstreth were known to have fallen. He expressed deep feeling, almost mortification, that the credit of that final coup had gone to him, instead of to me. His denial and explanation had been only a few soundless words in the face of a grateful and clamorous populace that tried to reward him, to make him mayor of Fairdale.

Longstreth had made restitution in every case where he had personally gained at the loss of farmer or rancher, and the accumulation of years went far toward returning to Fairdale what it had lost in a material way. He had been a poor man when he boarded the stage for Sanderson, on his way out of Texas forever.

Not long afterward I heard Steele talking to Miss Longstreth in a deep and agitated voice. "You must rise above this. When I come upon you alone, I see the shadow, the pain in your face. How wonderfully this thing has turned out when it might have ruined you. I expected it to ruin you. Who but that wild boy in there could ever have saved us all?

"Ray, you have had cause for sorrow. But your father is alive and will live it down. Perhaps, back there in Louisiana, the dishonor will never be known. Pecos County is far from your old home. And even in San Antonio and Austin a man's evil repute means little. . . . Then the line between a rustler and a rancher is hard to draw in these wild border days. Rustling is stealing cattle, and I once heard a well-known rancher say that all rich cattlemen had done a little stealing. Your father drifted out here, and like a good many others he succeeded. It's perhaps just as well not to split hairs, to judge him by the law and morality of a civilized country. Some way or other he drifted in with badmen. Maybe a deal that was honest somehow tied his hands and started him in wrong.

"This matter of land, water, a few stray

head of stock had to be decided out of court. I'm sure in his case he never realized where he was drifting. Then one thing led to another, until he was face to face with dealings that took on crooked form. To protect himself he bound men to him. And so the gang developed. Many powerful gangs have developed that way out here. He could not control them. He became involved with them, and eventually their dealings became deliberately and boldly dishonest. That meant the inevitable spilling of blood sooner or later, and so he grew into the leader because he was the strongest. Whatever he is to be judged for, I think he could have been infinitely worse."

When he ceased speaking, I had the same impulse that must have concerned Steele — somehow to show Longstreth not so black as he was painted, to give him the benefit of a doubt, to arraign him justly in the eyes of rangers who knew what wild border life was.

"Steele, bring Ray in," I called. "I've something to tell her."

They came quickly, concerned probably at my tone.

"I've been hoping for a chance to tell you something, Miss Longstreth. That day I came here, your father was quarreling with

Lawson. I had heard them do that before. He hated Lawson. The reason came out just before we had the fight. It was my plan to surprise them. I did. I told them you went out to meet Steele . . . that you two were in love with each other. Lawson grew wild. He swore no one would ever have you. Then Longstreth said he'd rather have you Steele's wife than Lawson's. I'll not forget that scene. There was a great deal back of it, long before you ever came out to Fairdale. Your father said that he had backed Lawson . . . that the deal had ruined him . . . made him a rustler. He said he quit. He was done.

"Now, this is all clear to me, and I want to explain, Miss Longstreth. It was Lawson who ruined your father. It was Lawson who was the rustler. It was Lawson who made the gang necessary. But Lawson had not the brains or the power to lead men. Because blood is thick, your father became the leader of that gang. At heart he was never a criminal. The reason I respected him was because he showed himself a man at the last. He faced me to be shot, and I couldn't do it.

"As Steele said, you've reason for sorrow. But you must get over it. You mustn't brood. I do not see that you'll be disgraced or dishonored. Of course, that's not the point. The vital thing is whether or not a woman of your high-mindedness had real and lasting cause for shame. Steele says no. I say no."

Then, as Miss Longstreth dropped down beside me, her eyes shining and wet, Ruth entered the room in time to see her cousin bend to kiss me gratefully with sisterly fervor. Yet it was a woman's kiss, given for its own sake.

Ruth could not comprehend. It was too sudden, too unheard of, that Ray Longstreth should kiss me, a man she did not love. Ruth's white, sad face changed, and in the flaming wave of scarlet that dyed neck and cheek and brow I read with mighty pound of heart that, despite the dark stain between us, she loved me still.

Chapter Nineteen

CONVALESCENCE

Four mornings later we were aboard the stage, riding down the main street, on the way out of Fairdale. The whole town turned out to bid us farewell. The cheering, the clamor, the almost passionate fervor of the populace irritated me, and I could not see the incident from their point of view. Never in my life had I been so eager to get out of a place. But, then, I was morbid, and the whole world hinged on one thing.

Morton insisted on giving us an escort as far as Del Rio. It consisted of six cowboys, mounted, with light packs, and they rode ahead of the stage. We had the huge vehicle to ourselves. A comfortable bed had been rigged up for me by placing boards across from seat to seat and furnishing it with blankets and pillows. By some squeezing there was still room enough inside for my three companions, but Steele expressed an intention of riding mostly outside, and Miss Longstreth's expression betrayed her. I was to be alone with Ruth. The prospect thrilled while it saddened me. How different this ride from that first one, with all its promise of adventure and charm.

"It's over," said Steele thickly. "It's done. I'm glad, for their sakes . . . glad for ours. We're out of town."

I had been quick to miss the shouts and cheers. And I had been just as quick to see, or to imagine, a subtle change in Ruth Herbert's face. We had not traveled a mile before the tension relaxed about her lips, the downcast eyes lifted, and I saw beyond any peradventure of doubt a lighter spirit. Then I relaxed myself, for I had keyed up every nerve to make myself strong for this undertaking. I lay back with closed eyes, weary, aching, in more pain than I wanted them to discover.

I thought and thought. Miss Longstreth had said to me: "Russ, it'll all come right. I can tell you now what you never guessed. For years Ruth had been fond of our cousin, Floyd Lawson. She hadn't seen him since she was a child. But she remembered. She had an only brother who was the image of Floyd.

"Ruth obviously loved Arthur. He was killed in the Rebellion. She never got over it. That left her without any family. Floyd and I were her nearest kin. How she looked forward to meeting Floyd out here! But he disappointed her right at the start. She hates a drinking man. I think she came to hate Floyd, too. But he always reminded her of Arthur, and she could never get over that. So, naturally, when you killed Floyd, she was terribly shocked. There were nights when she was haunted, when I had to stay with her.

"Vaughn and I have studied her, talked about her, and we think she's gradually recovering. She loved you, too, and Ruth doesn't change. Once, with her, is for always. So let me say to you what you said to me . . . do not brood. All will yet be well, thank God!"

Those had been words to remember, to make me patient, to lessen my insistent fear. Yet, what did I know of women? Had not Ray Longstreth and Ruth Herbert amazed and nonplused me many a time, at the very moment when I had calculated to a nicety my conviction of their action, their feeling? It was possible that I had killed Ruth's love for me, though I could not believe so — and it was very possible that, still loving me, she might never break down the barrier between us.

The beginning of that journey distressed me physically; yet, gradually, as I grew accustomed to the roll of the stage and to the occasional jars, I found myself easier in body. Fortunately there had been rain, that had settled the dust, and a favorable breeze made riding pleasant, where ordinarily it would have been hot and disagreeable.

We tarried long enough in the little hamlet of Longstreth for Steele to get letters from reliable ranchers. He wanted a number of references to verify the ranger report he had to turn in to Captain MacNeal. This precaution he took so as to place in MacNeal's hands all the evidence needed to convince Governor Stone. And now, as Steele returned to us and entered the stage, he spoke of this report.

"It's the longest and the best I ever turned in," he said with a gray flame in his eyes. "I sha'n't let Russ read it. He's peevish because I want his part put on record. And listen, Ray. There's to be a blank line in this report. Your father's name will never be recorded. Neither the governor, nor the adjutant general, nor Captain MacNeal, not anyone back Austin way will ever know who this mysterious leader of the Pecos gang might have been.

"Even out here very few know. Many supposed, but few knew. I've shut the mouths of those few. That blank line in the report is for a supposed and mysterious leader who vanished. Jack Blome, the reputed leader, and all his lawless associates are dead. Fairdale is free and safe now, its future in the hands of roused, determined, and capable men."

We were all silent after Steele ceased talking. I do not believe Ray could have spoken just then. If sorrow and joy could be perfectly blended in one beautiful expression, they were in her face.

By and by I dared to say: "And Vaughn Steele, Lone Star ranger, has seen his last service?"

"Yes," he replied with emotion.

Ruth stirred and turned a strange look upon us all. "In that case, then, if I am not mistaken, there were two Lone Star rangers . . . and both have seen their last service!"

Ruth's lips were trembling, the way they trembled when it was impossible to tell whether she was about to laugh or cry. The first hint of her old combative spirit or her old archness. A wave of feeling rushed over me, too much for me in my weakened condition. Dizzy, racked with sudden shooting pains, I closed my eyes, and the happiness I embraced was all that sweeter for the suffering it entailed.

Something beat into my ears, into my

brain, with the regularity and rapid beat of pulsing blood — not too late! Not too late! Not too late!

From that moment the ride grew different, even as I improved with leaps and bounds. Sanderson was behind us — the long, gray, barren between Sanderson and the Rio Grande beyond it — Del Rio for two days, where I was able to sit up — all behind us — and before us the eastward trail to Uvalde. We were the only passengers on the stage from Del Rio to Uvalde. Perhaps Steele had so managed the journey. Assuredly he had become an individual with whom traveling under the curious gaze of strangers would have been embarrassing.

He was most desperately in love. And Ray, all in a few days, while riding these long, tedious miles, ordinarily so fatiguing, had renewed her bloom, had gained what she had lost. She, too, was desperately in love, though she remembered her identity occasionally, and that she was in the company of a badly shot-up young man and a broken-hearted cousin.

Most of the time Ray and Steele rode on top of the stage. When they did ride inside, their conduct was not unbecoming. Indeed, it was sweet to watch, yet it loosed the fires of jealous rage and longing in me, and certainly upon Ruth. Gradually she had been losing that strange and somber mood she had acquired, to brighten and change more and more. Perhaps she divined something about Ray and Steele that escaped me. Anyway, all of a sudden she was transformed.

"Look here, if you people want to spoon, please get out on top," she said.

If that was not the old Ruth Herbert, I did not know who it was. Miss Longstreth tried to appear offended, and Steele tried to look insulted, but they both failed. They could not have looked anything but happy. Youth and love were too strong for this couple, whom circumstances might well have made grave and thoughtful. They were magnet and steel, powder and spark. Any moment, right before my eyes, I expected them to rush right into each other's arms. When they refrained, merely substituting clasped hands for dearer embrace, I closed my eyes and remembered them, as they would live in my memory forever, standing crushed together on the ridge that day, white lips to white lips, embodying all that was beautiful, passionate, and tragic. And I, who had been their undoing, in the end was their salvation. How I hugged that truth to my heart.

It seemed, following Ruth's pert remark, that after an interval of decent dignity Ray and Steele did go out upon the top of the stage.

"Archie," whispered Ruth, "they're up to something. I heard a few words. I bet you they're going to get married in San Antonio."

"Well, it's about time," I replied.

"But oughtn't they take us into their confidence?"

"Ruth, they have forgotten we are upon the earth."

"Oh, I'm so glad they're happy!"

Then there was a long silence. It was better for me to ride lying down, in which position I was at this time. After a mile Ruth took my hand and held it without speaking.

My heart leaped, but I did not open my eyes or break that spell even with a whisper.

"Archie, I must say . . . tell you . . ." She faltered, and still I kept my eyes closed. I did not want to wake up from that dream. "Have I been very . . . very sad?" she went on.

"Sad and strange, Ruth. That was worse than my bullet holes."

She gripped my hand. I felt her hair on my brow, felt her breath on my cheek. "Archie, I swore . . . I'd hate you if you . . . if you . . ."

"I know. Don't speak of it," I interposed hurriedly.

"But I don't hate you. I . . . I love you. And I can't give you up!"

"Darling! But, Ruth, can you get over it . . . can you forget?"

"Yes. That horrid black spell has gone with the miles. Little by little, mile after mile, and now it's gone! But I had to come to the point. To go back on my word. To tell you, Archie, you never, never had any sense."

Then I opened my eyes and my arms, too, and we were reunited. It must have been a happy moment, so happy that it numbed me beyond appreciation.

"Yes, Ruth," I agreed, "but no man ever had such a wonderful girl."

"Archie, I never . . . took off your ring," she whispered.

"But you hid your hand from my sight," I replied quickly.

"Oh, dear Archie, we're crazy . . . as crazy as those lunatics outside. Let's think a little."

I was very content to have no thought at all — just to see and feel her close to me.

"Archie, will you give up the ranger service for me?" she asked.

"Indeed, I will."

"And leave this fighting Texas, never to return till the day of guns and rangers and badmen and even breaks is past?"

"Yes."

"Will you go with me to my old home? It was beautiful once, Archie, before it was let run to rack and ruin. A thousand acres. An old stone house. Great mossy oaks. A lake and river. There are bear, deer, panther, wild boars in the breaks. You can hunt. And ride! I've horses, Archie, such horses! They could run these scrubby broncos off their legs. Will you come?"

"Come? Ruth, I rather think I will. But, dearest, after I'm well again, I must work," I said earnestly. "I've got to have a job."

"You're indeed a poor cowboy out of a job. Remember your deceit. Oh, Archie! Well, you'll have work, never fear."

"Ruth, is this old home of yours near the one Ray speaks of so much?" I asked.

"Indeed, it is. But hers has been kept under cultivation and in repair, while mine has run down. That will be our work, to build it up. So it's settled, then?"

She looked inquiringly at me, with a soft blush.

"Well, if you are so dense, try to bring back that Ruth Herbert who used to torment me. How you broke your promises! How you leaned from your saddle! Kiss me, Ruth!"

Later, as we drew close to Uvalde, Ruth and I sat in one seat, after the manner of

Ray and Vaughn, and we looked out over the west where the sun was setting behind dim and distant mountains. We were fast leaving the wild and barren border. Already it seemed beyond that broken rugged horizon with its dark line silhouetted against the rosy and golden sky. Already the spell of its wild life and the grim and haunting faces had begun to fade out of my memory.

Let newer rangers, with less to lose, and with the call in their hearts, go on with our work till soon that wild border would be safe. The great Lone Star state must work out its destiny. Some distant day, in the fullness of time, what place the rangers had in that destiny would be history.

About the Author

Zane Grey was born Pearl Zane Gray at Zanesville, Ohio in 1872. He was graduated from the University of Pennsylvania in 1896 with a degree in dentistry. He practiced in New York City while striving to make a living by writing. He married Lina Elise Roth in 1905 and with her financial assistance he published his first novel himself, BETTY ZANE (1903). Closing his dental office, the Greys moved into a cottage on the Delaware River, near Lackawaxen, Pennsylvania. Grey took his first trip to Arizona in 1907 and, following his return, wrote THE HERITAGE OF THE DESERT (1910). The profound effect that the desert had had on him was so vibrantly captured that it still comes alive for a reader. Grey couldn't have been more fortunate in his choice of a mate. Trained in English at Hunter College, Lina Grey proofread every manuscript Grey wrote, polished his prose, and she effectively managed their financial affairs. Grey's early novels were serialized in pulp magazines, but by 1918 he had graduated to the slick magazine market. Motion picture rights brought in a fortune and, with 109 films based on his work, Grey set a record yet to be equaled by any other author. Zane Grey was not a realistic writer, but rather one who charted the interiors of the soul through encounters with the wilderness. He provided characters no more realistic than one finds in Balzac, Dickens, or Thomas Mann, but nonetheless they have a vital story to tell. "There was so much unexpressed feeling that could not be entirely portrayed," Loren Grey, Grey's younger son and a noted psychologist, once recalled, "that, in later years, he would weep when re-reading one of his own books." More than stories, Grey fashioned psychodramas about the odyssey of the human soul. They may not be the stuff of the real world, but without them the real world has no meaning — which may go a long way to explain the hold he has had on an enraptured reading public ever since his first Western romance in 1910.

The employees of Thorndike Press hope you have enjoyed this Large Print book. All our Large Print titles are designed for easy reading, and all our books are made to last. Other Thorndike Press Large Print books are available at your library, through selected bookstores, or directly from us.

For information about titles, please call:

(800) 257-5157
To share your comments, please write:

Publisher
Thorndike Press
P.O. Box 159
Thorndike, Maine 04986